"Therefore I have no alternative but to sentence you to death. Your execution is so ordered. Signed: Kodos, Governor of Tarsus IV."

So unexpected were the words he heard that it took Lorca an extra moment to process their true meaning. He was not alone, as he exchanged shocked looks with his team even as a renewed rumbling erupted from the amphitheater audience.

"Did he just—" said Bridges, but the words died in her throat.

Lorca heard but did not acknowledge her, transfixed by the screen as the unimaginable began.

Howls of energy cascaded across the open-air venue, and Lorca immediately recognized the reports of large-scale energy weapons. Visible now in the tunnel entrances on the amphitheater's upper levels were oversized phaser cannons, variations of which were employed throughout Starfleet and the Federation for ground-based defense as well as more innocuous missions like drilling underground passages for mining efforts or tapping subterranean energy or water sources. Never in his life had Lorca seen them utilized in the manner he now beheld.

"Holy shit."

STAR TREK®

DISCOVERY

DRASTIC MEASURES

DAYTON WARD

Based upon *Star Trek*®
created by Gene Roddenberry
and
Star Trek: Discovery
created by Bryan Fuller & Alex Kurtzman

G

GALLERY BOOKS

New York   London   Toronto   Sydney   New Delhi   New Anchorage

G

Gallery Books
An Imprint of Simon & Schuster, Inc.
1230 Avenue of the Americas
New York, NY 10020

First Gallery Books trade paperback edition February 2018

GALLERY BOOKS and colophon are registered trademarks of Simon & Schuster, Inc.

For information about special discounts for bulk purchases, please contact Simon & Schuster Special Sales at 1-866-506-1949 or business@simonandschuster.com.

The Simon & Schuster Speakers Bureau can bring authors to your live event. For more information or to book an event, contact the Simon & Schuster Speakers Bureau at 1-866-248-3049 or visit our website at www.simonspeakers.com.

Manufactured in the United States of America

10 9 8 7 6 5 4 3 2 1

ISBN 978-1-5011-7174-1
ISBN 978-1-5011-7175-8 (ebook)

For Michi, Addison, and Erin

Historian's Note

This story takes place in the year 2246, approximately ten years prior to the "Battle at the Binary Stars" (*Star Trek: Discovery*), and nineteen years before the *U.S.S. Enterprise* under the command of Captain James T. Kirk encounters the energy barrier at the edge of our galaxy (*Star Trek: The Original Series*—"Where No Man Has Gone Before").

Prologue

Excerpt from *The Four Thousand: Crisis on Tarsus IV*
Published 2257

Unlike those found on Earth, the penal colonies located on other Federation worlds are somewhat lacking in modern amenities. Even so, when compared to the installations tasked with housing and treating patients diagnosed with severe mental disorders or who've been found guilty of the most heinous of crimes, the correctional facility on Garodon V is comfortable.

Its history as an inhabited world began as the site for a Starfleet long-range observation outpost, charged with monitoring a portion of the Neutral Zone separating Federation and Romulan territory. That duty was transferred decades ago to a series of observation stations designed to augment the line of monitoring stations deployed along the border a century earlier, following the cessation of the Earth-Romulan War. Now it serves as a Starfleet ship support facility. A small civilian community also thrives, albeit on the far side of the planet. The penal colony itself is similarly isolated, tucked into a valley between mountains a thousand kilometers from the nearest population center.

One of the main differences between this settlement and others, like Earth's New Zealand colony, is that those sent here accept that they are prisoners, remanded here for crimes against society. Those responsible for their incarceration believe these inmates are capable of achieving redemption. To that end, there are only a handful of inmates in residence convicted of more grievous offenses such as murder or assisting someone else to commit the act. One such prisoner is the subject of today's interview.

We stroll the narrow gravel path that winds its way around the grounds surrounding the cluster of buildings that make up the colony's primary settlement. Her hands bound by restraints and her ankles fitted with bands that allow her to walk but not run or kick, Hisayo Fujimura makes a point of ignoring the team of four security officers accompanying us this morning. According to her official schedule, Fujimura is supposed to report to the dining hall to assist in prepping the inmates' midday meal. It's a duty for which she harbors a deep loathing, so this is a welcome interruption. The sun is shining through the trees, and she seems to relish the warmth on her pale skin. She's rolled the sleeves of her yellow coveralls well above her elbows and her trouser legs above her knees, an apparent violation of the prisoner dress code but one which no one appears interested in enforcing. On the horizon, storm clouds threaten to chase away the peace and tranquility that's defined the day to this point.

"I only get to do this once or twice a week, depending on the weather," says Fujimura. "It's usually raining during my normal exercise period. I've asked to walk in the rain, but they won't let me." Holding up her wrists, she then points to the bands around her ankles. "It's not like they don't know where I am, or I can get away." Offering a knowing smile, she adds, "You realize the guards aren't necessary, right? I mean, for me. They're not here for me; they're here to protect you. They think I might try to kill you or something." She laughs at her own joke.

We walk in silence for fifty or sixty meters, navigating bends in the trail. This isn't our first meeting, of course; the first encounter was an introductory session, letting Fujimura know the potential topics of discussion and allowing her time to reflect on how she might respond to specific questions. It's a consideration extended to everyone interviewed for the book, and it's only fair that someone holding views in contradiction to so many of the other contributors be afforded the same courtesy.

"So," she offers after a few moments, "you wanted to talk to a follower of the cause. A true believer, as they say. I don't know if that's the perfect description, but I suppose it's still good enough. It was good enough for the people who sent me here, after all."

Reaching up to scratch her nose is a simple act, but it's one that attracts the attention of one of the guards. Though our four escorts have been maintaining a discreet if short distance, Fujimura's movements cause one of them, a blond human male who seems far too young to be in Starfleet, to break stride and begin walking in our direction. Once the prisoner drops her hands back in front of her, the guard relaxes, though he keeps his gaze fixed on us as he returns to his position on the loose perimeter he and his companions have fashioned.

Fujimura emits a quiet laugh. "They're so jumpy. I wonder how many times I can make them do that while we're out here?" As though she senses her attempts at self-amusement are already becoming detrimental to the interview, her expression turns more serious.

"I'm not a cold-blooded killer, no matter what the court transcripts say. I emigrated to Tarsus IV for the same reasons a lot of people did. The colony offered a chance at autonomy, a chance to decide for myself the life I wanted to lead, free from Federation interference." She shrugs. "Okay, so maybe not completely free, but we were far enough away that nobody seemed interested in us. We were just a little colony, carrying on with our farming and other efforts at creating a self-sustaining community that didn't need to rely on regular checks or supply shipments the way other settlements did." A derisive snort punctuates that comment.

"It might not have been the most glamorous life, but it was ours. All ours. Far away from the overcrowded central planets and even some of the larger colonies that were just working their way up to be Federation members all by themselves. I was born on Mantilles, but once the borders expanded in that direction it became one of the major ports of call for Starfleet and merchant ships, and thanks to the mild climate it was attractive to tourists. We natives hated that sort of thing."

An intersection where the path doubles back on itself after wrapping around a small pond gives us reason to stop for a moment. Fujimura says nothing else while watching a string of ducks milling along the pond's edge or swimming in the water.

"Nearly everyone living on Tarsus IV when I got there wanted the same thing: to be left alone. We weren't trying to secede, or anything silly like that. It wasn't about being anti-Federation. We just wanted to chart our own course, for better or worse. The colony had lived that way for decades before I was even born.

"We heard about the Epsilon Sorona disaster the same as everyone else, via the Federation news broadcasts. What we didn't know until it was already decided was that the refugees from that planet would be relocated to Tarsus IV." Fujimura holds up her hands. "Okay, that's not entirely true. The colony government knew about it. Governor Ribiero and the senior leadership welcomed the idea and the refugees with open arms. In and of itself, it was the right thing to do, of course. They needed a new home, and Tarsus was one of the few colony planets that could accommodate such a large influx of new settlers with minimal disruption. It was a big planet, with plenty of room for everybody. And it's not like the Federation just dumped them on us. They provided all sorts of assistance, in the form of new equipment, helping with building new housing, increasing our power and water distribution and other infrastructure needs, the works. In truth, New Anchorage grew about forty percent bigger within two years because of Federation aid, and our power grid and irrigation system for the farming communities was improved tenfold. We should've been grateful, and we were, at least for a while."

She pauses again, watching more of the ducks abandon the banks of the pond in favor of the water.

"They're not indigenous, you know," she offers, gesturing toward the waterfowl. "Like the colonists, Starfleet personnel, civilians, and us, they're imported along with all the other animal life, and some of the flora too. They didn't just dump them here, of course. Extensive research was conducted before introducing extraterrestrial animal and plant life into a new ecosystem. Kind of a novel idea, don't you think?"

It's obvious where she's going with this, and there's no need to prompt her with additional questions.

"If only they'd put that level of effort into the Tarsus relocation. Imagine how different things might be today. Something obviously wasn't done, or was just overlooked. I've read the official conclusions, along with some reports that dispute those findings." She shrugs. "It's been ten years, and I still don't know who or what to believe."

We start walking again, following the path around the pond's west side. There are no trees here, and the sun chases away the lingering morning chill. A glance to the horizon shows that the gray line of storm clouds has grown larger and darker. Rain will be here within an hour, perhaps two at most.

Much has been written about the cause of the fungal infection that ravaged the planet's food supply. In the years since the crisis, it has served as a cautionary tale about the risks of combining elements from two or more planetary ecosystems. The lessons taken from Tarsus IV continue to be taught, notably preventing another such calamity from ever happening again. Of equal importance is the need for proper crisis management.

"There was a lot of finger-pointing those first days," says Fujimura. "People were tying themselves into knots looking for something or someone to blame. Could the plague have been prevented? Was it something we even had a chance of stopping, or was it unavoidable? We had no way to answer those questions, and the simple truth was that none of it really mattered even though too many people were wallowing in pointless discussions. Think what you will of him, but Kodos had a plan. He didn't want to waste time on anything that didn't involve dealing with the situation going forward.

"I was there that night. With him, I mean. Kodos wasn't very talkative in the hours leading up to the gathering. We brought him meals, but he'd adopted this self-imposed policy about not eating until he'd implemented his plan to save us. A lot of books and news articles I've read over the years portray him as this cold, merciless man who didn't care about the people whose lives he was controlling." Fujimura shakes her head. "That night, you could see the doubt. Hell, you could *feel* it."

She stops, her gaze drifting away from the path not to the pond, but toward the horizon. It's obvious recalling the night of "the Sacrifice" weighs on her.

"That night, Kodos stood at the window of his office, watching as people made their way to the amphitheater. Most people were on foot, but there were a few vehicles. The streets and sidewalks were filled with people on their way to the gathering. Given everything, I figured Kodos would be nervous. It was going to be his first public address to the colony since taking on the governor's role, after all." She pauses, releasing a heavy sigh. "If it were me, I'd be terrified, but as the clock ticked down, a weird sort of calm seemed to settle over him."

Accounts from those few people who were in a position to observe Adrian Kodos in those last hours deviate in various respects, but all reveal a man consumed with the speech he was to deliver. Aides and members of the leadership council recall seeing him carrying a data slate all during that day. None of them knew the content of the speech he was crafting, of course, but they'd learn all about it soon enough.

"Since I was one of the few who knew what was going to happen, I was there as he worked on his speech. He would pace around his office, making this big circle as he practiced reciting it." Fujimura shakes her head as we resume our walk. "It wasn't just a simple reading; to me, he was treating it like a true performance."

Of course, there remains only a single real question. It's one that Fujimura has been anticipating since the start of the interview, and she does not flinch when it's finally asked.

"In a civilized society, can what Kodos did ever be justified or forgiven? We thought everybody on the planet was going to die. He was trying to save as many people as he thought possible. He obviously wouldn't have done it if he had any idea help was coming, but at the time? It was what he believed to be the best choice, from a selection of horrible choices."

She stops walking again, and our eyes meet. "But, let's not kid ourselves. He wasn't acting alone, and he didn't do it without support. I was there, from the beginning. I knew what was going to happen. I had a chance to voice my disapproval, but I kept my mouth shut. I didn't want anyone else to die, but I was okay with it being somebody other than me. I wasn't there when Kodos put his plan into motion, but I didn't do anything to stop it either.

"Why? Because I wanted to live. It was as simple as that. In a lot of ways, that makes people like me even worse than Kodos. After all, the truly horrible crimes were committed by those of us who were convinced he was right, and chose to help him. History's going to have its way with us . . . forever."

FEDERATION COLONY PLANET TARSUS IV

2246

1

Arms extended in front of him and with his phaser gripped in both hands, Gabriel Lorca halted his advance up the corridor as the door opened at the passage's far end. Standing on the other side of the doorway were two men, neither of them a member of Lorca's team. Both men were dressed in the uniform of the colony security forces, and each was carrying a phaser. Their eyes widened in surprise at seeing Lorca standing mere meters in front of them.

"You're not the maid."

He fired.

Only one of the men managed to raise his phaser, unconscious from Lorca's stun beam even before he fell to the floor. A single shot from his own weapon chewed into the floor as Lorca fired again. The other man dropped in a heap next to his companion, close enough to the door so that its sensors forced it to stay open.

Lorca gave brief consideration to the idea that he may have been better served by keeping one of the men conscious, at least long enough to extract some useful information. He dismissed the notion. The intruders were stunned, and the fact they had forced their entry into a Starfleet facility was enough for him to guess their intentions. They could be questioned once the situation was under control and the outpost was secure.

Moving closer to the fallen men, Lorca verified that both were out of commission before helping himself to their weapons. The scar in the floor from his opponent's phaser was enough to tell him that both weapons were set to kill, rather than stun.

But why?

Even with the emergency measures enacted by the colony's government in response to the current crisis, there was no reason for action so extreme as what these security officers from New Anchorage, the planet's main city, appeared to be undertaking. What could have motivated such a rash decision? Lorca and his team had already pledged their total support toward assisting Governor Gisela Ribiero and her staff to navigate the situation she faced. The relationship between the colony's civilian population and the Starfleet sensor observation outpost here on Tarsus IV was one of mutual cooperation that dated back to the colony's founding decades earlier. Had the governor taken leave of her senses? If she was willing to dispatch teams here on an apparent mission of murder, what else might she do?

I guess I'm just going to have to ask her that.

Adjusting each weapon's power level back to a stun setting, Lorca tucked them both into the waistband of his civilian trousers. Next, he used his foot to maneuver each man away from the door, then returned to the corridor and allowed the door to close. A single tap on the control panel set into the adjacent bulkhead activated the door's locking mechanism. Now it could only be opened from this side.

"Two down. How many to go?"

Running footsteps coming in his direction made Lorca turn to face back up the corridor, phaser at the ready, but he lowered the weapon at the sight of Ensign Terri Bridges, another of the outpost's five-person team, coming around a corner. Unlike him, the junior sensor-control officer was dressed in a standard Starfleet duty uniform, though her brown shoulder-length hair looked disheveled. As her gaze met his, her expression turned to one of relief.

"Thank god. A friendly face."

Happy to see a member of his team, Lorca felt his anxiety level drop, but only the slightest bit. "You okay?"

Bridges nodded. "Yeah." She pointed a thumb over her shoulder, back the way she had come. "I stunned two more of them near the secondary entrance. The weapons they were carrying were set to kill, sir. Internal sensors showed another dozen or so, moving in or around the outpost. Any idea what the hell this is all about, Commander?"

"I can guess, but it'd just be a stab in the dark." Lorca signaled for her to follow him before he began making his way down a junction corridor that would take them to the facility's primary control room. "It has to be connected to the emergency protocols the governor put into effect, but only if she's out of her damned mind. They can't just be after our remaining food stores. Besides, we already pledged everything we had to help out as best we could."

According to the latest reports coming from the governor's office, the fungal infection raging across the Tarsus IV settlements remained unidentified. Likewise, its origins were not known. Not in dispute was the effect the contamination was having on the colony's food supply. The fungus was ravaging organic foodstuffs at an alarming rate, leaving only prepackaged meals and field or emergency ration packs to feed more than eight thousand colonists. The fungus also had infiltrated colony farms and hydroponics facilities, permeating soil and forcing the eradication of crops and plants across New Anchorage and the smaller, outlying settlements. Food-processing equipment responsible for transforming raw, inedible material into actual meals was also affected. Engineers were dismantling and decontaminating the machinery, while the bulk of compromised food compounds were being destroyed in a desperate attempt to salvage at least some of the material. Until the infection could be arrested, however, all of this effort would be for naught.

The more immediate problem was that even the most generous estimates determined that the remaining food stores would never stretch far enough to support everyone for any appreciable length of time. A distress call had been dispatched and help was on the way, but there were concerns that assistance would not arrive before the already limited supplies were exhausted. In response to this dire predicament, the colony leadership enacted strict protocols governing the distribution of the remaining food. A curfew was also in effect, prohibiting citizens from being outside between the hours of 2200 and 0600. Security personnel were charged with enforcing the new restrictions and maintaining order, their new mandate a far cry from the regular, ordinary daily activities that exemplified life among the Tarsus IV populace.

From his back pocket, Lorca extracted his Starfleet-issue communicator and flipped open its cover. The device did not emit its telltale chirp to signal its activation. Was it inoperative?

"This is Lorca to any member of the outpost team. Respond." There was no reply from the contingent's other three officers, whose whereabouts and status remained unknown. Instead, he received only a low hiss, indicating a problem with the communications frequency. He gestured for Bridges to try her own communicator, waiting with growing dread while she repeated the call to the other members of the facility's Starfleet contingent and received the same result.

"If I had to guess," she said, "we're being jammed somehow. I'd need a tricorder or access to external sensors to be sure, though."

Lorca waved away the suggestion. "I'm sure enough. Come on." He indicated for Bridges to follow him. "We need to get to ops. After the computer signaled the unauthorized entry, I ordered it to seal that section and only open it to voice commands from the team. That won't stop somebody from cutting through the doors, but it should buy us a little time."

They encountered no resistance as they made their way through the facility's single level. Heading away from the crew's living quarters and recreation areas, they passed the compartments designated for the outpost's power generation and distribution systems along with the main computer, sensor, and communications equipment. Most of these components were automated, though they required routine maintenance and the occasional repair from Lorca and his people. Otherwise, the team's primary duties revolved around analyzing data received from a network of automated deep space sensor arrays. Each probe was aimed toward the distant reaches of the Alpha Quadrant, searching for signs of activity or civilization as well as being ever watchful for the approach of potential threats.

Unlike the observation stations constructed on asteroids and deployed along the Neutral Zone separating the Federation from space claimed by the Romulan Empire, the arrays were uninhabited. Immense constructs of metal framework protected the sensitive monitoring hardware cradled within them. Routine maintenance of the arrays fell under the purview of Starfleet's Corps of Engineers and usually was handled by the engineering staff of starships on patrol in the area. This left the small outpost crew with the often mundane yet still necessary chore of reviewing telemetry received from the arrays and transmitting relevant findings and other information back to Starbase 11, the designated Starfleet support installation for this sector.

It was time-consuming if undemanding work, and a far cry from fending off armed intrusions.

Observation Outpost Tarsus IV, or "OT-4," established nearly a century earlier, was a remote installation some distance from the nearest starbase and even farther away from the excitement of starship duty. Its presence on the planet predated the civilian colony and it continued to operate as its own entity following the arrival of the first settlers toward the end of the twenty-second century. The planet's location made it an ideal destination along the ever-expanding trade and Starfleet patrol routes in this sector of space. As colonization efforts continued to push ever outward from Earth and the more heavily trafficked regions of territory belonging to the still burgeoning United Federation of Planets, Tarsus IV became an anchor point on stellar navigation charts. After years spent in near isolation, Starfleet personnel assigned to the outpost welcomed the new arrivals with open arms.

Like the rest of the current contingent, Lorca arrived for duty only six months earlier. It was customary to rotate the entire five-person team every two years, following a brief transition period as the outgoing team ensured their replacements were up to speed on their new assignments. After serving for three years as leader of the security detachment aboard the *U.S.S. Helios*, and four years on two other starships before that, Lorca was looking for a change of pace and scenery. Duty at a regular Starfleet starbase or ground installation held little appeal for him, and it was his captain and mentor, Zachary Matuzas, who suggested the Tarsus IV billet at OT-4. Matuzas, as unconventional a commanding officer as Lorca had known at that point in his brief career, informed him that not only was the observation and relay outpost an important part of Starfleet's overall security mission, but it would provide him ample opportunity to rediscover his "land legs" in addition to an appreciation for wide-open spaces, fresh air, and actual sunshine. After reviewing the requirements to serve as leader of the small Starfleet team assigned to OT-4, the newly minted Lieutenant Commander Lorca decided it was a perfect counterbalance to almost a decade spent in space.

Space is sounding pretty good right about now.

Approaching the end of the corridor leading from the outpost's work and crew areas, Lorca stopped at the hatch that would give them access to the facility's command and control areas. It also contained an exit from the structure, which the intruders almost certainly would have exploited as part of their forced entry. Would there be invaders on the other side of the door? Without a tricorder or the ability to consult the outpost's sensor controls, there was no way to know.

"We might have company in here," he said, keeping his voice low. To emphasize his point, he raised his phaser and pointed it toward the door.

Bridges lifted her own weapon, cradling it in both hands. "Okay."

Like the other entrances to the crew's living spaces, this hatch did not automatically open when someone approached, but instead had to be unlocked by a code entered into the keypad set into the bulkhead. Entering his own access code, Lorca felt his grip tighten on his phaser as his other hand hovered over the control on the keypad that would execute the command to open the door.

"Here goes nothing."

Within the two seconds that passed as he touched the control and the door slid aside, Lorca noted two things. First, he saw the unmoving forms of the team's engineer, Chief Petty Officer Meizhen Bao, and communications specialist Lieutenant Piotr Nolokov lying slumped against the bulkheads to either side of the short corridor. Feeling anger welling up within him, Lorca shifted his gaze to two intruders standing before the door leading to ops. One of the men, a muscled individual with close-cropped blond hair, was holding his phaser close to his face and using it as a torch to cut through the reinforced hatch. Both were dressed in the uniform of the colony's security forces, and they heard the sound of the door behind them opening. The man watching his companion work, of slighter build and with black hair that reached his shoulders, reacted first, the phaser in his left hand coming up to aim toward Lorca and Bridges.

"Commander!"

Lorca felt himself pushed to his left, the intruder's phaser beam slicing through the air and just missing his right arm. Dropping to a crouch, Bridges returned fire, striking the security officer in the chest. He fell back against the wall behind him and slid to the floor at the same time his partner was crouching and twisting around to fire in their direction. Lorca was faster, aiming and firing before the other man could get off a shot. The intruder fell to his knees before slumping forward and falling to the deck.

"Thanks for that," said Lorca, offering a respectful nod to Bridges before stepping through the hatch and into the corridor. He kept his phaser leveled at the two stunned intruders until verifying their unconsciousness. Satisfied that neither man was going anywhere anytime soon, he kicked away their phasers before turning to where Bridges knelt beside the fallen form of Meizhen Bao.

"She's dead, sir," reported the sensor officer. She glanced to the body of Piotr Nolokov. "They both are."

Why?

What possible justification could there be for such a wanton act? Despite only serving with them for the brief period since being assigned to OT-4, these people had become more than colleagues. The remote nature of their present assignment saw to it that they were one another's best friends. Bao had been a formidable tennis player, as Lorca discovered the hard way during their frequent, spirited games on Sunday mornings, while Nolokov had fancied himself an amateur astronomer. It was not unusual to find him sitting in an open field a kilometer or so west of the outpost on clear evenings, using an old-fashioned refractor telescope to peer at the stars in Tarsus IV's night sky. Lorca had joined him on a few of those occasions, during which he also enjoyed samples of the latest bourbon produced by the lieutenant using a method of his own devising. The results were something that had to be experienced to be appreciated, as Lorca learned.

Now the two of them were gone, cut down in violent fashion for no sensible reason. Someone needed to answer for this. Lorca knew he would not be satisfied until he obtained a suitable explanation, no matter what it took or from whom he was forced to extract the answers. If that meant fighting his way through every member of the colony's security force and right up to the governor herself, then so be it.

Damn every last one of you.

His thoughts were shattered by the sound of the door to ops sliding aside without warning, and Lorca jerked himself around to face that direction, raising his phaser and aiming it toward whatever new threat might be coming his way.

2

"Hey!"

Lorca stared down the length of his weapon into the wide eyes of Lieutenant Aasal Soltani. The outpost's lead computer specialist put up his hands in surprise, and his eyes were riveted on the phaser hovering mere centimeters in front of his face.

Exhaling in relief, Lorca lowered the phaser. "Sorry." Drawing a breath as he congratulated himself on not shooting the junior officer, he said, "Glad to see you're okay, Aasal."

"You too, sir."

Soltani looked fatigued and worried, and if Lorca was reading his face with any accuracy, there might also be a hint of fear there as well. A tall, lean man with dark skin and hair, he was a native of Saudi Arabia on Earth, and when he spoke it was with a cadence that seemed almost musical.

Looking past Lorca, Soltani offered a small, joyless smile as he caught sight of Bridges. "Good to see you, too, Ensign. When the alarm sounded, I secured myself in ops and waited for the rest of you to arrive." His expression fell as his gaze turned to the fallen forms of Bao and Nolokov. "Piotr and Meizhen were being chased by these two men. They weren't armed. They never had a chance." He eyed the stunned security officers. "They shot them without ever saying a word, then just stepped past them and started cutting into the door. If you hadn't come when you did . . ."

Nodding in understanding, Lorca placed a hand on the other man's shoulder. "It's okay, Aasal. There was nothing you could've done."

The three officers worked to carry their fallen comrades into ops before Lorca sealed the door. Only then did he allow himself to relax the slightest bit. Adrenaline was still driving him, fueling his anxiety and his anger, and it required physical effort to get his emotions back under control. He wanted justice for Nolokov and Bao, but he knew there were more immediate concerns.

Soon. The word hammered the inside of his skull, repeating over and over as he gazed at the bodies of his colleagues. *You have my word, friends.*

Forcing himself to look away from their still forms, he took in the operations center. It was a simple, utilitarian affair: a rectangular room with workstations set into three of its four walls. A large viewscreen—bigger than the main display that was a common feature of most starship bridges—dominated the front wall, and was flanked by a pair of computer consoles. Stations dedicated to various primary stations lined the other two walls. Unlike on a ship's bridge, there was no command chair at the room's center. Instead, Lorca's place of authority resided at a workstation situated atop a raised dais near the wall opposite the viewscreen. Seeing Ensign Bridges already sitting at her sensor control station, he began moving in that direction.

"How many more intruders are we dealing with?"

Bridges nodded without turning from her console. "There are ten other life signs that aren't ours, sir." She pointed to one of her station's smaller computer displays. "It doesn't look like they're hanging around." Pausing to enter a string of commands across a row of control keys, she added, "They're definitely withdrawing. I'm seeing a pair of ground transports positioned about a hundred meters south of our position."

"We stunned six of them," replied Lorca, glancing to Soltani. "We'll need to secure them somewhere until I can talk to them." The outpost was not equipped with a brig or holding cell, so they would have to improvise a solution. "Put them outside and secure the exterior hatches, except for the two we found outside ops. Those two can go in the extra guest quarters. No windows there, and we can secure the hatch well enough. They won't need to be there very long." He had no intention of holding them any longer than was necessary, but he had not yet decided what he would do with them once he was satisfied they were of no further value to him. Besides, there was the matter of their having killed Bao and Nolokov, which could not go unaddressed.

One thing at a time.

Lieutenant Soltani, who had taken up position at his own workstation at the center of the room, said, "Commander, we have another problem. Communications are down. I thought they were only jamming us. Instead, it looks like the whole array is offline."

Before he could stop himself, Lorca glanced to the still form of Piotr Nolokov. Though every member of the OT-4 team was cross-trained in multiple disciplines in order to assist one another as needed, Nolokov was by far the most qualified of the group when it came to operating, maintaining, and repairing the outpost's communications equipment.

"I've checked the sensor logs," said Soltani. "It's only been inactive for about ten minutes. They must've done it on their way out. I can inspect the internal systems and provide an estimate on repairs."

Lorca nodded. "You and Bridges take care of our visitors, then see to that." He did not like the idea of being cut off, not just from the colony but also from transmitting or receiving messages from Starbase 11 or whichever vessels were en route to Tarsus IV to render aid.

Bridges turned in her seat. Her expression once again was a mask of concern.

"Sir, the people withdrawing from the area? They're carrying weapons crates. Five of them, on antigravity sleds."

"What?" Lorca leaned closer, looking at the readings for himself. "Son of a bitch. You've confirmed the armory was breached?"

Frowning, Bridges replied, "Yes, sir. The door lock's still engaged, but internal sensors show the intrusion. They probably cut through the hatch the same way their friends were trying to get in here."

"Could that be the reason they came here in the first place?" asked Soltani. "But why? The colony's security force has its own weapons."

Lorca turned and crossed the room to his workstation. "We have stuff they don't." He dropped into the chair behind his desk and reached for the tabletop computer interface. "What the hell did they take?"

Despite the outpost's size, it still maintained a substantial storage facility including an armory. The latter was a holdover from the days when OT-4 carried a larger contingent that accounted for the planet's entire population. There were concerns regarding the installation's safety in such an isolated, irregularly traveled area of space at the edge of Federation territory. With that in mind, the facility's active defensive capabilities were far greater than they were today. Most of the heavier weapons on hand for that purpose had been dismantled and placed into storage. Though they had been upgraded or replaced at normal intervals along with the rest of the outpost's equipment, they remained in their shipping containers, tucked away in the armory. The only exceptions were the personal side arms secured in lockboxes in each team member's living quarters.

Her attention once more on her console, Bridges called out, "The armory's internal sensors have been deactivated. I'm not able to get an inventory of the room's contents." She cast a look toward him. "Based on the size of the crates, I'm guessing phaser rifles, but we'd have to do a visual check to be sure."

Lorca, having just failed in his own attempt to call up the armory's contents via the outpost computer network, scowled. "No. I have a better idea."

3

Their wrists secured and sitting lashed to chairs procured by Lieutenant Soltani, the two men regarded Lorca with matching glares of disdain. Neither they nor he said anything upon his entry into the guest quarters, flanked by Soltani and Bridges, and the silence remained unbroken for the ensuing sixty or seventy seconds. It was then that Lorca was rewarded when the muscular man with blond hair—the one cutting into the ops door when they were interrupted—shifted in his seat, and his expression of defiance began giving way to uncertainty.

"I don't have a lot of patience for this sort of thing," Lorca said after several more seconds passed. "Let's just get to it. You both stand charged with murdering two Starfleet officers, aggravated burglary, unauthorized possession of Starfleet property, and pissing me off. It's the first and last things on that list that should concern you right now. Those two people were my friends. Neither one of you looks smart enough to have planned and executed this little raid of yours on your own, so you're going to tell me who sent you here."

"And if we don't?" said the blond man, earning him a frown of disapproval from his dark-haired companion.

To answer his detainee's question, Lorca stepped forward and drove the sole of his boot into the man's chest. The force of the kick was sufficient to send the other man and his chair toppling over until he slammed to the floor, lying on his back and with his feet pointing toward the ceiling.

Ignoring the man's groans of surprise and growing anger, Lorca turned his attention to his other unwanted guest. "Who sent you? Don't make me ask you again. Was it Governor Ribiero?" To his surprise, the man sneered in response to the question.

"Her? No. She's not even in charge anymore. She doesn't have experience with emergency situations like this." His look of contempt hardened. "So she was removed."

Lorca only knew Gisela Ribiero thanks to a handful of brief encounters since his arrival on Tarsus IV. The governor had been in office a short time following the most recent elections, which came about a few months before a sudden, unexpected influx of settlers transported from another colony world that had endured a natural disaster, necessitating evacuation and relocation. To that point, it was by far the most formidable test for Ribiero in her brief tenure as governor, and the growing pains from that abrupt expansion had caused no small amount of strife, from what Lorca knew of the situation. Among the other challenges this presented, she also faced conflicting sentiments from the original Tarsus colonists ranging from acceptance of the situation to outright protest. She won over the populace by playing to their basic humanity and empathy; Lorca recalled a not insignificant pushback from those adopting hard-line stances about what some perceived as a trampling of their basic independence and right to decide for themselves how best to utilize the home they had built here. As months passed and the Epsilon Sorona refugees continued to assimilate into their new home, much of the negative commentary offered by some news broadcasts and publications seemed to wane.

But it obviously didn't die out altogether.

Of course, the obstacles that came with resettling the Epsilon Sorona colonists paled in comparison to the present ecological crisis. Lorca thought it unfair to judge Ribiero too harshly on this point, given the speed with which the contagion spread. There had been precious little time to attempt understanding the contagion or finding a way to arrest it. Ribiero's first priority was seeing to the safety and security of the colonists.

Someone, it seemed, had other ideas.

"Who's in charge now?" asked Soltani.

Still on his back and tied to his chair, the blond man replied, "His name is Kodos. He apparently has some experience with crisis management, and he agreed to take over as governor until we get through this."

"And who's Kodos?" asked Bridges.

"I've heard the name, but never met him." Lorca knew only a handful of Governor Ribiero's staff, and he found it troubling that the colony's leadership council would see fit to remove her from office. How would such a seemingly rash action be received by the rest of the citizenry? As for Kodos, Lorca made a note to find out all he could about the new governor before making any attempt to speak or meet with him.

To the detainees, he asked, "And he's the one who sent you here?"

The two men exchanged glances before the blond man said, "Yes."

"With orders to kill us?" Lorca let his voice harden as he asked the question. It had the desired effect on both men, as their eyes widened in renewed concern.

"We were supposed to survey your weapons and your food stores," said the dark-haired man. "See how much escaped contamination."

Stepping closer, Lorca glowered at the man. "We already shared that information with Governor Ribiero. We offered to pool our remaining resources with the rest of the colony and stretch everything as far as we could."

Only a third of the raw compounds used for the outpost's food processors were unaffected by the fungal infection, with the rest quarantined and destroyed by Chief Nolokov. That accomplished, the engineer secured the untainted material in vacuum-sealed containers. What remained was still sufficient to feed the entire five-person team for almost two months without resorting to rationing. There also was a supply of emergency individual food packs that added another three weeks to that total. Earlier in the day, Nolokov confirmed trace amounts of the destructive fungus within two of the facility's six food processors, requiring the deactivation and decontamination of that equipment. The chief elected to clean all of the units, just to be on the safe side. With the infection still active, the decon procedures were a temporary measure, but it was Nolokov's desire to do everything possible to stay ahead of the situation to the maximum possible extent.

Armed with this information Lorca sent a message to the governor just prior to the end of his previous duty shift. He wanted to demonstrate to Ribiero and all of the colonists that he and the OT-4 team were a part of this community, in times of adversity as well as prosperity. This new governor, Kodos, should or would have known that before the dispatching of the team to the outpost on their bizarre mission.

"We offered our help," said Lorca, "and yet you came in here with no compunctions about killing us, and once it became obvious you wouldn't be able to do that, your friends stole our weapons before cutting and running. What are you planning to do with what you took?" When neither prisoner opted to answer, he felt his hands balling into fists, and it required force of will to keep his arms at his sides. The other men could see his rising emotions as both looked back at him with mounting fear.

Taking a moment to verify his temper remained in check, Lorca relaxed his hands, but kept his tone cold and hard. "We obviously can't remand you to colony security; at least, not until I've had a chance to verify who we can trust. I can't kill you, though the thought's crossed my mind more than once. For now, you'll stay here. Behave yourselves, and you'll be turned over to the captain of whatever Starfleet ship arrives to help us. Screw with me, and I'll throw you over whatever cliff I can find. Do we understand each other?"

He did not wait for a reply, but instead turned on his heel and exited the room. Only after he was in the corridor and out of sight of the prisoners did he allow his ire a small bit of freedom, channeled into his fist as he punched the nearby bulkhead.

"Commander? Are you all right?" It was Bridges, standing next to Soltani near the guest quarters' now-closed door.

Relishing the pain in his hand, Lorca said nothing for a moment as he flexed his fingers to make sure he had not broken anything. He leaned toward the wall that was the target of his rage, using his other hand to brace himself as he drew several deep, calming breaths.

"I'm sorry for that." Shaking off the residual pain in his hand, he gestured toward the guest quarters. "Make sure they're secure. We're going to have to keep them here until we can figure out what to do with them."

If it was true that the new governor, Kodos, had sent the team of intruders here, then it was possible the rest of the colony's security force could be similarly mobilized against the outpost. Now that Lorca and the others knew what they might face, they could prepare for further incursions, but they would not be able to hold off any sort of sustained attack. Lorca knew they had to get ahead of this situation before it spiraled out of control.

"Give me a minute," he told the others. "Aasal, get started on that check of the communications array. See if you can lend a hand, Ensign. I'll rejoin you in ops."

Bridges nodded. "Aye, Commander."

Once alone, Lorca moved down the short hallway to his own quarters, allowing the door to close behind him before releasing a tired sigh. What the hell was he supposed to do? This was not a situation for which he had received training. In his mind, there was only one course of action: confront Kodos, whoever the hell he was, and get to the bottom of this. As far as Lorca was concerned, and until proven otherwise, the governor was the one to answer for Meizhen Bao and Piotr Nolokov.

Crossing to his desk, Lorca noticed the small icon flashing in the lower right corner of his computer screen, indicating an unviewed message. The time stamp showed the message was received less than an hour ago, prior to the intrusion and the disabling of the communications array. Lorca tapped the control to access the message and saw it was from Balayna Ferasini, a civilian geologist whom he had met soon after his arrival on the planet.

"Gabriel, I know you said you weren't coming into town tonight because of the new curfew rules, but something's happening later this evening. Have you heard the news about Governor Ribiero? She's apparently been removed from her post, and the council's installed a new governor. I've never heard of him, but he supposedly has experience with emergency management during situations like what we're dealing with. His name is Kodos. Do you know him?"

A native of Alpha Centauri, Balayna was, in a word, beautiful, with dark, curly hair that fell to her shoulders and soulful, jade-green eyes that had drawn him in from the first moment he saw them. Lorca met her by chance at one of New Anchorage's more popular taverns. They struck up a conversation that ended up lasting well past the bar's closing, and their relationship had only grown during the intervening months. Her carefree nature, warmth of heart, and unrelentingly positive outlook on life was something that fascinated Lorca almost to the point of intoxication. Until that point, he had never been with anyone like her, and even his closest friends would describe him as conventional: prim and proper, if not outright boring. Balayna was the perfect counter to all of that, but rather than judge him, she instead coaxed him from a shell he did not even realize he inhabited until meeting her. By the end of that first evening, he was entranced.

It became a habit for him to spend weekends in town with her, and they had even discussed his moving in with her on a permanent basis. Though he had not come to Tarsus IV looking for a relationship, the idea of extending his tour here, or even leaving Starfleet and staying here, was one Lorca found himself considering with increasing frequency.

"*Anyway, he's called a special gathering for tonight at the amphitheater. He's going to speak to the entire colony face-to-face. Everyone's been sent a personal invitation to attend. It sounds like he's trying to address concerns and maybe boost morale. Given the size of the current population, they've sent messages to let us know they're splitting us into two groups, since only about half of us will fit in the stadium at one time.*" Balayna paused, sighing. "*It seems like a lot of trouble for a simple speech, but we could probably use a bit of camaraderie right about now. I know you said you wanted to honor the cur-*

*few and the other new rules, but I'd feel better if you were here
with me tonight. Maybe the new governor can give you and
your team special exemptions or something. If you get this message, I'm slated to attend the first gathering. Meet me here at
my place, and we'll go together. Talk to you soon."*

The message ended and Balayna's image disappeared,
replaced by a Starfleet insignia and leaving Lorca to ponder
this new development. A large gathering of colonists at the
amphitheater was not an unusual occurrence. The venue
was constructed with the idea of being able to accommodate the entire population while showcasing all manner of
live performances and other events. However, if the new
governor wanted to impart critical information to everyone
in his charge, why not make use of the colony's communication system? Perhaps Balayna was right, and this was a
means of putting the colonists at ease while keeping them
updated on the current situation.

Sounds like something we shouldn't miss.

4

Occupying space in one corner of the ship's cargo bay, the small field desk was awash with data slates and cards along with a few tools. There was also a small lamp and a computer terminal, along with an empty coffee mug and the remnants of a ration pack. Was that lunch, or dinner? She could not remember. Come to think of it, she could not even recall the meal's contents.

Maybe that's a good thing.

Philippa Georgiou sat up in her chair, both hands moving to the small of her back as she stretched and released a sigh of relief. A glance at the chronometer in the corner of the terminal's display before closing her eyes told her how long she had been sitting here, and the revelation only served to deepen the fatigue she struggled to keep at bay. What the chronometer also told her was that her day was far from over. A respite was still hours away, lurking behind a veritable pile of tasks that seemed to be growing even as she continued her efforts to scale it. If she was lucky, she might have time for a shower and quick nap before arriving at her destination.

And that's when the real work starts.

"Commander Georgiou?"

Opening her eyes, Georgiou looked up to see Lieutenant Enamori Jenn standing in front of the desk. How long had she been there? Long enough to say her name twice, Georgiou realized.

"I'm sorry, Lieutenant." Feeling a twinge of embarrassment, Georgiou forced a tired smile as she gestured to her desk. "These reports are pretty mind numbing."

Jenn grimaced, holding up a data slate of her own. "I'm afraid I'm only adding to that, Commander. I've got the final inventory counts you requested from the team leaders."

"Well, I asked for it." Georgiou took the data slate from Jenn and laid it atop the others demanding her attention. "Thank you for taking the lead on this. I'll review it once I get a break in a month or so."

Jenn smiled in understanding and sympathy at the weak joke. She was a striking Betazoid woman. Her species was almost indiscernible from humans, with the main giveaway being the black irises of her eyes. Her brown hair was pulled up and away from her face and held in place by a silver band at the base of her neck, the resulting ponytail falling below her shoulders. The top of her uniform tunic was unfastened, exposing her dark, Starfleet-issue undershirt. Her homeworld, Betazed, was a recent addition to the Federation, and Jenn represented Georgiou's first exposure to her people, meeting her for the first time during their joint briefing at Starbase 11 prior to boarding the *U.S.S. Narbonne*. From what Georgiou could tell, Betazoids preferred to keep to themselves, at least so far as sharing details of their personal lives. Jenn was a pleasant individual, she carried out her duties with precision and care, and in less than two days had become an invaluable assistant to Georgiou. The team into which they had both been thrown worked at a frantic pace to prepare themselves for the situation they all knew lay ahead.

"I need to get away from this," she said, pushing back from the desk and rising to her feet. She caught herself from emitting an involuntary groan of relief as the muscles in her back thanked her for the change in position. "Even if it's just for a few minutes."

Moving away from the corner she had established as her temporary office and with Jenn falling into step beside her, Georgiou moved into the oversized cargo bay. The chamber was one of twelve taking up the bulk of the *Narbonne*'s interior volume, and like two adjacent compartments this one was filled to overflowing with all manner of supplies and equipment. She did not have to review any of Lieutenant Jenn's inventory reports to know that food accounted for most of the space allocated to her and her team for this mission. It would also be the thing in highest demand where they were heading, and Georgiou knew that despite the sheer tonnage of materiel presently in her care, it was only the beginning of what would be needed.

But it's a start.

"Any updates from the captain?" asked Jenn.

Georgiou shook her head, recalling her last conversation with the *Narbonne*'s commanding officer, Aurobindo Korrapati. "Still no response from the colony, even though he's had someone trying to hail them since we left Starbase 11. He's also got his engineers pulling out every trick they know to extend power to the ship's long-range sensors, but we're still too far away. Maybe in an hour or so." At the ship's present speed, they were less than ten hours from their destination.

Tarsus IV.

It was but one of numerous Federation colony worlds about which Georgiou knew nothing. Calling up information from the *Narbonne*'s computer had done little to enlighten her beyond the usual collection of statistics regarding the settlement's founding and the number of people who called the planet home. Of particular interest was its selection as the new home for refugees from another colony that had suffered a disaster requiring total evacuation of that world; Georgiou recalled reading about that in some report. Such drastic action was uncommon enough that it would draw attention, but it was also one of the things she noted in her quest to understand the cause of the situation into which she and her team were wading.

"When I was at the Academy, I had friends who grew up on colony worlds," she said as they proceeded farther into the bay. "After we left Starbase 11, I reached out to a few of them I knew had lived through some tough times, such as extreme weather events, earthquakes, and even disease. Nothing on this scale, but I thought it'd be helpful to have an idea of what to expect from the colonists when we arrive."

To that end, Georgiou pestered Captain Korrapati and the *Narbonne*'s communications officer to locate and dispatch subspace messages to her former classmates, all of whom were scattered to various ships or installations. Her idea paid off, as she was able to get some fresh insight into the mindset of colonists besieged by crisis.

Jenn asked, "What did your friends have to say?"

"The Federation has contingency plans for all sorts of things," replied Georgiou. "Tarsus IV is a bit of a problem because its population is much larger than what you'd expect to see this far out from the major population centers." She knew this was the result of the relocation effort, which added six thousand colonists to the two thousand already living on Tarsus IV. Though the resettlement was unusual in its scope, the planet was more than capable of supporting a community of that size.

Or so we thought.

"Even the best plans take time to implement," said Jenn. "Especially when we're talking about planets light-years away from populated or well-trafficked regions. No matter how fast our ships can go, space is still very big."

Georgiou nodded. "And helping eight thousand people is no easy task."

The situation on Tarsus IV, as reported during her mission briefing from the commander of Starbase 11, Admiral Brett Anderson, was dire. Food supplies and the ability to create more savaged by a fungal contamination unlike anything previously encountered, placing the lives of the entire population in jeopardy. After the receipt of the original distress call, initial estimates from Starfleet put the arrival of rescue ships at the colony in just over a month, at which point any remaining food stores on the planet would be long exhausted. The Tarsus IV settlers were looking at hard times, barring a miracle, which had come in two-part form.

First was word that a ship of the line was presently speeding at high warp back from its patrol of the Federation-Klingon border. A *Constitution*-class starship, one of Starfleet's newest and most powerful vessels, would be able to provide all manner of support upon its arrival, including dedicated science and engineering teams that could tackle the problem of the still-active infection.

Assuming we strike out when we get there, of course.

Providing a more immediate response was the eclectic mix of officers and civilian specialists cobbled together by Admiral Anderson, placed under Georgiou's charge, and thrown aboard the *Narbonne*. Members of the team she commanded, many of whom she did not even yet know by name, maneuvered and worked around the stacks of cargo containers and other storage vessels taking up deck space here. Like her, these men and women had been working at a breakneck pace since leaving Starbase 11 less than forty hours earlier. Everything about this response was being executed in hurried fashion, because that was all for which there was time, but Georgiou was still working to assemble a viable plan that would deploy her people as well as the supplies they were bringing in the most efficient manner. She had pored over every scrap of information about Tarsus IV and its capital city, New Anchorage, using that data to configure her plan with an emphasis on distribution of materiel as well as the decontamination and restoration efforts of the colony's food manufacturing and processing infrastructure. All of that would have to be addressed within the first days of the *Narbonne*'s arrival, and Georgiou wanted her team to hit the ground running, as it would be up to them to hold the line until other ships arrived to augment the assistance effort. She and her people might be tired now, but she was certain their preparations would pay off once they made planetfall.

"Bridge to Commander Georgiou."

The voice of Captain Korrapati echoed in the cargo bay, and it took Georgiou a moment to locate a communications panel on a nearby bulkhead. Moving to it, she thumbed its activation control.

"Georgiou here."

"Sorry to interrupt your work, Commander, but I'd like to see you in my ready room."

Georgiou exchanged looks with Jenn, her eyes widening in surprise. What might this mean?

"I'll be right there, sir."

She severed the connection before turning back to Jenn. "I don't know how long this is going to take, but let the team know to finish whatever they've got going and to take a break. We'll get back to it in five hours." It was not the ideal reward for the hard work her people had been performing to this point, but it would have to suffice. There would be time for rest later.

"Aye, Commander," replied Jenn.

Georgiou exited the cargo bay, maneuvering down the corridor toward a ladder junction. It had taken her less than a day to acclimate herself to the *Narbonne*'s deck plan, owing to its size and layout. Not a ship of the line or even an advanced science vessel, this was a colony support vessel: a utilitarian craft designed for the sort of heavy-duty "grunt work" required to establish, refurbish, or even salvage or relocate planet-bound settlements. Essentially an overlong cylinder with warp nacelles tucked against its upper primary hull, most of its interior spaces consisted of immense cargo holds and berthing compartments of the sort needed to transport large numbers of people and even livestock. Designed for planetary landings, the vessel could also serve as shelter for newly arrived settlers until more permanent housing was constructed. The rest of the ship was a relatively simple network of connecting corridors and service conduits. Unlike starships with turbolift systems that ran horizontally as well as vertically, the *Narbonne* possessed only standard elevators connecting its eight decks, with pairs of cars located forward, aft, and amidships.

Georgiou learned on her first day aboard that it was more efficient to utilize the network of ladder wells if she wanted to get somewhere fast. Thanks to this, she arrived on the bridge less than five minutes after the captain's summons. She found him not in the raised seat at the center of the room, but instead standing at one of the perimeter workstations, hovering over the officer seated there. In his late fifties, at least according to the personnel file Georgiou had reviewed, Aurobindo Korrapati was a slender man, with close-cropped, stark-white hair that provided an acute contrast to his dark brown skin. His uniform appeared to fit him to exacting precision, and his boots were polished to a high gleam. Even without the captain's rank on his uniform, everything about the man seemed to yell "The one in charge."

"Thank you for coming, Commander," he said, upon noticing her arrival as she crossed the bridge toward him. "I apologize again for taking you from your work, but this is something I think deserves your input."

Despite his position as ranking officer on the ship, Korrapati was a man of unfailing politeness in all things. He had a calm, unruffled demeanor about him that Georgiou appreciated, all the more because she knew the captain had not always been the master of a simple colony support vessel. A review of his service record, prior to the *Narbonne*'s departure from Starbase 11, revealed to her that Korrapati was born on Mars to parents who migrated to the planet from Chennai, India, on Earth. He previously served as first officer and later captain of the *U.S.S. Glouchester*, a long-range patrol ship that had seen its share of tough scrapes and combat during his tenure. Most of that action was against marauders or Orion pirates, from whom Korrapati defended civilian merchant shipping and the occasional Federation colony. This was a man who had been tested beyond the confines of classrooms and computer simulations. That carried weight with Georgiou, who had left her former, more martial career path in favor of contributing to Starfleet's ever-expanding interstellar exploration mandate.

"What can I do for you, sir?"

Motioning for her to follow him, Korrapati began crossing the bridge. Like the rest of the ship, the *Narbonne*'s nerve center was a testament to function over form. Workstations encircled the bridge's command area, which contained the captain's chair as well as consoles for the helm and operations officers. At this time of ship's night, only a third of the stations were occupied. Everything about the bridge suggested a vessel that did not benefit from the regular maintenance and care afforded to ships of the line. Instead, it was the transport's crew of talented and dedicated engineers and other technicians who kept the *Narbonne* flying. That much was obvious to Georgiou within hours of coming aboard and assuming her role as "passenger."

The hatch leading to the captain's ready room was set into the bulkhead near the bridge's aft section, just to the right of the hatch connecting this compartment to a service corridor and the rest of the ship. Korrapati led the way into the adjoining room and Georgiou followed, stepping inside and allowing the door to close behind her.

"Coffee?" asked Korrapati as he moved to a counter extending from the wall at the rear of the room. The space held a food slot and, to Georgiou's surprise, a coffee pot sitting in its own brewing machine.

"You make your own?" she asked.

Korrapati nodded. "Absolutely." He gestured toward the food slot. "I've tried everything I can think of to program a proper recipe into that contraption, but it's hopeless." Holding up the cup in his hand, he added, "My brother sells his own blends to old-fashioned types like me. This one he made just for me, and I keep the recipe in my safe, along with the other documents and codes vital to Federation security."

Unable to stifle a chuckle as she accepted the cup, Georgiou nodded in appreciation. "I'm honored." She declined the offer of any sweeteners, preferring her coffee without additives.

"Help yourself, once you've decided it's the best coffee you've ever tasted."

After pouring a cup for himself, Korrapati moved to the chair behind his small, angled desk, which sat in one corner facing the door. He motioned for her to take the couch built into an alcove next to the desk. Georgiou took the opportunity to examine the small set of shelves built into the wall opposite the coffee maker, noting the selection of old-style hardcover books along with a few keepsakes. She smiled, admiring the collection and thinking of the small library she had amassed over the years and carried with her from one assignment to the next. Like hers, the books here were a blend of older, weathered volumes and recent facsimile editions. She noted that the captain's reading tastes ran the gamut from philosophy and history—human and otherwise—to classic literature and even a few modern fiction titles. The last category indicated Korrapati was a traditionalist in many aspects of his life beyond ceding his coffee needs to a machine. He seemed to share her preference for the look and feel of a physical book to its electronic counterpart.

"As you can imagine," he said after sipping from his coffee, "this isn't something I'm eager to discuss in front of the crew. Right now, only my first officer and my communications staff are aware of what I'm about to tell you. I'd like it kept that way, at least until we know more."

Cradling her coffee cup in her hands, Georgiou replied, "Understood, Captain."

Korrapati leaned back in his seat, leaving his cup on the desk and idly tracing its edge with the fingers of his right hand. "There's been no response from Tarsus IV. We're not even sure they're receiving our hails. To say I don't like what that might mean is an understatement."

"Particularly since there's been no other contact since Starbase 11 received the initial distress call three days ago."

"Exactly. According to Admiral Anderson, the colony didn't even acknowledge his message that rescue ships were on the way far sooner than originally anticipated." Korrapati frowned. "One would think that cause for celebration, or something."

Georgiou asked, "Any word from the other ships detailed to the rescue operation?"

Still playing with his coffee cup, Korrapati shook his head. "Not yet. At last report, two were pushing to get to Starbase 11 by the end of the day, loaded and heading out toward us twelve hours after that. The other ship is running silent until it's well enough away from the area of its last assignment. Apparently, Starfleet Command wants its movements kept under wraps as much as possible." He shrugged. "There are three others in that ship class due for deployment by the end of the year. We're not going to be able to keep the *Constitution*s a secret forever."

Given her pending assignment to the *U.S.S. Defiant* following her previous posting aboard the science vessel *Archimedes*, Georgiou had reviewed the technical specifications for the *Constitution*-class starships. They were the crown jewels in Starfleet's rollout of long-duration deep-space exploration vessels, intended for multiyear missions while operating well away from the support structure of starbases and other facilities. The initial fleet of twelve ships would also serve as the latest word in force projection toward the borders of Federation space. They would stand toe to toe with whatever might be thrown at them from the likes of interstellar adversaries like the Klingon and Romulan Empires.

There were those who questioned the need for vessels so overtly intended for military missions, given the present state of relations. No encounters with Romulans had been reported for more than eighty years, following the Earth-Romulan War that preceded the founding of the Federation. Beaten back by an alliance of Earth, Vulcan, Andorian, and Tellarite forces, the Romulans appeared content to retreat behind their borders and leave the rest of the quadrant well enough alone, but longtime Starfleet veterans like Georgiou knew that it was only a matter of time before the Empire resurfaced.

The same was believed true for the Klingon Empire, which also seemed to be ignoring Federation space and ships in favor of concerns elsewhere. It had been years since the last recorded run-in with a Klingon ship. How long would that uneasy peace last?

Not long enough.

His expression sobering, Korrapati leaned forward in his chair, resting his forearms atop his desk. "Commander, I don't mind saying I'm uncomfortable with how all of this is playing out. I don't like not knowing the colony's current situation, or what we may be walking into. There's something . . . just not right about all of this, but I'm damned if I can tell you what I think it is."

"I understand, sir." Experience and instinct told Georgiou that something odd was happening on Tarsus IV. Beyond the reported plague and its disastrous effects, what else could have befallen the luckless colony? Even without primary communications, there still were other methods of establishing contact. A distress beacon could be launched from the planet, for example, programmed to head for Starbase 11 or broadcast a message until it was detected by a passing ship.

After finishing her coffee, Georgiou pushed herself from the couch and made her way to the coffee maker, helping herself to another cup of the captain's personal brew.

It really is pretty damned good.

"Wait," she said, remembering something she recalled from her mission briefing. She turned from the counter to face Korrapati. "What about the Starfleet outpost there?"

The captain scowled. "No contact with them either. Their last status report was also three days ago, and indicated they had plenty of supplies to ride out the crisis until help arrived, but only if they isolated themselves from the rest of the colony. The leader of the team there, Lieutenant

Commander Lorca, reported that they would be donating their untainted supplies to the cause and throwing in their lots with the rest of the civilians."

"A small gesture, but an important one."

Georgiou recalled from her review of the colony's history that the outpost predated the settlement's founding; part of Starfleet's ongoing efforts to monitor Federation borders and potential threats from beyond the imaginary lines that served to divide territory on uncounted stellar cartography maps. As for the colony itself, despite its tendency to eschew as much direct Federation oversight as possible, the people living on the planet maintained a good relationship with the Starfleet contingent. She knew that whatever meager food stores the outpost team possessed would not go very far toward mitigating the larger crisis facing the colonists, but the act would still generate goodwill and a sense of shared sacrifice with everyone forced to endure such hardship.

Of course, now the question was: Why were Commander Lorca and his team also out of contact? Were they experiencing difficulties similar or related to those affecting the colony? Too many questions about this mission were piling up, with no easy access to answers, and Georgiou was beginning to sense some of the same uncertainty and even dread she knew Captain Korrapati must be feeling.

"I'm starting to feel like it's the first day of swimming lessons," she said, "and the instructor just pitched me into the deep end of the pool with a sandbag around my neck."

Korrapati was tapping his fingers on his desk. "About the only advice I can offer at this point is the same thing I'll be telling my crew: be ready for anything, Commander. We're walking into a dark room with no idea where the light switch is, or who might be hiding in there."

"That's how we've proceeded from the start, Captain."

With no real information about the situation, Georgiou
opted to develop a plan that envisioned the worst-case
scenario and relied upon no assistance from the colonists
themselves. If they arrived and it turned out the inhabitants
of Tarsus IV were able to help, so much the better, but until
she could prove otherwise, she was operating under the assumption that she and her team were on their own.

Not only were they tasked with rendering immediate
aid to the colonists, but Georgiou also carried the responsibility of determining whether the situation warranted a
full-scale evacuation of the entire population. Such a decision could not be made until she was on site and able to
assess the extent of the emergency and its impacts not only
on the inhabitants but the planet itself. Would Tarsus IV
even be capable of sustaining life once the present crisis was
addressed? That question would remain unanswered until a
comprehensive study of the fungal infection was completed.
It would also have to be prioritized behind the immediate
need to assist the Tarsus IV colonists through the calamity they faced. For all Georgiou knew, it would be up to
whoever was sent to relieve Captain Korrapati as the senior
Starfleet officer in charge of the response force.

At Starbase 11 while awaiting transport to her next assignment as first officer aboard the *U.S.S. Defiant*, Georgiou
found herself "drafted" by the admiral into emergency service and attached to the transport vessel for temporary duty.
Working with the resources at his disposal, Anderson pulled
together enough people to form a medical team, security
detail, various technical specialists, and a detachment from
Starfleet's Corps of Engineers. A third of the special detachment was pulled from Starbase 11's permanent crew, with
the balance filled out by personnel like Georgiou, all on
their way somewhere else when duty and fate came calling.
While Captain Korrapati retained command of his vessel

and overall authority for this first phase of Starfleet response to the emergency, she would be responsible for deploying her team as appropriate for whatever they might find once the *Narbonne* made planetfall. They were a stopgap measure, as the admiral put it—"first responders."

The whistle of the ship's intercom intruded at that moment, followed by what she recognized as the voice of Commander Natalie Larson, the *Narbonne*'s first officer.

"Bridge to Captain Korrapati. You asked to be advised when we entered maximum sensor range of the Tarsus system. We've crossed that threshold and initiated a sweep of the area. There are no signs of other ship traffic, and we're still not picking up any communications from the colony either."

Exchanging a glance with Georgiou, Korrapati asked, "What's our ETA?"

"Approximately nine hours, twenty minutes at our present speed, sir."

"Continue on course and maintain sensor sweeps. Keep trying to raise the colony at thirty-minute intervals. Notify me once we're close enough to scan the planet, or if anything else changes."

"Aye, sir. Bridge out."

Once the communication was terminated, Korrapati reached up to rub the bridge of his nose.

"They're being rather stubborn, aren't they?" he asked after a moment.

Georgiou nodded. "Looks that way, sir."

"Remember what I said about being ready for anything?"

"Yes?"

"Well, now you've got about nine hours to be ready for everything else too."

5

"I've never seen the streets this crowded."

Walking a footpath through the park that served as New Anchorage's central green space, Gabriel Lorca and Terri Bridges did their best to act as though they were just two more citizens making their way toward the amphitheater.

"Yeah," said Bridges. "Four thousand people heading in the same direction will have that effect. The curfew's not for two more hours, after all."

"Increased security presence." Lorca had noted dozens of uniformed officers, most standing at major intersections or at the entrances to various buildings. With the curfew in effect across the city and outlying settlements, he suspected their numbers would be stretched as they worked to enforce the new mandate. He did not doubt that a significant percentage of the force also was deployed to the amphitheater to help with crowd control. That was fine by him.

Like him, Bridges sported civilian attire, in accordance with his instructions. Traveling via transporter to the city's outskirts, all team members carried phasers, the weapons hidden beneath civilian jackets or under shirts so as not to attract undue attention. They did not have their communicators, as Lorca opted to leave them behind on the chance their frequencies could be tracked. After the incident at the outpost, he eyed every colony security officer they encountered. No one seemed to be reacting with any degree of recognition, but he already had decided against taking any unnecessary chances. That included entering the amphitheater or going where security personnel might be concentrated. He wanted the ability to escape and disappear into the crowd if circumstances required such action.

"It's this way," he said, pointing toward an apartment building situated along the park's western perimeter. Balayna Ferasini lived here. With the outpost's communications array still offline, Lorca was forced to rely on civilian systems in order to attempt reaching her. She had not answered his first call, so he left a message informing her of their imminent arrival. Even as he and Bridges approached Balayna's apartment from the south, Aasal Soltani was making his way there from the north. It was Lorca's hope that not traveling together would allow the team to further escape attention by colony security.

Entering the building proved to be no trouble. Even the one security officer they saw on the street appeared to pay them no notice. Likewise, gaining access to Balayna's residence also came without incident, as Lorca possessed the entry code for her door's keypad lock, which he had shared with the rest of the team in the event they were forced to split up and evade pursuit by the security force.

"Balayna?" he called out as he entered the apartment, and the foyer light came on in response to his presence. "Are you here?"

With Bridges following him, he stepped farther into the domicile, allowing the door to slide closed behind them. The front hall opened into the apartment's living room, which was decorated in understated fashion with a sofa and a pair of overstuffed recliners situated around a low-rise coffee table. Everything rested on a large area rug that Lorca knew Balayna had purchased from a Tellarite merchant in the city's market district. Bookcases lined the walls to his left and right, except for one section that was dominated by a viewing screen typical for a residence of this size. The screen allowed the viewer access to colony and Federation news networks as well as personal and community entertainment libraries.

The far wall was composed of bay windows extending from floor to ceiling. A door was set into the windows, allowing access to a large balcony upon which sat a pair of lounge chairs and a small round table. Art adorned what little wall space remained, and the bookcases were stuffed almost to overflowing with old-fashioned printed books of all shapes and sizes along with a smattering of smaller framed photographs and other keepsakes. Lorca's eyes paused at one picture, cradled in a silver frame, of himself and Balayna. He was shirtless while she wore a two-piece swimsuit, with brilliant blue water and fine white sand serving as a backdrop. It was from an excursion to the colony's one coastal village a month earlier, and he could not help smiling at the memories of the week spent there together.

"Nice place," Bridges offered.

Grunting in acknowledgment, Lorca moved to the small desk occupying the room's far corner. A square wooden bowl, the kind every vendor might swear was carved from the first tree felled on a colony, was filled with slips from the various fortune cookies he had given her to open. Why she kept them, he did not know, but it was one of those little quirks he loved about her. Absentmindedly, he selected one at random and glanced at it before putting it in a pocket. He turned on the small lamp, and atop the desk lay a notepad and pen. The pad's top sheet contained a message, written in what he recognized as Balayna's hand.

Gabe,

Went to the gathering. We'll never find each other in that crowd, so if you get this, watch the speech and wait for me.

Hope to see you soon.

Love, Balayna

After listening to him read the note aloud, Bridges asked, "She calls you 'Gabe'? That's sweet."

"She's one of the very few who can without risking serious injury." Lorca offered a small grin to show he was joking, but the truth was that he did prefer to be addressed by his proper name. Balayna ignored this wish, playfully of course, and in truth he had grown rather comfortable with her doing so.

The sound of the apartment's front door opening made Lorca and Bridges reach for their phasers, only stopping themselves at the sight of Aasal Soltani entering the foyer.

"Good to see you two," offered Soltani as the new arrival joined his companions. "Am I the only one who's happy to be off the street?"

"Not even close," Bridges replied.

Stepping away from Balayna's desk, Lorca gestured toward the viewing screen. "Balayna's gone to the amphitheater, and she's asked for us to wait for her. We can watch the whole thing here." It still struck him as odd that the new governor, Kodos, would opt for such a seemingly inefficient means of relaying information to the colony, when a speech broadcast over the colony news network would be faster and reach everyone simultaneously. Perhaps Balayna was right, and this was as much an assembly for morale and reassurance as it was for the dissemination of information, at least some of which would be less than pleasant.

Having moved to take a seat on the sofa, Soltani reached for the control pad sitting atop the coffee table, pressing controls to activate the screen and select the channel for the colony's primary news network.

"It's after eight p.m.," he said. "The speech should be starting soon."

The image coalesced into a montage of breathtaking vistas—lush forests, spectacular mountain ranges framed by brilliant blue skies, cascading waterfalls, ocean waves surging against bright white sands. Lorca recognized some of the locations, having visited them either with Balayna or one of his team. These soon were replaced by images of New Anchorage, a vibrant city teeming with activity. Impressive buildings along with the art and sculpture that adorned several of its public parks intermingled with pictures of men, women, and children engaged in a variety of work or recreation. Many of the city's landmarks were represented, including the spaceport and the governor's building, which faded and were replaced by striking views of expansive farmland and rows of greenhouses and irrigation systems.

"This is our world," said a deep, commanding voice. *"It was not a gift. All that is here—all that we've come to love, appreciate, and depend upon—is a product of our dedication and labor, along with those of your parents and their parents before them. Since this colony was founded, those who call it home have been driven by a single desire: the right of simple self-determination. For more than a century, that was the promise of Tarsus IV. Those of you descended from the initial settlers welcomed people like me into your midst, people who shared your values and who sought the same goals and purpose in life. Like so many others, I was inspired to follow*

your example, and to do my part to contribute to the greater whole."

The scenes of teeming landscapes and thriving agriculture disappeared, replaced with a new string of images that were far more sobering. Now the farms were blackened and dead, or were depicted as their crops burned, sending pillars of dark smoke spewing toward the heavens. When the pictures changed to those of people, gone was the happiness and promise of lives fulfilled. Instead, there were masks of concern, fear, and anguish. Children cried. Babies wailed. Adults appeared forlorn, as though ready to surrender or buckle in the face of overwhelming strife.

"Everything for which we've worked is threatened. The shortsightedness of a few has threatened us all. If we do not act, it will all disappear, yanked from us as a consequence of rash action, and also as punishment for crimes perpetrated not by us, but rather against us. Make no mistake: a reckoning is upon us; and it is how we respond to this challenge that will define the legacy of this world for all time."

The screen shifted to what Lorca recognized as a view of the amphitheater as if one was standing at its far end, looking across an expanse of people toward a dais that towered above those milling about on the ground. He noted that no one sat in the stands or along the walking paths or tunnel entrances leading to concourses underneath the rows of elevated seating, though security guards were stationed at random intervals along the walkway encircling the stands at their midpoint. Meanwhile, the thousands of assembled colonists stood on the grass. The lights, clusters of bulbs affixed to tall metal columns arranged around the venue's perimeter, illuminated the field and part of the raised platform, but Lorca saw that the area holding a podium was cast in shadow.

"Pretty crowded down there," observed Bridges, who had taken a seat next to Soltani. "Why not use the stands?"

Lorca, his arms crossed as he stood behind the sofa, shook his head. "No idea, other than maybe it's the fastest way to get people in and out?"

Pointing to the screen, Soltani said, "Something's up on the dais. I think it's starting."

All eyes turned to the screen as a figure moved from the darkness at the rear of the dais to the podium. Lorca saw what appeared to be a human—or at least humanoid—male, the upper half of his body still cloaked in shadows. Was this a consequence of the camera angle, or a deliberate choice? The effect was amplified by the bright illumination on the amphitheater field, upon which Lorca guessed there had to be somewhere in the vicinity of four thousand people, or about half of the colony's total population. Guards stood at each corner of the dais, with two more positioned behind the figure at the podium. Their uniforms were all but identical to those worn by the group that had infiltrated the outpost, and Lorca felt a twinge of irritation as he studied them. Though all carried sidearms, the weapons remained in holsters at each officer's waist.

"Has a thing for theatrics, doesn't he?" said Bridges. No one offered comments in response to her question.

There was a crackle of static, indicating the activation of an audio broadcast system, at which point a single voice boomed through speakers situated around the amphitheater.

"*Good evening, citizens of Tarsus IV. I am Governor Kodos, and I stand before you tonight not only as your new leader, but also as a member of this community, which finds itself at the brink of catastrophe. Rest assured that the contagion that has ravaged our food supply will soon be contained, but the damage it has wrought is severe and demands extreme action on our part if we are to survive. Distress calls have been dispatched, but the latest reports from Starfleet tell us that assistance is nearly a month away, far longer than we can*" *survive at our present food levels. As a consequence, a number of emergency protocols have been enacted for the safety and security of all citizens.*

"Many of those whom you have entrusted with leading this colony through prosperity and adversity have failed you. That they allowed the situation we now face to come about at all is crime enough, but then they compounded their offense by having no vision for how best to confront this crisis that threatens us all. Navigating this difficult time will present no shortage of challenges. Success depends on being able to make difficult, even impossible choices. The leaders you elected to shoulder this responsibility have proven unworthy of the trust you gave them.

"Because of this, I along with a group of equally brave and committed souls have stepped forward, answering the call to an unwanted duty. With their able assistance, it is I who will lead you through this most trying of circumstances. We've already assumed control of critical roles within the colony government, assessed our situation and the resources available to address this crisis, and made some difficult decisions.

"The unassailable truth is that we simply cannot feed eight thousand people until assistance arrives. Even with strict rationing, we will exhaust our supplies in just a handful of days. Help is weeks away, if not longer. We therefore face harsh, unforgiving choices. There were those who have taken issue with our methods and our conclusions, to the point that their dissension might well spell disaster for us all. We were left with no choice but to proceed despite such resistance. If we are to secure our future, we must free ourselves from the shackles of safe, conventional thinking, which can only lead us down a path toward doom. What we do from this point forward must be with the best interests of the community at its center."

Kodos paused in response to a chorus of murmurs and other sounds of concern and uncertainty emanating from the crowd assembled before him. Lorca watched as the security officers flanking him at the corners of the dais rested their hands on their holstered weapons.

Soltani asked, "What the hell is he going on about? He sounds like he's beating back total anarchy with a club, or something."

"Given what we're dealing with," replied Bridges, "some dissension is to be expected." She raised an almost Vulcan-like right eyebrow. "Hence the curfew and expanded security presence, among other things."

On the screen, the audience had quelled their various reactions to the governor's speech, and Kodos continued.

"We will press forward, and do what must be done if we are to preserve all for which this community was founded and what it has labored to achieve. We must do this despite the uncertainty and even cowardice that held back my predecessors. That means making sacrifices for the greater good, in accordance with a series of directives I am implementing immediately. What I do now, I do for the survival of our civilization and those best suited to carry our legacy forward. The revolution is successful, but survival depends on drastic measures. Your continued existence represents a threat to the well-being of society. Your lives mean slow death to the more valued members of the colony. Therefore I have no alternative but to sentence you to death. Your execution is so ordered. Signed: Kodos, Governor of Tarsus IV."

So unexpected were the words he heard that it took Lorca an extra moment to process their true meaning. He was not alone, as he exchanged shocked looks with his team even as a renewed rumbling erupted from the amphitheater audience.

"Did he just—" said Bridges, but the words died in her throat.

Lorca heard but did not acknowledge her, transfixed by the screen as the unimaginable began.

Howls of energy cascaded across the open-air venue, and Lorca immediately recognized the reports of large-scale energy weapons. Visible in the tunnel entrances on the amphitheater's upper levels were oversized phaser cannons, variations of which were employed throughout Starfleet and the Federation for ground-based defense as well as more innocuous missions like drilling underground passages for mining efforts or tapping subterranean energy or water sources. Never in his life had Lorca seen them utilized in the manner he now beheld.

"Holy shit."

It was all the reaction he could muster as the deadly beams swept across the field, slicing through the assembled colonists with vicious efficiency.

Then it hit him.

Balayna? No!

Cries of terror and anguish filled the air, punctuated by the shrill whine of the weapons playing over the crowd. Lorca realized with mounting horror that the shouts from the assembled colonists were decreasing in number and intensity with every passing second as bodies upon bodies disintegrated in the face of the onslaught. The weapons were set to maximum, both the larger cannons as well as the rifles wielded by dozens of security officers positioned in the stands high above the field. Their hellish attacks left nothing in their wake except the fading shrieks of men, women, and children who had unwittingly marched to their own deaths.

And somewhere in the midst of that slaughter was Balayna.

"We have to do something," said Soltani, but Lorca knew it was a reflexive response; a desperate bid to ward off the unspeakable massacre being carried out before their eyes. He understood and sympathized as waves of similar helplessness and torment washed over him.

As abruptly as it began, the execution was over.

Not simply execution, Lorca chastised himself. *Murder. Mass murder.*

Smoke hung in the air above the field, large portions of which were burned and pitted in the wake of the assault. A stifling silence descended over the scorched grass and dirt, upon which nothing moved—upon which nothing remained to move.

Tearing his eyes from the grisly scene, Lorca saw that the podium was empty. Kodos was gone. He had to still be there, somewhere at the amphitheater, likely being moved to a secured location. Save for the Starfleet outpost, there were no transporters in use anywhere in the colony, so Kodos and his escorts would have to rely on conventional transportation, but where would they go?

Lorca wanted him. He wanted the governor's throat in his hands. He wanted to feel the other man's pulse beneath his fingers, its rate increasing with each passing moment as he squeezed ever tighter, until the beats stopped or the windpipe cracked or he simply ripped that handful of tissue free as the light faded from Kodos's eyes.

Balayna.

"Commander?" It was Bridges, now standing so that she blocked Lorca's view of the screen. "Sir, are you . . ."

Looking past her, he saw that the image of the amphitheater was gone, replaced by a man standing before what Lorca recognized as the backdrop for one of New Anchorage's prominent news stations. The man was saying something about the curfew being once more in full effect and that violators would be arrested. Security forces were being deployed throughout the city, no doubt to contain what would be at least some demonstrations of resistance and violence once they finished absorbing the shock of the slayings they just witnessed. Warnings about confronting the colony's law enforcement officers also were issued, with severe penalties promised for any attacks or other acts of insurrection.

"It doesn't make any damned sense," he said after a moment, forcing words and thoughts to order themselves. "Even with help weeks away, they could have survived. Ration the available food. Find some way to hang on long enough for help to get here."

"Even with half the population," said Soltani, "the colony would be stretching the small amounts of uncontaminated food to a startling degree. They could survive, but it would by no means be pleasant."

Bridges added, "But to just decide that half the population needed to die? To save the other half? How does one make that kind of decision? Based on what criteria?"

"We have to take him into custody," said Soltani. "Somehow, but it won't be easy. How large is the security contingent?"

Lorca shook his head. "I don't know. A couple of hundred, maybe? The surviving colonists certainly outnumber them." He realized the magnitude of what that meant. Four thousand people cut down within minutes, while he was forced to watch them die.

"There's no way this Kodos decided to do this without a plan of some sort," said Soltani. "He had to know that there would be people who lashed out in anger and grief." The computer specialist gestured to the viewing screen. "If he was prepared to do that, then he's ready to kill anyone else who tries to move against him."

Bridges said, "But why? At first I thought he might simply be insane, but that doesn't explain the help he obviously had in order to pull this off."

"I don't know," said Lorca, "but I'm going to find out." He pushed aside the image of Balayna, which was at the forefront of his mind, forcing himself to concentrate on the matter at hand. "Before we can do that, we have to get a message to Starfleet. They have to know what happened here and what to expect when help arrives. For all we know, Kodos is planning something against whatever ship gets here first. We can't let anyone walk into this situation blind."

"It's a safe bet Kodos will be looking for us," said Bridges. "He has to know we can't let this go unanswered."

Soltani asked, "So, what do we do?"

"They'll be expecting us to run and hide somewhere," said Lorca. "We've got one chance at surprising them before they're onto us, so we need to make it count." He looked around the apartment, which was nothing more than a cruel reminder of what Kodos had taken from him. "This place is probably safe for tonight, but there's no way to know if they're aware of my relationship with Balayna, so we'll have to figure out something else. We can't go to anyone we know in the city." He cast an involuntary glance to the viewing screen. "Assuming any of them survived."

They could not return to the outpost; it was the first place security forces would look. Instead, they would need to hide, blend in, become invisible, and perhaps attempt to locate and detain Kodos, all while waiting for help to arrive.

One way or another, the executioner had to answer for his crimes. Lorca would make that his mission.

Balayna and four thousand other people deserved no less.

6

Could I have been so completely wrong?

The roof of the apartment building afforded Kodos a view offered by very few structures in the area. From here, he had what should be a wondrous panorama of New Anchorage. At this hour, well after sundown, streets and walkways would be illuminated, and lights from countless windows would appear as small constellations begging for acceptance from the stars far above.

Instead, as he leaned against the parapet encircling the building's roof and looked over the city, the vast majority of the windows he could see were dark, leaving only the streetlamps and other external light sources to paint New Anchorage's nighttime portrait. The scene tonight was punctuated by scattered fires of varying size. Alarms from street level were carried on the breeze, and if he strained to listen, Kodos could hear shouts and other sounds associated with bands of protesters.

"Reports are coming in from across the city," said his assistant, Ian Galloway. "Security units are responding to dozens of calls. Most are gatherings of fewer than ten people, but there's concern that small groups may band together the longer this continues."

There was a pause, and Kodos saw Galloway looking at something on the tablet he carried in his left hand. The younger man appeared tired. His clothing and his dark brown hair looked disheveled, as though he'd been awakened at a very early hour and working all through the day. To Kodos, Galloway also looked a little afraid.

"The bulk of the population seems to be complying with the curfew and the other emergency rules we've put in place, but some of the watch commanders are worried that won't last."

The unrest was to be expected, Kodos knew, once the surviving population was able to process the shock of "the Sacrifice," as he had taken to calling the event at the amphitheater. There was the initial, anticipated outcry, of course, but direct action in the first hours was muted, thanks to the efforts of security forces enforcing the curfew. Fewer than three dozen citizens were arrested that first night, but that number was exceeded long before nightfall today.

It would only get worse.

"Perhaps another speech is in order," said Galloway. "A new message to the people, asking for calm and reassuring them that everything's going to be fine."

Turning from the parapet, Kodos eyed his assistant with unabashed skepticism. "What is there to say? How can I possibly make them understand that we were acting in what we believed was the best course for the colony's continued survival?"

In the beginning, simple math had been the biggest driver of his decision. More than eight thousand colonists, with enough food to sustain less than half that number until Starfleet aid was supposed to arrive. In the face of such cold, incontrovertible facts, what else could he do? Rationing would only prolong suffering rather than alleviate it, and to what end? The loss of perhaps the same number of people as those chosen for the Sacrifice, and the continued suffering of those left behind? His solution, though harsh, at least possessed a virtue of mercy, and carried with it the possibility of protecting the community from dissolution. Would anyone believe as much, decades from now, once the story of this tragedy was committed to the pages of history?

"Yes, there are those who supported us, but how many will step forward and proclaim that allegiance?" Kodos shook his head. "I suspect that number will be very low."

"You were acting in all our best interests, sir."

Even as Galloway spoke the words, Kodos heard the faint hint of doubt in the other man's voice. That was understandable, he conceded. Upon witnessing the Sacrifice while standing at his governor's side, Galloway's immediate reaction was, like so many others', shock and disbelief. But to Kodos's surprise, his assistant seemed to process everything unfolding before him with quick efficiency before turning to the governor and saying what Kodos himself believed to be true. The words, uttered with a touch of uncertainty, still rang in his mind.

It is unfortunate, sir, but necessary.

"What we face are trying times, Ian," said Kodos, "but I have to believe that those of us who survive this challenge will come away better for the experience. Our true mettle will have been tested, and we'll be able to apply the harsh lessons learned here toward improving the quality of life for future generations."

Others expressed similar sentiments, including the majority of men and women who accompanied him to Tarsus IV a decade earlier in search of a fresh start and new opportunities. While there were hints of concern regarding the ramifications of the Sacrifice once Federation aid arrived, a number of people were beginning to express at least some degree of understanding for what he had ordered.

Or, was that merely his perception, viewed through a clouded filter of bias and desired validation?

It was something he had pondered at length while finalizing his decisions as to who would be submitted to the Sacrifice. The choices involved several factors, including each colonist's perceived value and potential future contributions to the community not just in the short term but for years and decades to come. How could such a determination be made, when the future was a vast unknown? Crafting his analysis was no easy task, and it could not be delegated to another party. Doing so meant inviting the possibility of emotion into the mix, rather than relying on objective facts and reasoned extrapolation and insight based on the available information. Kodos was certain only he could provide the proper dispassionate perspective necessary to make his final selections.

Likewise, Kodos knew only he would receive the full brunt of historical examination, persecution, and ultimate judgment.

So be it.

"You should say something, Governor," said Galloway. "The situation in the streets is escalating, but it's not yet out of control. There's still time to make the populace see reason."

Kodos blanched at the notion. "I fear that opportunity is lost. Now that people are learning help is on the way, the Sacrifice will be seen as unnecessary." Sadness welled up within him.

Despite his efforts to assert control over resources such as the colony's main communications center, Kodos and his followers were unable to keep one lone security officer from broadcasting to the city his receipt of a message from a Starfleet vessel that would be here within a day, if not sooner. How this was even possible, Kodos did not know, given the last report sent from Starbase 11 indicating help was several weeks away, if not longer. The circumstances behind that sudden change were unimportant, of course; all that mattered was the impact to the colony.

Armed with this news, more and more citizens felt emboldened. They were seeking retaliation, either in response to lost loved ones or friends or simply acting out against the Sacrifice. Unable to take out their anger on Kodos, they were channeling their increasingly runaway emotions on his surrogates, the security forces. Still others were launching or joining protests of varying size and intensity, the most visible signs of which were the fires Kodos could see from here on the roof. On the street in front of this building, he saw a group of seven people running down a sidewalk while being chased by security officers. Behind them was a ground vehicle consumed by flames.

"How many security officers do we have on hand?" he asked.

Galloway stepped forward until he stood just to Kodos's left. "Three hundred and seventy-four remain on the active roles. Twenty-two resigned their positions, and four have been injured during altercations." He paused, long enough for Kodos to cast a glance in his direction, before adding, "There's no way to know how many more we may lose, sir."

Nodding in understanding, Kodos said, "That also is to be expected. The past days have tried our souls. It's reasonable that there will be those who cannot find the strength within themselves to continue."

Only a small, trusted number of the colony's security officers knew of the Sacrifice before Kodos finalized his plans. Though he solicited advice from a cadre of trusted advisers, the ultimate decisions were his alone. He knew this would not matter once the Federation learned of what happened here, but it was his hope to mitigate the scope of people caught up in the affair once the truth came to light. When he informed the men and women who would be tasked with carrying out the solution, many of them balked, but Kodos had chosen his people well. Despite their initial uneasiness, those loyal to him accepted the necessity of the actions.

The remainder of the security details were caught up in the Sacrifice's aftermath. Kodos harbored no doubts that they were torn between their own personal feelings and their desire to uphold their duty to safeguard the surviving colonists. Indeed, he had already received reports to that effect, with officers remaining on duty even in the face of growing civil unrest and working to maintain order. How long could that last, given the startling news about Starfleet's imminent arrival and the growing awareness that the Sacrifice was as pointless as it was severe?

"Order all watch commanders to remain on station until further notice," he said, hoping it would not end up being a futile gesture. The officers on the ground only needed to hold out for another day at most, until the Starfleet ship arrived.

All of this was preventable.

"If only we had been left alone to live our lives in peace."

"Sir?"

Galloway's query made Kodos realize he had spoken the words aloud. It also made him aware that with his arms crossed, he once more had taken up the unthinking habit of stroking his thin, well-trimmed beard. It had become something of a nervous affectation in recent days, and it was beginning to annoy him.

"My apologies, Ian. I was only thinking that none of this had to happen, if we'd just been allowed to chart our own course. Instead, one could argue that our predicament exists only due to Federation interference."

Another colony world, Epsilon Sorona II, fell victim to a global catastrophe. Tectonic stresses far below the planet's surface subjected the six thousand colonists there to earthquakes that only continued to increase in frequency and severity. With just enough time to evacuate the planet before the quakes devastated everything, colony support services were left with few options relocating so many people in such a short span. Federation officials decided Tarsus IV was the best candidate for relocation. Though the planet was more than suitable for sustaining the new arrivals, some members of the colony's leadership council voiced concerns over strains on available resources. Officials overseeing the emergency relocation pledged all manner of support to alleviate such issues, and even Kodos was forced to admit that both the Federation and Starfleet exceeded the most generous estimates when it came to the provided assistance.

Still, there were those among the established colonists, Kodos included, who felt that their community's ability to weigh in on the choice was sidestepped if not outright ignored.

None of this was the fault of the relocated Epsilon Sorona colonists, of course. Indeed, many of the people brought here ultimately chose to stay rather than be taken elsewhere once opportunity and resources presented themselves. They did their best to integrate with the existing population and respect the vision of the colony working toward being a completely independent society. Some even seemed accepting of the more hard-line stance espoused by Kodos and others like him, who believed that everyone here should be educated, engaged, and productive citizens working toward a common goal of total autonomy.

Now all of that was in peril.

If the refugees from Epsilon Sorona II had simply been taken to another planet—any other planet—it was possible that what everyone had been forced to endure might never have happened. He would have been allowed to continue in his life as a simple scientist, immersing himself in Tarsus IV's geology and the untold stories it was waiting to tell, and spending the rest of his life learning whatever secrets the planet had managed to keep to itself before living beings chose to make it their home.

Why had he stepped forward? As much as Kodos might wish to deny the truth even to himself, the reasons were simple: the situation called for leadership his predecessor, Governor Ribiero, and her advisers were unable to provide. Unwilling to stand by and watch this leadership disaster, Kodos convinced a sufficient number of council members to vote for removing Ribiero from office. Despite his bold move and even with the support of his friends on the council, he assumed the governor's role with great reluctance.

Galloway asked, "Do you regret the choices you made, sir?"

"No. And yes." Blowing out his breath, Kodos shook his head. "Upon reflection, I moved too quickly to make my ideas known. Governor Ribiero and the others weren't able to consider the merits of my survival plan."

No sooner was he named governor than Kodos began communicating his initial thoughts on the colony's ability to weather the mounting crisis. He did not come out and say what he had in mind, but he did share his thoughts about how the community's weaker members—those who might not be able to contribute toward its preservation in the days and weeks to come—presented a liability, and even this mild point was met with resistance. Why could Ribiero and her council not be more open to the harsh necessities that survival demanded? If they had, Kodos might not have been forced to implement such a drastic action so soon after assuming the mantle of leadership.

Ignoring his initial temptation to include Ribiero and the council as part of the Sacrifice, Kodos instead ordered them placed into protective custody. Despite whatever differences in opinion or perspective they might have, the truth was that the former governor and the leadership council would be needed, once the emergency was over and the colony turned its attention to moving forward from the tragedy that had been forced upon them.

Of course, for all the help Starfleet and the Federation would provide, their assistance would also serve to undermine what Kodos felt compelled to do. Who, if anyone, might attempt seeing things from the perspective of those forced to live through this crisis? There was no way to know for certain, but Kodos did not find it likely. Of course, for all the help Starfleet and the Federation would provide, their assistance would also serve to undermine what Kodos felt compelled to do. Would any of them attempt to see things from the perspective of those forced to live through this crisis? There was no way to know for certain, but Kodos did not find it likely. It was more probable that the offworld authorities, and those who survived both the plague and the Sacrifice, would curse his name. Historians and other so-called experts, along with pundits and everyone else with an opinion, informed or otherwise, would be debating every aspect of this incident for years.

A tone emanating from Galloway's tablet broke Kodos from his reverie, and he looked over to see the other man consulting the device, his expression turning to one of renewed concern.

"Governor, there's been an update on the status of the Starfleet ship. I've just heard from the communications center that they received another message, advising us that they'll be here within two hours."

Kodos frowned. "So soon?"

"You can't stay here, sir," said the younger man. "They'll arrest you at their first opportunity. The spaceport isn't an option, as the port master has been ordered by the Starfleet captain to block access to either of the two ships berthed there."

The order, though prudent, was also superfluous. Once

it became obvious that the colony was suffering from the equivalent of a viral outbreak, quarantine procedures were automatically put into effect to prevent any threat of contamination from leaving the planet. That meant the shutdown of the New Anchorage spaceport, and the port master had overseen the process of locking out access to the onboard systems of both cargo transports docked there. Neither vessel could attempt a launch without those computer lockouts being rescinded, which required authorization from the Starfleet or Federation representative tasked with answering the colony's distress call. By activating the quarantine protocol, the port master had removed herself from the equation.

An efficient, if inconvenient, development.

"Alert the others," he said. There was no need to elaborate further, as Galloway understood he meant the small group of loyal supporters who would be traveling with him. "We've saved all we can, Ian. It's time to go."

7

"Look out!"

The warning from Terri Bridges came at the same instant Lorca registered movement in his peripheral vision. He ducked, pushing the ensign to his right as the chunk of concrete sailed over his left shoulder and slammed into the building behind him. The piece of shrapnel bounced off the wall and dropped to the sidewalk, cracking into several smaller sections.

Angered by the random attack, Lorca reached for the phaser concealed beneath his shirt. He stopped himself before drawing the weapon, focusing his attention on the group of four men less than ten meters from where he and Bridges stood. The piece of debris had come from that direction, but none of the men seemed to be paying any specific attention to him or Bridges. Instead, they were using crude clubs to smash the glass from the windows of buildings and ground vehicles, beat on doors, and break lighting fixtures along with anything else that happened across their path. One of the men wielded a longer staff similar to those employed by martial artists.

He sensed the men were not purposely attempting to harm anyone, but rather were taking out their frustrations on whatever inanimate objects they encountered. In the two days that had passed since the summary executions, he had seen the gamut of emotions coursing through those few people they encountered in the streets. What began as simple disbelief and astonishment now was monopolized by feelings of anguish and swelling rage. For the moment, simple vandalism and other methods of disturbing the peace seemed to be enough, but Lorca knew it could not last.

Some of these people, sooner or later, will pose a genuine threat.

"You okay?" he asked Bridges, reaching out to rest a hand on her forearm. The junior officer, though noticeably shaken, nodded and offered a thumbs-up gesture.

"Never better, sir."

Smiling at her ability to keep her wits about her, Lorca gestured for them to continue along their path.

"We're almost there," he said, pointing ahead of them. "The communications center is on the next street over."

After taking refuge in Balayna Ferasini's apartment on the night of the mass executions, Lorca and the others had done their best to maintain low profiles. Uncertain as to whether the security forces were still hunting them or if they were forgotten with all of the other issues plaguing New Anchorage, the Starfleet officers had taken advantage of the mounting confusion to secure a new hiding space. Governor Kodos and his people had even aided in that task, through the simple act of publishing the names of those killed at the amphitheater. It had taken Lieutenant Soltani mere moments to cross-reference that list against the other occupants of Balayna's building and find those occupants who would, unfortunately, never return home. At first uneasy about the unconventional tactic of seeking refuge in a dead person's home, Lorca knew such measures would be the only way to stay ahead of any potential pursuers until they formulated a better long-term strategy or the Starfleet ships arrived.

It was while watching the news broadcasts from their new hideout that Lorca and the others first learned that someone assigned to the New Anchorage government's communications center dispatched news of the Starfleet vessel's pending arrival. Far ahead of even the most optimistic estimates, the ship was due to arrive within hours. The news served only to heighten Lorca's grief and seething anger at the horror inflicted upon the colonists.

Balayna.

Her face filled his mind, as it had countless times during the past two days. Once more he forced the image back, wanting to lose himself in it and yet knowing that was impossible, at least for now. He still had two friends and subordinates looking to him for leadership. Until Starfleet arrived and got this situation under control, it was just him and his team, doing whatever they could to find Kodos and perhaps glean some answers for the senseless tragedy inflicted on the people of Tarsus IV. The first item on his agenda was making contact with the approaching Starfleet ship. Comm systems at the outpost were still down, and without access to a transporter or ground vehicle, the facility was out of reach for the moment. That left the colony communications center, even if getting there meant plowing through whoever stood in their way.

Bridges asked, "Do you think Soltani's all right, sir?"

"We'll know soon enough."

After leaving the apartment, the team had once more split up for the movement to the communications center, which was located adjacent to the offices of the governor and the rest of the colony government. Soltani departed first, following a route that would take him through this part of the city and toward the comm center from the east, while Lorca and Bridges approached from the west. The plan was to meet near the building's main entrance before surveying the scene and figuring out how best to gain entry. That it might mean putting a security officer or two out of commission was a possibility Lorca could accept.

Once they were moving again, he saw ahead of them that the four rioters had crossed the street and now had something else on which to focus their interest, in the form of a single colony security officer.

"Hang on."

Lorca looked around to see if anyone else was reacting to the developing situation. While there were other people visible on the street, no one seemed to be taking any notice of this group. Without saying anything more to Bridges, he stepped from the sidewalk and crossed to the street's opposite side, maneuvering into the shadows cast by the building as he approached the men. A quick glance to Bridges told him she was following his lead while making sure no one else was trying to move in behind them. Her hand was at the small of her back, where he knew she had secreted her phaser. It was his preference to avoid drawing their weapons and the attention they would attract, but that would depend on the men's intentions. As he closed the distance, he was better able to hear what they were saying.

"Here's one of them."

"Walking out here all by yourself? Bad idea, buddy."

"Were you there? Were you one of the people killing my friends?"

The voices were becoming louder and more belligerent in tone with each passing moment, and Lorca saw that two of the men were brandishing their clubs in what could only be an aggressive manner. Realizing he was about to be cornered, the security officer reached for the phaser at his waist, but one of his adversaries was faster. A fit-looking blond in his late thirties or early forties, by Lorca's estimate, he did not present the appearance of a trained fighter, and his attack was clumsy but still sufficient to knock the officer's phaser from his hand.

The weapon clattered to the sidewalk and one of the

men kicked it away. Holding his wounded hand, the officer uttered a grunt of pain that earned him derision from the four men. He was looking for a path to escape, but his assailants had spread out, forming a semicircle in front of the man, forcing him backward toward the building behind him. The one wielding the staff and the group's apparent leader, a gangly man with thinning dark hair and wearing what might be an engineer's coveralls and heavy boots, began waving the weapon toward the officer. The way he carried himself indicated he might be a greater threat, so Lorca adjusted his approach, deciding this man needed to be confronted first. There were easier ways to go about neutralizing this potential problem, of course, but the simple fact of the matter was that after two days spent hiding in empty apartments, alleys, and other dark corners of New Anchorage in the wake of what happened in the amphitheater—after what had happened to Balayna and so many others—he was feeling mean.

"Cover me," he said to Bridges.

"Commander."

Lorca heard the ensign's implied warning, but ignored it as he approached his chosen target and lunged forward with a fist to the right side of the other man's head.

The single punch, though not enough to kill his would-be adversary, still dropped him to the sidewalk like a puppet with severed strings. He was unconscious on the way down, and Lorca caught the staff as it fell from the man's grasp. Spinning it in his hand to get a better grip, he turned to face the man's companions. Without shifting his gaze, he noted Bridges moving closer, her right hand held tight against her side. She had drawn her phaser and was ready to use it. None of the three remaining men had taken notice of her presence. With that in mind, Lorca moved to keep their attention on him.

"Four against one?" He made a clucking sound of mock disapproval. "That's not very sporting, is it?"

Rather than answer the taunt, the blond man chose to step forward. He held his own makeshift club in both hands and attempted to assume what he likely thought to be some flavor of offensive pose. Lorca saw the attack coming and with a single movement swung the low end of his own staff upward. Its tip caught the other man just under his chin, stopping him cold. Lunging closer, Lorca shifted the staff and brought it back the other way. Its opposite end whipped down across the man's face, eliciting both a scream of pain and a thin line of blood from his forehead down the left side of his nose. He staggered backward, tripping on the edge of the sidewalk while reaching for his face and falling into the street. Hitting his head on the hard ground, he released a muted grunt of pain before slipping into unconsciousness.

The pair of strikes had taken less than three seconds and were over before the man's remaining friends even realized what was happening. Lorca returned his staff to his two-handed grip, holding it before him. He ignored the look of warning from Bridges, who seemed ready to stun the remaining two men with her phaser, but she held her position, her expression and wide eyes asking Lorca for direction.

"You can either collect your friends and move on, or we keep going." Despite his desire to bring a quick end to the confrontation, part of him was hoping his adversaries might choose the latter option.

The first man, balding and slightly overweight, was wearing stained work clothes that reminded Lorca of a mechanic's uniform. He moved to pick up his fallen friend's club while his partner—a wiry fellow with dark hair and sporting civilian clothes one might wear for camping or hunting—pulled a long knife from somewhere beneath his light gray jacket. Lorca saw that the man's trousers were tucked into black boots that rose to his shins, hinting at a military background. The way he held the knife, low and to one side while presenting his left forearm, suggested at least some training in hand-to-hand combat.

Lorca was fine with that.

What the hell is wrong with you? Finish this.

As with Bridges, he ignored his own warning.

"Who the hell do you think you are?" asked the knife wielder.

"A concerned citizen."

The man was smarter than he appeared, waiting for his friend to try something. Lorca did not catch the ploy until the other man was advancing toward him and swinging his club. Deflecting the attack was easy enough, with Lorca using his own staff to push the other man to one side before kicking him in the shin. The man's leg crumpled beneath him and he fell to one knee, close enough that Lorca had to scramble to his right to avoid tripping or losing his own balance.

The man with the knife was moving. Light from a nearby streetlamp reflected off something shiny, and Lorca saw the long blade slicing toward his abdomen. A frantic swipe with the staff blocked the other man's forearm but his opponent pulled back the blade, dragging it down the length of Lorca's arm. Gritting his teeth in sudden pain, Lorca swung his staff with his other hand, an awkward strike that was still sufficient to make the knife wielder step back to avoid the hit.

A high-pitched whine filled the air, and bright blue light chased away the darkness for a moment as Bridges opened up with her phaser. The beam washed over the man with the knife, and he collapsed to the street. Before his one remaining conscious companion could react the ensign turned the weapon on him. Then, being thorough, she applied a stun beam to the two men who still lay on the street.

"Thank you," said Lorca.

Bridges gestured to his wounded arm. "Are you all right, sir?"

Dropping his staff, Lorca gripped his arm where he had taken the knife cut. A quick inspection told him the wound was long, but not deep, and had not hit a vein. The injury was superficial and easily treated.

"I'm fine. It's not quite a scratch, but close enough." He used the sleeve of his shirt to dab at the thin line of blood oozing from the wound. "I'll take care of it once we get where we're going."

He looked to where the security officer had moved to stand against the wall, still holding his hand where one of the assailants had struck him. The man's expression was one of relief but also uncertainty as he beheld his saviors.

"You're from the Starfleet outpost, aren't you?"

Lorca ignored the question and instead gestured to the man's hand. "How bad is that? Do you need medical attention?"

The man nodded. "I think he broke a couple of fingers."

"We can help with that," said Bridges.

Stepping closer, Lorca eyed the man. "What's your name?"

"Jacob Clancy."

Lorca replied, "All right, Jacob Clancy. As you can see, walking the streets by yourself can be hazardous to your health." His eyes narrowed. "Were you at the amphitheater?"

Realizing the implicit question entwined with the words, Clancy's eyes widened in renewed fear.

"No! No, I wasn't. I was on street patrol. I swear, I had no idea that was going to happen." He paused, clearing his throat. "I still can't believe it *did* happen."

"I know the feeling." Lorca gestured again to the man's hand. "As I said, we can help you, but we need your help."

8

Located on grounds adjacent to the colony's center of government, the communications center occupied a building separate from the bulk of the administration's offices and was accessible to the civilian population. At least, it was prior to the governor's declaration of martial law. Lorca expected to find an armed presence guarding entrances to the building and was not disappointed. A short path leading from the sidewalk to a grassy courtyard ended at a stone archway marking the building's main entrance. Standing just inside that portico was a pair of security officers, a man and a woman, both wearing uniforms identical to Clancy's and with phasers on their belts. Lorca saw glowing energy strips lining the archway's underside, and cast a knowing look at Bridges, who stood just behind him as they and Clancy huddled out of sight next to a building south of the entrance and used the darkness for concealment.

"I don't remember them using a force field before," said the ensign.

Still cradling his wounded hand, Clancy replied, "It's been there all along, but we never had a need to use it." The security officer shook his head. "This entire situation is . . . I'm just doing what I can to keep it from going to hell. Keep any more people from getting hurt, you know?"

"I know." Lorca gestured to the entrance. "Do you have access?"

"Yeah. We all do."

"Good. You're our ticket inside."

Clancy cast him a skeptical look. "They won't let you in."

"Sure they will. We were attacked on the street, and you came to our aid." Lorca held up his bloodied left arm. "I need medical attention, and this is closer than the hospital."

His expression communicating his uncertainty in the impromptu plan, Clancy offered a nervous nod. "Okay."

"Commander."

Lorca felt Bridges's hand on his arm, then saw she was looking at something on the far side of the street. He turned to look in that direction and saw a lone figure moving up the sidewalk at a brisk pace toward the entrance and the guards. Even before the new arrival passed under a streetlamp, he recognized Aasal Soltani. As per Lorca's plan, the lieutenant had made his way from the apartment, but he seemed uninterested in joining his comrades. Instead, he appeared focused on the comm center entrance and the guards.

"What's he doing?" asked Bridges.

Lorca had no clue. That seemed as good a reason as any to act.

"Let's go."

Advising Clancy to stick to their ad hoc scheme, Lorca indicated for the security officer to lead them toward the entrance. The trio was halfway across the street when Soltani arrived at the archway, and Lorca could hear the hum of the active force field.

"Officer!" Soltani said, waving his hand to get the guards' attention. "I need your help!"

Stepping forward, the male guard, a man of perhaps forty years with gray-black hair cut in a severe military style, eyed the lieutenant with obvious suspicion. "What's the matter?"

"It's them!" replied Soltani, then surprised Lorca by pointing at him. "They've been following us and threatening us!"

I'll be damned. Lorca forced himself not to smile at the lieutenant's quick read of the situation and improvisational skills. *Nice job, Aasal.* Adopting a hard expression, he continued his advance toward the entrance.

Behind the force field, it was evident the guards were confused by what was playing out before them. The female officer, a trim human with red hair pulled back into a ponytail, noticed Clancy's uniform but to Lorca did not appear to recognize him.

Adapting to the evolving deception, Soltani said, "He tried to arrest me. It's not past curfew, and I did nothing wrong!"

Lorca and Bridges stopped moving closer to the guards. Even Clancy, now up to speed on the ruse, halted his advance as, inside the archway, both guards drew their weapons. Looking up and down the street, Lorca saw that no one else was outside, or at least in this immediate vicinity. If they were going to do something here, it would have to be fast.

"Everybody just stay calm for a minute," said the female guard. She nodded to Soltani. "Please step back from the entrance."

Then the male guard granted Lorca's wish and dropped the force field.

To his surprise, it was Bridges who took immediate advantage of the situation. Her movements partially blocked by Lorca and Clancy, the ensign was able to draw her phaser. She fired between the two men, her shot striking the male guard in the chest. Already unconscious, he was staggering backward as his partner reacted to the unexpected attack. She started to duck behind the archway but Bridges was faster, her second shot catching the other woman in the side and sending her stumbling into the courtyard.

Eyeing the ensign with amusement, Lorca stifled a chuckle. "I think you're beginning to like that thing a bit too much."

Bridges replied, "I was just aiming to avoid an argument, sir."

"Nice aim." To Soltani, Lorca said, "And well played, Lieutenant. How did you know we were here?" He had not seen Soltani until they were almost at the archway.

"I . . . played a hunch," replied the lieutenant, his expression wistful.

After relieving the stunned guards of their weapons, Lorca and the others stashed the unconscious pair out of sight behind a row of hedges along the courtyard's near wall. With the force field reactivated, he led his team and Jacob Clancy into the comm center, with the security officer guiding them through the building's two-story interior. At this hour there were few people working, but Clancy's knowledge of the center allowed them to avoid encounters with any on-duty personnel until they arrived at the main communications broadcast hub on the second floor. The oversized chamber with high walls was a rectangle, consisting of workstations lining the longer sides as well as the far wall. Several viewscreens were set into the walls above the workstations. Though none of the controls were immediately familiar to him, they reminded Lorca of consoles one might find crammed into a spaceship's bridge or engineering room.

"Where is everybody?" he asked.

Clancy replied, "After nineteen hundred hours, the center shifts to a minimal staff. There's a watch commander on duty, but they'll be in an office on the first floor. If anything requires their attention in here, an alert is sent to the computer terminal there."

Turning at Soltani's approach, Lorca saw that the computer specialist had retrieved an emergency medical kit from a supply locker tucked into a corner of the room. He extracted an emergency field dressing and offered it to Lorca.

"You can clean and bandage your cut, sir. At least until I figure out how to use the dermal regenerator."

"Thanks, Aasal." Lorca took the bandage and began rolling up his bloodied left sleeve while Soltani gestured with the kit to Clancy.

"I can treat your injuries too."

The security officer nodded in relief and gratitude before he and Soltani moved to a small circular conference room just off the hub's main floor. Soltani set to work with a medical diagnostic scanner he found in the kit.

As they were still close enough to converse, Lorca said, "I'm surprised there isn't a greater security presence, given the increase in unrest and violence outside." As he spoke, he opened a packet containing a disinfectant pad and used it to dab at the cut on his forearm. The cut had clotted a while ago, and the moist pad made short work of the dried blood along the wound's length.

"Force fields are active at all points of entry on all colony government and administration buildings," replied Clancy. His right hand lay atop the table as Soltani ran the scanner over it. Then the lieutenant pulled another device from the medical kit and held it over the wounded hand.

"I apologize if this hurts a bit," said Soltani. "It's a bone knitter. Your fingers will be as good as new in a minute."

After Lorca finished sizing and applying the field dressing to cover his cut, he stepped away from the conference area and back onto the hub's main floor. Rolling up his right sleeve so that it matched its counterpart, he eyed Bridges and Soltani.

"I'd rather not spend a lot of time here." He was worried about random inspections of the area by the watch commander or someone else just wandering around who might find them in the comm center, or the two stunned officers out in the courtyard. "We need to make contact with the incoming Starfleet ship. Can either or both of you figure out how to work any of this equipment?"

Soltani dropped into a chair situated before a nearby console as Bridges moved to an adjacent station. After a moment, the lieutenant said, "This is all fairly standard, Commander. All of their systems are up and running, and we can make use of the communications array to transmit offworld."

Sitting to Soltani's left, Bridges added, "I've got access to the network of sensor buoys deployed within the Tarsus system, sir. The incoming ship is the *U.S.S. Narbonne*, a colony support vessel. According to long-range scans, it should be here within two hours."

"Open a hailing frequency," Lorca ordered, feeling a small sense of relief beginning to build within him. Even the thought of being able to speak to someone else about their current plight, knowing that help was on the way, made him feel just a bit better.

A moment later, Bridges said, "Frequency open, sir."

Stepping closer to her console, Lorca leaned toward the console's audio pickup. "*U.S.S. Narbonne*, this is Lieutenant Commander Gabriel Lorca, commanding officer of the Starfleet observation outpost on Tarsus IV. Please acknowledge this transmission."

It took only a moment before Bridges reported the hail had been received and answered. She tapped a control and one of the console's screens flared to life. Its image was what Lorca guessed to be a middle-aged human male of Indian descent with short, salt-white hair and dark, piercing eyes.

"This is Captain Aurobindo Korrapati of the Narbonne. It's good to hear from you, Commander. We're coming loaded to the rafters, but we were fearing the worst for a while when we got no response to our hails. The information I have on your present situation is a few days old, so hopefully you can fill me in."

Lorca exchanged looks first with Bridges and Soltani, then with Jacob Clancy, who had rejoined the group now that his hand appeared to have been healed.

"I assume you already have the initial reports sent to Starbase 11, sir. However, there's been . . . an incident here that will require immediate attention upon your arrival."

"Where's Governor Ribiero?"

Korrapati's voice was level and composed, the mark of a confident, experienced leader. Lorca neither knew him nor was familiar with him, but guessed the captain and his ship and crew were assigned to this mission because they were best suited to handle things like natural disaster or disease or some other calamity that might befall a colony. On the other hand, maybe once the distress call was received only the *Narbonne* was available to journey with haste to Tarsus IV. Lorca doubted Captain Korrapati and his people were ready for what they were about to face.

"I honestly can't tell you Governor Ribiero's location, sir. She and her staff are no longer in any position of authority here. The governor was removed from her post and replaced by another individual, Adrian Kodos. He's a colonist, but as far as I know wasn't in any leadership role here until three days ago. After declaring martial law, he—"

The words caught in his throat, refusing to be spoken aloud.

"What is it, son?" prompted Korrapati. *"What happened? Some new viral outbreak that's affected the colonists? Does the planet need to be quarantined?"*

Lorca shook his head. "No, sir. It's not like that. We . . . we just need you, Captain. Right now."

Unable to look Korrapati in the eye, he let his gaze fall to the floor. The captain was waiting for the rest of his report, but grief and fury were threatening a comeback, and he knew he needed time to process his shifting emotional state. The past two days seemed to him like months or even years had passed, draining him of strength or even the desire to keep moving. He did not want to go anywhere or do anything—not without Balayna. Drawing a long, deep breath, Lorca willed himself to return his attention to Korrapati.

Help was coming far earlier than anticipated.

For too many people, help was far too late.

9

Despite herself and even the assistance of the ship's internal environmental systems, Philippa Georgiou still felt the queasiness knotting her gut. With nothing to do but watch the activities of the *Narbonne*'s bridge complement, her imagination could run wild as it conjured all manner of disastrous endings for what the ship was doing.

"Initiate landing sequence," ordered Commander Natalie Larson, the ship's first officer, from where she sat at the bridge's environmental systems station along the starboard bulkhead. A blond human who looked to be Georgiou's equal in age, Larson had positioned herself at the workstation so that she could watch her instruments as well as the main viewscreen and other members of the bridge crew assisting with the landing operation. As second-in-command, Larson did not have a dedicated seat on the already cramped bridge. Instead, Georgiou noted that she tended to divide her duties between that of executive officer and different bridge stations based on current need.

Lieutenant Melissa Parham, seated at the helm console at the bridge's center, replied, "Sequence initiated. Warp drive is offline. Increasing power to inertial damping systems."

"Continue landing procedures," said Larson.

The helm officer reported, "Placing atmospheric thrusters on standby."

A young human woman, Parham handled the ship's controls with the easy self-assurance of a skilled pilot. Her reports to Captain Korrapati sitting in the command chair behind her and the rest of the bridge crew were crisp and precise, with no wasted words or time. She was also the only one, for example, who did not react when the *Narbonne* began descending through the atmosphere and was buffeted by the thickening, superheated air surrounding the transport. Whereas Georgiou's attention and that of everyone else was drawn to the onrushing clouds and bright morning sky, all distorted by waves of heat roiling across the ship's hull, Parham's focus was on the controls beneath her fingertips.

"Engaging atmospheric thrusters. Inertial dampers at maximum." She turned from her station and glanced not to Korrapati or Larson but instead to Georgiou. "This could get a little bumpy, Commander."

It took Georgiou a moment to understand what Parham meant, then she realized she was the only person on the bridge not occupying a seat. Nodding in acknowledgment, she moved to the vacant engineering monitoring station at the rear of the bridge and took the chair. She noted Korrapati swiveling his chair to look at her. The captain offered a small, sympathetic smile.

"First time on a ship that doesn't stay in orbit?"

Georgiou nodded, unable to hold back a small chuckle. "Yes, sir. I've been on shuttles and smaller transports that made landings, of course, but nothing this big."

"Relax. Even seasoned planet hoppers get a little queasy on occasion. Don't worry, though. Parham is one of the best there is at this sort of thing. She can do it with her eyes closed."

"I'd prefer she didn't."

Given the circumstances and what they were about to face head-on, no one seemed moved to laugh at her attempt at humor, though Korrapati offered another look of understanding before turning back to face forward. All around them, the buffeting became more pronounced as the *Narbonne* descended through the atmosphere, its engines battling the planet's gravity for supremacy. Within moments the maneuvering thrusters gained the upper hand and the shuddering subsided.

"Extending landing struts," reported Parham.

After another ninety seconds passed, Georgiou felt the slightest tremor as the ship's set of eight squat landing struts made contact with the ground. The helm officer's touch was so soft that the touchdown was all but imperceptible.

Parham glanced toward Korrapati. "Struts down and locked, sir. Commencing post-landing shutdown procedures."

"Deactivating artificial gravity," added Larson, tapping controls on her own console.

"Maintain atmospheric integrity," ordered the captain. It was a point of discussion between him and Georgiou prior to landing that the ship would continue to observe standard ingress and egress procedures as though still in space. Until the viral contamination currently plaguing the colony could be isolated and dealt with, no chances would be taken with contaminating the *Narbonne*'s own vast food stores.

Rising from his chair, Korrapati turned to the officer on duty at the communications station, Ensign Richard Doherty. "Send a message to the colony leadership. Notify them we're here and commencing post-landing operations, and that I'll make myself available to whoever's in charge over there as soon as possible." He turned his attention back to Parham. "Lieutenant, let's have a look around. Put New Anchorage up on the viewer."

"Aye, sir." The helm officer tapped a control on her console and the image on the viewscreen changed to offer a look at the main city as though seen from someone standing atop the *Narbonne*'s hull.

Georgiou knew from her review of the colony and its infrastructure that the main spaceport that was their present location occupied a broad expanse of relatively flat terrain four kilometers south of the main city, New Anchorage. A sensor scan prior to their landing revealed only two small cargo transports occupying berth space at the port, though neither vessel had its engine activated. There also was a single shuttlecraft attached to the Starfleet observation outpost. Scans showed that the tiny craft was powered down and resting on its landing pad near the outpost. After arriving in orbit hours earlier, Captain Korrapati's first order was to the port master, forbidding access to the two transports and declaring that no launches or landings would be made without his personal authorization until further notice. As for taking his own ship down, he made the decision to wait for daybreak before attempting a landing and use the intervening time to conduct sensor sweeps of the entire area.

Only then did the *Narbonne*'s crew get its first confirmation of the horrific story relayed to them by Lieutenant Commander Gabriel Lorca. According to the scans, the population of Tarsus IV had been reduced by half, and sensors were able to detect residual indications of concentrated energy weapons use in New Anchorage's main amphitheater.

Georgiou pushed herself from the chair at the engineering station and turned at the sound of the hatch behind her sliding open to admit the ship's chief medical officer, Sergey Varazdinski.

"You asked for a preliminary report as soon as possible, Captain," he said by way of introduction. His voice was thick with a Russian accent, which Georgiou knew from her review of his personnel file came from his having been born and raised in the Bulgarian region on Earth.

Korrapati's eyes widened. "Already? That's fast work, Doctor."

"I was anxious to see the results for myself." As soon as the words left his mouth, Varazdinski paused, frowning. "Perhaps anxious isn't the right word."

A short balding man of indeterminate age, he wore a rumpled physician's lab coat over his Starfleet uniform, and his hands were jammed into its pockets. Georgiou noticed his uniform was missing its top, as Varazdinski tended to shun it in favor of a regulation dark undershirt. Like the lab coat, the shirt also lacked rank or department insignia. His round face sported several days' worth of beard growth, and his hair, like the coat and trousers, was unkempt. Even though he held the rank of lieutenant commander, it appeared as though he was doing everything in his power to prevent drawing attention to his status as an actual, commissioned Starfleet officer. Having met the doctor shortly after coming aboard the *Narbonne*, Georgiou came to realize that Varazdinski was in reality a civilian down to the subatomic level, who for reasons surpassing understanding had wandered into a Starfleet recruiting office before stumbling his way through the Academy. From Captain Korrapati, she knew the doctor had already completed his medical training and certifications prior to joining Starfleet. This begged the natural question of why a man of his accomplishments would choose such a career path, but even Korrapati lacked an answer to that question. Further, from her own dealings with Varazdinski and what she had learned from other members of the crew, she guessed that it was a topic he was not interested in discussing.

"What did you find?" asked Korrapati.

The doctor's expression, which already seemed to have a default setting of "annoyed," turned even darker. "We ran bio-sensor sweeps of the amphitheater and picked up massive traces of disrupted and deconstructed bio-matter, along with residue from synthetic materials that are likely clothing and things of that nature. It's as Commander Lorca reported: A large number of humanoid life-forms in that contained space were subjected to an intense barrage of concentrated energy weapons fire. They were disintegrated, en masse."

"No," said Larson, who had moved to stand next to Korrapati. "Four thousand people . . . ?"

For Georgiou, trying to process the magnitude of Varazdinski's report was proving difficult. Present on the bridge when Commander Lorca's hail was received from Tarsus IV, she and everyone else was aghast at what they were hearing. Having the unbelievable story corroborated by the ship's CMO was like twisting a knife after being stabbed.

"This is unbelievable," said Korrapati. It was not the first time the captain had made the statement, but it was no less true for being repeated. Turning to Ensign Doherty, he asked, "Have you gotten a response from the colony?"

"Yes, sir," replied the communications officer. "I'm in contact with Governor Ribiero's aide. Apparently, she's been allowed to resume her office."

Larson said, "I bet there's an interesting story behind that."

Ignoring the first officer, Korrapati asked, "Where the hell is Kodos?"

Doherty replied, "She doesn't know, sir. He seems to have disappeared, along with a number of other people."

"Supporters?" asked Georgiou. "Others who helped him?" It dawned on her that Kodos could not have done all of this without help. How had she not considered that before now? Of course he had followers, people who either believed in what he was doing or were somehow forced to do his bidding out of fear for their own well-being.

Who the hell is this maniac?

"We'll find them, sir," offered Larson. "He can't hide forever. Not from sensors."

Korrapati held up a hand. "One thing at a time." To Doherty, he said, "Is Ribiero available?"

"Yes, sir. She and her staff are waiting to meet with you at your convenience."

From the helm console, Parham said, "Captain, there are several hundred people gathering near the spaceport's main entrance. They obviously knew we were coming, and there's no doubt our landing attracted attention."

"Are the entrances secure?" asked Larson.

Parham nodded. "Scans show all five gates are locked and can only be opened with pass codes from port personnel."

"Tell the port master I want those entries to remain locked down until I say otherwise," said Korrapati. "As for the governor, let her know we will meet in her office." He gestured toward the viewscreen. "Tell her about the people gathering. There may be an opportunity to address the public and perhaps ease some anxiety. A reassuring word certainly can't hurt." Snapping his fingers, he added, "What about Commander Lorca and his people? Have they contacted us yet?"

"No, sir," said Doherty. "I'm monitoring all frequencies, but so far they haven't reached out to us."

According to Lorca's report, he and the surviving members of his outpost staff believed their lives might be in danger, following an attack on their facility by agents possibly acting on behalf of Kodos. Given the possibility of Kodos loyalists within the security force's rank and file, Lorca felt it prudent to avoid any official colony government facility until personnel could be vetted. The commander's last report indicated he and his team would make their way to the *Narbonne* in due course.

"They've been on the lam pretty much since this whole thing started," said Georgiou. "They'll be thrilled with the break." She knew from Lorca's report that the outpost's team were on the run, avoiding all unnecessary contact with members of the colony's security forces. The commander and his team would be grateful for the respite, rather than being forced to make do in the city while at the mercy of whatever emergency supplies could be found.

After watching the bridge crew turn to various tasks for a moment, Georgiou looked to Korrapati. "I can at least get my team started with whatever preliminary work needs to be done before we start deploying people, sir." She would not know who was needed where until she got an updated report from the governor or whomever she appointed as liaison to the Starfleet personnel. Even without that information she could make educated guesses. "According to Commander Lorca's report, there was a lot of civil unrest. Help will likely be needed at the hospital and wherever else they're treating any injured."

Korrapati nodded in approval. "Sensors didn't pick up any fluctuations in the colony's utility services, but let's stick to our plan anyway. Make sure the infrastructure is secure."

The planning discussions hashed out by the captain and Commanders Larson and Georgiou had established a priority for the *Narbonne*'s relief teams once the ship landed. A team of engineers would be sent to the main power distribution center to ensure the facility was operational and not in danger of being invaded by angry colonists. Similar inspections were laid out for water and sewage systems as well as computer access and other services. Commander Lorca's report had not mentioned damage to any of these areas, but neither the captain nor Georgiou wanted to take chances.

Korrapati said, "Naturally, the first priority is the colony's food-processing facilities, farms, greenhouses, and any other places where food can grow on this planet. It's critical that absolutely everything be inspected. We want the contagion identified and isolated or destroyed before we break out any of the supplies we brought with us." His expression fell. "We apparently have more time to work until the existing food supplies are exhausted."

The captain's words gave voice to feelings harbored by Georgiou and everyone else aboard the *Narbonne*. Assembling in such short order a team capable of providing all manner of aid to the Tarsus IV colonists was no easy feat, but she and the people pulled together by Admiral Anderson were ready to answer the call. They were motivated by a desire to help others. Georgiou and the group of specialists—many of whom she barely knew—were set to hit the ground running in order to offer that assistance, and hopefully alleviate even a bit of the fear and uncertainty gripping the stricken population. To discover that fully half of the people they were sent to help were gone—removed from existence with a single hellish command—was a gut punch. Everyone on the ship was still reacting to the news, and while that was not sufficient to sway them from their mission, the apparent mass execution cast a pall over the relief mission before it even got under way.

Straightening his posture, Korrapati said, "Commander Larson, I'm going to prepare for our meeting with Governor Ribiero. You have the conn. Feel free to start a sensor sweep of the entire area, because I want to know where every living person on this planet is right now. Doctor, you're with me." He turned his gaze to Georgiou. "All right, Commander. You're up. Let's see what we can do to help these people."

"Aye, sir."

Following Korrapati and Varazdinski through the hatch leading from the bridge, Georgiou found herself still struggling to find her bearing. How could something like this happen in this day and age, when technology had solved nearly every problem that plagued humanity before its discovery of faster-than-light travel and other inhabited worlds? It was a sudden, brutal slap across the face, a grim reminder that complacency and an overreliance on technology were fraught with risk, and that was before someone decided to introduce other elements into the mix.

And what of Kodos, the apparent arbiter of this horrific act? The reasons that drove him to sacrifice fifty percent of the colony in a bid to extend the survivability of the remaining half were suspect. Surely other options were available that might have sustained the colony until help arrived? The threat of starvation, while real, was also not as dire as one might think at first. Children, the elderly, and the infirm would have been at greatest risk, of course, but even then there were means of addressing the immediate issue.

That left Kodos, his motives, and his judgment.

Stay on target, Commander.

Coming to grips with the situation they were entering needed to happen quickly if she was to function efficiently during this mission. Georgiou knew there would be time for reflection and even grieving for the loss of the four thousand colonists, but it would have to be later. Likewise, the search for Kodos, his followers, and answers would also have to wait, likely for people better qualified for such pursuits.

For now, she had a job to do.

10

"I know that many of you are scared. I know that many of you are angry. You want answers. You want closure, and you want justice. We will seek all of those things, together. We will not rest until those responsible for the unspeakable tragedy we've suffered are made to answer for what they've done. Not just for ourselves, but also for those who are no longer with us. We owe them that much. For their sake, we must rededicate ourselves to the continuing betterment of our community, and do so in living, eternal memory of those we lost. Thank you."

Georgiou watched as an aide standing before the transmission pickup signaled to Governor Gisela Ribiero that the frequency was closed following the conclusion of her speech. Along with Captain Korrapati, Georgiou stood in one corner of the room from which this and other speeches were broadcast, be they from the governor or other public officials. The centerpiece of the room was a raised dais upon which stood a podium bearing the governor's seal and a representation of the New Anchorage flag.

Ribiero stepped from behind the podium and moved to the edge of the dais, casting a look to the small gaggle of assistants and other members of her staff. She was a human woman of Brazilian descent, and Georgiou guessed her age to be mid to late forties while suspecting the events of the past few days would serve to make her feel even older and careworn. Despite help from a makeup assistant and vitamin and nutrition supplements provided by her personal physician, as well as a light gray women's pantsuit tailored to fit her trim frame, Ribiero looked tired. That much was understandable, given that she and members of the colony's leadership council had been incarcerated by Kodos soon after he succeeded her as governor. Neither Ribiero nor any of the other hostages were worse for wear after their brief ordeal, and she in fact had refused to discuss the subject. In her mind, two days locked in a jail cell was nothing compared to what the colony had endured.

Following Captain Korrapati's lead, Georgiou and Varazdinski moved to stand with Ribiero at the front of the platform.

"Thank you for staying," said Ribiero. She reached up to wipe a lock of curly brown hair from her eyes. Her voice was almost lyrical, thanks to what Georgiou recognized as a Portuguese accent. "I just wish I could've given the speech to an actual audience."

"Not a good idea, Governor," said Korrapati. "At least, not until we're sure the situation is secure. After all, it remains to be seen how your return to office will be greeted by the rest of the colony."

Ribiero replied, "I appreciate your concern for my safety, Captain, but it's the least of my worries just now. We can't pretend this tragedy didn't happen, but we also can't allow ourselves to wallow in our grief. The people we lost deserve more than that. We will remember, but we will also proceed forward, as we always have."

During their first meeting in Ribiero's office, the governor had expressed a desire to deliver her speech outside the amphitheater, hoping to reconnect with citizens as they each confronted their shared pain. Korrapati pushed back on that idea, worried that being so close to the place where loved ones were lost might provoke extreme responses from someone in any gathering. There was also the visceral reality of what had taken place in the stadium. As the executions were performed with particle beam weapons, there were no bodies requiring attention, but there would be a lingering, unnerving scent of smoke along with burned wood and other synthetic materials. Georgiou was all but certain the air would also reek of the haunting odor of scorched flesh. All of this, she knew, carried the potential to act as emotional triggers.

Korrapati moved to one of the windows on the room's far side. "There's a pretty large gathering out there. A hundred people, at least."

Stepping away from the podium, Ribiero made her way to the room's far wall, where a table had been arranged with carafes of water as well as dispensers for tea and coffee. The lack of food was noticeable, and though there was a food processor set into the wall above the table, it was a subtle yet practical way of reminding Georgiou about the food crisis that—though being addressed with the *Narbonne*'s arrival— was still very much a serious consideration.

"Some of those people have been there since before sunrise," replied Ribiero as she helped herself to a cup of tea. "I wish I could say they were all supporters celebrating my return to office, but I know better."

Crossing the room to stand next to Korrapati, Georgiou saw the assemblage of citizens from her vantage point three stories above the street running in front of the governor's building. The people were not a single mass, but instead broken into small groups of varying size. Some talked among themselves while many more stood in silence, staring at the building as though waiting for something to happen.

"I know I've repeated this several times already," said Ribiero, "but I can't thank you enough for being here.

Now that people are realizing the Federation and Starfleet never abandoned them, it's my hope that we'll all find a way to work through this together."

Georgiou said, "From what we've been led to understand, it's not being abandoned by the Federation that has so many people upset. Quite the opposite, in fact."

"That's true." Ribiero sighed. "There will be many who ultimately blame the Federation for what happened to us. Many of those descended from the original settlers, and quite a few more who came later, live here because of what Tarsus IV has always represented: a life of independence and self-determination."

"Every Federation world enjoys that same right," said Korrapati. "It's been a fundamental component since the beginning."

Teacup and saucer in hand, Ribiero replied, "But then that same Federation comes here and tells us that they're taking away part of our planet and giving it to a group of outsiders. A *large* group of outsiders, larger than the community that was already here." Before Korrapati could respond, the governor held up a hand. "Don't misunderstand me, Captain. Bringing the Epsilon Sorona refugees here after the disaster that befell their world was a correct, humanitarian thing to do. But there were those among us who saw it as a gross overreach of power by people light-years away, who hold no regard for the lives we've made for ourselves here."

"Yet you agreed with it," said Georgiou. While the *Narbonne* was in transit, she reviewed the speeches Ribiero presented to the people of Tarsus IV, explaining the dire situation on Epsilon Sorona II and the need to transfer its six thousand inhabitants from that colony to here. The governor's impassioned plea to her constituents was compelling, but it did not protect her from all manner of pundits representing a number of publications and news programs who took issue with the relocation. Some expressed concern that the rushed process might have unintended harmful effects, not just for the original Tarsus IV residents but also the refugees.

Turns out those people might not have been so far off after all.

Ribiero said, "It was the only rational option, even setting aside the fact that Tarsus IV is not an independent world but instead a Federation colony and protectorate. Even if I'd had the power to do so, I wasn't about to tell the Federation to take their problem somewhere else. There was no reason to deny the request, but my point was that it was never a request. It was a decision, made by someone else, implemented by someone else, and put into motion without even a passing attempt at respecting the sovereign status of this planet or my authority as its duly elected leader." She looked to Captain Korrapati. "So let's kindly dispense with the lectures about core Federation values. They're of precious little use to me at the moment."

Her words were flat and icy, matching the momentary flash of anger in her eyes. It was the first time Georgiou had seen genuine emotion from the governor since arriving on Tarsus IV. Having all but forgotten the tea she prepared, she set the cup and saucer back on the table before returning her gaze to Georgiou and Korrapati.

"Yes, I accepted the relocation, because it was the right thing to do, and I convinced the leadership council to back me. Then we pitched it to the rest of the colony. There were a few objections, mostly about the need to verify that anything brought from Epsilon Sorona II wouldn't present a danger to us. I shared those concerns with the Federation and Starfleet, and they did the usual round of studies and checks that are always done when you blend elements of disparate ecosystems." She paused, shaking her head. "Obviously, that wasn't enough."

"So, when the contagion began, people blamed you," said Korrapati.

Ribiero nodded. "Not everyone, but enough. Despite the initial resistance to the relocation and their desire to be left alone, these are good people. It was the suddenness of the change that upset them. Still, there was that percentage of people who were never going to agree with me, about anything. You know how politics works; from the instant you enter this arena, you always have those people who will never support you but instead will find every opportunity to tear you down."

Crossing her arms, Georgiou said, "The early confusion and indecision—or at least their perception of indecision—couldn't have helped."

"We were just figuring out what to do." Ribiero scowled, casting her gaze around the room. "I've dealt with emergency situations before, but nothing on this scale. We had eight thousand people depending on us to make the right choices and see them through this crisis. We were all conscious about screwing it up, but I never had any chance to really do anything. We were still getting our feet under us when Kodos convinced the council to push for a no-confidence vote. Then there was nothing I could do."

Georgiou asked, "But why bring someone like Kodos into your inner circle? He was a known voice of dissent regarding the relocation, was he not?" She already knew the answer to the question, having reviewed what limited information was on file for Adrian Kodos.

"I didn't bring him in," replied Ribiero as she began pacing the room. "I'd never even met him before this all started, but he was friends with a few of the council members, and he had experience dealing with emergencies."

She shook her head. "I'm still waiting to hear what exact situations he dealt with. Part of me thinks it was a ruse so that he could move into position to take over. He certainly didn't waste any time turning several of the council members against me." Reaching the window, she looked out at the gathering Georgiou knew was still there. "And after all of that, they had no problem putting me back in charge to deal with the aftermath of what he did."

Crossing the room toward her, Georgiou said, "Governor, one of the things I've been ordered to determine is whether a full evacuation of the planet is the best option for everyone involved. Before, when it was just the contagion, there was an argument to be made for defeating the infection and helping the colony get back on its feet, but now? The massacre will hang over everything you try to do here. There will still be people who blame you, not just for the outbreak but for what Kodos did. They'll argue that if you hadn't accepted the Epsilon Sorona refugees, Kodos would never have been in a position to do what he did."

"They'll lay the whole thing at your feet," added Korrapati.

Ribiero turned from the window. "All those people can go to hell. We have real problems to solve, and we need real solutions. You and your people represent those solutions, Captain, and with your help, we'll get through this."

"It won't be easy," said Georgiou.

"Nothing worth doing ever is." The governor smiled. "If anything, it's that attitude that exemplifies this planet and its people. This colony wasn't founded because it would be easy. The people who came here knew what they were getting into, but their hopes and dreams were enough to fuel them. Getting past this tragedy won't be easy, but they'll want that chance to try. Yes, we must find and apprehend those who supported Kodos or who aided in the massacre, but I have to believe the majority of those still with us want nothing more than to live in peace and to put this terrible ordeal behind them. They deserve that chance."

Georgiou could not help thinking that if Ribiero had put forth this level of confidence from the outset of the crisis, events might have unfolded in far different fashion. Even now, after returning to her office, some news broadcasts continued to attack her. Polls supposedly taken to gauge public sentiment showed an alarming percentage of people who preferred to condemn Ribiero for the executions, rather than Kodos. What Georgiou wondered was how many people sat in silent solidarity with him. There had to be some, even if they played no actual role in carrying out Kodos's plan.

As for the governor, she could be criticized for her lack of experience in the face of the calamity affecting her people, and even her early indecision as she struggled to formulate a course of action, but her concern for the well-being of those she was elected to lead was palpable.

"I know it will be difficult," said Ribiero, after a moment. "There were several arrests made soon after your landing, along with a number of assaults. Our hospital was already stretching its resources to the limit with the previous days' influx of patients, but this new surge has caught them all off guard."

"I've already sent our medical team to the hospital, Governor," said Korrapati. "And we have equipment and supplies being moved into position as well."

Upon being briefed on the hospital's most pressing needs, Doctor Varazdinski shifted into high gear, dispatching the medical staff assembled by Admiral Anderson back at Starbase 11. Three doctors along with a team of nurses and even a handful of field medics were already on scene and contributing to the triage and treatment for more than two hundred patients. Georgiou could not help but be impressed by the doctor's speed and organization as he put into motion his components of the assistance plan.

"And we also have teams deployed to the main food-processing facilities," said Georgiou. "Neutralizing the contamination is the first priority, including machinery used to convert the raw food compounds. Decontaminating farms, hydroponics facilities, and food processors in residences and other buildings will take longer, but we have plenty of rations aboard the *Narbonne* to cover the gap while that work proceeds." Colony scientists had made progress isolating the source of the fungal infection. Developing a counteragent was proving to be a greater challenge, but early reports from agricultural specialists brought in with the ship were encouraging.

"I appreciate everything you've done already," said Ribiero, "and everything you'll be doing in the days ahead. Your response to all of this has been amazing. We will never be able to properly show our gratitude."

Korrapati said, "We're just the first wave, Governor. Other ships are on the way; at last report, the next one won't be here for at least two weeks. Starfleet has been scrambling all available resources, but it's still a lot of space to cover." He smiled. "Until then, you'll have to put up with us."

"Gladly."

The room's front entrance opened to reveal one of Ribiero's assistants. An older man; his weathered features were framed by close-cropped gray hair, and he wore a simple blue civilian ensemble that seemed to Georgiou a bit formal for the current situation.

Then thoughts about his fashion sense were shattered as Georgiou caught sight of his right hand and the dark cylinder it held.

"Grenade!"

She uttered the warning as she saw the man's arm cock back to throw the object. Instinct took over and she lunged toward Ribiero, who was reacting to the shout of alarm before Georgiou slammed into her and forced her to the floor. Korrapati was also moving for the governor and the three of them ended up in a tangled heap.

Twisting her body, Georgiou was looking for the grenade to come bouncing into the room, but instead saw the man's attack thwarted by the appearance of a second person. Another human male dressed in civilian clothing had lunged into view, covering the other man's hand with his own and preventing him from throwing or dropping the grenade. Lean and muscled, the new arrival punched the would-be attacker in the side of his head, trying to subdue him. The first man grunted in obvious pain, struggling as they both held the grenade between them. He reached with his free hand for his opponent's throat, but the second man was faster, landing another vicious punch to his rival's head.

"Stay here," snapped Georgiou, pushing away from Ribiero and Korrapati and moving toward the scuffle. She was too late to offer any help as their apparent savior landed a third brutal punch to his adversary's head. The first man collapsed, sagging against the nearby wall before sliding down to the floor. All the while the new arrival kept his grip tight on the grenade until he had it free of the other man's hand. That accomplished, he studied the device before pressing a recessed control, deactivating it. Making eye contact with Georgiou, he offered her the grenade.

"Pretty rude way to say hello, don't you think?"

Wary of a second attack, Georgiou said nothing until a pair of security guards arrived to take the unconscious intruder into custody before shifting their attention to the other man.

Returning to Ribiero, Georgiou placed her hand on the other woman's shoulder. "Governor, are you all right?"

Ribiero nodded in response, as did Korrapati when Georgiou checked on him.

"He's one of my most trusted aides," said the governor as they watched the security officers pull the man to his feet.

"You might want to think about firing him," Georgiou offered.

"We got lucky," said Korrapati, "but we need to do a better job screening for weapons and other devices. My security people can help with that."

Georgiou said, "There's something else to consider. We may not be able to trust every member of the colony's security force."

"Kodos," said Ribiero. "You think some of the officers may still be loyal to him?"

"Somebody let that guy in here with a grenade."

Korrapati added, "And some were involved in the execution. Others likely helped him hide and eventually escape."

"If there are Kodos supporters among the civilian populace, there will damned sure be some within the colony government, including others among your staff, Governor."

It was a terrible thing even to consider, but Georgiou knew they had to weigh all the possibilities. Anyone who backed Kodos, for whatever reason, would be taking steps to conceal their identity and affiliations in the hopes of evading arrest.

Reaching up to wipe tears from her eyes, Ribiero released a heavy sigh. "It's been . . . difficult maintaining my composure, even just with my staff, and now this? Everyone, including me, lost someone that night. My fiancé was one of those chosen. I didn't even know until I was released from the cell where Kodos's people threw us." She drew a deep breath, wiping one last tear from her right eye before looking once more to Korrapati and Georgiou. "Can you help us find him and anyone who assisted him?"

"I volunteer for that duty, Governor."

The answer came from a voice near the room's entrance, and Georgiou saw that the man who had arrived in the nick of time was back, no longer flanked by members of the governor's security detail. Only then did Georgiou realize she recognized him.

"Lieutenant Commander Gabriel Lorca," the man said, offering a formal nod first to Ribiero, then to Korrapati and Georgiou. He gestured to two new arrivals—a man and a woman—who stood just outside the room in the adjoining passageway. "Along with the remains of my team, reporting as ordered, Captain." His expression flat, he added, "Welcome to Tarsus IV, sir. With your permission, I'd like to hunt down Adrian Kodos and bring him to justice."

11

After two previous attempts to reheat it, the tea had lost its flavor and no longer held any appeal for him. With a grunt of disgust, Kodos tossed the metal cup's bland contents against the cave wall. Watching the tea run down and into the cracks within the rock, he shook his head at his own temper and stupidity.

Do you feel better?

Drawing a deep breath, Kodos considered his surroundings. Though he had never believed himself to be claustrophobic or otherwise troubled by confined spaces, he tried not to buy into the notion that the walls of the underground caverns were indeed closing in around him.

"You're being silly," he said to no one.

"Governor?" someone asked.

Startled that he was no longer alone, Kodos turned toward the mouth of the small cave serving as his private quarters to see a younger man studying him. In the dim light provided by the portable lamp, it took him a moment to recognize Joel Pakaski regarding him from near shadow. Dressed in a drab green jumpsuit of the sort favored by pilots and others who worked around vehicles or other large machinery, the security detachment commander was a quiet man perhaps ten years younger than Kodos. Pakaski preferred to shave his head, a practice Kodos had witnessed earlier in the day, and he was renowned among the security forces for the intense exercise regimen he followed almost without fail each morning.

"My tea and I were having a disagreement, Joel," said Kodos, forcing a smile. "What can I do for you?"

Pakaski pointed a thumb behind him. "Charlynn has finished linking into the information network. We're able to receive broadcasts."

"Excellent."

One of the drawbacks to hiding in the mountains well away from New Anchorage was the lack of communication or other connection to the city. Despite his preparations that included this refuge and the supplies they acquired to sustain them and his eventual departure from the planet, his plans were disrupted by the arrival of the relief ship far ahead of estimates. This resulted in a number of tasks being completed in hurried fashion. From the moment it became obvious Kodos and his people would have to flee New Anchorage, the transport of personnel and equipment began. A caravan of ground vehicles, loaded and positioned well outside the city, was waiting for them after Kodos gave the withdrawal order. Pakaski had not been able to secure everything they wanted to take with them, but the equipment already on the vehicles provided a decent start. The journey to the mountains was slow and circuitous in a bid to avoid detection. Once here, however, hiding became somewhat simpler, owing to geomagnetic instabilities throughout the region. These anomalies would interfere with sensors and transporters, making it difficult for anyone hunting them. On the one hand, the mountain range's natural properties made it an obvious choice for a hiding place. However, anyone conducting a search here would have to do so the hard way, on foot or by ground vehicle, giving Kodos and his people the advantage of anticipating the arrival of any unwanted guests.

He accompanied Pakaski to the larger cavern, which acted as a command post. Equipment and worktables were scattered in something resembling a circle around a larger table that held a quartet of portable computer workstations. Stored along the cave walls were packing containers, most able to be carried by a single person, that contained food rations as well as medical and other supplies. The chamber felt in many respects like a military camp, though Kodos himself had no experience with such things. He suspected this was Pakaski's doing, in keeping with the man's past as a Starfleet ground forces officer.

"Did you have trouble obtaining the other supplies?" asked Kodos.

Pakaski shrugged. "It was a challenge, but we managed. If we go back again, there could be problems. The Starfleet ship is already working with the security forces to keep things under control. You can be sure they'll be monitoring anyone entering or leaving the city."

"Then it's a good thing we know the city better than they do."

New Anchorage, being an open city on a planet where crime was low and civil unrest all but unknown, did not possess any sort of barriers to entry. Even the spaceport, the most controlled area in the region, allowed entry to the city once new arrivals were processed through the colony's immigration support center. All of that changed with the onset of the fungal infection, first with Governor Ribiero enacting curfews and later when Kodos instituted martial law. Even with the arrival of the Starfleet vessel and others still on the way, extra security measures remained in place throughout the city. A curfew remained in place, and access to certain sensitive areas around the city was still restricted. Pakaski, leading a small group of people back to the city in order to abscond with some needed supplies, was able to learn much about the current security situation.

"I think we'll still be able to get in and out unde- tected," said Pakaski. "We'll just have to pick our entry points and times very carefully. Plus, I've already got some people looking into whether we can worm our way into the Starfleet ship's sensor feeds without being detected. Assum- ing we can pull it off, that'll be a big help."

Kodos nodded in approval. "Impressive. You obviously have some training and skills that aren't listed in your per- sonnel file with the security forces."

With a knowing smile, Pakaski replied, "I learned a long time ago that as long as no one asks the pertinent question, choosing not to share certain things isn't really lying."

"Situational morality, Joel?"

"All morality is situational, Governor."

"Indeed."

Crossing the cave floor to the cluster of portable com- puter terminals sitting atop the central table, Kodos moved to stand behind a young woman working at one station while sitting on a folding camp stool. It took him a moment to recall that her name was Charlynn Schmidt, daughter to another of the security officers who had rallied to his cause. She was perhaps too young for this life, Kodos decided, but it was still gratifying to see people her age supporting their cause.

"I'm told we're able to receive broadcasts, thanks to your efforts," he said, and the young woman shifted on her stool so that she could face him.

"That's right, Governor. It took some doing, but I've been able to patch into the data feeds being transmitted between New Anchorage and the outlying settlements. We can monitor anything that comes across them, and they'll never know we're watching."

Pakaski added, "We recorded a news broadcast that aired just a few minutes ago. It's something you'll want to see." To Schmidt, he said, "Queue it up."

Pressing a string of keys on her terminal's console, Schmidt called up a visual log before moving to her right in order to give Kodos and Pakaski an unobstructed view of her computer's display. On the screen, a middle-aged man in civilian attire sat behind a desk on the familiar stage of one of New Anchorage's prominent broadcast news providers.

"The arrival of the Starfleet ship Narbonne *appears to be lifting spirits across the city. Though colony security continues to report instances of civil unrest, including vandalism and assaults against citizens, those incidents look to be on the decline. Many people remain understandably upset by the events of recent days, and community leaders are demanding answers, even as Governor Ribiero and her staff continue their efforts at keeping things under control. Security commanders stress that everything possible is being done to rein in these protests, while praising the community for their efforts to help them minimize further injuries to persons or damage to property."*

Kodos knew from the moment he first conceived of the Sacrifice that implementing it would come with repercussions. Stunned at first by the scope and audacity of what he had put into motion, the remaining colony population seemed to undergo something of a delayed reaction to the reality of what was done. In fact, the resulting displays of unrest and retaliation, against figures or symbols of authority or just one another, ended up being more subdued than what he expected. He was both surprised and relieved. Might it mean on some level that a segment of the remaining population at least understood if not outright approved of the drastic actions undertaken to ensure the colony's survival?

One can only wonder, and hope.

On the computer screen, the newscaster continued, *"Around the colony, members of the Starfleet assistance team are digging in and working hard on a variety of tasks. Medical personnel are on hand, assisting the staff of New Anchorage Hospital to treat the patients they've received in the wake of ongoing protests and other acts of civil unrest. Foremost among these is the eradication of the fungus that contaminated our food supplies and endangered us all. Reports on this front indicate the science and engineering specialists are close to a solution, which will allow food-processing and delivery facilities to be brought back on line. In the meantime, citizens are encouraged to visit one of the designated locations in order to receive food rations brought by the* Narbonne, *all of which have been verified as not affected by the contamination. Efforts to develop a way to defeat the contagion are ongoing."*

Kodos reached for the computer interface and pressed the control to pause the playback. He let his hand remain on the terminal, and only after a few moments did he realize he was propping himself with his arm.

"Governor?" he heard Pakaski prompting. "Are you all right?"

Had he really just sagged against the table? For a handful of fleeting seconds, the strength seemed to ebb from his body. The sensation faded with the same abruptness that it appeared, leaving him to wonder if there was something physically wrong with him, or was this a form of mental malaise that had chosen to manifest itself?

Guilt?

Of course, he felt remorse at the necessity of the Sacrifice. How was anyone to know assistance would arrive so much sooner than originally estimated? Should he have waited, exercising greater prudence before carrying out his final decision? Perhaps, but no amount of second-guessing would undo what happened. There was only the future to contemplate, both for the colony and for himself.

Without answering Pakaski, Kodos touched the control to resume the playback.

"Also continuing are efforts to locate and detain Adrian Kodos, who authorities report has not been seen since the night of the mass executions at the amphitheater. Officials asked for comment on the manhunt indicate they are following a number of leads, but they've had no luck even ascertaining his last known location. There are rival theories as to Kodos's whereabouts, with some believing he's still hiding somewhere in New Anchorage, while others think he's fled the city, likely with the assistance of at least some of the individuals who helped him carry out the merciless executions."

"They can look all they want," said Pakaski. "They won't find us, sir."

Kodos did not believe the other man, but saw no reason to diminish his confidence, at least not in front of subordinates. There would be time enough later to discuss contingencies.

"Complicating matters is the fact that very few people seem to even know what Kodos looks like, and most of the colony administrative staff, with the notable exception of Governor Ribiero and a few council members, did not survive the executions. A preliminary examination of colony computer records reveals that all imagery of Kodos has been deleted, suggesting he sought to complicate efforts to search for him before making his escape. Authorities are asking for assistance from the community and for anyone with information pertaining to Kodos to please come forward."

"That's enough." He indicated for Schmidt to stop the broadcast. Thanking the woman for her assistance, he gestured to Pakaski, and the two men began walking among the worktables and stacks of supplies and equipment.

"They will not stop looking for me," he said, keeping his voice low. "The public will demand my capture and trial. For all we know, people will look for me on their own, and justice will be far from their minds while they hunt for me."

"Hunt for *us*." Pakaski regarded him with an expression of unfettered conviction. "You're not alone, Governor. They're hunting all of us."

The man's devotion was admirable, and Kodos was moved by his assurances. If and when the time came to confront pursuers—be they interested in justice or vengeance—Kodos knew full well that he may be forced to make some difficult choices. The people who had sworn allegiance to him could find themselves placed in the position of choosing between him and their own freedom or well-being. Left with no other alternatives, how many of these people would sacrifice themselves? He was certain that Pakaski, Ian Galloway, and a handful of others would. But the rest? There was no way to be sure. The situation had turned drastic with the Starfleet ship's arrival, and what seemed so clear and righteous just days earlier now was consumed by doubt.

His own choices were simple. Kodos needed to plan for the worst. If he was to have any measure of peace, he likely would have to discard everything about his current life and identity and begin anew. A simple getaway by fleeing offworld was not a viable option, at least at present. The Starfleet captain and his crew would be expecting something like that and taking appropriate precautions to prevent his escape. Even getting to a transport would be all but impossible, with the spaceport under close watch and those few ships occupying berths prohibited from departing without extreme screening.

"We can't wait for opportunity to present itself, Joel. We must act in order to maintain control of our situation for as long as possible."

Pakaski replied, "We need to stay ahead of whoever they send to find us. Seize the initiative, instead of waiting for them to come to us. Better yet, we can disrupt their work with the colony. Divide their attention, divert their focus."

"Exactly."

As they continued their stroll, Kodos waited until they were past a cluster of six men and women, each working to unload supplies from a trio of packing containers. He said nothing until he was sure they were out of earshot.

"There's something else to consider. Blending back in with the population may be our best option. Perhaps if we waited until the initial searches for me are completed. The rest of you should have no problem. On the other hand, I'll have to take prudent steps."

Knowing there was no obvious means for him to escape the planet, the Starfleet teams rendering assistance to the colony would search the entire planet for him. Assuming he did nothing, they would find him, sooner or later. Even with whatever ended up passing for a fair trial in a Federation court, there was no chance he would escape conviction or incarceration. He had no intention of spending the rest of his days consigned to a penal colony or—worse—a psychiatric facility such as the remote planet Elba II, an asylum for the criminally insane and other miscreants viewed as unsuited for existence in the idyllic paradise the Federation had labored to create. Once banished to such a place, he would become an object of scrutiny and scorn, doomed to endless questioning, study, and judgment by doctors, curiosity seekers, and other, weaker beings.

Never.

Kodos would die before he allowed that to happen.

How many people would have to die along with him?

12

The window shattered, sending an expanding cloud of glass shards along with the brick responsible for it into the hallway. People, some of them injured along with others who accompanied them to the hospital, scrambled for cover. One man, older and slower than those around him, was the unfortunate target of the brick, which struck him in the head. Grunting in pain, he stumbled to the other side of the corridor before sagging against the far wall and sliding to the floor.

"Help! I need help over here!"

Georgiou was running for the fallen man even as she shouted. Pushing past people who had ducked away from the window and now were packed into the corridor's confined space, she did not reach him until he had settled into a heap on the floor. He was leaning against the wall, his arms hanging limp at his sides as his chin rested against his chest. Blood ran from a wound where the brick struck his head, and Georgiou could see the indentation in the right side of his skull marking the point of impact.

"What the hell is going on out there?" she snapped at a *Narbonne* security guard who was running toward the nearest exit. The younger officer paused, his eyes wide with concern.

"Some kind of protest outside, Commander. Apparently, a few members of the colony's governing council are here in the hospital, and there are a number of people out there who are upset about it." His gaze seemed to fix on the fallen man. "I guess people are looking for someone to blame for . . . what happened. Things took a turn, but colony security people are already on it. We're heading outside to help."

"Be careful out there," offered Georgiou before returning her attention to her latest patient. How many people had she treated in the last six hours? She quit counting after she ran out of fingers. It was all she could do to keep up, doing her best to assist the New Anchorage hospital staff and the *Narbonne* medical staff.

With everyone shorthanded and little time for any single point of focus, Georgiou and the rest of the relief team found themselves doubling and even tripling up in order to carry out various tasks, regardless of individual expertise. Trained years ago as a field medic, Georgiou quickly found herself lending a hand with the triage activities both here at the hospital and at the emergency treatment stations set up at a school gymnasium a short walk from here. Setting aside her supervisory duties as she tried to keep track of various *Narbonne* personnel working around the city, she found herself elbows deep in assisting with the diagnosis and first response treatment of dozens of patients. Most of the wounds she had seen to this point were minor, lacerations along with the odd broken bone, and all treatable with nominal effort. More serious cases, including life-threatening issues, were being handled by Doctor Varazdinski as well as physicians from the hospital. None of those people were around at the moment, leaving Georgiou to deal with what her trained but not expert eyes told her was a serious injury.

"Commander," said a voice behind her, and Georgiou

looked up to see Ensign Dralax, one of the medics pulled from the Starbase 11 staff and hurriedly assigned to the *Narbonne*'s relief team. He was a Denobulan, and his pale complexion and the pronounced ridges framing his face set him apart from the humans comprising the bulk of the people packed into the hospital's halls and waiting areas. Dralax was carrying a field medical kit slung over his shoulder, which he unlimbered and set on the floor as he took a knee next to Georgiou and the injured man.

"He was next to the window when the brick came through," reported Georgiou. "Definite skull damage. Could also be intracranial hemorrhaging." The amount of blood coming from the wound worried her. She reached for Dralax's medical kit, expecting to find a portable diagnostic scanner.

Resting one hand on the man's arm, Dralax replied, "I think you're right." The ensign's tone was crisp and professional, forgoing ranks and protocol as his medical training and the patient before him pushed aside all other considerations. "Help me get him to a treatment room."

No sooner did Georgiou move to help lift the man than she felt his entire body go limp. There was a final, pitiful exhalation, and she knew in that moment that they were too late.

"Damn it!" The fatigue of the past hours pushed the words from her lips before she even realized she was speaking. Without thinking, Georgiou shifted herself in order to leverage the man up and onto her shoulders in a firefighter's carry before heading at a trot toward the treatment rooms. She heard Dralax behind her, running to keep up.

"Commander, I'm afraid he's gone."

She knew he was right, but the anger at having watched the man killed before her eyes—in the corridor of a hospital, no less—drove her onward. Reaching the treatment room, she saw it was unoccupied and she lowered the man onto the treatment table. Once he was prone, lying faceup, there was no denying that he had passed. His eyes, thankfully, were closed, and she found herself transfixed by the wound and blood marring the right side of his head, face, and neck.

From behind her, she heard Dralax say, "I'm sorry, Commander. His injury was just too severe."

Two nurses, a man and woman both looking as tired as Georgiou felt, entered the room. The woman looked to the unmoving man.

"We just got the call about this. Is he . . . ?"

Georgiou shook her head. "There was nothing we could do. It was just . . . too fast." Stepping aside, she allowed the nurses to inspect the man's unmoving form. "It happened almost right in front of me."

"A woman outside the hospital was hit the same way," replied the male nurse. "They're rushing her into surgery. It looks like security's getting the situation under control." He sighed as he looked down at the dead man. "Too late, unfortunately."

Activating the patient bed's antigravity controls, his companion lifted the bed from its frame and began guiding it toward the door.

"We'll take care of him, but we're going to need this room."

"Understood." Georgiou watched the two nurses maneuver the bed out of the room and disappear down the corridor, swallowed by the constant stream of people heading in all directions toward points unknown.

A moment later, she heard the sound of something heavy falling against the wall, and she turned to see Dralax sitting on the floor.

"Are you all right?" she asked, moving toward him.

The Denobulan's brilliant blue eyes seemed to be staring at nothing. His lips moved, but Georgiou heard no words. Crouching beside him, she touched his shoulder.

"Ensign?"

The touch seemed to bring him out of his trance—or whatever it was—and he blinked several times in rapid succession before looking at her. His jaw was slack, and his eyes were watering.

"I'm . . . I'm sorry, Commander. I don't know what just came over me. I . . ."

"When was the last time you ate or got any sleep?"

Blinking some more, Dralax replied, "I arrived here yesterday evening with the first group of medics from the ship. I've been working since then." He frowned. "I don't understand why I'm so tired. Denobulans can go far longer than a single day without the need for sleep."

"We're all working much longer and harder than normal, Ensign. Stress only contributes to our fatigue, so we have to remember to take care of ourselves. You should know that." Realizing she was in danger of lapsing into full "command mode," Georgiou softened her tone. "I know it seems a bit overwhelming, but if we start collapsing, we're no good to anyone here."

Dralax nodded. "You're absolutely right, Commander. It's just . . . I'm still having a problem processing all of this." When she did not reply right away, he added, "As I've been treating patients, it's impossible not to listen as they talk about what they've been through: what happened before we arrived. Even with the evidence right in front of me, it's still so hard to believe."

"You've never been involved with something like this, have you?" Georgiou asked.

"Only mock training exercises. Starbase 11 is my first duty assignment since graduating the Academy and medic training. I'm supposed to be spending a year getting practical experience treating real patients while learning from the starbase medical staff."

Georgiou resisted the urge to observe that he was getting far greater experience here than he would while working at a starbase, but such a comment felt inappropriate at the moment.

"I wasn't born on Denobula," Dralax continued. "My parents were scientists living at the Federation colony on Arvada III. We were among a very small number of nonhumans, but it was a wonderful place to live. I have so many friends there, and so many happy memories." He closed his eyes, drawing a breath. "I can't stop thinking about something like this happening there. My parents, my friends; the idea of them being forced to . . ." The sentence faded, and he placed a hand over his mouth. "I'm sorry, Commander."

"It's okay. I want you to get some rest." Seeing the look on his face and knowing he would protest, she held up a hand. "Just a couple of hours. You don't have to leave the building. Use the rooms we've set up as break areas for our people. I'll personally come and get you if I need help with something. And get something to eat. You need to keep up your strength."

"Aye, aye, Commander." Accepting her extended hand, he pushed himself to his feet. "And thank you."

"Thank you for your hard work, Ensign. If we're going to tackle all of this, we're going to have to keep working. Don't burn yourself out too quickly."

Nodding in understanding, Dralax gathered his medical kit before leaving the room, presumably in search of the rooms designated for *Narbonne* personnel to catch brief respites from the ongoing work.

A nap sounds pretty damned good right now.

No sooner did the errant thought cross her mind than

Georgiou forced it away. Despite the gentle lecture offered to Dralax, there were still a number of things she needed to check on before resting. She needed to get updated reports from her various team leaders, not just here at the hospital but at other key locations around the city, and she also was due to provide Captain Korrapati with an updated status report.

If I can't sleep, I can at least have the biggest cup of coffee I can find.

Giving the treatment room a last, sad look, Georgiou shook her head and straightened out her uniform before moving back into the hallway. The crowd here was thinner than she remembered, and the commotion from minutes earlier seemed to have subsided. There were faint sounds of shouting, likely coming from somewhere outside the building, but the situation in here had returned to its previous level of controlled chaos.

The hospital was constructed as four structures, each containing five levels, and connected by a central hub. On patient treatment floors, these junctions contained the nurse's stations and doctor's offices. As Georgiou made her way toward the second-floor nurse's station, she caught sight of a uniformed colony security officer standing outside one of the patient examination areas. The man, who looked like he should be studying for a high school test rather than standing guard, noticed her approach and his posture stiffened.

"Commander Georgiou?" he asked.

"That's right." She indicated the exam room's closed door. "What's going on?"

The security officer, whose name tag read CUSHMAN, replied, "I'm on escort detail. I was told to wait outside until a doctor came to see this patient."

"What patient?" Moving past the guard, Georgiou reached for the keypad next to the closed door and pressed the control to trigger the chime alerting the person inside that they were about to receive a visitor. A moment later the door slid aside, and she found herself staring at a young human girl sitting on the edge of the room's single patient examination table. The child was perhaps seven or eight years old, with blond hair pulled back into a ponytail. Her clothes—dark pants and a red shirt—were soiled, and her left pants leg was ripped from the cuff up to the middle of her thigh. Two pieces of what looked like plastic slats were secured on the inside and outside of her leg in a field-expedient splint. Sitting next to her on the table was a stuffed doll that resembled an Andorian, its blue skin faded and worn and one of its two antennae hanging limply from its head. A data slate rested in the girl's lap, its screen dominated by the graphics of some kind of game. She looked up at the sound of the door opening and smiled at Georgiou.

"Hi."

"Hello," replied Georgiou as she stepped into the room. "What's your name?"

"Shannon. Shannon Moulton."

"I'm Philippa. What happened to your leg?"

"My mommy says I broke it when I fell down some stairs."

Still outside the room, Cushman said, "All of the hospital's bone knitters are being used, both here and at the school triage site. A few are broken, so the others are stretched thin. Shannon's mother went to find a doctor."

"Does your leg hurt?" asked Georgiou, her gaze still on the girl.

Shannon shook her head. "It did before, but not now. A nurse gave me something to make it feel better."

"Well, we'll get you fixed up." After the incident with the poor old man, it was nice to be able to offer attention to someone she might be able to help.

"Are you a doctor?"

Georgiou smiled. "No, I'm just someone helping the doctors."

"Okay." Satisfied, at least for the moment, the girl returned her attention to her data slate.

Stepping closer, Georgiou reached for the doll. "What's your friend's name?"

"Vran." Shannon's eyes were wary as she watched Georgiou handle the toy. "He's supposed to bring me good luck, but I guess he's not working today."

"Maybe he's just confused." Georgiou indicated the spot where the broken antenna hung from a piece of torn fabric. A portion of the doll's stuffing protruded from the small opening. "Once we get your leg taken care of, I can probably fix this for you."

"Okay."

"Commander?"

Looking to where Cushman still stood in the hallway, Georgiou saw that he was joined by a human woman. Despite her tired, worn expression, the resemblance to Shannon was obvious.

"Hello. I'm Commander Georgiou, from the—"

"The *Narbonne*, yes." Stepping into the room, the other woman extended a hand. "I'm Eliana Moulton, Shannon's mother. Thank you for being here, Commander." Offering a weak smile to her daughter, she added, "Maybe you'll have better luck finding a doctor for us?" She even sounded tired when she talked.

"I'm sure we can do that." Looking to Cushman, Georgiou said, "Would you please see about that?"

Cushman glanced at the other woman before replying, "I'm sorry, Commander. With all of the riots and other problems, I'm really not supposed to leave Doctor Moulton or her daughter."

Frowning, Georgiou said, "I don't understand."

"Council members and advisers have been given security escorts," answered Moulton. "Those of us who are still alive, I mean. Colony security is worried that people might try to come after us as retaliation for . . . for what happened."

"You're on the leadership council?"

Moulton grimaced. "I'm an adviser. Specifically, I'm an agricultural scientist. I work with other scientists to better understand the planet's ability to be farmed for both indigenous and imported seeds and crops."

"So, you're one of the people who can help us identify and eradicate the fungal contamination?"

"Identify? Yes." Shame and regret clouded Moulton's features. "Eradicate is another thing, though."

Georgiou knew that Governor Kodos had included members of the council and others like Eliana Moulton in the roster of colonists he sentenced to death, but how or why had this woman survived?

"You obviously know about the contagion," said Georgiou.

Again, Moulton's gaze shifted to look down toward the floor. "Oh, yes. I know a lot about it, for all the good it did."

13

Excerpt from *The Four Thousand: Crisis on Tarsus IV*

Transcripts and visual recordings of Governor Ribiero and the twelve elected members of the colony's council depict a leadership team gripped by uncertainty. Although things had not yet descended into chaos, events had served to push Ribiero and her trusted advisers to the precipice.

Exploring all possible means of containing the plague wreaking havoc on colony food supplies was beginning to place a strain on resources, personnel, and emotions. This much was obvious to Doctor Eliana Moulton as she stood before the governor and the council, armed with information she knew they would not want to hear.

"Looking at the numbers wasn't going to change anything," she says, as the two of us sit on the front porch of her home on Midos V, a long-established, thriving Federation colony world. "I'd done the computations five times. I remember staring at them, willing them to change, or for my math to be completely wrong, but it wasn't. Numbers are merciless, the way they present cold, harsh truth, and it was this truth that I had to present to Governor Ribiero and the others." She shakes her head. "I remember thinking it was a lot like having to give a patient a terminal diagnosis. There was just no way to make what we'd found come off sounding anything less than what it was: dire."

Being a scientist, Moulton delivered the unwelcome news the only way she knew how, by presenting the facts and the supporting evidence as collected by her and her colleagues.

According to their research into its origins and rate of expansion, Moulton and her people determined that the fungal contamination was the result of extreme reactions by the Tarsus IV soil to seeds and crops imported from the beleaguered colony on Epsilon Sorona II. Despite a battery of tests to ensure compatibility, something in the genetic makeup of the foreign seeds responded to the new environment by mutating into something never before seen.

At first the change was small and undetectable, and by the time the initial oddities were noticed by farmers preparing to harvest crops, it was too late. Within days, the contamination was raging out of control, defying all attempts to stop its advance using every measure at the colony's disposal. The fungus seemed possessed of its own consciousness, advancing from farm to farm, at first contained to New Anchorage and the areas in close proximity, but scientists like Moulton quickly learned that even outlying villages were falling victim to contamination. Other plant life was affected, but not to the extent suffered by food crops.

Only scorching entire fields and greenhouses with phaser fire eradicated the infection, but it was a localized solution. Worse, raw compounds such as those used in food processors were also being exposed to the contagion, and they were carrying the contamination into the inner workings of the machines that took those compounds and created edible offerings for the population. Only quick thinking on behalf of Moulton's people and others working to confront the mounting crisis saw to it that the colony's remaining food supply escaped infection. Even as she stood before the council, work was under way to move uncontaminated food stores to protected locations around the city, namely pressurized storage facilities at the colony's main spaceport.

Such measures were helpful, but they did not represent a solution.

"We were in trouble," says Moulton, sipping tea she made by hand for us to enjoy during the interview. "The steps we were taking were keeping existing supplies free of infection, but until we found a way to eradicate the infection, we couldn't grow any more. We also had to clean food processors. I'm talking disassembling them down to the smallest piece, scrubbing them clean with decontamination gels and whatever else we had on hand or could dream up from raw materials. Even that was only a temporary fix, because unless you can run those systems in an airtight chamber, they'd still be susceptible to being contaminated all over again." She shakes her head, the frustration in her voice evident even after ten years.

"And with all of that, the council still seemed to be having trouble believing the crisis was not only real, but out of our control. Every test we ran, everything we tried in order to develop a counteragent, came up negative. Within two days, every farm had been razed by phaser fire, and every greenhouse emptied down to the bare metal walls and floors. That stopped the immediate problem, but it's not as though we could start growing new crops. We needed to stop the contamination, erase all traces of it, or we risked just giving it a second chance to hammer us all over again."

Once Governor Ribiero and the leadership council were convinced of the immediacy of the threat and the problems it was creating, attention turned to what else could be done. One obvious first step was to call for help, so a distress call was dispatched to Starbase 11, which in addition to its considerable Starfleet presence also included offices and representatives from the Federation's Department of Colony Support. So far as Ribiero was concerned, the crisis gripping Tarsus IV rose to the level of planetary emergency.

"That's when we got the bad news." Moulton offers that

simple observation free of sarcasm or other negativity. Like so much the scientist has said, the comment is delivered without emotion and in matter-of-fact fashion. "Help was available, but it was a month away. At first, that seemed ridiculous, but then you remember that Tarsus IV was quite some distance from Starbase 11 or other inhabited planets, Starfleet only has so many ships available in any given sector, and space is really, really big."

She laughs, but it's a laugh devoid of humor. "People tend to forget that part. Warp drive is great, but it still takes time to get from place to place. Even so, that wasn't what was working against us so much as the simple lack of ships. The starships assigned to Starbase 11 were deployed for various reasons. We learned later that a couple of them were dealing with issues relating to our always interesting relations with the Klingon Empire. Others were sent on missions that, as far as I know, are still classified."

Further questions aren't needed at this point, as Doctor Moulton is content to keep talking without additional prompting. She pauses only to refill our tea before continuing. "So, there we were, facing at least a month before help might arrive. Admiral Anderson at Starbase 11 tried to put a positive spin on things, noting that he'd recalled certain ships from their other missions in order to warp back to help us." Her voice then turns conspiratorial. "There were rumors that the ships that ended up arriving so soon after the massacre were actually closer than what we were told, but the classified nature of their missions required Starfleet brass to put out disinformation about their status." She shakes her head. "Nobody ever admitted that, of course, and if they had, I'd bet heads would roll."

Despite initial hesitation before the magnitude of the crisis began to sink in, Ribiero set into motion several efforts that even her harshest critics deemed proper and necessary. First, there was the immediate collection and protection of the colony's remaining food stockpiles, which were estimated to be well short of what was needed to sustain the entire population if the estimates for the arrival of rescue ships were accurate. What food had escaped contamination was placed under guard at the New Anchorage spaceport. Next, the governor instituted a strict rationing procedure, including directing nutritionists from the hospital to devise a caloric intake that could be shared by the bulk of the population while also favoring children and the elderly as well as the infirm and anyone with special dietary needs. Even with such emergency measures in place, it was quickly apparent that even extreme rationing would see available food stores depleted well before help's estimated arrival.

"They really didn't have a choice but to institute a curfew," laments Moulton. "Sealing off access to the spaceport and other government buildings made sense, and increasing street patrols by the security forces. Ribiero didn't go all the way to declaring martial law." The scientist shrugs. "Maybe she should have, but at the time most people were being cooperative. Of course, a big part of that was not letting on the truth about the remaining food reserves. I think if that knowledge had become public, there would've been a much stronger reaction." Her gaze drops, as though examining some invisible point on the floor at her feet. "But there was never a chance for anything like that to happen."

Transcripts from the council meeting included Moulton's presentation to the assembled leadership, and Governor Ribiero's reaction to the news is depicted as one of uncertainty, indecision, and doubt. Such characterizations were bolstered by her eventual removal from office and the council appointing an interim governor for the duration of the crisis. In the wake of the massacre, this led to protests calling for her to be held accountable for the executions. Her approval ratings among the population were affected by the entire incident, and it took her years to recover the trust she lost.

Moulton is more forgiving. "The problem with using transcripts and news reports as a source is that they tend to boil away the humanity of a situation and the people caught up in it. Gisela Ribiero was a good governor, before and after the massacre. She was simply ill-equipped to handle something on this scale. Very few people are, except maybe those who receive training for this sort of thing. I read that she'd once dealt with a disease outbreak on another colony, not as a governor or other elected leader but just someone who pitched in to help. She was a nurse of some sort, and I remember reading that she and other nurses and medics did a first-rate job caring for victims of the disease until a cure was found. They ended up saving a lot of lives that may have been lost otherwise. So it's not like she was a stranger to difficult challenges.

"But Tarsus IV was a whole other level of emergency, and this time it was on her shoulders. Okay, hers and the council's, but she was the governor. We were already guaranteed to be at least a few paragraphs in a history book, somewhere and someday, but no matter what happened, good or bad, hers was the name that would be linked to it forever. I can understand how that might give someone pause. The problem was that she lost the confidence of the council, and by implied extension the rest of the colony."

This lack of faith in their governor compelled the council to take unprecedented action by removing Gisela Ribiero from her post as governor of Tarsus IV. While many critics praised the move, those expressing kinder opinions categorized Ribiero as a victim of circumstances, unfairly blamed for the crisis the colony faced. This was borne out by initial public reaction to the decision, with many people taking issue with the abrupt and perhaps premature removal from office. Regardless of where people landed with respect to the action, it did make way for the council to install a leader better equipped to guide them through such troubled times.

The process of appointing a successor would prove to be short and direct, with the council already possessing what they considered to be a suitable replacement. From the emergency's outset, there had been one voice that remained calm, offering level-headed suggestions and support to Ribiero and the others. In hindsight, those council members who survived the massacre would realize his dispassionate manner was itself a warning of what was to come, but in the moment? All anyone saw was composure under pressure and resolve in the face of uncertainty and fear.

In a unanimous vote, the leadership council selected as their interim governor a quiet, thoughtful man of science named Adrian Kodos.

14

To the casual observer, it might appear the food-processing plant's warehouse was the victim of nothing more than a crime of opportunity. It would take a trained eye to notice the slight yet undeniable clues left behind by the perpetrators, alluding to something more than a simple robbery. Without that insight, there would be no reason to suspect anything sinister taking place. It could be assumed that any items missing from the inventory were taken by scared men or women motivated by nothing more than a desire to survive, or perhaps provide for a family.

Even before having his gut instinct confirmed, Gabriel Lorca knew.

"This was calculated," he said, more to himself than the plant director or any of the Starfleet security officers walking with him as he completed his visual inspection of the warehouse's interior. Having already reviewed a complete inventory provided by the facility's director as well as a report on what was missing, he needed little time to examine the actual storage racks and shelves and the rows of larger storage containers and make his determination. "Someone looking to hoard supplies or equipment would've just taken what they wanted, rather than trying to cover their tracks."

Walking alongside Lorca, the plant's director, Christian Apodaca, replied, "It's even better than that. Someone accessed our inventory database and altered the counts to cover what they took."

Lorca nodded. It made sense, though it only served to reinforce his initial feeling that the responsible party was something more than a desperate opportunist.

"What tipped you off that something was wrong?"

Apodaca held up the data slate she carried in her left hand. "I had no idea at first, but I was walking the floor when I noticed that two portable generators were missing. Our inventory says we're supposed to have eight, and there's eight on the racks in here, but I did the count less than a week ago, and we had ten. I checked the logs, and there were no transfers of generators. I verified a couple of other items where I remembered the counts and found similar discrepancies. So I went into the protected archives and pulled a backup of the database from our last official full inventory audit, and compared it to what's currently on file." She waved the data slate. "Nothing was taken in any large numbers, but once you start looking at the list, you can see that everything they took would've been perfect for—"

"For setting up a base camp somewhere." No sooner did he speak the words than Lorca turned to face his companion. "My apologies. That was rude."

"It was, but I'll get over it." The remark was neither terse nor teasing, and instead delivered with almost no emotion, in keeping with the rest of Apodaca's interactions with Lorca since his arrival. A trim Earth woman of perhaps forty years, she carried herself with the air of an experienced manager used to having everything organized and under control. That made sense, given her responsibilities overseeing one of New Anchorage's primary food-processing and distribution centers. Her eye for detail was obvious, given the quick way she determined something was amiss in her warehouse and the steps taken to confirm her own initial suspicions. Lorca could also appreciate the easy way she brushed aside his momentary lack of manners and instead turned it back on him.

"Well, I promise that's not my usual style." Lorca gestured to her data slate. "I didn't see how many field ration packs were taken."

Apodaca replied, "A little over two hundred."

"Why weren't the field rations secured with the rest of the food stores at the spaceport?" asked Lorca.

"More than half of what we had on hand was transferred there." Apodaca gestured around, indicating the rest of the warehouse. "Along with whatever raw food materials managed to escape infection. That was right before we shut down all processing operations, pending a full decontamination of the facility."

Taking all of the colony's food processors offline had been a concerted effort, though simplified somewhat due to the fact that most New Anchorage residents eschewed personal processors in their homes in favor of actually cooking their meals. The majority of the city's restaurants also observed this practice, leaving such operations to larger facilities like this one to transform raw bulk materials into edible food items for commercial and residential use. Though the unrefined compounds were resistant to the contagion, it was only a matter of time until the concentration of that material in the machinery suffered contamination just like processed foods.

"We were instructed to keep the rest of the field rations here," continued Apodaca. "Sort of a contingency reserve, I guess. Not too many places around the colony have pressurized storage areas that could protect food from the fungus, and everything at the spaceport was already being used. This plant, the other two, and the hospital were the main alternate storage sites."

Lorca had made a similar proposal to Governor Ribiero with respect to the outpost's storage facilities, even offering whatever space remained at OT-4 for housing other food supplies. The message he sent never received a response before Ribiero's authority was transferred to Kodos.

Well, we did get a response.

Pushing aside the errant thought, which brought with it images of Meizhen Bao and Piotr Nolokov lying dead in the outpost corridor, Lorca forced his attention back to the matter at hand.

"All right, so somebody knew you'd have supplies here, and not only knew precisely what to take, but also how to hide what they were doing, at least for a while. Not to accuse you or any of your staff, Director Apodaca, but this sounds to me like an inside job."

Behind Lorca, a new voice said, "I think I can confirm that, sir."

Along with Apodaca, Lorca turned to see Ensign Terri Bridges approaching them. She was accompanied by another woman he did not recognize at first, but as they drew closer he saw the emblem of Starfleet's Corps of Engineers above the left breast pocket of her olive-green utility jumpsuit.

"Commander, this is Lieutenant Haley Carroll," said Bridges. "She's with the *Narbonne* team."

Nodding in greeting, Carroll offered, "Good to meet you, Commander." A human woman, Carroll appeared somewhat older than Bridges, with blond hair cut in a short style that left her ears and the base of her neck exposed while allowing a brushy mop to adorn the top of her head. Lorca had seen similar styles sported by female members of Starfleet's ground forces. Between that and her toned forearms, which were visible thanks to her having rolled the sleeves of her jumpsuit above her elbows, Carroll looked as though she may have done a stint with that group before transferring to the SCE.

"Likewise, Lieutenant." Lorca gestured to the data slate in Carroll's hand. "What did you find?"

The engineer replied, "Whoever made the updates to the inventory database was no slouch. They either had or were able to forge the necessary credentials to get past system security, then updated not just the master database but also duplicate files transmitted to the colony administration offices along with the other processing plants and even the smaller facilities in the outlying settlements. I'm actually surprised they didn't get into the protected archives and manipulate the counts in the backup files, but those are safeguarded by another level of security that requires management approval for access." Looking up from her data slate, Carroll eyed Apodaca. "Somebody poached you pretty good, Director. I'd bet all the credits in my pockets it was somebody on your staff."

"Never saw who it was." Apodaca drew a deep breath. "A week ago, I'd have punched you both in the mouth for suggesting something like that, but now?" She shook her head. "I just don't know."

"What do you mean?"

Before answering, the director cast a glance to the pair of Starfleet security officers accompanying Lorca before indicating for Carroll, Lorca, and Bridges to step away from the guards. Once they moved to what she must have felt was out of earshot, she said in a lower voice, "When everything started, we were all worried, of course. It hit everyone so quickly, we weren't able to process it all before having to act. There was definitely some initial dissatisfaction with the way Governor Ribiero seemed to be moving too slow, not making decisions, that sort of thing. I actually felt sorry for her, to be honest. This had to be like being thrown into the ocean and not knowing how to swim. However, when Kodos took over, a few members of my team seemed reassured. That's when I remembered that they were among the group that came with Kodos to Tarsus IV, so it made sense that they'd know and feel comfortable with him."

She frowned and made a waving motion with one hand as though she were trying to erase what she had just said. "I mean, we all felt a little better at first, because we'd heard Kodos had prior crisis-management experience, and the word from Ribiero and other members of the council was that he was pretty cool-headed. From the sound of it, he wasn't rattled by the situation, and his early decisions and actions bore that out. Calm, focused leadership in the face of fear and chaos. It was exactly what we needed right then." When she paused, Lorca realized her eyes were reddening and her gaze began to falter, dropping to the warehouse floor.

No.

"Director, are you all right?" It was Bridges who asked the question, but Lorca already knew the answer.

Blowing out her breath, Apodaca reached up to wipe her eyes. "A third of my staff, twelve people, were among those . . . the people Kodos picked. Someone I'd been seeing was one of them too. I didn't have a complete list until the next day, when they didn't show up for work. A couple of others didn't come in either. As for my . . . other friend, he'd left me a message saying he was going to the gathering at the amphitheater, but I was here, working late." Her voice wavered, and it was Carroll who placed a reassuring hand on her shoulder.

"We're very sorry for your loss," said Bridges.

Lorca knew the ensign was channeling her own feelings about the deaths of their friends at the outpost. For his part, Lorca was thinking of Balayna again, feeling sadness and anger threatening to overwhelm him. Closing his eyes for a moment, he pushed the image of her face from the forefront of his mind, banishing it to some dark corner of his thoughts. She deserved more of his mourning than he could afford just now.

I'm sorry.

Oblivious to all of this, Apodaca forced a small, weak smile. "We'd only been dating a couple of weeks. You know, still figuring out all of the awkward, silly stuff. He worked at one of the news stations as a field reporter. Human interest stories, that sort of thing. I ran into him when he was covering one of the culture festivals we have every few months." Her eyes brightened, as though she was recalling a fond memory. "It might not have been love, but it was certainly something at first sight." Clearing her throat, she wiped her eyes again. "I'm sorry. You didn't come all this way to hear this sort of thing."

"We did, actually," said Carroll, and Lorca saw that the lieutenant also was affected by the director's story. "We came to help in any way we can."

"Thank you. It's just . . . it's just such a damned *waste*. All those people, dead, and for what?" After taking another moment to compose herself, Apodaca returned her attention to Lorca. "I know the rumors are circulating everywhere, but it's my understanding that Kodos had help from some members of the security forces in carrying out the . . . executions. There may have been a small group of close confidants who also knew beforehand." She paused again, and took another calming breath. "While I can't believe any of my people helped with that, I can certainly see anyone who felt some loyalty to Kodos helping him escape from the city." Her words seemed to catch in her throat. "Actually, no I can't. It doesn't make any sense. Who could support someone like that?" With new conviction, she shook her head. "At least they're gone. Fine. They can stay gone."

"Well," said Lieutenant Carroll, "that's the thing. I don't know that we can count on them staying gone."

Lorca regarded the engineer. "You think they'll come back?"

"Maybe not here, but somewhere." She indicated her data slate. "The stuff they took won't last them forever, and that's assuming whatever food rations they took don't end up getting hit by the fungus. If they're a decent-sized group, they'll need resupply at some point, sooner rather than later."

Bridges said, "They wouldn't hit the same place again, would they?"

"Maybe," replied Lorca. "Whoever they are, they're not stupid. They had the skills to pull off this robbery and cover their tracks. I'm betting they weren't counting on Director Apodaca getting wise to them so quickly. Still, they might think they can do something similar."

"We can be ready for them," said Apodaca. "It will take some doing, but we should be able to secure this place and the other plants against this sort of intrusion." She was speaking with more confidence, and even a new hint of determination. "No way am I letting them get away with something like this again."

"They'll have plans for this sort of thing," said Lorca. "The trick will be trying to anticipate them: get ahead of their thinking somehow, so we can be ready for them."

Lorca did not expect their quarry to be quite so cocky as to repeat themselves or make some other stupid mistake. Whoever Kodos and his followers were, they had planned their escape well and in short order, and successfully fled the city to parts unknown. Kodos would have to know that Starfleet security teams were at this moment searching for him and anyone who may have aided him, either in preparing or carrying out the mass execution, or his escape to avoid capture and prosecution. Perhaps he even had a plan to flee Tarsus IV altogether and to do his best to outrun the hand of justice.

Lorca, haunted once more by visions of Piotr Nolokov and Meizhen Bao, to say nothing of Balayna, was not about to let that happen.

You want off this planet, Kodos, then it's going to have to be through me.

15

An eerie calm seemed to grip the ground around her, and Georgiou was almost afraid to move for fear of disrupting the welcome if uncomfortable silence.

She stood in the middle of the New Anchorage amphitheater's main field. Large patches of the grass were burned if not blackened. There remained a layer of fine, almost ashen residue discoloring the ground, which Georgiou knew was a by-product of organic matter being disrupted by phased energy delivered at extreme frequencies. The effect on a single item—or individual—was often much less obvious, at least in her experience. She had seen the effects of larger concentrations of phaser fire, but never anything like this. An involuntary shudder coursed down her body, and it took her a moment to realize she had crossed her arms and was hugging herself in response to the abrupt chill now gripping her.

And the smell.

The errant thought was enough to invoke another shiver. Carried on the light breeze wafting across the arena field was the unmistakable odor of burned flesh. She clamped her mouth shut, wrinkling her nose in protest of the fetid stench assailing her nostrils. The amphitheater's design all but assured the smell would persist here until the field was cleaned of the carbonized remains. As she pondered this, Georgiou trembled again and gripped herself tighter, and the more she did that, the angrier she became.

Bastards.

"Commander Georgiou?"

Startled by the unexpected voice, she turned to see Lieutenant Commander Lorca walking toward her. Unlike the last time she saw him with the other members of his staff from the observation outpost, he wore a Starfleet uniform complete with equipment belt that held a phaser pistol slung low along his right thigh, communicator, and a pair of accessory pouches. He needed a shave, and there were dark circles under his eyes. Given that it was still early in the day, Georgiou guessed the commander had been working through the night.

"Mister Lorca."

The commander replied, "I came as soon as I got your message. Captain Korrapati said you'd be here."

Watching him as he spoke, Georgiou noted how the man's eyes moved to look past her, taking in the scene around them with short glances. He did not like being here, she decided, and could not fault him.

"You look exhausted. When did you last sleep or eat anything?"

Lorca seemed to force a small, grim smile. "It's been a while. I have to admit I've been pushing myself a bit hard, but this is . . . important." He paused, his gaze moving once again past her to take in the ashen grass. Per her instructions and his own desire to help, Lorca had been immersed in the search for Kodos and anyone loyal to him.

No, not searching for him, Georgiou reminded herself. *Hunting him.*

Lorca's own words, uttered with cool resolve during their first meeting, still rang in her ears. He presented himself as a man possessed, if not obsessed, with the singular goal of finding Kodos and bringing him to justice.

Georgiou was okay with that, to a point.

"Your dedication is commendable, Commander, but we can't afford to have anyone working themselves to death." Lightening her tone, Georgiou added, "Don't make the captain unleash Doctor Varazdinski on you."

"Understood. I promise I'll see to it right away, but I wanted to make a report to you as soon as possible."

Georgiou realized this was the first time she had been alone with Lorca. Things had been moving with such speed and the demands on her were so formidable that she needed to remind herself about sleep and meals. For his part, Lorca had set to work attempting to determine Kodos's whereabouts. He was driven—that much was certain.

"You've seen the crowds outside the amphitheater," he said. "Tempers have been running hot, even before your arrival. Some of them are getting pretty riled up. Now that you're here, they want to see results. They want answers to their questions. They want us to *just do something*. Some of them probably don't even care what we do, as long as we're doing it. They're hurt. They're scared and mad, and they want someone to blame. We can't give them what they want, so they'll take out their frustrations on us or anything else that fits the bill."

"I can't say I blame them." Georgiou cast another look over the field.

Some distance from where they stood, sealed gates and other entrances were reinforced by active force-field generators positioned around the amphitheater's perimeter. According to the *Narbonne*'s overnight watch officer, the first few dozen had arrived just before dawn. They had not said or done anything to attract undue attention from security guards stationed near the entrances, but instead stood in silence, as though holding vigil. Daybreak brought with it more people—men, women, even children—and the silence gave way to the low, rumbling murmur generated by uncounted conversations laced with the occasional shout toward one of the officers from the *Narbonne*'s security contingent providing security for the outdoor arena. Now, at the morning's halfway point, there were at least two hundred people standing outside the force fields.

She could only imagine what they and so many others had to be feeling. Like her, they felt a need to come here, to walk on this grass and see for themselves what little remained of those lost. In some respects, the tragedy would not be real until they saw with their own eyes where it had happened. Such revelations would bring with them more pain as those left behind struggled to process this insanity. Georgiou felt herself gripped by the same emotional turmoil. The longer she stared at the desecrated field, the more the weight of what happened here seemed to press down on her.

"I can't believe something like this could ever happen on a Federation world."

Lorca said, "Utopia's easy when everything works and all your basic needs are met. We tend to think we've traveled this long path toward peace and prosperity, but take away the necessities of living and it's a short walk back to our baser instincts. Kodos's mistake was allowing that to cloud his judgment."

"This wasn't about clouded judgment." The words were delivered with more venom than she intended, but Georgiou made no apologies. "And it wasn't about noble sacrifice for the greater good. If that were the case, he'd have cast himself down with those he *sacrificed*. Push past his fancy speech, and it was just him playing god, and ultimately about saving his own ass. How many more might he have killed if we never came?"

It was a thought she had considered more than once, despite there being no evidence to suggest Kodos intended such a thing. However, anyone who could murder four thousand people in one stroke surely had no compunctions about killing more, if he believed he was acting for the right reasons. How many more innocent men, women, and even children would he have slaughtered if the *Narbonne* arrived even a day later? The very thought made Georgiou shiver.

"Are you all right, Commander?" asked Lorca.

She drew a breath to calm herself. "I'm sorry. I think I'm having a sort of delayed reaction to all of this. I can't imagine what someone who's been here the whole time has been dealing with."

"It's a lot to absorb," said Lorca. "Trust me, I understand. It's why I prefer to keep working, rather than sit around. The people need to know that we see the individuals caught up in all of this, that it's more than just getting them past the immediate crisis. We have to be about what comes tomorrow too."

Georgiou replied, "We're doing everything we can. I know it's not enough, but it's a start."

The effort had begun within an hour of the *Narbonne*'s landing, with her detachment of first responders and the ship's crew hitting the ground at the proverbial run. Doctor Varazdinski, despite his evident disdain for the pomp, circumstance, and other trappings of the service, was a first-rate physician whose assistance proved invaluable at both the hospital and the triage center. Working with the New Anchorage doctors, nurses, and other volunteers, Varazdinski and his medical team had ensured each patient requiring care received timely and effective treatment.

Other areas of the city, though vulnerable as a consequence of the protests that erupted after the executions, were also under control and food distribution had started with no major obstacles. Although it would be some time before things returned to anything resembling "normal," the immediate danger of the crisis was at least being addressed. With the origin of the fungal contagion identified, scientists from the *Narbonne*'s team were continuing their work to develop a means of arresting its effects. The most recent report detailing test results and projections was encouraging, and impressive considering the Starfleet crew had been on the scene for less than two days. Georgiou had no idea if Admiral Anderson knew what he was getting when he assigned Aurobindo Korrapati and the *Narbonne* as an initial response to the Tarsus IV crisis, but his gambit looked to be paying off in spades.

Still, Georgiou knew it was only one part of a much larger puzzle still missing a key piece.

"Along with everything else we're doing, we need to find those responsible." She felt her jaw clenching. "Maybe Kodos actually thought he was doing the right thing, but that makes him a monster. For that reason alone, we have to find him and drag him back here."

"Agreed."

Doing her best to set aside her personal feelings and growing disdain for Kodos, Georgiou tried to focus on more constructive topics. "You've made some progress?"

Shifting to a more professional, reserved tone, Lorca said, "I conducted an investigation of one of the food-processing plants, as well as a maintenance facility, a supply warehouse for a couple of merchants in the city, and one of the colony administration's transportation depots." The commander reached up to rub the bridge of his nose, the almost unconscious gesture an indicator of his fatigue. "Each of those locations was targeted. Whoever conducted the raids knew exactly what they wanted, and how to take just enough to avoid immediate notice. They also modified computer logs to cover their tracks with respect to what was taken. This was well planned, even if they were forced to kick things into high gear once they learned a Starfleet ship was arriving far earlier than anticipated. The director of the food plant was the first to notice something off, and that led to similar discoveries at the other locations. Based on what was taken—food, tools, equipment, and so on—I'm betting Kodos and whoever's with him aren't in the city."

"You think they tried to disappear in the wilderness somewhere?"

"It's what I'd do. They couldn't leave the planet thanks to the quarantine protocols initiated after Governor Ribiero declared a viral outbreak, and staying in the city presents too many dangers. They'd be outnumbered, either by the security forces, our people, or even just regular citizens looking for retribution." Lorca nodded in the direction of the amphitheater's main entrance.

"Even if he's fled the city," said Georgiou, "he likely still has supporters here. As you said, somebody helped him steal those supplies, so it stands to reason he had help getting out without anyone noticing. That would probably mean people staying behind to cover any tracks or clues he may have left." She felt a renewed wave of anger. "I want those people too."

"Right there with you, Commander." From the thigh pocket running along the left side of his uniform trousers, Lorca extracted a standard Starfleet-issue computer data card. "That contains copies of personnel databases taken from the colony administration offices. All of the biographical information pertaining to Adrian Kodos has been purged from the system, including contingency archives. We did find a medical file in the hospital's computer system, and that includes data like blood type, DNA, and so on, but no visual record. As far as I can tell, there's not a single image of Kodos in any computer system, anywhere."

Georgiou frowned. "How is that even possible?"

Shaking his head, Lorca held up the data card. "It shouldn't be. I'm actually surprised the medical file's still intact, but its encryption levels are different from those used by the colony administrators. It could simply mean Kodos or whoever was helping him with this worked in the administration offices, but he didn't have a similar point of contact at the hospital."

"And no images of him were captured at any point after he assumed the governor's duties?" asked Georgiou.

Lorca blew out his breath. "He stood in the shadows the night of the . . . executions. I watched it as a live broadcast." When he paused, Georgiou recalled how he described that night, and the immediate reactions offered by him and his companions. She felt as though Lorca might be holding something back. Had he suffered a personal loss? Neither he nor his fellow officers from the outpost volunteered anything on that topic, and Georgiou felt uncomfortable prying any further.

"There's more," Lorca continued, handing her the data card. "This also has the arrest records for three members of the colony's security force who are believed to be Kodos's collaborators. They were on duty the night of the massacre. Records show they drew heavy weapons from the armory earlier that evening, and returned them just before midnight. Armory maintenance records show the weapons' individual energy cells were depleted as much as sixty percent, indicating a long period of sustained fire—"

"Or a short period of fire with the weapons set to high power," finished Georgiou. "Dear lord."

"None of the three seem eager to talk, but I expect that'll change once formal charges are drawn up and presented. They'll talk, if not about Kodos, then at least about somebody who helped or supports him and who's still in the city."

Georgiou said, "They can't possibly be hoping for some kind of immunity agreement."

"Only if they're idiots," replied Lorca. "I honestly believe they're stalling. Perhaps they think they're buying time for Kodos and anyone with him to get farther away, or deeper into whatever hole they've picked for a hiding place."

"There will be more like them. We could crosscheck identities with known Kodos associates. If necessary, we'll verify the identity of everyone. We have to start with the assumption that administration databases have been compromised. Whoever helped Kodos may have altered the memory banks, but they wouldn't be able to get to those maintained by Federation Colony Support. We'll compare the two sets of data, and see what shakes out." She made a mental note to ask the *Narbonne*'s captain to dispatch a request to Starbase 11 for copies of that information for comparison.

Lorca said, "In the meantime, we can still be looking for Kodos and any followers, wherever they might be hiding."

"Assuming they've left the city," said Georgiou, "finding them could prove more difficult than we originally thought. If they didn't just head to one of the outlying villages or some other place with a decent population, there are large areas of the planet that don't react well to sensors. The mountain ranges east of the city are just one major source of geomagnetic interference." She had examined the topographical data on file with the colony administration offices, as well as information gathered by the *Narbonne*'s sensors. "We're talking thousands of square miles of terrain that we can't examine from a distance, let alone get a transporter lock on anything we find. Kodos is no fool, that's for sure. If we're going to search for him in areas like that, it's going to have to be the old-fashioned way."

"Time's on our side," said Lorca. "Nobody's allowed offworld without their identity being verified. We don't even know how many people we're looking for yet."

"It'd be a small number," guessed Georgiou. "Kodos would've wanted to keep the circle close, not just for those helping him but probably those who knew the executions were going to happen. Based on what was taken from the supply warehouse and the transport depot, I'd guess no more than a few dozen people at most."

"And some of them are still in the city," added Lorca.

"All right, so we outnumber them by a significant margin, we've got more help on the way. My biggest concern is avoiding any direct confrontation with Kodos or his supporters. After all of this, he won't be willing to come peacefully. With that in mind, we've got to plan this and do it right. From what I know of those *Constitution*-class ships, their sensors can find pretty much anything. There won't be anywhere for Kodos and his loyalists to hide."

Even from this distance, she could hear the low drone of hundreds of colonists milling outside. "The people who've lived through this catastrophe need to know that we're doing everything in our power to find Kodos. They need to see justice being served, for the sake of the dead as well as those left behind. We can't present anything less than total commitment to apprehending him and anyone who helped him. And while we're at it, anyone who might be a silent supporter of Kodos needs to know that Starfleet is not leaving any stone unturned searching for them as well." The anger she tried to push down was attempting to reassert itself. "Those people in particular need to know they can't hide from us. They need to be terrified at the very idea that we'll find them."

Easy, Philippa.

A dull thump from somewhere near the amphitheater's front entrance made both officers flinch and reach almost in unison for their holstered phasers. Georgiou ran toward the sound with Lorca right beside her, and within moments she could hear dozens of voices shouting over what was a sizable crowd. The assemblage of colonists had swelled since her arrival less than an hour earlier, and she guessed five or six hundred people were standing outside the arena. A glance around her showed an increased presence of Starfleet security from the *Narbonne*. Farther from the entrances and occupying discreet positions from which they could monitor the situation were members of the colony's security forces. Even with the added level of protection offered by the force fields, Georgiou wondered if the barriers would be enough to keep out the burgeoning crowd should the mob's collective mind decide to advance as a single unit. Scanning the crowd, she listened to the steady drone of shouts and other noise and tried to pick out faint, individual cries of protest.

"We want Kodos!"

"Bring us the butcher!"

"Where is he? Why haven't you found him?"

"Death to Kodos!"

A flash of light to her left caught Georgiou's attention just before she saw a dark object trailing flames arcing through the air. The makeshift explosive—likely a glass container with a crude fuse fashioned from a fuel-soaked rag—smashed against the stonework of the amphitheater's outer wall and exploded into more fire. Many members of the nearby crowd pumped clenched fists into the air as flames clung to the wall, feeding off the liquid accelerant. Then automatic fire suppression systems activated, making short work of the momentary disruption.

"Molotov cocktails," said Lorca. "That escalated quickly."

"Ladies and gentlemen," said a calm voice over the arena's array of recessed speakers, and Georgiou looked toward the entrance to see Captain Aurobindo Korrapati standing just inside the force field and speaking into a personal communicator, which she guessed was patched into the amphitheater's broadcast system.

"What are you doing about Kodos?" yelled another voice.

"Who helped him? Where are those people?"

Korrapati continued in the same composed manner, *"Please remain calm. You have my word that we're doing everything we can to assist you, and to apprehend anyone responsible for the tragedy you've endured. We will not rest until those goals are met."*

Another improvised device was hurled from the crowd, smashing against the force field itself almost directly in front of Korrapati. The captain stepped back as the glass container burst apart and there was a brief rush of flame as the fuel it contained ignited, but the effect was momentary with nothing to continue feeding the resulting fire. Nevertheless, a fire suppression unit addressed the issue, extinguishing what little remained of the small blaze.

"Damn it," said Georgiou.

Lorca replied, "If we try to disperse them, we'll only make it worse. They need to know they're being heard." He gestured to Korrapati. "He's got the right idea, but it's going to take a while."

He was right, Georgiou knew, but while the anger, fear, and uncertainty on display here were justified, violence could not be tolerated. Still, any attempt to quell the crowd through force was just asking for more trouble. Dealing with such situations was not something with which she had experience, but Korrapati was acting as though he had done it all his life. Appearing unperturbed by the disruption, the captain climbed onto a cargo container moved into position near the force fields, standing upon it so that he was more visible to the crowd before him. Still protected by the electronic barrier, he raised his free hand while speaking once more into his communicator.

"We feel your pain. We feel your anger. We will bring those responsible to justice, and we will need your help to do so. Let us work together, for the good of everyone and for the memories of those you lost."

Though Georgiou thought she heard at least a few voices of agreement, there also was another chorus of shouting, followed by another of the crude cocktail bombs. This one landed short of the wall, shattering on the ground and erupting into a pool of flame before one of the auto extinguishers snuffed it out.

"Yeah," said Lorca. "This is definitely going to take a while."

"Then I suggest we use that time wisely." After weighing everything, including the human factor and the need to show the colonists that they were doing everything possible to apprehend Kodos while not exposing her people to unnecessary risk, Georgiou knew that inaction was not an option. They needed to move, and they needed to move fast. She turned to face Lorca.

"Start with Kodos loyalists who might still be in the city. Find them. We'll use them to get to him. Wherever they're hiding, root them out. I want him running and I want him scared, and then I want him in chains."

Lorca offered a single, curt nod, and she noted his subdued expression of agreement and approval.

"Aye, Commander."

16

Crouching in darkness with his back against the rough, thermoconcrete wall, Gabriel Lorca felt his body tensing in anticipation. His fingers tightened around his phaser's handgrip, and he reminded himself to relax. It had been a few years since he last participated in an armed entry, or even practiced the tactic. However, training and muscle memory were bringing everything back, including the rush he felt in those last moments before the initial breaching action.

Breathe. Relax. Focus.

From his present position, the door they were about to enter was to his left. Past the door and positioned in a manner similar to Lorca was Lieutenant Jason Giler, the officer in charge of the *Narbonne*'s security detail. A muscled blond man of European stock, Giler looked as though his Starfleet uniform were a second skin. He wielded a phaser rifle, and the weapon looked like a toy in his massive hands. Lorca had declined the offer of a rifle from the ship's armory, having long ago grown accustomed to the portability of the phaser pistol variant. It was another habit formed from countless hours of training and a few hours of actual tactical operations like this one, all part of a life he thought he had left behind years ago.

The more things change . . .

Acting on information pulled from the security forces personnel database as well as sensor logs of the night of the executions, Lorca and his colleagues were about to breach the suspected location of Alexander Simmons, one of the colony's senior security commanders and—according to logs of the night in question—someone who was on duty at the amphitheater. There also were other records of his visiting the governor's office on the day prior to the executions, suggesting he may have possessed advance knowledge of Kodos's plans. According to other members of the security contingent, Simmons had failed to arrive for duty at his precinct headquarters the following day, and no one could remember seeing him since the *Narbonne*'s arrival. With all major methods of entering and exiting New Anchorage under tight control, it was unlikely Simmons had fled the city, but neither was it probable that he would return to his own residence. After discovering Simmons had wiped his information from his official computer access profile as well as his personal correspondence account, Lorca put Aasal Soltani to work. The lieutenant dug into the colony administration's computer records in search of any information or connection, no matter how tenuous, between Simmons and any other member of the community.

It took little time for Soltani's expertise and tenacity to pay off, in the form of archived electronic exchanges between Simmons and a woman, Joanna Robarge, whom he appeared to have been seeing socially for the past few months. From there, it was a simple matter to determine Robarge's address, and obtain authorization from Governor Ribiero, Captain Korrapati, and Commander Georgiou to effect an arrest.

After waiting until nightfall and upon arriving at her apartment complex, a surreptitious tricorder scan was enough to tell Lorca that there were two people inside her dwelling, along with at least two phaser pistols of the sort employed by the security forces. There seemed to be no other sensors or other security devices that may have detected his and Giler's presence, which he found odd.

Too good to be true?

Lorca raised his free hand, offering a thumbs-up to Giler. The lieutenant returned the gesture, communicating to Lorca that he was ready to proceed. As he did so, he shifted his position, bringing his phaser rifle up as he rested the weapon in a two-handed grip across his chest.

Reaching into one of the pouches on his equipment belt, Lorca extracted a magnetic lock override device and placed it over the keypad set into the wall next to the residence's rear door. Known as a P-38, or "skeleton key" in Starfleet parlance, the tool was normally used by engineers and security personnel aboard starships as a means of bypassing the locking mechanisms of a starship's interior and exterior pressure hatches. They could also be programmed for use by military and law enforcement personnel for situations like this one.

Lorca pressed the control to activate the P-38 and the unit worked its magic, bypassing the door lock's access code. An indicator on the keypad changed from red to green, and Lorca pushed himself to his feet, gripping his phaser in both hands as he stepped forward. The door slid aside at his approach, and with his weapon leading the way, he stepped into the residence. Once inside, he stepped to his left, allowing Giler to enter behind him. The lieutenant moved right, and both men quickly surveyed what appeared to be the apartment's kitchen. A single light was active, illuminating a small, round breakfast table. More illumination filtered from a source in the adjoining room, part of which was visible through an arched entry.

"Alexander Simmons," Lorca called out in a commanding voice. "This is colony security. Make your presence known."

Instead of a reply, Lorca heard running footsteps.

Damn it.

"Simmons!"

Lorca shouted the second call as he crossed the kitchen, phaser out in front of him. He crossed into the next room, which resembled a sitting area. A small lamp on a corner table was the light source he had seen from the kitchen, and the center of the room was devoted to a pair of large recliners and a sofa with a low-rise wooden table situated before it. A viewing screen was set into the wall to his right, and he could see light from a source outside the large window that dominated the room's far wall.

Movement to his left made him turn in that direction, and he leveled his phaser at the shadowy figure still trying to hide behind a sofa. The figure crouched, head and shoulders just visible above the top of the couch, but Lorca saw that it was not Simmons. Long, dark hair framed a slim face, which matched the description Lorca had for the apartment's listed resident, Joanna Robarge. Despite knowing this as he looked at her, for a split second he was reminded of Balayna.

That fleeting distraction was all the woman needed to make her move.

Lorca snapped back to the here and now upon catching sight of the phaser in her hand. She was attempting to aim it at him while still hunkering behind the couch and her shot missed the mark, passing over his left shoulder as he stepped right. Lorca fired a single shot that caught the woman just below her throat, the bolt of phaser energy washing over her before she collapsed out of sight. Stepping around the couch, he trained his weapon on the prone body, now able to verify that his would-be shooter was indeed Joanna Robarge.

"Nice try, lady."

He had to admit to admiring her audacity at choosing to remain in the apartment while covering her lover's escape. Kicking away the phaser lying next to her right hand, Lorca was relieved to see that the pistol's power level was set to stun.

My lucky day.

"Up front!"

Giler's call was enough to send Lorca lunging for the short hallway connecting the sitting room to the apartment's foyer. Ahead of him, Lorca saw that the dwelling's front door was open, and Giler was already running through it. Following on the other man's heels, he saw that the entrance led to an open-air passage between apartment units, beyond which lay a grassy courtyard. Giler turned right and sprinted out of the corridor, and Lorca looked several meters past the lieutenant to see another figure, with dark hair and clothing, running across the grass toward an adjacent building.

Idiot, Lorca chastised himself. *You should've had Giler cover the front. Why the hell didn't you bring more people?*

The easy answer was that Simmons, if the available evidence and Lorca's own gut were correct, was a high-value suspect with connections to Kodos. He might well be involved in whatever support the governor was receiving from people still in the city. It was possible Giler even knew Kodos's location, or at least where to start looking. Lorca, unwilling to leave this to the colony security forces for fear of alerting sympathizers to Simmons or Kodos, instead opted to keep the situation contained and the circle of people who knew about this operation limited to as small a number as possible.

For all the damned good that did you. Son of a bitch is getting away.

Out in the open, Giler stopped his running and took aim at the fleeing figure, who looked over his shoulder and realized what was about to happen. Just as Giler fired, the other man dodged to his right, causing the stun bolt to miss wide left. At the same time, he turned and raised his arm. Lorca saw that it was indeed Alexander Simmons, and he had a phaser in his hand.

"Giler!"

The lieutenant dropped to one knee, and by a hairsbreadth missed catching head-on a phaser bolt of his own. Despite his distance from the fleeing man, Lorca fired on the run, the shot skirting past Simmons's right arm. The fugitive turned to aim toward the new threat, and Lorca and Giler fired in unison. Simmons took both phaser blasts high in the chest, staggering backward from the double impact. He dropped unconscious to the grass.

"You all right, Lieutenant?" asked Lorca as he closed the distance, covering the unmoving Simmons with his phaser.

Giler rose to his feet. "Yes, sir." He gestured to Simmons. "I hope he's worth it after all this."

Regarding the stunned man, Lorca nodded. "Me too." He was already getting tired of hunting small game like Simmons. He and anyone else cowering in the shadows were like rats, afraid to face the light and the consequences for their actions. The question was whether Simmons—or whomever else Lorca and his people were able to find— would turn on the recipient of their misplaced loyalty.

We'll find out soon enough.

17

One warning indicator was an isolated issue. Two was an anomaly. Three was a pattern.

Seven, in Georgiou's opinion, was a big damned problem.

"What the hell is all this about?"

Looking up from the console where she was working in the colony administration's communications center, Georgiou turned to behold the master status board set into the room's north wall. The board was little more than a collection of indicators, each representing a key location somewhere in New Anchorage. Government offices including the headquarters and precinct locations for the security forces, the spaceport, public utilities, and other facilities were linked to a central alert system, designed to connect every location to the administration offices. During times of emergency or other incidents requiring the rapid dissemination of information, the main comm center could be employed by the governor or members of the leadership council to connect with any or all of the networked locations.

Except for rare, predicable occasions, all of the indicators on the master board were supposed to glow green, indicating all was well. A yellow color signified a location was experiencing technical difficulties with any of its facilities or equipment, or else was offline for routine or unscheduled maintenance. Red meant some serious deviation from normal operations, either in the form of equipment failure or some manner of security breach.

Seven of the indicators were red. Flashing, angry red, as though doing everything within the limited scope of their operation to announce to anyone who might care that something was very, very wrong.

"Multiple alerts," said Lieutenant Enamori Jenn. Working at a nearby console, she vacated her chair to get a better look at the master board. "I've confirmed it's not an error. We're showing alarms at seven different locations around the city." Beneath the rows of status indicators was a workstation, its rows of controls and compact display screens reminding Georgiou of a typical starship console. "I'm retrieving information from each location."

A moment later one of the station's displays began scrolling data in rapid-fire fashion, only some of which Georgiou was able to decipher.

"Some kind of breach," she said, just before another set of data appeared on another of the workstation's screens.

Jenn nodded. "Internal scanners at these locations are all reporting explosions targeting power distribution nodes." She turned from the console. "Commander, this has to be a coordinated attack."

"Of course it is," Georgiou said. "I should've known we couldn't count on more than one night's peace."

The previous evening was uneventful, aside from security having to deal with a couple of minor protests and a handful of younger people being drunk and disorderly in public. Following the *Narbonne*'s arrival and its crew pitching in to help restore order, things finally were looking to settle down. Her teams were carrying out various tasks that did not require her immediate supervision as they continued their assistance efforts at the hospital or bolstered the security forces to help maintain order in the city. With Commander Lorca preparing to expand the search for Governor Kodos beyond the city, Georgiou found herself all but delegated out of any meaningful work. Unable to sleep, she volunteered to work in the comm center with Jenn this evening, assisting the staff in sifting through volumes of computer and communications data from the period before the crisis up through the tragic events at the amphitheater. The task was daunting, but its goal was simple: find anything that might shed light on Adrian Kodos or any of the people who apparently pledged him their support. Even with the citywide curfew still in place, reports were coming in of protest groups and other clashes between security personnel and the civilian populace. None had reached the level seen at the amphitheater, and even that disturbance seemed to have blown itself out after a few hours. Captain Korrapati remained on site throughout that incident, continuing to talk to the crowd until he began to win over more people to his side. Not everyone left satisfied with the action that was being taken, but it was progress. At this point, Georgiou would take any victory she could get.

This, however, was something else altogether.

Behind them, a door slid aside to admit Kerry Abela, the comm center's second-shift supervisor. A human male in his late forties, Abela had thin, receding blond hair and was dressed in a simple blue jumpsuit with his last name stitched over his left breast pocket. The front of his overalls was covered with a dark stain, and it took Georgiou an extra second to realize the other man had sloshed the contents of the coffee cup in his left hand in his haste to return from his dinner break.

"There are alarms sounding throughout the building," he said. "What's the problem?" His attention was on the master board. "Seven alerts? That never happens."

Jenn replied, "So we gathered." Her attention still on her workstation's displays, she added, "The locations in question are at one of the schools, a water treatment facility, a library, two restaurants, a fire station, and an open-air shopping district. According to this, security teams and emergency response personnel are already en route to those locations."

Using the adjacent workstation, Georgiou called up a city map, highlighting those areas corresponding to the active alerts. They were at different points around New Anchorage, and she noted nothing that might indicate a pattern to the targeted locations. They seemed to be random selections.

Except they're not. They were chosen for a reason.

"The only one that presents any immediate concern is the fire station," said Abela. "It's the closest one to here, and other stations will be sent to deal with that."

Jenn asked, "What about security personnel?"

"They'll go too. Any available officers in the immediate area will be dispatched." Stepping closer to Georgiou's workstation, Abela reached for the console and tapped a string of controls. In response to his commands, a city street map appeared on one screen, highlighted by six glowing points of blue light. "Those are the communication units carried by our security people. The dispatch center tracks every officer who's in the field, but we can monitor those signals from here too."

To Georgiou, the timing of the explosions indicated a premeditated, coordinated effort, but whose, and for what reason? Though she possessed no evidence, instinct told her this was more than simple protests or other expressions of dissatisfaction or even outrage on the part of aggrieved citizens.

Her gut feelings seemed to strengthen when she caught sight of another alert indicator flaring to life. Turning to look at the new alarm, Georgiou frowned upon seeing that the red status light shifted back to green, mere heartbeats after its first change.

"What was that?" asked Jenn, who also saw the fleeting alert.

Georgiou replied, "I don't know." An odd feeling was growing in the pit of her stomach as she noted the reading indicated the building in which they now stood. "Mister Abela, what does this status mean?"

"The same as with the other facility alarms," replied the supervisor. "Security system failure, a breach of the outer perimeter fence, or some other intrusion alert, that sort of thing."

Jenn was already tapping controls on her console. "I'm calling up the external monitors." A moment later two of her station's screens shifted their images to show feeds from visual recorders positioned around the building's exterior. As she tapped another button, the views shifted to show other areas of the structure and the surrounding grounds. Nothing appeared out of the ordinary.

"Looks all quiet," offered Abela.

Georgiou scowled. "That's what bothers me."

On the screen, the icons were moving along streets toward the red icon indicating the fire station, and Georgiou noted from where half of the blue dots were moving.

"They dispatched security from here as well?"

Abela nodded. "Makes sense. There's a precinct headquarters on the first level, and it's closer than others."

"How many officers would be sent?" asked Jenn.

"One locator typically means a pair of officers, so six from here. It's okay, though, as we usually have eight on duty for second shift."

"Wait," said Jenn. "Don't you have holding cells here too?"

Shrugging, Abela replied, "Sure. All the precincts do."

"Right," said Georgiou, "but what does this one have that the others don't? People arrested for suspected ties to Kodos."

That could be it.

She pointed to the screen showing the alerts. "These could all be distractions, diverting attention for whoever set off the explosions."

"That seems pretty far-fetched," countered Abela.

Ignoring the supervisor's doubts, Georgiou reached for the control to activate the intercom system. "Comm center to security desk." There was no response, even after she repeated the call, and she exchanged knowing looks with Jenn.

"Commander," said the Betazoid, "I just checked the internal sensors. They're offline in that part of the building."

Here we go.

"We can play that game too." Moving to a nearby workstation, Georgiou called up a set of technical schematics for the building. Once she found what she wanted, she entered a long string of instructions to the console's interface and was rewarded by several status readings shifting from green to red.

"What did you do?" asked Abela.

"Disabled the internal sensors throughout the building." Georgiou frowned. "It won't last if anyone tries to circumvent what I did, or matter if they have tricorders. I'm hoping whoever's here is looking to get out fast and won't have time to counteract it." Taking an additional moment to study the schematics, she tried to commit the internal floor plan to memory. It was impossible to absorb everything, so she concentrated on the section that contained offices for the security detail as well as the holding cells.

Already feeling her pulse rate increasing in anticipation of what might be coming, Georgiou moved back to her workstation and retrieved the satchel she brought with her. She extracted from the satchel her equipment belt with its holstered phaser. Strapping the belt around her waist, she looked to see Jenn mirroring her movements. Indeed, Jenn was ahead of her, having pulled her own weapon from its holster already on her hip to examine its power settings.

"What do you want me to do?" asked Abela, and Georgiou heard the nervousness in the man's voice.

Pointing to the workstation, Georgiou replied, "Is there any way to seal all the building entrances from here?"

The supervisor shook his head. "No. Only from the security desk."

"Forget that, then," said Jenn.

"Okay," replied Georgiou. "Contact the *Narbonne*. Let them know what's going on, and have them beam over reinforcements. Jenn and I will have a look downstairs."

Neither she nor Jenn even made it to the door before Abela called out with the next bit of concerning if not unexpected news.

"I think somebody's jamming communications."

Of course they are.

"Damn." Reaching for the communicator on her belt, Georgiou flipped open the device's cover, but saw the indicator informing her the unit was unable to establish an outgoing frequency.

Jenn, holding her own communicator, said, "Mine too. Can you get around the jamming?"

"It'd take too long. Come on."

After directing Abela to lock the door behind them, Georgiou and Jenn made their way from the comm center. Phasers drawn and ready, both officers proceeded down the corridor, searching for threats that did not appear.

"Forget the lift," said Jenn. "Whoever's in here may have cut off access to those."

Georgiou nodded. "Or they're waiting to trap anyone who might try to use them. That leaves the stairs."

"You don't think somebody will be covering those?"

"I absolutely think they will."

"That's not the answer I was hoping for."

The door leading to the stairwell on this floor was unguarded, and neither did Georgiou and Jenn find anyone waiting for them on the stairs. Recalling her quick review of the building's interior layout, Georgiou knew that they were on the opposite end of the floor from where the security force offices and holding area would be, one level below them. The stairs did not come out into the corridor leading to that section of the building, so there was a chance they could make their descent and emerge unobserved into that passage.

Only one way to find out.

Traversing the stairs proved uneventful, but as Georgiou reached the first-floor landing and proceeded toward the door leading to the corridor, she stopped when she felt a hand on her arm. She glanced over to see Jenn regarding her and shaking her head.

"What?" Georgiou whispered the question, the single word all but inaudible. Had Jenn heard something she missed? Was she acting on some odd intuition, or was she just exercising simple caution before they exposed themselves to danger?

Instead of replying, Jenn pointed toward the door. The look in her eyes told Georgiou she was expecting *something* from the other side. Using hand gestures, she moved to stand a few paces from the door, positioning herself so that she faced it at an angle before dropping to one knee. She held her phaser close to her chest, cradling the weapon in both hands, and seemed to pause a moment before drawing a single breath and nodding to Georgiou.

Her heart feeling as though it might punch a hole through her chest, Georgiou gripped her own phaser before reaching for the keypad set into the wall and tapping its control to open the door.

No sooner did the door slide aside than she caught sight of the single man wearing dark clothes, including a balaclava to cover his face. He was standing just far enough to the left of the door that Georgiou would have to sidestep to get a shot. The man knew he was not alone and was already reacting, bringing up his own weapon and starting to aim in their direction.

Jenn, still kneeling and in perfect position to engage their adversary, fired first. The single stun burst was enough to drop the man before he had any hope of defending himself. He collapsed against the wall behind him, sliding unconscious to the floor.

"Nice job," said Georgiou as she exited the stairwell and confirmed the man was no longer a threat. She glanced to Jenn, who was now also in the corridor and taking up a defensive stance near the door. Her phaser still gripped in both hands, she seemed to be listening as well as looking for other signs of activity. "Are you psychic or something?"

"Or something."

Without expounding on her reply, Jenn began moving the length of the short corridor, then turned right ten meters ahead of them. Georgiou remembered from the floor plan that this was a service passage, connecting to the main corridor that ran the length of the building. Pausing near the junction, Jenn rested her back against the nearby wall.

"There are others." Her voice was low and quiet.

"I don't hear anything," said Georgiou. She strained to listen for whatever it was Jenn detected, but shook her head.

Then the lights went out.

"Damn," she snapped as the corridor was plunged into darkness.

It lasted only a second before backup lights activated, casting dim illumination from where they were set into the ceiling at five-meter intervals the length of the corridor. Then the shadows were sliced apart by a hailstorm of phaser fire coming from somewhere around the corner.

"Get back!" Georgiou dropped into a crouch as the firing ceased, pressing her left shoulder against the wall as she tried angling herself toward the corridor. She heard voices speaking in crisp, curt bursts, but she could not make out words. Shadows played along the walls of the main corridor, and she got the sense of someone approaching even as Jenn was backing away from the junction, holding her phaser out in front of her and retreating toward the door.

"Commander, we have to move. Now!"

Georgiou saw the first figure moving into view and fired a poorly aimed shot in that direction. The stun blast missed its target, and the figure ducked to one side, out of sight. Georgiou pushed herself to her feet and started back-pedaling in the direction of the stairwell. More shadows bounced off the walls ahead of her, and her muscles tensed. She made it to the door before something broke the plane of the wall at the corridor junction, and a dark object came around the corner. Then the passageway was filling with dark-clothed figures.

"Watch out!"

Jenn's warning came just before Georgiou heard the hum of multiple phasers and the near darkness erupted in a blue-white explosion of light.

18

"Easy, Commander. You want to take it slow."

Opening her eyes, Georgiou saw Doctor Sergey Varaz-dinski standing at the foot of what she now recognized as the hospital bed she occupied. Her attempt to sit up brought with it a pounding in her head that made her wince, and she reached up to find a swollen lump near the back of her skull.

"I guess I'm alive?"

"You're alive, Commander," offered the doctor. "You apparently hit your head when you were stunned. There was some bleeding but no serious damage. One of the security officers who found you administered first aid and sealed the cut, but even with pain meds you'll probably have a headache for a little while yet."

"You're also very lucky," said Captain Korrapati from where he stood at the bed's left side. "You and Lieuten-ant Jenn both. Those people could just as easily have killed you."

As though deciding that the remainder of this conver-sation was unimportant to him, Varazdinski said nothing else to Georgiou before stepping away from her bed. He did offer a perfunctory nod to Korrapati, who smiled as the doctor exited the room without so much as a parting glance in the direction of the captain or Georgiou.

"His bedside manner could use some work."

"I've been telling him that for years," replied Korrapati. "I'm thinking it's irreversible at this point."

Smiling at the mild joke, Georgiou asked, "Where's Ena?"

"With security," replied Korrapati. "Other than being stunned, she wasn't hurt. She's working to figure out how the intruders were able to gain access to the administration building and free the prisoners."

Grimacing, Georgiou asked, "We figured that's what they were up to. They all got away?"

"Yes," said the *Narbonne*'s captain. "After entering the building, they were able to defeat the internal sensors and jam communications. They didn't bother getting fancy with breaking out their friends. Instead they just cut through the walls of the holding cells with phasers. Since the sensors were offline, there's no record of their escape. We don't even know which exit they used to get out of the building, or where they went once they were outside."

"Not a great day for the good guys, then." Closing her eyes, Georgiou rubbed the back of her head. "Sorry, Captain. We screwed up."

Korrapati countered, "It wasn't your fault, Commander. You were outnumbered, outgunned, and had no way of knowing you'd be targeted. We think you may even have upset their timetable. There are indications they were trying to break into the precinct's armory, but gave up for some reason. That could be due to you discovering what they were doing."

"One little victory." Georgiou grunted. "I guess I'll take it." Her brow furrowed. "Not that I'm ungrateful, but why are we alive? If the people behind this are from the same group who hit the outpost, why didn't they kill us too?"

"It's a good question," conceded Korrapati. "The only guess I've got is that they know we're here to help the colonists and search for Kodos, and they're avoiding making things any worse for themselves than they already have. At least, I hope that's the case. Surely someone in that camp who didn't know the massacre was coming was shocked by what happened."

"It's a nice thought," replied Georgiou. Then she frowned. "Wait. What about the other alarms? We picked up signs of explosions around the city."

Korrapati said, "Seven altogether. According to sensor logs, improvised explosives were detonated at the target locations within seconds of one another. None of the explosions were large enough to do any real damage, and no one was hurt."

"Small favors," said Georgiou.

Shaking his head, Korrapati replied, "More like diversions. I spent twenty minutes reviewing preliminary reports from each of the scenes. As you and Lieutenant Jenn suspected, this was a coordinated strike. From what we can tell, a series of distractions meant to draw attention and first-response resources to those areas."

Something about this did not add up for Georgiou. "It seems like a lot of effort just to liberate three people from detention, sir. According to the transcripts from their questioning, they weren't really valuable members of whatever group Kodos put together to help him escape authorities. Something here's not adding up."

"There may be some help with that," said Korrapati. "Commander Lorca has found and apprehended Alexander Simmons."

Georgiou's eyes widened in surprise. "Already? That was fast."

"Mister Lorca is rather highly motivated."

"Tell me about it." Georgiou had authorized Lorca's plan to locate and apprehend the senior security offer, Alexander Simmons, and bring him in for questioning. She expected the effort to take days, at minimum. Instead, Lorca had delivered in less than twenty-four hours.

Damn.

"Where is he?"

"He's being processed, both by the colony security forces and our people." Korrapati's eyes narrowed. "We're taking extra care, given his position in the security forces and his alleged connection to Kodos. Lorca told me he would notify us when Simmons is ready for questioning."

"Excellent." Grimacing at the knot on her head, she added, "He can wait a bit, though. So, we think the diversions were cover for something besides the brig break?"

Korrapati said, "There were no other disturbances reported. Security forces checked each of the explosion sites as well as the colony administration building and found nothing else out of the ordinary. We're missing something, but I just don't know what that is yet." He gestured as though trying to wave away the conversation. "This can wait. How are you feeling?"

"Aside from the headache, I'm fine." Swinging her legs off the bed, Georgiou said, "I'd like to get back to work, sir."

The captain nodded. "Understood, but don't overdo it until you've had a chance to get some rest."

She patted the bed's mattress before forcing a small smile. "That was the best sleep I've had in three days."

After dressing in her uniform while trying to ignore the dull ache at the back of her skull, Georgiou exited the treatment room and made her way to the stairwell at the near end of the hospital wing. She ascended to the next level, grateful to find the scene here quieter than even just twelve hours earlier. With the bulk of the patients requiring immediate treatment having been cared for and either moved to rooms or sent home, the passageway and waiting areas were mostly empty of people.

The nurse's station at the hub where the corridors for the different wings converged was a small hive of activity. Two nurses, a woman and a man, busied themselves with the administrative detritus that was the unglamorous aspect of providing medical care. The male nurse's attention was focused on a computer terminal, paging through some dense report, while his female companion worked with one of several data slates cluttering her desk. Georgiou nodded in greeting as both nurses took notice of her approach.

"Commander," said the woman, rising from her seat. Georgiou noted the patch above the pocket on her nurse's smock, which gave her name as WATSON.

"Yes?"

Watson pointed down one of the other passageways. "You've got a visitor in the waiting area."

Curious as to who might be here to see her without going through official channels, Georgiou made her way toward the waiting area and felt her whole mood lift as her eyes fell on young Shannon Moulton. The girl was wearing a light blue shirt and white pants, and her blond hair was shiny and pulled into a high ponytail. It was a complete transformation from the last time Georgiou saw her. The only thing that carried over from their previous encounter was the plush Andorian doll in her hands. Gone was the hasty splint used to immobilize her broken leg, and she demonstrated how her injury was healed by jumping up from her chair in the waiting area and crossing the room toward her.

"Commander Philippa!" Her face was all but consumed by her wide smile.

Accepting the girl's energetic hug, Georgiou said, "Shannon, you came to see me?"

"My mom said it was okay. She's visiting a friend who's still sick, but who's going home today."

Georgiou asked, "Don't you have school?"

"I do school at home, but not today."

The girl's words were tinged with a hint of sadness, which Georgiou understood.

"How's your mother?" Georgiou left the question at that, allowing the girl to answer as she saw fit.

"She's okay. I don't think she's sleeping very well. She misses my daddy, just like I do."

Following their first encounter, she had reviewed reports from the colony administration office and found a Zachary Moulton listed among those killed on the night of the executions. From there, it required little effort to determine that the man was Shannon's father. That Eliana Moulton was able to maintain her composure while carrying out her duties and dealing with the fallout of everything was—in Georgiou's opinion, at least—an amazing feat of will in the face of personal grief.

"You're probably right." Attempting to change the subject, Georgiou asked, "What brings you to see me today?"

Shannon shrugged. "I mostly just wanted to say hi." She held up the doll. "But you said you could help me fix Vran."

Taking the doll, Georgiou saw that it was still in need of a new antenna, and perhaps some stuffing to replace whatever had escaped the hole in its head where the missing appendage used to be.

"I think we can do that." Finding suitable material here at the hospital to complete the task should present little problem, Georgiou guessed, and the minor yet welcome distraction would be good for her as well as the girl. "Let's go find your mom, and tell her what we're going to do."

"Okay."

As they left the waiting area, walking in the direction Shannon indicated in order to track down the girl's mother, Georgiou noted a tall, middle-aged man of African descent walking toward them. He was accompanied by a single uniformed member of the colony security forces, indicating he was a person of some importance who required an escort. He was dressed in well-tailored civilian attire consisting of dark trousers and jacket worn over a matching shirt. Black hair cropped close to his scalp harbored a liberal smattering of gray. Though she did not recognize him, he appeared to know her. He smiled upon seeing her, moving toward her and extending his hand in greeting.

"Commander Georgiou? I'm Donovan Eames, director of the New Anchorage hospital system. We haven't had a chance to meet before now, and for that I apologize."

Taking the man's hand, Georgiou replied, "Director Eames, it's good to finally meet you as well. I'm only sorry it couldn't be under more pleasant circumstances."

"Agreed." Eames looked down to Shannon. "Hello, young lady. Are you a friend of the commander's?"

"Uh-huh." Standing close to Georgiou, Shannon held her doll in both hands and returned the man's gentle smile.

"May I borrow her for just a moment?"

Looking up to Georgiou, Shannon nodded. "Okay."

"Why don't you go find your mother, and I'll catch up," offered Georgiou.

"All right." Shannon held up the doll. "Don't forget Vran."

"I promise I won't."

Georgiou waited until the girl was out of earshot, wandering down the passageway toward the patient rooms on this floor. Once Shannon was gone, she redirected her attention to Eames.

"What can I do for you, Director?"

The man's expression lost some of its warmth. "It's what I'm hoping I can do for you, Commander. I understand some of your Starfleet officers are conducting a search for Governor Kodos."

Though details regarding any efforts of Commander Lorca or anyone else involved with the manhunt weren't available to the public, Captain Korrapati had released a series of generic statements indicating the ongoing effort was under way, and that the *Narbonne* crew was assisting local law enforcement entities to locate Kodos and any of his followers.

"I understand you're having difficulty finding people who can identify Kodos," said Eames.

Georgiou nodded. "That's right."

"In my role as director, I'm one of the advisers to the governor and the leadership council. I was there the night Kodos took over as governor."

"People like you are in very short supply, sir." Though she did not say it aloud, her research as well as the investigations carried out by Lorca and other members of the Starfleet team were illustrating a common, disturbing theme: Kodos included among the lists of people to be "sacrificed" anyone who could identify him. This led to speculation that Kodos may well have had intentions to remove everyone else who knew him, but his plans were thwarted by the *Narbonne*'s arrival.

"I know what you're thinking," said Eames. "Why am I even still alive? Don't think it's a question I haven't asked myself at least a dozen times since that night. The only thing I can think of is that my role here made me valuable in the governor's eyes; at least, valuable compared to others." His expression turned to one of shame. "It's horrible to even consider something like that. I try not to think too much about it, in all honesty."

It was a stance with which Georgiou could not take issue. Were she in his position, she harbored no doubts that she would feel the same way.

"You were there when Kodos took over as governor," she said. "That means you got to see him make his first decisions and issue his first set of instructions."

Eames grimaced. "In hindsight, a better descriptor might be 'directives.' Don't get me wrong; at the time, it was just the sort of resolute leadership we needed. Gisela Ribiero simply wasn't suited to crisis management. On the other hand, Kodos acted as though he was born to do it. Looking back on it, he came off somewhat less emphatic than I remember. Instead, he was cool, almost detached in a way." He shook his head. "If only one of us had been smart enough to see that, and understand it for what it was."

19

Excerpt from *The Four Thousand: Crisis on Tarsus IV*

Low, thin fog shrouds the small lake that lies some thirty meters from the cabin's oversized dining room window. The transparent aluminum panel takes up the room's entire eastern wall, providing an unfettered view of the forest surrounding this modest home. In the distance and yet still towering above the trees is the single mountain, known by the locals as Sentinel's Peak. No one seems to know or remember the meaning behind the name, but one popular story explains it as a consequence of the mountain seemingly always being visible, regardless of weather conditions.

"It's there every morning, rain or shine," says Donovan Eames. "Even if the fog is dense and it's storming like the end of the world, you can still see it, plain as day. It's like the clouds are afraid to go near it."

Despite being retired, he is still an early riser, making a point to be out of bed almost every morning before sunrise. "I like to go for a run before the sun comes up," he explains. "Though sometimes I'll go fishing instead." He pauses, looking around as though ensuring his remarks aren't being overheard. "And every so often I do like to sleep in. Don't tell my wife that, though. She likes it when I get up first and cook our breakfast."

Following his retirement as the director of the New Anchor-

age hospital system, less than ten years after the brief yet un-
forgettable rein of Governor Adrian Kodos, Eames and his wife,
Imani, left Tarsus IV in search of a new beginning. They found it
here on Benecia, a Federation colony planet.

Despite knowing the reasons for this interview, Eames
takes his time warming to the subject. By his own admission, it
is not something he speaks of with any frequency. One of the
reasons he and his wife moved here was because it offered
them a chance to put the events of Tarsus IV behind them
forever. Aside from a small circle of close friends, no one here
knows of their troubled past. Eames prefers to keep it that way,
but he agreed to the interviews for this book knowing it likely
would cost him and Imani their relative anonymity on Benecia.

"So be it," he says at the beginning of the first interview. "It's
a story that needs to be told, if for no other reason than telling
it might prevent something like it from happening ever again."

The official transcripts of all meetings between Tarsus
IV's governor and the colony leadership council are matters
of public record. For almost a decade as of this writing, historians have pored over those notes, remarks, and even sensor
records where they exist, searching for heretofore unrealized
context, nuance, or other hidden meanings. Even with these
available resources, it is all but impossible to get a sense of
what meeting participants were thinking and feeling. This ne-
cessitates personal reflections such as the one Donovan Eames
provides.

"The tension was so thick in that room, I thought I might
choke," he says, his expression growing wistful as he recalls the
event of that first evening. "Gisela Ribiero was out, removed by
majority vote of the council after they formally cited a loss of
confidence in her leadership. In her place was Kodos, whom
they'd appointed as an interim governor. None of us had ever
seen anything like this before. A few of us who had lived on
other colony worlds had experienced a governor being re-

moved or replaced due to illness or death, and even criminal activity in one case, but this was completely different."

With the source of the fungal contagion determined, at least with a significant degree of certainty, attention was being directed toward countering the infection's effects. Also of immediate concern was the impact of the contamination not just on the colony's existing food supplies but also on its ability to grow or manufacture more. The problem was severe, and was already beginning to generate concern among the populace.

Eames recalls, "We had people counting everything, down to the last piece of fruit or packaged field ration. Governor Ribiero had already asked everyone in the colony to dispose of contaminated food as quickly as possible. Collection centers were set up around the city, and security officers were going door to door, gathering whatever they could find. Basically, if it wasn't prepackaged or kept in some other sealed container, it had to go. Some colonists grew their own vegetables and fruits and canned them, the way early settlers used to do before food processors or even centuries ago before refrigeration. Some of that was spared, but everything had to be scanned to make sure. Once the fungus hit something, that food became inedible, even toxic. Plus, it would spread so quickly if left unchecked. No matter how fast we moved to contain it, that damned stuff seemed to move faster." He shakes his head. "It was frightening."

Despite these measures, it was becoming apparent that such efforts would not be sufficient. Quarantining and protecting existing food stores was just one part of a problem exacerbated by the contagion's ability to pollute food-processing machinery, and by extension the raw compounds it worked with to produce edible foodstuffs. This resulted in an almost immediate crippling of the colony's ability to provide for itself.

"Even with the technology, we had our farms and greenhouses." Eames smiles. "I don't care how good they make it, no machine will ever produce a reconstituted apple that tastes as good as the real thing. One of my favorite things to do was go to the produce markets for fresh fruits and vegetables." He leans back in his overstuffed chair, recalling the pleasant memory. "It doesn't matter what planet you're on, there's nothing like biting into a crisp Fuji apple first thing in the morning. Some of the best apples and corn I've ever eaten were grown on Tarsus IV." His expression turns somber. "I almost cried as I watched an entire orchard burned to the ground. It was necessary, of course, but that didn't make it any less tragic. Even after the crisis was over, there was something different about the produce. I could never put my finger on it, but things were never quite the same after that."

Returning to the subject of the colony's mounting food situation and the public's reaction to such extreme measures, Eames grows thoughtful. "It didn't take long for people to understand that we had a serious problem on our hands. The colony leadership tried to downplay things at first, but when you see news broadcasts of entire farms being torched, it's pretty obvious that something is very wrong. Within days, the truth was beginning to circulate, and people were starting to worry, but we hadn't gotten to full-blown panic just yet."

Understanding the extent of the problem far better than the general population, Governor Ribiero and the council had already taken steps to maintain order. The first curfew directive was issued within forty-eight hours of the governor's public declaration of emergency, along with her instructions to collect all uncontaminated food so that it could be stored and hopefully protected against the ongoing contamination. Once Adrian Kodos assumed the role of governor, he began issuing edicts designed to further those efforts, for the protection of both the community and the security officers charged with keeping the peace.

"I was as stunned as anyone when he implemented martial law." Eames shifts in his seat, clearly uncomfortable with revisiting these events. "That sort of thing was unheard of except in very rare circumstances: things like floods, earthquakes, and other natural catastrophes that impacted entire populations. Sure, what we were facing was at least in the same league as those other things, but it still took us all by surprise. Looking back on it, what seemed to bother me the most was how casually Kodos went about it. He wasn't cold or cruel, but rather just matter-of-fact, as though everything were a mathematical equation with a single correct solution. In the meetings, his expression was unreadable. He was almost like a Vulcan that way. You could see in his eyes that he was thinking, considering his options, and calculating odds of success or failure." Eames shrugs. "It's almost as if he forgot he was dealing with people rather than objects. Or he just decided it was easier to view them that way."

Then, before moving on to the next question, Eames holds up a hand. "There were those who chose to view what Kodos did through another lens. I didn't particularly like the idea at the time, but over the years I've come to realize there has to be at least some truth to the notion that Kodos was acting more like a military commander than a governor of a civilian community. We weren't people. Instead we were markers on a map, being maneuvered into position to fight an enemy represented by marks of a different color. Kodos was the general, moving troops around the map and plotting how best to commit his forces to fighting that enemy and securing an objective. To be able to succeed at that kind of thing, generals have to detach themselves from the people they're sending into harm's way. If you don't think of them as living beings, with families and goals and dreams, then it's easier to cope with the reality that you're probably sending a good number of them to their deaths. It's the same reason ancient farmers didn't typically give names to the animals they were raising to slaughter as a food source, but on a far larger scale."

Martial law did not come without resistance. There were several demonstrations around the city, including outside the governor's house as well as the offices of the leadership council and other prominent advisers and public figures. Dozens of protesters were arrested that first day, though formal charges were filed for only a handful of individuals. Otherwise, citizens were released and sent home, as security forces personnel were stretched thin trying to enforce curfews and other restricted access to various buildings and other facilities around the city. Manpower became an issue in short order, but the bulk of the populace began scaling back their protests, concentrating their energies on the governor and the council in hopes of garnering attention and sympathy.

"The protests never seemed to faze him," Eames reflects. "Other members of the council raised concerns, as did I and a few of the other advisers. I was worried about the hospital and the outpatient clinics around the city. You know, providing security for my staff and our patients. Kodos, on the other hand, took it all in stride, at least in front of us. The public remarks he made in response to protests offered reassurance and resolve. I guess it worked, at least to a degree, because even at their worst, the people causing most of the trouble seemed to understand that even when you've got grievances, there are still lines you don't cross."

Eames pauses, as though uncomfortable with where his recollections are beginning to take him. "In that regard, Kodos was exactly the kind of leader we needed. If he'd kept that up the entire time, maybe things would've gone differently."

He sighs. "If only this. If only that. If only we'd known what he was really thinking."

20

"Get your hands off of me!"

Hearing the commotion from somewhere ahead of her in the corridor, Georgiou broke into a jog. She rounded a bend in the passageway and saw a member of the hospital's security staff with his hands full as he tangled with someone almost half his size. It took her an extra beat to comprehend that it was an adolescent giving the guard such a fit: a human male likely in his early teens with a mop of unruly brown hair. The boy was wiry, all motion and fury as the guard pulled him from a patient room into the hallway.

"Let me go!"

Though outsized by the guard, the boy compensated with speed, agility, and tenacity. No sooner were they in the corridor than he broke free of the guard's grip on his arm. Pivoting away from the older man, he sprinted up the hallway, his expression turning to shock as he saw Georgiou standing in his way. He slowed to a stop less than five meters from her. Though his hazel eyes burned with a defiance that would not be uncommon for a teenager, she sensed something more at work here.

Her arms folded across her chest, Georgiou asked, "What's going on?" She did not react to the sight of another security guard coming around a corner in the corridor ahead of her, and neither did she turn her head as she heard running footsteps behind her. Beyond the guards she could see, a handful of hospital staff members as well as civilians were beginning to gather.

"Security breach, Commander," offered the guard who had pulled the boy from the room. The tag affixed to his uniform shirt identified him as PEARSON. He gestured behind him. "We detected an unauthorized access of the hospital's encrypted system from a terminal in that patient's room. From what we can tell, he was trying to access an outside network."

Georgiou cocked her right eyebrow. "Really?" She regarded the boy, who remained silent, his expression cold and unyielding but offering not the first hint of fear. "Is this true?"

"Yes."

The blunt answer was surprising, but Georgiou realized she should have expected it. Nothing in his demeanor suggested he believed his actions, whatever they might be, were wrong. He appeared unworried about any repercussions he might incur.

"Jimmy!"

The new voice made Georgiou look up to see a woman jogging down the corridor toward them. She was perhaps in her mid to late thirties, and a look of concern clouded her features. Her hair was a light brown, not quite blond, but there was an intensity to her hazel eyes Georgiou quickly recognized. It did not take much in the way of deduction to see that the new arrival had to be the boy's mother.

"I'm sorry, Commander," said the woman as she approached, and the way she offered the rank without hesitation told Georgiou that she was familiar with Starfleet. "My name is Winona Kirk. I'm a xenobiologist working with the colony's science institute. I hope my son hasn't been causing any trouble." To the boy, she said, "I've been looking all over for you. There's a curfew for children, you know."

"I told Sam I'd be here."

"Then you can bet I'll be having a little chat with you *and* your brother when we get home." Winona turned to Georgiou. "What's he done now?"

"Well, we were just getting to that." She directed her gaze to Pearson. "What exactly are we talking about here?"

"We're not sure," replied the guard. "He locked the terminal before we could stop him, and we can't access it, directly or remotely."

"It's not my fault you don't know your own system."

"James," said Winona, her tone one of warning.

For her part, the boy's comment almost made Georgiou laugh, but she managed to maintain her composure. Glancing past Pearson and the boy's mother, she saw that more people were gathering in the hallway, drawn to the minor standoff taking place in their midst. It was time to defuse this situation while it was still under control.

"What were you doing?" she asked the boy.

The boy's eyes narrowed. "Looking for a picture of Kodos."

While it might not be the last thing she expected to hear, Georgiou admitted it had to be close. "I beg your pardon?"

"A picture of Kodos. I already tried to search his publicly available files, but they've either been erased or else anything that might identify him has been purged."

Winona asked, "Why were you doing that?"

"Because I *saw* him, Mom. I saw his face, on the screens. He tried to hide it, but I got a good look at him. So did Tommy. We both saw him, but I can't find a picture of him anywhere."

Georgiou's gaze shifted between the boy and Pearson. To the guard, she said, "Can you confirm any of this?"

"No, Commander." Pearson's face was reddening. "We tried to monitor his activity, but he was able to mask it."

Though she thought she might regret it later, Georgiou gave the boy a look of appreciation. "I'm impressed."

"It wasn't me. Tommy showed me how to do the hard stuff. He's the smart one."

"Is Tommy here?"

Waving back the way he had come, he replied, "He's in his room."

Georgiou searched her memory, recalling another teenager first admitted to the hospital before the *Narbonne*'s arrival and still assigned to a patient room on this floor.

"Thomas Leighton?"

The boy nodded. "Yes."

"The Leightons are friends of ours," offered Winona. "We traveled together to the colony." Her expression fell. "Tommy's parents, well . . . they . . ." The rest of the words faded on her lips, but she did not need to say anything further.

Georgiou said, "I'm sorry for your loss." After a moment, she redirected her gaze to the boy. "And your name's Jimmy?"

"Kirk. James Tiberius Kirk." He cast a quick glance toward his mother. "You can call me Jim."

When he spoke, there was an obvious pride in the words that bordered on defiance. No doubt the boy took his share of ribbing with such a pretentious-sounding name, but rather than express shame he instead seemed to wear it like a badge of honor. Indeed, there was a maturity in his entire stance and demeanor that belied his youth. He stood ramrod straight, hands at his sides. While he might not be preparing to attack or flee, he also seemed unfazed at the prospect of reprisal. Watching him, Georgiou observed how he remained aware of his surroundings, including what might be happening behind him. His eyes glanced left when Pearson stepped closer, as though he were anticipating the guard attempting to again lay hands on him. Even then, there was no apparent concern.

Holding up a hand to stop Pearson's advance, Georgiou stepped forward, indicating for the boy to accompany her. "I'd like you to show me what you were doing."

"Commander," said Pearson, and she saw the skepticism in his face.

"It's all right. I'll take care of this."

After assuring him, the other security officers, and Winona that she had the matter well in hand, Georgiou directed his colleagues to return to their regular duties. With that settled, she let the boy lead her and his mother to his friend's room. Drawing closer, she noted the signage on the door listing the current occupant as LEIGHTON, T. Inside was a single patient bed occupied by another male teenager with a build similar to young Jim Kirk's. The medical monitor behind and above his head provided his current vital signs, and Georgiou saw that his pulse, respiration, temperature, and blood pressure were all well within acceptable parameters for an adolescent human male in good physical health. Another indicator showed his medication level, and she noted his having received a dose of pain suppressant within the last hour.

As for the boy himself, the bed's upper portion was raised so that he could sit upright, with a pillow tucked behind the small of his back. His white hospital gown provided sharp contrast to the orange-yellow bed linen covering his lower body. He was awake, but rather than reading from the computer terminal positioned atop a movable arm next to his bed or looking at the viewing screen set into the wall before him, he instead was staring out the window to his left. Standing in the room's doorway, Georgiou saw that his head and the left side of his face were swathed in white bandages.

"Hello?" she said. "Tommy Leighton? May I come in?"

Next to her, Jim offered, "It's okay. I've been coming to visit him every day since we brought him here. He hasn't said anything."

"What happened?"

"The night of the killings," said Winona. "His parents were there, on the field in the amphitheater. Tommy was supposed to go, but his parents told him to stay home."

Jim cast a sad look toward his friend. "He wanted to see what it was all about, so he talked me into going with him."

It took a moment for Georgiou to grasp the boy's meaning. "Wait. You were there, in the amphitheater? You saw what happened?"

"Yes. There are a couple of ways to sneak into the amphitheater." He gestured to his friend. "Tommy knew how to bypass the lock on one of the gates, and that's how we got in. We hid in one of the concourse ramps." He paused, swallowing as he regarded Tommy. "From there we could see everything."

He did not offer anything more, but Georgiou knew what he was not saying aloud. They had borne witness to the murder of four thousand people, including Tommy's parents.

Dear god.

She glanced to where his mother stood nearby, and she wondered if the woman's haunted expression was a match for her own. Winona certainly had far less need for the boy to elaborate about the events of that night.

"Once the shooting started," continued Jim, "there was a lot of commotion in the stands and walkways as guards reacted to what was happening. One of the guards saw us and we ran, and he shot at us." He paused, swallowing an apparent lump in his throat. "He wasn't trying to stun us. His phaser was set to maximum, and he just barely missed us. The beam was close enough that Tommy's face was grazed."

Winona's face was a mask of horror. "You didn't tell me that before."

"Because I knew you'd be upset." Jim wiped his face. "I don't even know how we got away, but I dragged Tommy down a maintenance passage and we hid in the dark. The guard tried looking for us, but then I think he got called away. That's when I got us both out of the amphitheater and I brought Tommy here."

Astounded by the boy's bravery and presence of mind during what had to be a terrifying situation, Georgiou offered a sympathetic smile. "That took a lot of courage, Jim. A hell of a lot of courage."

"He'd have done the same for me."

Georgiou looked to Winona. "You weren't there, I presume."

"No." Winona shook her head. "I was working at our lab, and my husband's not even on the planet. He's in Starfleet, and they're always sending him on secret missions, so I don't see him very much." She dropped her gaze to the floor, and Georgiou saw tears forming in the corners of her eyes. "I wish he was here now."

"We don't even know if he knows what's happened," added Jim.

Georgiou said, "I'm sorry, Jim." She wondered if she might be able to dispatch a message to his father, and made a mental note to ask Captain Korrapati about it.

Drawing a deep breath, Jim looked up to her, and when he spoke this time his own voice was subdued. "You wanted to see what I was doing."

He led the way into the room, with Georgiou and Winona following. Once inside, Jim moved to the computer terminal near Tommy's bed, swinging it around so that he could access its interface. Winona moved to the bed itself and reached out to stroke the boy's dark hair. If he took any notice of their presence, he chose not to acknowledge it. Georgiou watched his face for nearly a full minute before Tommy blinked his one uncovered eye, which along with the medical monitor behind his bed was the sole indicator he was even conscious.

Meanwhile, Jim had activated the computer monitor, and Georgiou saw that with a few quick commands, he unlocked whatever program he was running when Pearson found him. He was entering long strings of instructions to the device. The image on the display screen showed several columns of text scrolling past in rapid fashion. Though she possessed solid computer skills, she felt like something of an amateur while watching the boy work. After a minute or so of this communing with the machine, Jim pressed a final control and the display coalesced into an image of nine people: five women and four men. Jim pointed to one of the men, who was dressed in formal attire. His red hair was receding on top but thick and wavy on the sides. He also sported a trimmed beard and thin mustache.

"That's Kodos."

Staring at the image, Georgiou asked, "You're sure?"

"Absolutely. It was only for a few seconds, but I saw him plain as day. Then he issued the order and . . ."

The sentence drifted away as Jim's attention seemed to lock on the picture. It lasted just a handful of seconds, and she watched him shake off the wave of emotions he had to be experiencing. After a moment, he gestured to the computer terminal.

"That's why I went looking for a picture. I heard you and the others didn't seem to know what Kodos looked like, so I thought if I could find something, you'd know who to look for. This picture is from a friend of his. They worked together, or something, before all of this. Kodos wiped all of his own pictures, but I thought maybe someone who knew him might have one."

Winona asked, "You thought of all this on your own?"

"Sure. It wasn't that hard. It just took a while."

Continuing to study the image of Adrian Kodos on the computer screen, Georgiou nodded in open admiration.

"This is very impressive, Jim."

This kid is pretty damned sharp.

He carried himself with a determination, a simple grit that was uncommon in his peers. Georgiou wondered if it was a product of having to assume greater responsibilities at such a young age to compensate for a father called away by duty for months or perhaps even years at a stretch. While she sensed his innate respect for authority figures and rules, neither did he feel constrained by such things if he felt the need to circumvent or even defy them. He carried himself with a self-assurance that allowed him to disregard them while not crossing the line of willful insubordination. Even while harboring memories of what he witnessed on the night of the massacre, he was able to set aside his own emotions while doing what he could to help others. How much of this was upbringing, as opposed to some natural trait? From what Georgiou could see, he was a fount of raw, untapped potential, lacking only age, education, and experience. If he was anything like his parents had to be, and assuming his own desire to pursue such a path, young Jim Kirk had the makings of a first-rate Starfleet officer.

A short electronic chirp echoed in the room, and Georgiou glanced to the communicator on her belt. Retrieving the device, she flipped open its cover.

"Georgiou here."

"It's Lorca, Commander. We're ready to question Alexander Simmons. You said you wanted to be here for that. Are you able to join me at the security forces main precinct?"

Georgiou exchanged looks with Winona and Jim, seeing their expressions brightened at the report. "Indeed I am, Mister Lorca. I'm on my way."

Closing the communicator, she gestured to the computer terminal. "Send this to me." She provided Jim with the information needed to transmit the picture and other data to her on the *Narbonne*. "I'll see to it that it's distributed to our security people."

His task completed, Jim moved from the computer terminal to join his mother near the bed, and Winona wrapped an arm around her son's shoulder. Only then did Georgiou realize that Tommy Leighton had moved for the first time since they entered the room. He had shifted his head so that he no longer stared out the window, but instead was studying them. He said nothing, but it was easy to see that he was aware of his visitors, and she wondered what had to be going through his mind. There was understandable pain, grief, and loss in his eye, but Georgiou thought she saw something else as well.

Hope?

"They're going to find him, Tommy," said Jim. He glanced to his mother before turning to Georgiou. His expression softened. "So you think this will help?"

"Oh, yes," she replied. "It's going to help a lot."

21

By design, the interrogation room was a dull, uninviting box. Formed from thermoconcrete, its walls, floor, and ceiling were painted a drab gray. A single lighting panel was set into the ceiling, sealed behind a seamless, translucent screen. The panel also housed sensor equipment that allowed for the monitoring and recording of interview sessions. A single door in the east wall, also painted gray, was the room's only exit. A rectangular table, formed from some composite material and painted to match the room's monotone scheme, sat in the middle of the room, flanked by two chairs on the side closest to the door and a single chair opposite them. Even the chairs were gray.

Sitting in the single chair, his hands secured to the armrests and his yellow jumpsuit providing the room's only other source of color, was Alexander Simmons.

"Nice job, catching this guy," said Georgiou as she stood before a small viewing screen set into the wall of a control room adjacent to the interrogation room. Here a member of the security staff was able to oversee all interviews, making a record of each session and ensuring that such activities were carried out in accordance with applicable laws and regulations.

Standing next to her, Lorca replied, "Thanks. He did a pretty good job hiding, but his mistake was staying in the city. Once Soltani had a trail to follow, it was inevitable we'd track him down."

"My compliments to your team." She studied the array of small monitors dominating the wall to her right. Each screen offered a piece of the biometric puzzle that was the process of monitoring the interview subject's vital signs and reaction to any stimuli, be it a change in the room's lighting or temperature or an introduction of various sounds designed to place the person on edge. There also were indicators that could reveal the subtle changes in respiration or pulse rate that almost always accompanied a subject's attempt at deception.

"What do we know about him?"

Lorca said, "He's a watch commander at one of the larger precincts in the city. I've pulled his personnel file and it shows that he arrived on Tarsus IV from Earth with the same group of colonists that included Kodos. He's been a civilian security specialist for fifteen years, mostly at various facilities on Earth and Mars. Coming here was the first time he'd even left the Sol system."

Georgiou was surprised by that bit of information. Given the relative ease and convenience of modern space travel, it was rare to encounter someone who had never ventured beyond the confines of their home solar system. Even her own parents had traveled to Vulcan, as that planet along with other Federation planets was always expanding its capacity and willingness to host "outworlders" curious to experience firsthand the culture of another world and civilization.

"What about his girlfriend?" asked Georgiou.

"Joanna Robarge. She's a local. Already told us everything she knew, which wasn't much. Simmons came to stay with her the night of the massacre and took off a couple of times in the middle of the night. He didn't tell her what he was up to."

Georgiou frowned. "She shot at you."

"She says she thought we were protesters. A few security officers have been attacked and harassed since all this started." Lorca grunted in annoyance. "She doesn't know anything useful, but I might still be able to use her when talking to Simmons."

"Do we know if Simmons knew Kodos before they came here?"

Frowning, Lorca shook his head. "No, but I do know a way to find out." He gestured toward the viewing screen.

"Lead the way, Commander."

They exited the room into a narrow hallway, which like everything else on this underground level of the security force's main precinct headquarters was also constructed of thermoconcrete. There were no windows, but the passage was well illuminated thanks to lighting panels set at regular intervals into the ceiling. Someone had taken pity on the men and women working here and painted the walls a soothing beige. Colored lines ran along the floor, and Georgiou guessed they were intended as visual cues for prisoners moving or being escorted within the holding facility. Signage along the walls provided directions to different offices and other rooms, or listed some rule or regulation that needed following by anyone in this section of the building, prisoner and law enforcement officer alike.

It was but a few steps to the interrogation room, which at present was guarded by a single female security officer. She was dressed like her male counterparts in dark uniform shirt and trousers, her pants legs tucked into her polished black boots. Her blond hair was cut short, with no ponytail or long tresses to be grabbed by an unruly prisoner. There was no holstered phaser on her belt, but instead a thin cylinder Georgiou recognized as an extendable stun baton. The guard, whose security badge identified her by last name as SULLIVAN, nodded at their approach.

"Good evening."

Lorca said, "We're here for a chat with our guest, Officer Sullivan."

Instead of replying, the guard turned to the keypad mounted to the wall beside the interrogation room's door and entered a six-digit code Georgiou did not see. The pad's status light changed from red to green, and the door slid aside.

"You've got a visitor," said Sullivan, poking her head into the room. "Behave yourself, or no dessert."

"Still not funny," replied a voice from beyond the doorway.

Allowing herself a small smile at the guard's joke before schooling her features, Georgiou followed Lorca into the room. She took in her surroundings, verifying that the gray paint was as dreary and perhaps even as soul-crushing as she gathered from the sensors. She then directed her attention to the room's sole occupant, taking in her first unfettered view of Alexander Simmons. The man sported several days' worth of beard growth, and his brown hair was unkempt. There were dark circles under his eyes, and for a brief moment Georgiou wondered how long it had been since he last slept.

Actually, I don't really give a damn.

Instead of taking one of the chairs, Lorca moved to stand behind them, his hands held at his sides. Georgiou stepped into the room and moved far enough from the door that it slid closed behind her, and she heard it lock once it cycled shut. She watched as Simmons turned and locked gazes with Lorca, the two men sizing each other up. According to Lorca, it was the first time the two were seeing each other since the other man's capture. It seemed to take Simmons a moment to realize how he knew the commander, after which he nodded in apparent recognition.

"You," he said. It was a single word, but as Simmons was the first one who spoke, Lorca was the winner of the little staring contest, along with the battle to see who would initiate a conversation. Georgiou knew that such minor victories actually were helpful tools for the person conducting the interview, as a subject's need to break their silence was a potential weakness to be exploited. It indicated an openness to suggestion, as well as a strong if misguided sense of self-preservation. She harbored no doubt that Lorca knew all of this.

"Are you enjoying your stay with us, Mister Simmons?" Letting the question hang in the air, Lorca said nothing else. It did not take long for his prisoner to rise to the bait.

"Another comedian. Wonderful." Shaking his head, Simmons added, "I've been a security officer for twenty years. I know how this works."

Lorca crossed his arms. "Fifteen years. I've read your file, moron. If you're going to start this with a very bad and very obvious lie, it's just going to piss me off. Since I'm already pissed off at you for shooting at me, imagine how fun I'll be when you add to that."

Georgiou could not help glancing at Lorca as he spoke, listening to the hard edge in the man's voice. Was it her imagination, or was she detecting something more than the tough-guy act the commander was affecting?

"Whatever." Simmons scowled. "It's easy to talk when I'm strapped to a chair. Let me up, and we can see how things go."

Grunting in apparent amusement, Lorca began moving to his left, making his way around the table. "That's probably not a good idea. You see, while you're in the chair, I'm not allowed to hurt you. I'm not even allowed to touch you. I free you, and all bets are off." Pausing less than an arm's length from Simmons, he leaned forward until his face was mere centimeters away from the other man's right ear. In a low voice, he added, "Right now, the only place on this entire damned planet where your sorry ass is safe is in that chair."

If it was an act, Lorca was very good at it, Georgiou decided. If it was something else, then she began to wonder if there might be potential trouble here.

"We know you're a friend of Adrian Kodos," she said, attempting to ease the room's brewing tension. It earned her a momentary glower of contempt from Lorca as he backed away from Simmons, but he said nothing, so she continued. "You came here from Earth with him and several other colonists. We know you helped him on the night of the murders."

Simmons glared at her. "I didn't—"

"We know you were on duty that night, and you were at the amphitheater. We also know from visitor logs that you met with Kodos at the governor's office the day before his execution order came down. Those same logs indicate you've been there more than once, even though your duties don't typically require you to interact directly with the governor." Georgiou stepped closer to the table. "Why were you there?"

His features twisting into a mask of anger, Simmons all but snarled at her, but said nothing.

"Why didn't you report for duty the day after the murders?" asked Lorca, getting back into the game. Stepping behind Simmons, he began pacing a circuit around the table. "You disappeared. Didn't go to work. Didn't go home. You were a damned ghost, until I found you last night cowering like a rat in your girlfriend's house." Once again back in front of Simmons, he stopped and placed his hands flat on the table, resting on his extended arms as he faced the other man. "You help murder four thousand defenseless people, then crawl into some hole like the coward you are. Mothers, fathers, husbands and wives, friends and lovers. You just burned them to the ground like the crops you had to torch to keep the fungus from spreading. Is that what you thought those people were? An infection to be wiped out in order to have a better chance of saving your own hide? You're not worth the time it'd take to re-charge my phaser after I kill you while you're sitting in that damned chair."

Returning Lorca's fierce stare, Simmons said, "I thought you said I was safe in this chair."

"I lied."

Georgiou flinched at the sudden explosion of move-ment as Lorca used one hand to sweep the table out of his way. It slid left across the room and clattered against the thermoconcrete wall, but by then Lorca was already on Simmons. His right hand closed around the restrained man's throat, and Georgiou could see that he was applying great pressure to his grip, as Simmons's face began turning red. His eyes were wide with surprise and terror, and he muttered something indecipherable.

"Mister Lorca!"

It took a second shout before Lorca reacted to his own name. He released his grip on Simmons, who began sputtering and coughing as he leaned forward in his chair. Spittle escaped his mouth and dampened the front of his yellow coveralls.

"Wait outside," Georgiou snapped, fixing Lorca with the hard glare she reserved for junior subordinates who did something stupid through apathy or laziness.

The commander said nothing. Instead, he drew a deep breath before nodding in acknowledgment of her order. With a final, accusatory look in Simmons's direction, Lorca turned and walked toward the door. Georgiou waited until he was in the corridor and the door once again closed before returning her attention to Simmons.

"He could've killed me," snapped the prisoner.

Georgiou shrugged. "I should have let him." That got the man's attention, and he sat straighter in his chair. "On the other hand, a dead man can't answer any questions. The ball's in your court, Mister Simmons."

"I'm not saying another word until I talk to a lawyer."

Shaking her head, Georgiou replied, "I guess you're forgetting the colony is still under martial law, and Governor Ribiero has granted us wide latitude to search for Kodos. That includes how we deal with anyone who helped him." She stepped closer. "You don't have many options at the moment. I'd think carefully about how you want this to go."

In truth, she was not comfortable with the suspension of civil liberties that came with imposing military rule over a civilian populace. It was a tool for use in extreme circumstances, and while the current situation qualified, Georgiou knew it was a practice that was vulnerable to abuse. Despite the pressing need to restore order and locate Kodos, she and the rest of the Starfleet contingent were obligated to proceed with caution and awareness here.

Though Simmons's breathing had returned to normal, his face was still flushed. "What about Joanna?"

"She's been very cooperative. Told us everything she knew. I guess she hates the idea of ten years in a Federation penal colony for firing a weapon at Starfleet officers."

"She's not involved in any of this." Simmons was testing his restraints, but his wrists moved not one centimeter from the chair's armrests. "I told her you were rioters, looking for a fight. She didn't know who you really were. She doesn't know anything except what I told her, and I lied to her to keep her out of it."

"Out of what?"

Simmons rolled his eyes. "All of this." Still strapped to the chair but without the table in the way, to Georgiou he somehow looked even more vulnerable.

"Fine. What doesn't she know?"

Sighing, Simmons said, "She has no idea I was there that night, or that I had anything to do with it. The less she knows, the better."

It was Georgiou's first encounter with someone who admitted to having any involvement in that night's horrific events. This was different from people like Gabriel Lorca who witnessed it from afar, or even young Jim Kirk and Tommy Leighton, who watched the massacre unfolding just meters before their very eyes. Here was a man who just admitted to being responsible—or complicit, at the very least—to the mass murder of thousands of people.

I should've just let Lorca choke him.

"All right," she said. "You were there. Give me one reason why I shouldn't just throw you into the deepest, darkest hole I can find."

Simmons hung his head, a gesture that to Georgiou appeared motivated by a combination of shame, guilt, and simple resignation over his current situation. When he did look up again, it was to cast his gaze toward the interrogation room's dull gray ceiling.

"Because I didn't kill anyone. In fact, I was one of the people Kodos wanted to die that night."

22

Excerpt from *The Four Thousand: Crisis on Tarsus IV*

The visitor's courtyard, like most of the New Zealand Penal Settlement, is oddly welcoming. Well-manicured lawns, trees, and gardens are interspersed with low-rise buildings featuring large windows, balconies, and rooftop pavilions. People move about in the open air free of restraint, with light gray uniforms the only distinguishing feature separating guards from residents. Those sent here as punishment and for rehabilitation are not called "prisoners" or "inmates," and neither is other jargon normally associated with a detention facility used, at least by the staff. To the casual observer, the settlement is more gated community or retirement village than prison.

"Oh, it's still a prison, all right," says Alexander Simmons, the subject of today's interviews. "They treat us very well, of course, and there are all kinds of rules residents have to follow, but so long as you do what you're supposed to do, they maintain a hands-off approach, for the most part." He offers a wry smile. "All that changes if you try going over the wall, though."

It's an expression, of course. There is no wall surrounding the penal colony, which sits on a bluff overlooking the ocean on New Zealand's northeastern coast. The air is a bit cool, but not so uncomfortable that it prohibits sitting outside and enjoying the early spring sun and breeze. Except for a transporter inhibitor field and restricted air space around the facility, there are no barriers preventing exit and entry to the facility. Every resident is fitted with an ankle bracelet that constantly transmits biometric information as well as the individual's location to the colony's central computer system. Any attempt to leave the colony or to circumvent or remove the monitor would trigger an alarm as well as initiate a stun effect on the wearer's nervous system before dispatching an alert to the computer notifying security staff of the incident. Would-be escapees are then remanded to the colony's enhanced detention section—or "the Box," as residents call it—to serve out whatever punitive duration they receive in relation to their violation. A check of the section's current population shows that there are no occupants, a statistic that has remained unchanged for nearly five years.

"Somebody tried it, back when I first arrived," says Simmons, running a hand through his thinning hair, which has gone somewhat gray since his being remanded to the colony in 2247. "Thought he could reprogram the locator and feed it updates with a portable scanner to fool the guards. He got as far as the beach before the locator figured it out and zapped him." He laughs. "Guy spent six months over in the Box. Idiot."

Simmons is eight years into a twenty-year sentence, and records indicate he has been a model resident from his first moments at the facility. The punishment he received could have been much more severe, and he is well aware of that fact.

"They could've sent me to Elba II or one of the really remote penal colonies. I guess nothing we have is as bad as a Klingon gulag, but that doesn't mean it would've been a picnic, either. So I'll take what they give me and keep my mouth shut."

A check of his record shows that due to his good behavior while in residence, Simmons has been considered for parole. He has refused that opportunity, instead making personal requests to the facility's director to stay here in order to carry out the full term of his incarceration.

"I deserve worse. The judges didn't think so, but that doesn't mean I can't believe otherwise. They sent me here, and I intend to serve out every last second of my term. It's the least I can do." During his stay, Simmons has made himself available to facility staff as an instructor and mentor to other residents, teaching classes and even assisting in the training of officers in various security-related subjects. According to his quarterly reviews, he has never given any cause for concern or complaint by any member of the staff.

Alexander Simmons looks around the garden where today's interview is being conducted. We occupy a park bench situated at the edge of a large open meadow. Other residents are nearby, either walking, jogging, or just lying in the afternoon sun. A few guards are visible, but their presence is obvious without being obtrusive. They patrol the paths that encircle the meadow and wind through the gardens and clusters of trees. Sensors and other monitoring devices track residents' movements, so the guards are on hand mostly to respond to alerts issued by the colony computer system.

He raises his head, enjoying the feel of the warm sun on his skin. "Fresh air instead of an underground bunker on an asteroid or planet with a poisonous atmosphere? I'll take it. They let us have visitors, and even furloughs after so many months of good behavior. Joanna comes to see me a couple of times a week, and I'm due for a furlough next month." He casts his gaze toward the small meadow's lush green grass. "Truth be told and when it's all said and done, I got off easy."

During his trial, it was revealed that Alexander Simmons was a friend and follower of Governor Adrian Kodos. They were acquainted on Earth prior to their departure for Tarsus IV, members of a group interested in beginning a "new chapter" in their lives.

"The main thing that's wrong with life on Earth is that there's pretty much nothing wrong with life on Earth." He gestures, indicating the meadow and the rest of the facility grounds. "This is jail, for crying out loud. The only real challenges regular people face are the silly ones they make up to alleviate boredom. Mountain climbing, orbital sky diving, exploring the bottom of the ocean." He frowns. "People with too much time on their hands do that kind of thing, or they just lie around reading or doing pretty much nothing of any consequence."

He points toward the sky. "For a real challenge, you have to get out there. If you join Starfleet or work for them as a civilian, you can at least go and explore new worlds, maybe meet some alien race we've never seen before, or find the ruins of a civilization that died out millions of years before life even existed here on Earth." There's a pause, and a nod of appreciation. "I can respect the people who choose that sort of life, but it was never for me. Instead, I wanted to get away from the easy life on Earth and try something different: to make something out of nothing, or almost nothing. That's what colony life means to a lot of people. Kodos felt very strongly about that sort of thing too."

Tarsus IV was an established colony decades before Kodos arrived along with Simmons and other like-minded individuals. The planet still offered plenty in the way of opportunity for those seeking a challenge. Though many of the settlers and their descendants preferred life in or near the colony's main population center in the city of New Anchorage, others chose to put down roots, figuratively and literally, all across the planet.

"I couldn't shake being a security specialist," says Simmons. "I was barely off the transport ship when the head of the security forces found me. He'd already read my record from my Earth career and wanted me to join his unit. There wasn't a lot of crime on Tarsus IV, but still more than what I dealt with back home. It seemed like it would leave me time for other things, so I said yes, and I was right. The job had its share of minor excitement, but nothing that kept us working overtime."

He sits straighter in his chair, exhibiting an air of pride. "I was able to build my house with my own two hands. It took me almost a year. With the exception of an antigrav unit or help from a friend to get some of the heavier materials into place, I placed every brick, every shingle, and every piece of lumber or tile myself, from the foundation up. None of my tools were self-powered. I cut every piece with a hand saw, and hammered every nail. Ran all the cabling, and did all of the plumbing. If a friend helped me, then I returned the favor while they worked on their house." With a smile, he flexes his right hand for emphasis. "Lots of aches, pains, and blisters in those days, but it was damned satisfying watching it all come together and knowing it was through my own hard work. I miss that house. I hope whoever's living in it now is taking good care of it."

Other colonists, including several who had come with Simmons to Tarsus IV, followed pursuits that were even more ambitious. In an age when machines can create meals out of inedible compounds, one might question the need or desire to farm, but agriculture remains a time-honored vocation even on Earth. It is even more prevalent on colony worlds.

"Most of the larger farms are within a hundred kilometers of the city, but there are a number of others, in all shapes and sizes, here and there. Those, along with hydroponics plants and greenhouses—everything from small versions in someone's backyard to big combines—contributed to a pretty diverse selection of locally and regionally sourced produce and other foods."

Simmons pauses again, closing his eyes before releasing a small sigh. "That's why it was so devastating when the infection hit. All that work, and that damned fungus just chewed through it without breaking a sweat. I'm not a farmer, but I know plenty of people who were, and saw a lot of them cry when we had to burn their farms to the ground."

With the source of the contagion believed to be the unforeseen consequence of introducing crops and seeds imported from Epsilon Sorona II into the Tarsus IV ecosystem, public tensions rose quickly in response to the escalating crisis. Driven by fear and uncertainty, many colonists—including descendants of the original settlers who had called Tarsus IV home for their entire lives—began searching for something or someone to blame for their plight.

"There was a group of us who were never happy with the Federation's decision to relocate the Epsilon Sorona colonists to our planet." Simmons shakes his head. "We all had our own ideas about being left alone to live our lives as we saw fit. Kodos in particular harbored strong feelings on this subject. Sure, you can't get completely away from the Federation, and we couldn't help that a Starfleet outpost was there before a colony started, but we're about self-determination and all that, right? And for the most part, we were allowed to go about our lives—within reason, of course. That's why we went there, and for years we never had any problems with Federation bureaucracy, and we had great relations with the Starfleet people assigned to the outpost." He sighs. "Then somebody sitting in some office a hundred light-years away makes a decision that upsets everything."

Simmons seems to feel some guilt over his remarks. "Don't get me wrong. Of course you want to help someone when they're in need, and of course we welcomed the Epsilon Sorona refugees. There was no other choice. What if the situation was reversed, and it was us needing a new home?" He grimaces. "I know it sounds selfish, but I guess we just wanted to have a say before we opened our world to strangers."

With the fungal contamination, however, skeptics and those otherwise opposed to the Federation's decision to relocate those evacuated from Epsilon Sorona II found a measure of vindication. It was a short-lived and meaningless victory, as attention turned to battling the contagion and dealing with the aftermath of its effects. Governor Gisela Ribiero, who many felt was to blame for the whole thing by accepting the refugees, was removed from her post. She was replaced by Kodos, who got right to work asserting his newfound authority.

"Those first council meetings after Kodos took over were pretty tense." Simmons raises a hand, waving away an insect choosing that moment to strafe his ear. "In addition to the usual group of advisers, they also wanted senior security commanders present, to make sure we had the latest information so far as dealing with the public and being able to prepare for possible civil unrest. Some of the council members were still upset by Ribiero's sudden ousting, but none of that seemed to faze Kodos. He let them vent for a short while, but when he started talking it was like he'd been in charge forever. He wasn't interested in assigning blame for what happened. We needed to focus on getting through the crisis we were facing. It was a matter of simple survival."

Simmons turns pensive for a moment, as though deciding how best to give voice to unpleasant memories. "Survival was the word Kodos kept going back to, survival of the fittest and all that. He was fascinated by cultures on Earth or other planets where such beliefs were celebrated. The ancient Spartans, the Klingons, the Andorians. He didn't care much for the more militaristic tenets of those societies, while thinking that other aspects of those civilizations were worth emulating. Even before he left Earth, Kodos had this idea that embracing such a philosophy was the only way to survive if humans were to continue expanding their influence in the universe. We had to take hold of this belief if we were going to survive encounters with other species who might not share our idealistic and somewhat naive views about living and working in harmony and all those other things we're supposed to value."

Further, the people of Tarsus IV harbored goals and dreams of creating a self-sustaining community that was home to the best representatives of various Federation worlds. Long-term plans included the expansion of scientific and technological knowledge as well as the advancement if not outright evolution of individuals and perhaps even entire species. Though things like genetic engineering are against Federation law, this does not preclude scientists and engineers from seeking other means of improvement. Is this a form of eugenics? There are those who might see things that way, and many people with opposing views called Tarsus IV home.

Everything for which the community had worked, including its very survival, was at risk. As Kodos and the council focused their collective attention on their current situation, it was impossible not to dwell on the unpleasant prospect that awaited them all if they did nothing. Distress calls had already been dispatched, and the colony leadership knew that aid was far too distant to be of timely help. The people of Tarsus IV were on their own for the foreseeable future, facing a severe food shortage and far too many mouths to feed. Public reaction to the news was what might be expected during troubling events. In the absence of real information, speculation began filling in knowledge gaps.

"People were spinning all sorts of theories and worst-case scenarios," says Simmons. "Did we know if the fungus might end up having an effect on us, the way it had already destroyed our food sources? What if it mutated and spread to us? What if Starfleet took too long deciding if we were a contagious biological threat before sending someone to help us? What if they decided to just raze the planet to keep infection from spreading? It was insane."

It was Kodos who put forth the notion that such trying circumstances must call for extreme and perhaps distasteful yet necessary measures.

"He called it a revolution," says Simmons. "At first, he presented it as a way to divide the colony's original settlers from those relocated from Epsilon Sorona II. With that done, the two groups would be further segmented and sent to other parts of the planet. It was believed that relocating to areas that had not been exposed to the fungus was a way of defeating the contamination and beginning again. Food processors could be brought online, and accelerated farming techniques could be employed to generate new produce. It would be rough going at first, but with determination, cooperation, and a little bit of luck, we'd make it."

Simmons grows somber again. "That was just the story for the masses. After the meeting was over, Kodos held back a handful of us." He rubs his hands together before reaching up to cover his face for a moment, releasing a long, loud sigh. "There were about a dozen of us, all people who came with him from Earth. Some I knew, but others were just faces I'd seen either on the transport ship or after we arrived on Tarsus IV. Only then did I realize that these were all people who had closer relationships with Kodos than I did, and shared many of his beliefs.

"When he laid it all out, it was completely without emotion. He reduced the entire thing down to simple arithmetic. This much food, this many people needing to eat, this much time until help arrived. Even with rationing, we were still going to come up too short. That's when he dropped the bomb on all of us: we could all die, or some of us could be sacrificed to ensure the colony's survival."

More than a minute passes with Simmons sitting in silence, his face conveying the pain that comes from dredging up unpleasant memories.

"Kodos said we had to remember that the future of the community had to be the primary objective. At first we thought he meant helping the children, the elderly, and those needing additional care, but he wasn't thinking like that at all. He wasn't thinking along traditional lines about simple survival. Instead, he wanted to remove the weak, the sick, and those who it was decided had no relevant contributions to make to the community going forward. It was to be survival of the fittest and those deemed useful."

A tear runs down Simmons's left cheek. He makes no move to wipe it away, but instead sits still as it is joined by another, both of which run down his face.

"To this day, I can't believe I actually believed what he was saying, even for a minute. I was stupid and scared. I didn't want to die, and I didn't want to be one of those chosen to die."

When asked whether he thinks Kodos actually believed the views he was espousing in the hours before the massacre, Simmons nods with conviction.

"He absolutely believed he was doing the right thing for the good of the colony. In his eyes, he might be damning himself, but it was the chance to save at least part of the community. He seemed resigned to the idea that history would judge him, if not for the act itself, then in how he went about deciding who'd be sacrificed."

Leaning back on the bench, Simmons releases a grunt of annoyance. "It's almost ten years later, and I know better, but I can still remember what I was feeling. It was so overwhelming as we all tried to process what we were talking about, but there was also an odd sort of nobility to what he was suggesting. We all knew it was a hard, terrible choice, but it felt . . . right." He shakes his head. "Damn him, and damn me for believing him. At least, I thought I did. I had doubts, but standing there in front of Kodos, trying to put them into words, I just couldn't do it. I could tell from his eyes that he wasn't convinced I was behind him, and that's why he did what he did."

Questions about the massacre itself are met with resistance, but Simmons eventually offers his version of the events as described in official records and the transcripts of his trial.

"I couldn't go through with it. People were gathering in the amphitheater, and Kodos had picked a small group he could trust to help him carry out his order. Yes, I was one of the chosen, but it was crap. Kodos must've known he couldn't count on me, and though I didn't get it at the time, it's obvious he wanted to make sure I couldn't come back to make things difficult for him. He'd taken great pains to conceal his identity from all but a close circle of trusted friends, not wanting to show his face until after he'd carried out what he was calling 'the Sacrifice.' Looking back on it, he was simply getting rid of eyewitnesses in case it all went bad, and that meant people like me. I just had the honor of being one of the first people to die before he carried out the larger crime."

Simmons grasps his hands in front of him, squeezing them together in a rhythmic fashion as he recalls more disturbing memories. All these years later, and having lived every day with the consequences of his choices and actions, it's apparent that he's unwilling to forgive himself for his role in the events of that terrible day. A check of the archives for subspace messages dispatched from the planet in the aftermath of the executions reveals that it was Simmons himself who broadcast to the people of New Anchorage that a response to the colony's original distress call had been received. A ship was coming, far sooner than originally anticipated. Simmons had made that broadcast at great personal risk, as it turned out, but in his own eyes that was not nearly enough to grant him even some small measure of forgiveness.

"We were in position at the amphitheater when Kodos sent one of his people to kill me. All the years we'd known each other, and he didn't even have the courage to do it himself. Even with all his big words and supposed bravery in the face of crisis and saving the community at all costs, he was already taking steps to insulate himself from the fallout of what was about to happen.

"It was just blind luck I saw it coming. I won't bore you with the details, but the short version is that I killed the guy before he could kill me. Then I ran like hell. I didn't try to stop what was about to happen; I was too busy trying to save my own ass. I wasn't a block away from the amphitheater when the executions started. The sounds of phaser fire and the screams carried on the night air and echoed off the buildings. To this day, when I lie awake in my bed in the dark? I can still hear them. I'll hear them until the day I die, and maybe they'll haunt me forever after that."

Simmons shrugs. "Seems just."

23

Standing in silence, Lorca waited before Georgiou's desk while the commander consulted some report or other correspondence on the data slate she held in her hand.

She looks pissed. Well, that was certainly predictable.

Georgiou had not so much as looked up at his entrance after summoning him following her questioning of Alexander Simmons, leaving him to examine the decrepit office the security force's watch commander had seen fit to provide her. The walls, formed from thermoconcrete like everything else in this building, were painted a dull white. Georgiou's desk along with its chair and the table to her left were a matched set of gunmetal gray, all scuffed and scratched with age and abuse. On the desk was a standard computer interface as well as Georgiou's equipment belt and a second data slate that was a companion to the one in her hand.

After another minute or so of the silent treatment, she placed the data slate on the desk. Leaning back in her chair, she folded her hands in her lap and regarded him with obvious disapproval, but also a hint of concern.

"Simmons is back in his cell. Security is doing what it can to corroborate his story. What do you think of what he said?"

Surprised by her opening line of questioning, Lorca replied, "Biometric readings indicate he was telling the truth."

"I asked what *you think*."

"I agree with the biometrics." He was watching as Georgiou had continued to question Simmons, and even without studying the monitors and their information, Lorca knew without doubt Simmons was not lying. He may have thought he wanted to carry out Kodos's order, but at the moment of truth, Simmons wavered. His conscience, though already compromised, had won the day.

"What makes you so sure?" asked Georgiou.

"He could've killed us at his girlfriend's apartment. It's not like other people working for Kodos had a problem with that sort of thing." The comment elicited images of Meizhen Bao and Piotr Nolokov. He slid his hand into his pocket, not realizing he was reaching for the small fortune cookie slip until he felt it slide between his fingers.

Georgiou's eyes narrowed. "You're going with your gut?"

Lorca took his hand out of his pocket and crossed his arms. "And the biometrics. Also, when we found Simmons and his girlfriend, their weapons were set to stun. What happens to him now?"

"He'll stay in holding until Captain Korrapati gets a response to the messages he's sent to Starfleet Command and Federation authorities. Until Governor Ribiero rescinds the martial law order, we've got broad discretion here, and we'll still keep an eye on things, but the captain and I think Simmons should remain in the custody of local civilian law enforcement officials."

"I think that's probably a wise choice."

At first, Lorca worried that there might be individuals within the New Anchorage security forces who still harbored loyalty to Kodos. He need not have worried, as Captain Korrapati had also anticipated that problem, assigning members of the *Narbonne*'s security detail to the precinct headquarters where Simmons was being kept. Governor Gisela

Ribiero had kept the martial law order in place, along with the curfews and other restrictions that remained in effect. This allowed her to make use of Korrapati and his Starfleet contingent to assist wherever she thought necessary.

Rising from her chair, Georgiou placed her hands flat on the desk and leaned toward Lorca. "Simmons is taken care of. You want to tell me what the hell all that was about with you in there?"

Lorca replied, "No excuse, Commander. I let my emotions get the best of me, and I crossed a line." It was a frank answer, offered without embellishment and which also had the virtue of being true.

"Well, thanks very much for not making me beat a confession out of you."

"I didn't want to waste more of your time." Georgiou was too good an officer to have to put up with whatever excuse he might choose to employ. Lorca could not defend his inappropriate actions. Assaulting a prisoner was a direct violation of at least a half dozen Starfleet regulations and civil laws. The only way to retain Georgiou's support was to respect her and give her straight answers.

She made her way around the desk, her gaze hardening as she stared up at him. "You're confusing me, Mister Lorca. Do you want me or the captain to bring formal charges against you?"

"I'd rather you not. I'm simply acknowledging my responsibility in this matter, which I accept along with whatever consequences there might be."

Georgiou held his gaze for several more seconds. "As long as we're being honest, I can't say I blame you. Even if he didn't actually help to carry out the executions, Simmons was on board with the idea until he backed out at the last minute. At some point, he was okay with the idea of murdering thousands of people, so let's not pretend he's a precious flower in dire need of our protection." The command presence returned. "I might disagree with your actions, but having reviewed your record, I'm confident it was an atypical occurrence. Therefore, I don't expect I'll be seeing a repeat of that performance. Am I clear?"

Lorca nodded. "You are, Commander."

Given the sharpness in her tone, he was surprised to see Georgiou sigh.

"I know you've had to deal with a lot since all of this started. Losing two members of your team. Simmons had nothing to do with that, but he confirmed the raid was ordered by Kodos. He wanted Starfleet out of the way, because he knew how you'd react to the executions. If you couldn't stop them, then you'd damned sure try to find those responsible. In that respect, it's probably good for him that we arrived when we did. Were I Kodos, I wouldn't want you hunting me."

"I'm still hunting him." For Lorca, this would be over only when Kodos was in custody or in a morgue. At the moment, Lorca had no real preference.

Georgiou eyed him for a few seconds, saying nothing, and he got the sense that she was weighing whatever question she might pose.

"You knew someone among the colonists who were executed, didn't you?"

The question came out of nowhere, catching him completely off guard. Lorca felt himself all but flinch in response to the direct query, which by itself was enough to confirm Georgiou's suspicions.

Good, he decided. *Let's get it all on the table.*

"Yes, Commander. I did."

Georgiou's features softened. "Someone close to you? I know Meizhen and Piotr were your colleagues and friends, but . . . well, you know what I mean."

Nodding, Lorca felt his jaw clenching. "Yes, I do. She was a colonist. Her name was Balayna."

"I'm sorry, Commander." There was no doubting her sentiment was genuine. Lorca saw the anguish in her eyes and was grateful for it. He also knew that duty compelled her to look at this new development with a professional, dispassionate eye.

"I can't even imagine what you're going through. I wish there was something I could do. Anything I could do."

Lorca squared his shoulders. "Don't relieve me of my duties."

"Commander, you've suffered a personal tragedy. Not only are you obviously emotionally compromised, but it's simply not fair to ask you to compartmentalize your feelings like that. Not this quickly, at the very least. I have a responsibility to your well-being too."

"And I appreciate that," he countered. "But we've got our first tangible lead on Kodos's whereabouts. I honestly understand what you're saying, but I'm asking you to let me stay with this." He paused, feeling his anxiety level rising. Drawing a deep, calming breath, he clasped his hands before him. "I need to finish it. Not just for Balayna, but for all of them." Standing on the sidelines was unacceptable; he needed to be on the playing field. He could not even imagine discontinuing the pursuit. Not now.

"Let's not get ahead of ourselves," said Georgiou. "First, we need to verify this information we're getting from Simmons. If what he's saying is true, then rooting out Kodos isn't going to be easy."

"I've already started, Commander." Even as he watched Simmons responding to Georgiou's questions during the extended interview session, Lorca began the process of piecing together a plan to act on what the prisoner was revealing about the former governor and his followers. According to Simmons, he was a member of the group that helped Kodos locate and establish a refuge of sorts in the mountains east of New Anchorage. The minerals and geo-magnetic anomalies permeating the region provided the ideal cover from sensors and transporters, all but allowing anyone to hide from the eyes of modern technology. Kodos and anyone with him could hide for weeks if not months among those mountains without any risk of detection. The location would be a closely guarded secret, known only to a precious, trusted few of Kodos's inner circle.

Simmons had been in that circle at one point. None of the information he was providing could be trusted on its own, of course, but Lorca already had an idea on how to deal with that.

"There's one way to guarantee his full cooperation. Let me take him with me."

Having reclaimed her chair behind her desk, Georgiou began tapping the desktop with her fingers. "A guide?"

"Guide, or bait. Whatever works. As far as he knows, Kodos thought he was dead, but we can't trust that to last forever." Lorca could not help looking around the cramped, uninviting office. "We don't know if Kodos has any loyalists around here, but I'm not betting against it." With that in mind, Lorca had taken steps from the moment Simmons was brought in to keep his presence known only to people with a strict need for that information. He was hoping to preserve the secret of their having arrested someone with crucial knowledge about Kodos, but he knew that would not last. If they were going to make the most of whatever advantage Simmons might provide, they needed to seize the initiative, before Kodos or any of his followers could act.

"We can offer him a reduced sentence to secure his cooperation," said Georgiou. "His lawyer will love that." After the interrogation incident, the commander had seen to it that Simmons was afforded the opportunity to speak with legal counsel. Despite the civilian attorney's warnings to the contrary, the security officer had agreed to cooperate with Georgiou and Lorca. "Assuming I let you do this, what's your plan?"

"A simple manhunt, Commander. Simmons claims to have knowledge of the base camp Kodos established, so he can lead the way. With all the geomagnetic interference lacing the region, the *Narbonne*'s sensors won't penetrate too far belowground, but they can still be used to monitor activity on the surface. Even if we don't find their camp, our movements may still flush them out." Lorca sighed. "Assuming they're actually in there somewhere." It was an unsophisticated strategy, but with the information and resources available to him—at least until more help arrived—Lorca believed it was the plan with the best chance of success.

"If he is there, it could be dangerous," said Georgiou. "You have to think anyone who goes to all that trouble to set up a hiding place is going to take steps to protect it."

Lorca offered a grim smile. "That's why Simmons will be in front."

"We probably shouldn't tell that to his lawyer." Georgiou eyed him with obvious concern. "And you're sure you're up for this?"

"Absolutely. Besides, it's certainly better than sitting around here and wallowing in . . . it's better than just sitting around here. I need to *do* something, Commander."

As though contemplating the potential consequences of her decision, Georgiou dropped her gaze to her desk, and her fingers continued their rhythmic tapping for several more seconds before she drew a deep breath and nodded.

"Outline your plan for Captain Korrapati, then draw whatever equipment you need from the *Narbonne*. I'll release Simmons into your custody. Promise me you won't kill him while you're out there."

Lorca replied, "Only if he tries to kill me first."

"Fair enough," said Georgiou. "You'll have support from the *Narbonne* while you're in the field. Sensors, transporters, whatever we can scrounge up. We've got a team of SCE engineers with us. Maybe they can build a prison barge out of cargo containers before you get back." She paused, and her expression changed as though she was processing a sudden, concerning thought. A moment later, she rose from her chair and fixed Lorca once again with another hard stare.

"I understand and appreciate what you've been through, and based on what you've told me, I can accept your actions against Simmons were motivated by stress and fatigue, and even anger. Given the circumstances, I'm willing to consider them an abnormality, but this is important, Mister Lorca: I want Kodos punished just like you do, but we are *not* vigilantes. It's not our job to dispense justice. Bring Kodos back—alive."

Lorca offered a single, crisp nod. "He'll face trial, Commander. You have my word."

He had every intention of taking Kodos into custody and dragging him back to New Anchorage, in chains if he managed to find some, and throwing him at Governor Ribiero's feet. It was the only way justice could truly be served for Piotr Nolokov, Meizhen Bao, and the four thousand slain colonists—including Balayna. Their families and friends deserved to witness firsthand the architect of their death receiving the punishment he deserved.

On the other hand, if Kodos decided to fight, Lorca would have no trouble putting him down without a second thought.

24

Sunrise on Tarsus IV.

The air was crisp and cool but not so cold as to require heavy outer garments. It revitalized him, pushing away the last tendrils of fitful sleep. For Kodos, this was his favorite time of day. It had long been his habit to awaken before dawn; that had evolved over the years to include the ritual of sitting on the veranda of his home to greet each new day. Living in the city, he preferred to greet the dawn alone, sipping his tea and watching the darkness fade as vivid oranges and reds pushed outward from the distant horizon before the sun made its first appearance.

Without his tea and having only a flat rock on which to sit in lieu of the chaise lounge on his veranda, he still held to his morning routine. As always, he felt the new day pushing away at the fatigue lingering within him. It was a temporary measure, Kodos knew, but nevertheless one that gave him a small degree of satisfaction. These past days spent living in virtual exile wore on him. His own thoughts ate at him, forcing him to question the wisdom of his choices and the magnitude of their consequences. Would his consciousness—and his conscience—ever cease to torment him? He found that possibility unlikely.

And perhaps that is as it should be.

The thought occurred to him as he dropped his gaze

to the worn hardcover book sitting in his lap. It was not an original edition but a facsimile, created to resemble a tome from centuries past. The faux leather was worn and scuffed in places, and the gold lettering on its spine was faded and chipped but still legible: *The Complete Works of William Shakespeare.*

While it was true that much of Earth's ancient literature and poetry was lost to time, certain authors and their creations had somehow managed to persevere through the ages. Though he read the usual selections of *Romeo and Juliet* and *Hamlet* in primary school or while attending university, it was only within the last few years that Kodos took an active, ongoing interest in the celebrated playwright's life and writings. The book in his lap was one of the few physical tomes he had brought with him from Earth. For reasons he still didn't understand, reading its electronic equivalent on a computer screen or data slate—as he had done with almost everything else since childhood—did not provide the same sense of satisfaction. There was an energy to the words that was somehow diminished when reduced to pixels on a screen. Here, in a tangible form he could feel beneath his fingers, they exuded the passion, pain, and life captured by their author all those centuries ago.

What would Shakespeare think of the situation in which Kodos found himself? It certainly had the makings of a tragedy in the classical mold. Surely the story lent itself to a saga, one of conflict between heroes and villains, to say nothing of long soliloquies filled with reflection and angst. Perhaps a modern playwright would one day pen such an epic tale worthy of the Bard himself.

I rather doubt that.

"Good morning, Governor."

Kodos glanced over to see Ian Galloway standing behind him. How in the world had his assistant maneuvered so close without being heard? Despite being relatively flat, the plateau near the summit of Mount Bonestell still presented challenges to a novice or untrained hiker, which Galloway had proven himself to be during the overland trek here through the mountain passes.

"You move with surprising stealth, Ian."

Galloway, slightly out of breath, offered a small smile. "Practice, Governor. It's not like I've got a lot of choice, given our current accommodations."

"It's the remoteness of our location and the effort required to get here that is our greatest advantage."

Kodos and the others were able to make use of all-terrain vehicles to get them from the city into the unforgiving region, as whatever roads and trails that may have existed beyond the city proper ended well away from here. The small convoy was able to make it a few dozen more kilometers into the wilderness, but even that soon came to an end, necessitating the group to cover the remaining distance on foot. This complication was factored into the overall movement plan with the same attention to detail that had helped to decide on the location in the first place. Even as Kodos and the majority of his followers proceeded into the mountains toward their camp, the vehicles were returned to the city and their drivers remained there, doing their best to verify that the escape was made without detection.

As for their choice of refuge, there were other areas within this region that afforded easier access, but they lacked the higher concentrations of minerals and other subterranean geomagnetic activity that thwarted sensor technology of the sort the Starfleet ship would be employing. Indeed, the levels of interference here were so pervasive that he was able to emerge without worry from their hiding place, stealing a few moments for himself each day to greet the dawn.

If his hunters wanted him, they would have to work for it.

"What can I do for you, Ian?" he asked.

Galloway stepped closer. "You wanted to be informed if we received any word from our friends in the city. There's been a development. One of our people has been taken into custody."

"That was to be expected. Perhaps it was inevitable."

"Yes, Governor, but the person they've captured is Alexander Simmons."

It took Kodos an extra few seconds to process the report. Shifting his seat on the rock serving as his perch, he eyed his assistant. "You're certain?"

"The information comes from our contact at security forces headquarters. They saw him brought in after being apprehended by two Starfleet officers."

"How is this even possible?" Kodos stopped himself, remembering that Galloway did not know the truth about his plans for Simmons on the night of the Sacrifice. It was a bit of information restricted to himself, Joel Pakaski, and the man sent to carry out his order, Markus Seidel. Himself a security officer, Seidel was given specific instructions with respect to Simmons, but in his rush to move to a temporary hiding place while planning his escape from New Anchorage, Kodos had somehow overlooked obtaining a final determination regarding Simmons—or Seidel, for that matter. Neither man arrived to join the group leaving the city, and Kodos realized his oversight. He should have had Pakaski look into the matter, both to ascertain Seidel's whereabouts and to verify that Simmons was dead.

"According to our contact at security headquarters, Simmons was able to escape being killed by Officer Seidel."

Galloway's matter-of-fact statement caught Kodos by surprise. He regarded his assistant with new appreciation of his apparent resourcefulness, but also a small amount of apprehension.

"How do you know this?"

"Simmons recounted his version of the story to his interrogators. Seidel attempted to kill him, but Simmons turned the tables and escaped the amphitheater. He then laid low at his girlfriend's apartment until he was found by the Starfleet search party." Galloway paused, his expression turning thoughtful. "He was originally supposed to be part of our group, was he not?"

A gust of wind coursed through the valley and up to the plateau, chilling Kodos to the point that he pulled his collar tighter around his neck as he considered how best to respond to his assistant. Deciding truth was his best option, he said, "Simmons was not a believer. He doubted that what we were doing was just. That much is reasonable, as what I was suggesting would be overwhelming for anyone. However, I was concerned that he would falter at the moment of truth, when we most needed him to set aside his personal feelings and act for the greater good. So I sent Seidel to make sure Simmons carried out his duty or, failing that, to make sure he couldn't compromise us."

"I understand, Governor," said Galloway. "This is what Simmons communicated to his captors. For whatever my opinion's worth, I think you made the right decision. Anyone holding such doubts puts us all at risk."

Kodos was surprised to hear such conviction from his assistant. Why had he not perceived such feelings from Galloway before now? Was he so consumed with everything that had transpired over the past several days that such subtle clues escaped him? Perhaps there were other details that had evaded his attention. That could be dangerous, given his current surroundings. Did he trust everyone around him? There was Galloway and Joel Pakaski, both of whom had more than proven their loyalty, but what of the other twenty people hiding with him? Before all of this, he would never have needed to question their devotion, either to him or the cause into which they all had entered. How many of them were driven more by personal survival than any other consideration? Under any other circumstances, it would be a reasonable stance to take, but none of those involved him. On the other hand, the desire to survive and—in this case— avoid arrest and criminal prosecution would provide power- ful motivation to work together in pursuit of this mutual goal. It was only when the situation began to deteriorate that the true character of those he had chosen to help him would be revealed.

Here's hoping it doesn't come to that.

"What else did Simmons tell the authorities?"

Galloway replied, "The Starfleet response team is en- gaged in a major search effort. They're sweeping the city looking for us. A few of our people have been rounded up, but Simmons was their most significant capture. It's a safe bet they'll use him to expand their search." He paused, and Kodos saw the younger man was nervous. "One of the of- ficers who found Simmons was the commander of the out- post garrison. According to the report I received, this man seems particularly driven to find us."

"To find me, you mean."

Not for the first time, Kodos shook his head as he con- templated the folly of sending a team to raid the Starfleet observation outpost. It seemed a prudent move, given that the five-person detail possessed weapons and other equip- ment that might prove useful to resisting the security forces if circumstances called for that sort of action. The outpost also had its own food supply, which, according to the facil- ity's ranking officer, had escaped infection by the rampant fungus. The officer, a man named Lorca, even offered their uncontaminated food stores to be added to the colony's remaining supplies. It was a show of solidarity welcomed by

Governor Ribiero and the leadership council, and appreciated even by Kodos. However, Lorca and his team were liabilities to be dispatched lest they become legitimate problems for Kodos and the Revolution.

"The teams we sent to the outpost killed two of the Starfleet officers," said Galloway. "Therefore, this Commander Lorca almost certainly knows you ordered that action. According to our contact, he was rather . . . animated during his questioning of Simmons. It stands to reason he has a personal interest in finding us."

Kodos realized that he had underestimated the abilities of the Starfleet personnel, who he assumed were technicians rather than trained security specialists. It was a mistake that was coming back to haunt him. Lorca, in particular, seemed to possess some tactical training and experience. Would he seek justice for the death of his colleagues? Perhaps. What if he was motivated by other factors? Like so many others impacted by the Sacrifice, he may have had personal relationships with one or more of the civilian colonists. Vengeance could be a powerful motivator, and now it seemed this Lorca had access to pertinent information to assist his search.

"He'll use Simmons," said Kodos. "He'll use him to find us." Turning from Galloway, he took in the grand vista before him. With the sun now above the horizon, the mountain valley was cast in an ethereal glow that soothed him. It was utter serenity, a scene in which he could lose himself forever.

Such is not to be.

"We can't stay here. Sooner or later, the search will be brought to our doorstep. They'll find us. We need to plan for that eventuality."

Galloway said, "If we leave, won't they be able to track our movements?"

"Ultimately, yes." Kodos knew he and his followers possessed the advantage. The terrain was their ally, but the Starfleet forces would soon overcome that obstacle. What he needed was a diversionary action: some sort of distraction that might provide the cover necessary to go . . . where? Back to the city? Was the answer to double back on his pursuers, somehow finding a way past the security cordons in order to lose himself within New Anchorage? It was a ploy worth considering, but it would take planning and no small amount of luck to achieve success.

They could not wait.

Time was running short.

25

Lorca saw the man ahead of him stumble, his right foot slipping on a slick section of flat rock outcropping. His leg went out from under him and the man pitched backward, the weight of his pack pulling him off balance and casting him toward the sloping ground. Others in proximity shouted various warnings as he started to tumble. His arms were flailing in an attempt at catching on to anything to keep from rolling down the hill. Stepping to his left to avoid getting swept away, Lorca extended his right arm and seized one of the man's hands in his own. The speed and extra weight almost managed to drag him down but Lorca was able to set his feet and lean against the abrupt pull on his arm. Within seconds the man's fall was arrested and he was lying on his back, wincing in momentary pain from the unexpected shock.

"You okay?" asked Lorca, shaking his right arm to throw off the minor discomfort of nearly having it yanked from its socket.

The other man, a civilian whose name Lorca could not remember, nodded. "Yeah. Thanks for that. I didn't see the moss on that rock."

Lorca gestured to the soles of the man's shoes. "That's not the best footwear for being out here." The tread was decent enough for streets and sidewalks, but lacking for uneven or wet terrain such as what the group was traversing. "You'll need to watch your step. Don't want to be getting a twisted ankle or a broken leg." He offered a small grin to remove some of the sting from his rebuke. "It's a long way back to base camp, and I really don't want to carry you."

"I've actually got a pair of boots in my pack. I just didn't think I'd need them until we got a bit higher up in the mountains. I guess we both know how that worked out. I'll be careful, Commander. Thanks."

Offering his hand, Lorca braced himself as he pulled the other man to his feet. "What's your name?" he asked.

"Denham. Brian Denham."

The name rang a bell, and Lorca recalled seeing it on the list of civilians who had been vetted as having no known ties to Kodos. While screening personnel for the team that would help with the search for the fugitive governor, preference was given to those with military, law enforcement, or outdoors experience. However, the need to avoid bringing in possible Kodos sympathizers forced Lorca to consider alternative candidates. Despite lacking certain desired skills, people like Denham were eager to help in any feasible manner.

"What do you do, Brian?"

Straightening the straps of his pack and resettling it on his back, Denham replied, "I'm a computer specialist. My wife is a molecular biologist."

"Ever been hiking or camping?"

The other man's face reddened. "That obvious, huh?"

"A bit, yeah." In addition to the man's ill-suited footwear, his outer garments were not sturdy enough for the unrefined outdoors. His jacket, some kind of lightweight polymer, was torn thanks to his accident, and his backpack appeared stuffed to overflowing, likely with items that would serve little to no practical purpose out here. In contrast, Lorca carried a standard-issue Starfleet field pack on his back containing only those items he knew from experience would be of practical value in this environment. He had added a sheathed hunting knife to his equipment belt, and his pack was fitted with a compartment that held drinking water, complete with a tube he could access without removing his gear from his back. Its side pockets held field rations and extra power cells for his phaser. Suitable clothing to handle the various elements rested in the pack's main compartment. Anything else the pack contained would be categorized by Lorca as "luxury items."

Stay warm, stay hydrated, and stay ready to fight, his combat and wilderness survival instructors told him, over and over, during training that felt as though it had occurred a lifetime ago. *The rest of it will sort itself out later.*

"What made you volunteer for this, Brian?"

Denham's expression turned somber. "My father was in the amphitheater that night. I want to help find the man who did that to him and all the others."

"Your father?" Lorca estimated Denham to be in his mid to late forties, meaning his father would likely have been twenty-five to thirty years older. Kodos had included a number of elderly colonists in his "sacrifice" action, and the very thought once again set his teeth on edge. In a cold, calculating sense, the governor's actions could be seen as motivated by a certain practicality, but it did not lessen Lorca's desire to pummel the man with his bare hands.

Heartless prick.

"I was born on Epsilon Sorona," said Denham. "My parents were among the original settlers on that planet, and we were all brought here as part of the relocation." He paused, looking around the magnificent vista surrounding them. "This is our home, and I want to help find the bastard who took my father away from me, and all the other mothers and fathers he took from everyone else."

Whatever he might think of the man's outdoor skills, Lorca could admire Denham's convictions. After all, there was a risk to what they were doing here, including a good chance that Kodos, if found and realizing he had nothing to lose, might decide to stage a last stand. Assuming that happened, there could be injuries—or worse. Denham, like the other civilian volunteers, was not carrying a phaser, as there were not enough of them to cover every member of the search party. The man had a knife on his belt along with a hatchet, and what Lorca recognized as a cricket bat sticking out of the top of his backpack. Lorca was not sure how effective such improvised weapons might be should a firefight break out, but he had to concede that the idea of employing the bat held some appeal.

Steady, Commander.

"Thanks for joining us, Brian. I appreciate it. You might want to think about switching to those boots before too long."

Denham smiled. "Sure thing."

Allowing the other man to move up the mountain path to rejoin his group of fellow volunteers, Lorca waited for Ensign Terri Bridges to catch up to him. Walking beside her and carrying a field pack similar to hers was Alexander Simmons.

"How's our guide?" asked Lorca. "Giving you any trouble?"

Bridges threw a sidelong glance toward Simmons. "Are you giving me trouble?"

"You threatened to throw me off a mountain if I did."

Grinning, Bridges looked to Lorca. "See? No trouble."

Lorca stifled the urge to laugh. "How are you holding up?"

"Well, I haven't hiked like this since Academy survival training, but I'll be okay. I think I should add something like this into my exercise routine, though."

"Maybe we can revise the training schedule once we're all back to our regular duties." Lorca turned his attention to Simmons. "Anything around here look familiar to you?"

The other man scowled. "It's a mountain. It looks a lot like the other ones."

"You understand I'm okay with Bridges throwing you off this one, right?" When Simmons made the wise choice not to reply, Lorca added, "You're here to help us home in on Kodos's location. If you can't do that, then I'll give you the push you need to roll your worthless ass back down to base camp. Do we understand each other?"

Simmons nodded. "We do."

The disgraced security officer had said little since the search party left behind the ground vehicles that could no longer traverse the rugged, angled terrain. The vehicles formed a perimeter around the small base camp established as a support station for Lorca and the group of twenty-five people who were continuing the hunt on foot. The search party was one of four distributed throughout the mountain region, each converging on the center of the area from a different direction while using whatever trail or other means available to maneuver over the unforgiving ground.

Unforgiving in more ways than one.

Lorca and the others knew going in that the natural geomagnetic activity taking place far beneath the surface would interfere with sensors and all but cancel out the ability to use transporters to beam anyone or anything to or from the region. Communications and even personal tricorders were other casualties of the situation, as Lorca quickly discovered once they were well away from the base camp and into the first of the mountain valleys assigned to his group's search grid. Tricorder scans of the area were inundated with the background interference, inhibiting their usefulness for anything beyond twenty to thirty meters. Communicators operated in similar fashion, unable to establish a reliable signal much beyond one hundred meters.

Anticipating this twist, Lorca had taken the precaution of preparing printed topographical surface maps of the region, generated from the *Narbonne*'s sensor scans of the entire mountain range. The maps would serve them only on the surface, but they—along with special compasses developed for use even in areas of the planet where the geomagnetic interference was strongest—would at least provide a sense of direction and distance traveled. He took it a step further by having Simmons mark on the maps where he believed Kodos and his followers had hiding places or caches of equipment, and even possible escape routes. Simmons was lacking when it came to information in that department, and some of his selections on the map made Lorca suspicious, but comparing his marks to sensor data of the region had given him no reason to either accept or deny the security officer's insights. Given that reality, Lorca reminded himself of what he told Georgiou about this entire plan.

There's only one way to find out if it'll work.

He could adapt to the lack of tricorders, sensors, or transporters, but the inability to summon reinforcements, either from the camp or the *Narbonne* crew, was more than a little concerning. They would just have to adapt and rely on the tried and trusted method of "sweep and clear" search missions the way he conducted them as a junior ensign undertaking reconnaissance forces operations and later during Starfleet security training. As his instructors took great glee in reminding him, technology was never a substitute for "boots on the ground."

Lorca fell into step beside Simmons, taking the opportunity to scan the column of men and women working their way up the hill behind and ahead of him. The route they were traversing was not so much an established path as it was simply a natural groove cut into the rolling hillside, likely the result of water runoff over the course of millennia. At his instructions, the column proceeded through the valley and into the foothills while maintaining intervals of four to five meters between individuals. It was a habit from his ground forces days that Lorca had never shaken, and being in here, in this place, under load and carrying a weapon while hunting an enemy, had brought long-dormant skills and experience to the fore.

At the head of the loose formation was Lieutenant Jason Giler, who along with a dozen members of the *Narbonne*'s security detachment accounted for half of the search team. Four members of his detail were spread to either side of the column, acting as sweepers to ensure no one approached the group from their flanks. The rest of the party was comprised of civilians like Brian Denham, who were doing their best to compensate for their lack of field skills with an eagerness to contribute to the cause. However, a couple of the people Lorca chose to join the search did possess at least some outdoors experience, along with a rough familiarity with this region. This he welcomed, as relying on Alexander Simmons for all of his on-site intel was not a sound tactical plan. Lorca was still expecting the security officer to pull some kind of play, either to escape or to warn Kodos or anyone else who might be nearby that danger was approaching. His gut told him Simmons would not betray them so much as act in his own self-interest, but that would be enough for Lorca to make good on his threat.

We'll see.

"Are there any landmarks we should be looking for?" he asked, glancing toward Simmons. "Subtle clues left for anyone coming to join Kodos and the others?" Even knowing what to look for with respect to detecting passage through an area, Lorca had seen nothing to indicate the presence of anyone who had no reason to be here. No footprints, dislodged rocks, or flattened vegetation, and no trash or other evidence of sentient yet sloppy beings on the move. Experience told him this was conclusive of nothing, either because Kodos and his people knew how to conceal their movements, or else they had taken a different path through the region.

Assuming they came through here at all.

A flash of light and a muffled explosion from somewhere ahead of them made Lorca flinch, and he looked up the hill to see a body being thrown off his or her feet several meters through the air before landing with a heavy thud on the hillside. A cloud of dirt shrouded the figure as it rolled a few extra meters along the ground before coming to rest against a rock outcropping.

Hearing the shouts of alarm from other members of the search party and without thinking, Lorca grabbed Simmons with his left hand and dropped to one knee, dragging the other man with him. His other hand had drawn the phaser from its holster on his waist, and he brought up the weapon, glancing at its power level and confirming it was set to stun. From the corner of his eye, he saw Ensign Bridges mimicking his movements. Around them, he noted how other members of the team were crouching or lying on the ground, weapons up and assuming defensive positions as everyone scanned for other threats. No one spoke, and Lorca listened and looked for telltale signs of an approaching attack, but heard nothing.

"Dear god," said Bridges, keeping her voice low. "Was that Giler?"

Lorca was already attempting to determine who the casualty might be, and it took little time to figure out based on where the explosive detonated that it had to be Giler. The security detachment commander was leading them all up the hill, and would be the likely victim of any sort of . . .

Booby trap?

"I don't believe this."

Instructing Bridges to remain with Simmons, Lorca rose to a low crouch and began moving up the hill toward the fallen figure. As he passed other members of the search party, he gestured for them to maintain their positions. His eyes darted about the ground ahead of him, searching for anything that appeared out of place or otherwise did not belong. He saw nothing, and yet every rock or clump of grass was a potential danger. It took him the better part of a minute to reach what he saw was the unmoving form of Jason Giler. The lieutenant had landed on his back, his torso elevated by the field pack beneath him. Blood ran from several wounds on his face, and a significant portion of his torso, including his uniform jacket, was blackened. Kneeling next to him, Lorca pressed the first two fingers of his left hand against the side of the other man's neck, searching for a pulse. He found none.

"Damn it."

Phaser held before him in both hands, Lorca swept the weapon from side to side, but saw no signs of anyone else ahead of him along the hillside. His eyes did fall on a section of ground, just beneath a large hunk of rock protruding from the soil. Damp, dark soil along with bits of stone littered the ground leading to the hole, scattered in an undeniable blast pattern.

A proximity trigger.

It was the one thing that made the most sense, given the visual evidence. Lorca was familiar with the devices, having received training long ago on their use in tactical situations. In those cases, they were employed as defensive measures, such as aiding to secure a perimeter in anticipation of an attack. Even then, they were meant as deterrents, used to activate sensory disruption devices by releasing bursts of intense light or sound. The use of proximity triggers to activate antipersonnel explosives had been outlawed by the Federation and Starfleet for nearly a century.

"Commander?"

Glancing over his shoulder, Lorca saw Ensign Bridges working her way toward him, prodding a very reluctant Simmons to walk ahead of her. When her eyes fell on Giler's stricken form, her eyes widened as the color drained from her face.

"Oh, no," was all the ensign could muster before averting her gaze.

Lorca stepped toward Simmons. "What the hell is this?" He grabbed Simmons by the strap of his backpack and pulled, flinging him toward the ground, where he landed on his hands and knees next to Giler. "Goddamned booby traps?"

"I don't know anything about it!" pleaded Simmons, holding up his empty hands. "I swear I don't know why they'd do something like this."

"To slow down anybody trying to track them," said Bridges. "Or maybe it's a signal, and now they know we're here."

Lorca said, "They likely wouldn't bother with something like this if they weren't protecting something, either their camp or a supply or escape route. It could be part of a security perimeter. For all we know, we've wandered into their damned backyard." He turned to Simmons. "Care to comment?"

"I think we may be close." The other man all but stammered his reply.

"Uh-huh."

Behind Bridges, other members of the search party were clambering up the hillside, their expressions all displaying varying degrees of shock and horror as they got their first look at Giler. Lorca waved to one of the Starfleet officers, Lieutenant Reece O'Bannon, whom he knew only as Giler's assistant security detachment commander. As he stepped closer and saw the body of his friend, O'Bannon's face clouded with sorrow and anger.

"I'm sorry, Lieutenant. He was killed instantly."

O'Bannon nodded. "Thank you, Commander." He paused, looking around as though taking stock of the rest of the search party and their surroundings. "There may be more of those things, sir. What do you want us to do?"

"First, secure Lieutenant Giler." Lorca checked the chronometer he wore strapped to his left wrist. "It'll be dark soon, so we'll make camp here for the night. I hate to leave Giler here once we move out again in the morning."

"I've already done the math, sir," O'Bannon replied. "Two of my men can take him to base camp and be back here well before sunup." He glanced once more to Giler. "I won't have any trouble finding a couple of volunteers."

Uncomfortable with that idea, Lorca said, "I'd rather no one walk around here after dark, at least not beyond any area we clear of other . . . surprises." He could not help glancing to Giler as he spoke. "We'll organize a sweep party with tricorders to scan the immediate area and secure it for the night, and disable any other devices we might find. In the morning, your volunteers can take the lieutenant back to base camp. When the rest of us head out tomorrow, anyone leading the column will be scanning the ground ahead for possible threats." Once more, he regarded Giler's unmoving form, and this time he felt anger rising within him. "We're not losing anyone else to those damned things."

"Finding a volunteer to walk point might be harder, sir," said Bridges, before turning her attention to Simmons. "But I do have a suggestion."

"That's a mighty fine idea, Ensign." Lorca smiled at the security officer, who appeared none too happy about the conversation's new direction.

"Don't I get a say in this?" asked Simmons. Fear laced his every word.

Forcing himself not to give voice to his barely restrained annoyance with the man and any companions of his who might be lurking nearby, Lorca gestured to Giler.

"Talk it over with him."

26

Enamori Jenn was tired, and the easiest way to demonstrate her mounting fatigue was to release a long, loud yawn.

"That's pretty good," said Aasal Soltani, keeping pace beside her as the two of them walked the service corridor of the power distribution station.

Jenn eyed him. "What is?"

"I thought you were imitating the mating call of the Kreemorian fangor beast. It's a worthy impression."

Unable to stifle a laugh, Jenn shook her head. "No, that's not what I was doing, and how do you know what such an animal sounds like anyway?" Though she knew of the Kreemorian system, she had never visited the lush jungles of the second planet where the fabled predators thrived.

"We undertook survival training there during my third year at the Academy," replied Soltani. "They warned us about them several times during our premission briefings, but nothing prepares you for seeing one up close." He grimaced. "Nothing."

"You saw one? Up close?"

The computer specialist nodded. "Pretty close. Until I started running, that is. Thankfully, they don't like the water, so I swam a lot that day."

Laughing again, Jenn offered him a mock scowl. "Now you're joking with me."

"Would I lie to you? Check the Academy's archived historical documents. Our training mission reports are all there."

For the briefest of moments, Jenn wondered if Soltani might be having a bit of fun at her expense. She considered breaking her personal rule of not reading the thoughts of coworkers and other colleagues. Doing so would be simple enough, but was also a betrayal of trust, so far as she was concerned. There were many Betazoids who harbored no compunctions about such things, and in truth it would be far easier for Jenn to do so, instead of blocking out the minds of those around her. On her homeworld of Betazed, the ethics of such choices were left to the individual to determine for themselves. Still, in a society where almost everyone could know everyone else's innermost thoughts and feelings, anything less than total honesty seemed a waste of time, and Betazoid civilization evolved over generations to embrace the tenets of openness and transparency.

This was fine, so long as Betazoids remained isolated unto themselves. Such views could not last once it was learned that other planets harbored their own advanced societies, and interaction with them became inevitable. The first challenge to Betazoid cultural mores came less than a decade ago, when scientists successfully launched a ship capable of traveling faster than light and discovered eyes from worlds not their own were watching. Jenn had only just reached adolescence when the Starfleet ship settled into orbit around Betazed and government leaders were visited by travelers from a distant star system. No, not just a single star, as the vessel brought with it representatives of several civilizations. Faced with an unprecedented decision, the planet's various government representatives met in secret, making the determination that keeping their psionic abilities a private matter was the best course, at least until more could be learned about their new interstellar acquaintances.

The issue arose once more after Betazed joined the Federation, and Jenn was among the first Betazoids to attend Starfleet Academy. Once more, it was decided to keep this information from non-Betazoids, but even government leaders knew that should their world apply for full Federation membership, they would no longer be able to maintain their secret.

For now, though, she was content to abide by her people's wishes.

"Are you all right?" asked Soltani, and Jenn realized she had allowed her mind to wander.

"I'm fine." Another yawn was threatening to escape and echo within the passageway, and she covered her mouth. Their inspection of the distribution station at Commander Georgiou's request was the cap on what already had been a very long day. Indeed, the fourteen hours she had worked today was but the latest in what was threatening to become a string of long days. Jenn comprehended the need to pitch in where needed and the priority of making sure all of the city's utility services were online and functioning, but that did nothing for her mounting fatigue.

"We're almost finished," said Soltani, and she heard the sympathy and understanding in his voice. "Another hour at most, and we're out of here."

Jenn replied, "On the other hand, I'm not really looking forward to sleeping on that shelf aboard the ship." She had to think for a moment to recall when she last slept in a decent bed. The berthing compartment provided for her aboard the *Narbonne* lacked much when compared to her quarters on Starbase 11.

Footsteps echoed from the corridor ahead of them, announcing the arrival of Vanessa Chandra, the power plant's operations manager.

"Good evening," she said, smiling upon seeing the two

Starfleet officers. "I was sure you'd have finished and made your escape from this dungeon."

Returning the greeting, Jenn said, "We're almost finished. Even though the interruptions you experienced weren't that extensive, Commander Georgiou insisted we give the entire place one last once-over before finalizing our inspection. So we're doing another walk-through and then calling it a night."

Chandra's smile widened. "Have to keep the bosses happy, right?"

Jenn recalled from her review of the manager's personnel record that she was a native of Tarsus IV, born soon after her parents' arrival thirty-four years earlier. Despite her heritage, traces of an accent were still detectable, at least to Jenn's ears, hinting at her family roots somewhere in the Indian subcontinent region on Earth. Chandra was dressed in a set of gray coveralls with her access credentials pinned to her collar. This, along with her black hair pulled back from her face and secured in a tight bun, made Chandra look every bit the hardworking, dedicated engineer thrust unwillingly into a leadership position. Jenn knew this to be true, as the other woman had made a point of announcing that to anyone who might be within earshot at any given moment. Despite her recent promotion to the manager's billet, Chandra insisted on maintaining a hands-on approach to the plant's operation. If that meant crawling through a service conduit to repair a piece of equipment at the expense of finalizing a status report to her supervisors, then so be it. Jenn had taken an instant liking to her.

Soltani asked, "Anything new we should know about before we wrap up for the night?"

Shaking her head, Chandra replied, "Not a thing. I've just come from the control room and all the status lights are green. I was about to do my own last rounds before turning it over to the second-shift supervisor. You can tag along with me if you like."

The trio set off, heading deeper into the distribution center's maze of corridors, catwalks, service crawlways, and access conduits. Despite all of the machinery and support equipment contained within this three-story structure, noise-suppression materials saw to it that any potentially harmful sounds were shielded. This allowed the plant's crew to move about the facility without the need for hearing protection, except for those areas where coming into proximity with the equipment was unavoidable.

"Most of the damage we sustained was confined to outside the building," said Chandra as they walked, passing a pair of engineers working in front of an open access panel that looked stuffed with all manner of computer and electrical circuitry and other components. Both technicians, a man and a woman, nodded at their approach and offered polite greetings.

Soltani said, "The report indicated the damage wasn't all that extensive."

"A couple of distribution conduits and some protective shielding, but nothing too serious," replied Chandra. "Taking the plant offline was more a safety consideration, while my people finished the repairs, than anything else. Besides, it gave us a chance to test our disaster recovery and backup procedures. Most people in the city didn't even notice anything, as the other two plants were able to shoulder the load."

She paused, and Jenn saw her expression change. It was a look she had seen many times since all of this began, and once more she sensed a surge of emotions as Chandra recalled unpleasant memories. Despite this, Jenn resisted the urge to take in the other woman's thoughts. The feelings alone were sufficient to communicate the grief being confronted. She had lost someone to Kodos and his executioners, and the level of emotional intensity was enough to tell Jenn that it was someone close.

As though realizing her change in demeanor was being noticed, Chandra cleared her throat and redirected her attention back to Jenn and Soltani. "I'm sorry. It's just that . . ." She let the sentence fade on her lips.

"It's all right," said Soltani, laying a hand on her forearm. "We understand."

"I'm sure you've heard similar stories since you got here." It was a noble attempt to erect a brave front, though Jenn saw through the ruse.

"But we haven't heard it from you," she said.

Reaching up to wipe a tear from the corner of her right eye, Chandra offered a small laugh that Jenn knew was forced.

"We'd only been seeing each other for a couple of months. I met her at one of the bars in the arts district, and we just sort of hit it off. She'd had a bad breakup and didn't want to stay on Tarsus IV anymore. There was a bag packed and lying at her feet in the bar when we met. Anything that didn't fit, she was happy to leave behind."

Chandra's wide brown eyes were watering as she recalled the memory. "I'd been out of a bad relationship for about six months, so I knew where she was coming from. We talked all night, and she decided to stay. I didn't even see her for a week after that, and then one day she's standing at my front door." Once more, the smile returned. "I was happier than I'd been in a long time, and so was she. We were already talking long-term plans, and then . . ." She waved a hand in the air in front of her face. "Then all this happened."

Feelings of catharsis and even relief washed over Jenn as Chandra spoke. It was apparent that the mourning woman had spoken with no one about her personal tragedy and had been looking for an outlet. She needed to give voice to her grief and finally was finding some sense of inner peace. After a moment, Chandra wiped her eyes, and her expression softened.

"I'm sorry. I didn't mean to burden you with all of that."

"It's fine," replied Jenn. "Really."

A beeping tone echoed in the passageway, making Chandra turn toward a communications panel set into the nearby wall. A red indicator was flashing, and the panel's speaker grille erupted with a loud, anxious male voice that Jenn recognized.

"Attention, all personnel. This is Supervisor Maharaj. We have an unauthorized entry. First level, west entrance. Emergency lockdown protocols are in effect. Secure your stations, and report to central control."

Confusion and concern darkening her features, Chandra looked to Jenn and Soltani. "What the hell?" Reaching for the comm panel, she slapped its activation control. "Chandra to control room. Ravi, what's going on?"

Over the open channel, the distribution plant's second-shift supervisor, Ravishankar Maharaj, replied, *"We're still figuring it out, Vanessa. The west entrance access lock is off-line, and internal scans show that door was opened from the outside. Then everything on the main board went dark. I don't have any of the sensors or—"*

The rest of Maharaj's report was lost in a burst of static followed by a low hum coming from the comm panel's speaker.

"Ravi?" Chandra tapped the panel's control pad again. "Ravi, are you there?" Looking back to Jenn and Soltani, she said, "It's dead."

Jenn, drawing her phaser from its holster on her belt, motioned to Chandra. "If there are intruders, we can't stay here." Soltani's memories of losing Piotr and Meizhen came rushing back, threatening to pummel her. "There's no way to know what they want, or what they'll do to get it."

"There's a stairwell at the end of this corridor," said Soltani, holding his phaser in both hands. "We can use it to get to the control room."

They made it halfway to the stairs before Jenn reached for Soltani's arm, halting their advance.

"Wait," she warned, her voice just above a whisper.

Soltani looked around, sweeping the passageway in both directions. "What is it?"

"On the stairs. Someone's coming."

Turning to aim his weapon toward the stairwell, Soltani said, "I don't hear anything."

"Neither do I," added Chandra.

Jenn had not heard anything either. Instead, she had picked up the two sets of thoughts growing closer with every passing second. It had taken little effort to detect the pair of individuals, both males. One of the men was worried about making noise on the stairs while keeping from slipping. Unable to explain any of this, Jenn instead motioned her companions to back away from the stairwell before advancing on the doorway, phaser up and ready.

The first man appeared at the threshold leading to the stairs. Dressed in dark clothes and a mask covering his face, he made a perfect target. Jenn saw his eyes widen in surprise as she fired, the single stun beam catching him in the chest. He was still falling back into the stairwell when Jenn stepped forward, seeing the man's friend reacting to the sudden attack. She pressed the phaser's firing stud again and the other man crumpled.

"Ena!"

Jenn whirled at Soltani's shout of warning to see the lieutenant and Chandra crouching against the wall of the passageway. Soltani was firing his own weapon at another pair of figures near the corridor's far end. The new arrivals were responding to the threats in their midst but Soltani was faster, taking both intruders in seconds.

"Never mind," he said, tossing a sheepish grin toward Jenn.

"Want to bet there are more of them?" she asked.

Chandra said, "They may be heading for the control room. We have to get up there, or at least warn somebody."

"Yes." Jenn reached for her communicator. "We definitely need to warn somebody." She had no idea if anyone on the *Narbonne* was monitoring critical facilities like the power distribution plants and watching for any deviations from their normal operation. Maybe the intruders were able to mask their infiltration. If that was the case, then she along with Soltani, Chandra, and everyone else in this building might well be cut off from help. She flipped open her communicator.

"Jenn to Commander Georgiou."

Nothing. Not even static.

This can't be good.

Her initial feeling was only strengthened when the lights went out, and she heard the telltale sound of equipment shutting down.

Everything seemed to be going offline. Right now.

27

"Are we ready?"

Cradling in his left elbow the phaser rifle he had taken from one of the New Anchorage security forces armories, Joel Pakaski stood behind his computer specialist, Hisayo Fujimura, watching as the young woman's hands moved over the workstation's array of multicolored buttons and switches. He noted that the other three members of his team, all of them dressed like him and Fujimura in black jumpsuits, were positioned at each of the doors leading from the power distribution plant's entrances, making sure no one would disturb them during these next critical minutes.

"Almost there. Just a few more minutes," replied Fujimura without looking up from her work.

Pakaski tried not to look at either of the room's two wall chronometers, or even the smaller model strapped to his wrist. It would not help to stare at their numbers as they advanced with agonizing slowness while he and the others waited for Fujimura to complete her infiltration of the plant's computer system. With nothing to do, he looked to the three unconscious technicians in their midst. One lay on the floor where she had fallen after being stunned, and her two male companions were slumped in the chairs at their respective workstations.

Studying the three insensate plant employees, Pakaski

was satisfied with his decision not to kill them. There had been enough death in the last handful of days, and he would be glad to be liberated from it. That freedom was in his grasp, perhaps less than an hour away, if all went according to plan.

"I'm in," reported Fujimura. "I've accessed the system's security protocols. Starting my bypass." The thin, petite Asian was all business, her attention moving between the control console and the portable computer interface she brought with her just for this task. After uncounted hours spread across the past three days, forgoing decent sleep and taking her meals at a field desk in the underground hideaway far beneath Mount Bonestell, her efforts were about to pay off in a major fashion.

She had already circumvented the plant's internal security sensors, having accomplished that by plugging into a data terminal in the first office they found upon entering the building. The bypass was easy enough to mask, at least long enough for Pakaski to lead his team to the plant's main control room and incapacitate the employees on duty here. The supervisor, a middle-aged man of Indian descent who took his job seriously, was already figuring out something was wrong when Pakaski and the others arrived. A general alert to anyone else in the building could not be prevented, and Pakaski was forcing himself not to count seconds before someone decided to take action. His growing nervousness was not helped when Fujimura put into motion the next phase of her attack on the plant's infrastructure by disabling computer access and main power throughout most of the complex, with the notable exception of the control room along with the plant's primary power source and the outgoing distribution network. That action carried with it the risk of being detected from somewhere beyond the plant itself, a reality that only heightened Pakaski's anxiety.

He consulted his wrist chronometer. In truth, almost ten minutes had elapsed since their taking of the plant's control room. How had their presence gone undetected for such a stretch of time? Were Fujimura's efforts to hide their activities that effective, or was their good fortune a product of simple luck? Pakaski had no desire to learn the answer to that question.

"Hisayo," he prompted.

"Working on it." Her tone was one of mild irritation, and Pakaski let her have it. Fujimura was a former civilian employee of the city's security forces, and her habit was to become hyperfocused on the task right in front of her, almost to the exclusion of all other stimuli. Distractions only served to stoke her annoyance, and she had no qualms about making her displeasure known, regardless of the recipient of her ire. Supervisors and watch commanders had long ago quit bothering to counsel her on her behavior, as they learned her greatest value lay in her technical acumen rather than people skills.

Of course, none of her work or eccentricities would matter if Fujimura was unable to execute the results of that labor, or if the plant's other employees were able to stage an organized defense of the building, or if they received help from the Starfleet crew, of which Pakaski knew two were somewhere in the building. They were an unexpected crimp in his overall plan, but they could be handled, provided no reinforcements were summoned. As part of her preparations, Fujimura had anticipated this possibility and brought with her the equipment necessary to jam communications to and from the plant. With the exception of their own communications devices, all of which were locked on a specific frequency, all other channels were inaccessible. This included the communicators carried by Starfleet personnel.

"Hey! Somebody's coming!"

Pakaski heard the warning from one of his men mere heartbeats before phaser fire erupted from somewhere outside the control room. The man guarding the door closest to that action flinched, trying to press himself against the wall while aiming his weapon into the passageway and returning fire. Recognizing the distinctive high pitch of the weapons being fired from the corridor, Pakaski knew the identity of their new adversaries.

Starfleet.

"Hisayo!" he shouted as he moved to help the man holding position at the door. "Damn it, they're here!"

Fujimura turned in her seat. "I'm in. I've circumvented all the safety protocols, and we can initiate the sequence whenever you're ready."

"Do it," snapped Pakaski. Moving closer to the door, he fired three times into the corridor, shooting more to provide cover than with any real hope of finding actual targets. He was sure he caught sight of at least two figures lurking in the shadows of the dimly lit passageway, but he could not be sure.

Glancing behind him, he shouted, "Now, Hisayo!"

Nodding, Fujimura flashed a knowing smile before turning back to the workstation. Once more, her fingers moved across both the keypad of her portable computer terminal and the rows of buttons on the console as she entered yet another sequence of instructions. Then, she leaned back in her seat, the index finger of her right hand poised with dramatic flair over a blinking red button.

"Time to wake the neighbors."

She pressed the button, and only then did Pakaski realize he was holding his breath and clenching his jaw. Then he saw one of the figures moving in the hallway again and fired in its direction. His effort resulted in another miss.

Come on, Hisayo. Come on!

Looking to where Fujimura remained at her station, Pakaski saw several indicators on the control room's main status board had flipped from green to red. An alarm began sounding from a recessed speaker in the ceiling, which Fujimura disabled by touching another control. From his vantage point, Pakaski could make out the status board's display screens, each of which was scrolling lines of text generated by the plant's automated oversight system. The monitors were all providing him with small portions of a larger, multifaceted story that he was eager to see.

"Power surge is at one hundred eighty-four percent of normal energy flow," reported Fujimura. "Just as I expected, no safety protocols are kicking in. That should be more than enough."

"Hey! Somebody's coming!"

Damn it.

Hearing the shout of alarm, Enamori Jenn wondered what she had done to give away her presence to the man standing watch a mere ten meters in front of her, just inside the east door leading to the power plant's control room. Not that it was important anymore. What mattered was that the pale man with red hair and brandishing a security forces phaser had seen her. Further, his reactions were in keeping with someone who was the recipient of extensive law enforcement or military weapons training, which is to say that without hesitation he took aim and fired at her.

Jenn felt a hand on her arm an instant before she was yanked to her left. The intervention was fortunate, in that it removed her from the line of fire just as a bright red energy beam sliced through the space she had occupied a second earlier. It was Soltani, pulling her to the other side of the corridor, which was afforded small measure of concealment thanks to the orientation of the control room door and the position of the guard just inside it. Without a direct line of sight to his quarry, the guard was forced to shift his position in the hopes of getting a better shot.

Soltani was not about to give him that, and instead fired his own phaser three times, then twice more in the direction of the door. The man inside ducked away from the entrance.

"Watch out!"

Vanessa Chandra's warning gave Soltani time to move aside just before more phaser fire emerged from the control room. Emergency battery-powered lighting provided the only illumination in the corridor, and the resulting shadows served as meager concealment. So long as their opponents stayed within the well-lit control room, it would be harder for them to see who was shooting at them.

"What do we do?" asked Jenn.

Chandra replied, "They have access to the entire plant from that room. I have no idea what they want, but if it's in there, then it can't be good."

Then everything went dark. Again.

Unlike the power loss that had plunged most of the plant into near-darkness, this time a massive, metallic snapping sound accompanied the outage. Ahead of hers, she saw the control room fall victim to this latest failure.

"Oh, shit," said Chandra. "I think they just took the entire plant offline."

Soltani asked, "Do you have backup generators?"

"For the offices and workspaces, sure," replied the plant supervisor. "But the distribution network itself is down. All the power requirements for the city are being handled by the other two plants, until this one can be brought back online, and that doesn't happen automatically. There are diagnostics to be run, switches and relays to be reset, and a few other checks before we can bring it all back up. The whole process takes over an hour, and that's assuming whoever did this didn't destroy everything we need to do that."

"We didn't."

The voice echoed in the corridor, followed by the three of them being bathed in the bright beam of a flashlight. Then phaser fire lanced forward from the direction of the control room, catching Chandra in the chest. She sagged against Soltani, who barely managed to keep her from falling face-first to the corridor floor. Jenn turned toward the control room, bringing up her phaser.

"Don't even think about it!" The warning came with another energy beam that tore into the wall to her left, slicing through the metal. Jenn froze as the male voice that had given the command instructed, "Drop your weapons."

Both Soltani and Jenn did as they were told, holding up empty hands. Next to her, she heard Soltani trying to hold Chandra's limp form. Glancing in his direction, she saw him lowering her body to the floor.

"Ena," he said, his tone low and anxious. "Chandra's dead."

There was no chance to process this latest unsettling news before Jenn heard footsteps and the beam's source began drawing closer. She could not see who was holding the flashlight, but she could sense at least three sets of thoughts.

"What do we do with them?" asked another voice.

Jenn heard a metallic click before the man who gave the initial orders—and perhaps killed Vanessa Chandra—spoke again.

"Take them with us."

28

Darkness swallowed the passageway around Georgiou as the lights went out. Sparks swiped at the blackness around her as circuits overloaded and lighting fixtures exploded, triggering alarms in the corridor. No sooner did the primary illumination disappear than it was replaced by emergency lamps positioned at regular intervals along the passageway. She was also aware of the omnipresent thrum of the *Narbonne*'s internal generators fading. Even the airflow from the ship's environmental control processes ceased, making more prominent the sounds of clicks and beeps as battery-operated backup systems activated.

What the hell just happened?

A dull hum was beginning to emanate through the deck plating, and as she leaned against a bulkhead Georgiou felt a mild reverberation in its metal surface. To her left and right, members of the ship's crew were stumbling into the passageway through half-open doorways—the ones they had been able to pry apart, at least.

"Commander Georgiou," said a voice, and she saw Lieutenant Melissa Parham making her way up the corridor toward her. "Are you all right?"

Georgiou nodded as the *Narbonne*'s helm officer closed the distance. "I'm fine. Just a little disoriented. What's going on?"

"No idea, but if I had to guess, I'd say some kind of overload or power surge. We're hooked into the spaceport's primary power hub, which gets fed from a distribution plant that also supplies energy to the city. If all our onboard generators and regulators are offline, this is likely a shipwide problem. I'm on my way to the bridge."

Indicating she would follow the lieutenant, Georgiou fell in behind Parham as the younger woman led the way through the dimly lit passageway that was the ship's main thoroughfare on this level. They passed other members of the crew, most of whom appeared to have gotten past their initial, momentary shock and were moving to duty stations or participating in damage control parties. Georgiou overheard snippets of instructions and reports as training and procedures came to the fore and the crew turned to their various tasks.

"Captain Korrapati trains you all very well," observed Georgiou.

Parham replied, "We may not pass too many fancy inspections or be the prettiest to look at, but don't let the grungy coveralls fool you, Commander. When we have to, we can turn and burn just like any ship of the line."

As they moved forward, the more Georgiou saw that the crew's efforts were already having an effect, with at least some of the main corridor lighting being restored. Upon their reaching the bridge, all of the alarms that had been sounding in the passageways were gone, replaced by rhythmic sequences of beeps and tones as diagnostic protocols were activated on various workstations, access panels, and other control surfaces.

Georgiou followed Parham through the doorway to the bridge, and saw Captain Korrapati standing at the center of the room, overseeing the controlled chaos around him. The smell of smoke, from burned insulation, optical cabling, and other composite materials, fouled the air, along with the recognizable odor of fire suppressant. Members of the ship's crew were at every station, and Georgiou saw that several screens were blown out, along with scorched control consoles and more than a few blown illumination strips.

"Welcome to the party," said Korrapati upon noticing them.

Parham, moving to the helm console, asked, "What happened, sir?"

"An immense power surge from the distribution plant. It's affected the entire spaceport and a good portion of the city as well. There are overloads and circuit burnouts everywhere, and the plant itself appears to be offline."

"What about emergency facilities?" asked Georgiou. "The hospital?"

Korrapati frowned. "We don't know if they got hit, but they have emergency generators and other backup systems if they need them. I suspect the same is true for other first-response assets. Once we get everything sorted out here, we can start checking with colony administration to assess the damage."

"Looks like we got hammered pretty good," said Parham. The helm officer had eschewed her chair and instead was leaning over her console. Georgiou could see from the rows of indicators and other readouts that the lieutenant was running status checks and collecting information being relayed to the bridge from other areas of the ship.

"We lost about forty percent of our power relays," offered Commander Natalie Larson as she stepped from the primary sensor control station along the bridge's starboard bulkhead. "There are more blown breakers than I can count. Engineering's going to have their hands full for a while."

Georgiou asked, "Aren't we shielded from this kind of thing?"

"We are, at least to an extent," replied the *Narbonne*'s first officer. She let her gaze drift around the bridge. "On the other hand, this is an older ship, and we don't have state-of-the-art systems like line ships are getting. They'll likely scrap us before giving us that kind of upgrade."

Standing next to his command seat, Korrapati laid his hand on the chair's armrest. "That said, she held up pretty well, all things considered."

Larson nodded. "True enough, sir." For Georgiou's benefit, she added, "Primary power distribution was knocked offline, but not damaged. Backup systems are up and running, which is good enough for now. Primaries will be back online within a half hour or so. After that, it'll mostly be overloads and burnouts that'll need replacing or rerouting until engineering can get to everything."

A hum from the front of the bridge caught Georgiou's attention, and she looked to see the main viewscreen coming back to life. The screen flashed a sequence of colors and then a string of indecipherable, encoded text indicating the imaging software was resetting and running through its startup diagnostics. A moment later the picture coalesced into a view of the spaceport as though Georgiou was looking through a window in the *Narbonne*'s bow.

Almost everything was dark.

"Sensors are still rebooting," reported Commander Larson from where she had returned to the sensor station she was using to oversee damage control and repairs. "But we've got enough to give us a look around the area. The entire spaceport went offline thanks to the surge, and at least thirty-seven percent of New Anchorage is also affected." She tapped several controls before consulting one of the console's readouts. "Commander Georgiou, the hospital looks to be running on their backup generators."

"Thank you, Commander." Georgiou frowned. "Aren't

there procedures in place to prevent this kind of thing from happening? At the power plants, I mean."

Larson nodded. "There should be. The plants are supposed to have multiple redundant protocols designed to prevent surges like this from running unchecked. According to our sensors before they were knocked out, the power surge that hit us was nearly twice what we're supposed to be receiving. Assuming the plant's safety protocols are active and there are no maintenance issues with the physical equipment, that sort of overload should be impossible, two or three times over."

"So the plant that's supplying us with power while we're on the ground just happens to produce an uncontrolled energy surge," said Korrapati. "And we get caught in the middle of it? Am I the only one who thinks that sounds suspicious?"

"No, sir," replied Georgiou. Then, recalling something she should have remembered sooner, she cursed herself and pulled her communicator from a uniform pocket. "We've got people there. Soltani and Jenn. They were assisting with final inspections of the plant after the damage it took during some of the protests."

"The communications array's still offline," said Larson. "It'll be up in a couple of minutes."

Georgiou glanced toward the hatchway leading from the bridge. "I can go check on them myself then." To Korrapati, she said, "Request permission for a security detail to accompany me, sir."

"Our transporters are offline and won't be back for at least thirty minutes. By the time you get there, comm will be back up," replied the captain. "Let's just take a breath and make sure we're not running off in all directions without a plan. If this was a coordinated strike, there may be more to it." As though sensing Georgiou's imminent protest, he raised a hand. "If we get comm and are unable to reach the team at the plant, then you can go."

Returning to her work, Larson called out, "I think you may be onto something, Captain. Something's going on." Both hands were working different sets of controls at the sensor station, and without looking away from the console, she continued, "We can receive incoming transmissions. I'm tapping into the city's news feeds." She moved toward the communications station. "Ensign?"

"Already on it, Commander," replied Richard Doherty, the *Narbonne*'s communications officer. "We're not completely up and running just yet, but I can compensate. Pulling in one of the feeds now."

The ensign pressed another control, and the image on the main screen shifted again, displaying a well-dressed woman sitting at a desk and framed by a backdrop of the New Anchorage skyline. At the bottom of the screen was a red banner highlighting a line of white text scrolling from right to left, informing viewers of a series of unexplained explosions occurring at various points around the city. Ensign Doherty had caught the broadcast with the news anchor midsentence, and when she spoke, her demeanor was composed and her tone was one of utter seriousness.

"*—six separate explosions have been confirmed. The targets appear to be buildings or facilities overseen by the city government, including the amphitheater, courthouse, two administration buildings, one security forces precinct, and a fire station. Authorities have no leads on who might be responsible, and no one has yet come forward to claim responsibility. Also unconfirmed is whether the incident at Power Station 2 and the problems it's caused since the unexplained power surge are connected to the bombings.*"

"Anybody want to wager against them being connected?" asked Korrapati.

Georgiou shook her head. "No, sir, and I'm betting we also know who's responsible."

A new alarm from the sensor station made them all turn to where Larson was consulting new readings being fed to her console.

"There's been a breach of the force field at the spaceport perimeter. The fields are being supported by backup generators, but one of them just went offline." She tapped another control. "I'm picking up an unauthorized vehicle entering the port grounds."

"Go to red alert," ordered Korrapati. "Recall anyone who's still outside, and secure all exterior hatches. Where is that vehicle heading?"

Larson replied, "Not for us, sir." A second later, she looked away from the console. "It's heading for one of the other transports. I just scanned them, Captain: only one was impacted by the power surge. The other one wasn't touched."

"Damn it," said Georgiou. "Somebody's trying to run for it." Could it be Kodos? Had the fugitive governor finally emerged from hiding, in a daring bid to make an escape?

Korrapati asked, "Do we have security people on the ground over there?"

"Just two, sir," replied Larson as she stepped away from the sensor console. "Request permission to—"

"Go," snapped the captain before gesturing to Georgiou. "Take the commander and a security detail. Secure that ship."

29

While the illumination from the trusty flashlight taken from her engineer's tool satchel was helpful, it did little to assuage Haley Carroll's unease.

"Wow, but it's damned dark out here. And spooky too." The moon was somewhat helpful, casting a pallid blue veneer over everything while doing little to chase away the shadows cast by the surrounding buildings.

Standing next to her, Ensign Dralax replied, "I am able to see well enough even without your light."

Carroll could not help but smile. "Sure, wave your Denobulan eyes in my face. How is it every species we humans meet ends up having something about their physiology that's superior to whatever we're born with?" She offered a grunt of mock disapproval. "Life is so unfair."

"Whatever the biological differences between our species," said Dralax, "it's not as though humanity has failed to make significant contributions to the interstellar community. You and your people have much to be proud of."

She chuckled as she reached for the communicator on her equipment belt. "Sure. Bring a bunch of planets together to form a club. Fight a couple of wars together. Help each other out during times of crisis. Still doesn't help me see in the dark, or live . . . how long do Denobulans live anyway?"

"Our average life spans can be as much as three hundred years as measured on Earth, Lieutenant."

"And you're practically immortal compared to us too. That's just great." She laughed to show she was having a bit of fun at her friend's expense. "And didn't I tell you to call me Haley? If we're going to be working together in the dark at all hours of the night, there's no need to be so formal."

"Very well, Haley."

Satisfied with her minor victory, Carroll smiled. The two of them were paired together for a four-hour shift of guard duty at the docking slips where the port's only two civilian transports were berthed. With the *Narbonne*'s crew stretched thin as it supported various efforts around New Anchorage as well as the search parties currently hunting Governor Kodos, anyone and everyone who could relieve the ship's overworked security detail for guard duty and other mundane tasks was being called into service. Even medics like Dralax and the civilian members from Starfleet's Corps of Engineers were not exempt from the boring yet necessary duty, and fate had seen fit to partner Carroll with the affable Denobulan. In truth, the walk with Dralax from the *Narbonne* was the most time she had spent with him since being assigned by Admiral Anderson to the ship and the Tarsus IV response team at Starbase 11. There had been little opportunity for socializing en route, with every member of the ship's baseline and extended crews focused on various preparations so they could be ready to render aid upon making planetfall. After the ship's arrival, everyone had turned to one task or another, working all hours of the day and night. The medical personnel in particular had been very busy, to the point that most of them, Dralax included, were taking brief sleep periods at the New Anchorage hospital.

We'll have at least four hours to get acquainted, assuming this little power hiccup isn't anything serious.

"Carroll to *Narbonne*," she said into her communicator after flipping it open. Static was the only reply to her call, which she repeated with the same result. She turned the device over in her hand, removing its back cover and inspecting its internal components. "There's nothing wrong with it. The problem must be on their end."

Dralax had also attempted to contact the ship with his own communicator, and was no more successful than Carroll. He said, "Perhaps the *Narbonne* was affected by whatever has caused the spaceport to lose power."

The two of them were walking from the ship toward the spaceport's other berthing spaces when darkness descended upon the entire area. Every exterior light and any visible illumination inside the surrounding buildings was extinguished, and Carroll heard the sound of an alarm as the force field encircling the spaceport failed. That was followed moments later by backup generators kicking in to ensure the field's continued operation, but power to the exterior lights was slower in returning, for reasons she did not understand. Faint glows were visible in some of the nearby lamps positioned along the walking paths and the service roads utilized by ground vehicles. In the distance, she could see the berthing spaces for visiting ships coming back to life.

Shouldn't take this long, should it?

"We should keep heading to the docking slips," she said. "Maybe the guys we're relieving will know something."

"That seems a prudent course of action," replied Dralax as the pair resumed walking in the direction of the docking berths.

The path they traversed led them past one of the spaceport's equipment hangars, which Carroll knew from her initial inspection was used for servicing small atmospheric craft and the one-person work pods used to deploy, retrieve, and service satellites in orbit around the planet. Beyond that structure, she could see the metal columns and immense sections of thermoconcrete forming the port's perimeter wall. On the wall's far side was the reassuring orange-yellow glow of the force field, which appeared to once again be operating at full strength following its brief interruption. One of the spaceport's secondary entrances was also visible, connected by a paved surface from the wall to the rest of the open tarmac at this end of the massive field. As for the hangar, its external lighting was restored, and she saw a few people milling about outside one of the open hangar doors. Inside the bay was a pair of work pods and an atmospheric skiff in various states of assembly. Carroll smiled, understanding and sympathizing with the crew assigned to such tasks at all hours of the day and night. The spaceport, like a starship, was in a constant state of operation.

Something, a new sound from somewhere near the wall, caught her attention, and she saw the section of force field protecting the nearby entrance wink out. It was followed by the revving of an engine, and then Carroll caught sight of the ground vehicle bearing down on the entry's metal gate arm. The vehicle's running lights were not active, cloaking it in the near darkness until it passed beneath one of the lamps overlooking the service road.

"Dralax?" was all she could muster before the vehicle crashed through the gate, wrenching it from its base and sending it flying away from the road to land in the nearby grass. The vehicle's speed did not diminish but instead increased as it passed through the entry and onto the spaceport tarmac.

Its arrival was not going unnoticed, as alarms began shrieking across the field within seconds of the breach. New lights snapped on across buildings and from lamps along the service road, adding brighter, more intense illumination to the entire area. The large, almost tank-like vehicle was plainly visible as it sped along the road, turning at the first intersection and accelerating as it headed directly for the berthing slips.

And the two transports docked there. Holy shit!

"Come on," she said, pulling at Dralax's arm as she started jogging after the vehicle. The Denobulan fell into step beside her and Carroll increased her pace, holding her satchel at her side and watching as the vehicle turned from the service road onto a connecting path toward the nearer of the two occupied docking berths. She changed direction, running across the grass in a bid to make up ground, but they were a hundred meters away and the vehicle was still moving.

"We cannot hope to overtake them," said Dralax.

Carroll replied, "No, but we can try to help whoever's at the gate when they get there." Even from this distance, she could see the gate separating the roadway from the docking slip, and two figures emerging from a small building near the entrance. Thanks to the glow of lamps above the building, she recognized the Starfleet uniforms they wore. Beyond them and inside the docking area, other people were moving about, dressed in different civilian attire. They had to be spaceport workers, perhaps dispatched following the power outage to assess damage.

The vehicle was not slowing down.

Joel Pakaski braced himself against the bulkhead of the personnel carrier's passenger compartment as his driver accelerated, pushing the machine ever faster toward the gate. Through the forward canopy, Pakaski saw two Starfleet officers drawing their weapons and taking aim, then throwing themselves out of the way to avoid being hit before the vehicle smashed through the docking slip's entry gate.

"What the hell are you doing?" snapped one of his Starfleet prisoners, who had given his name as Soltani. Both he and his companion, a woman named Ena-something Jenn, were doing their best to keep from being thrown from their own seats while their arms were secured with restraints behind their backs.

Ignoring Soltani, Pakaski kept his attention on the forward canopy. "Keep going!" He reached for a passenger strap dangling from the compartment's ceiling as the driver guided the carrier into a right turn. The impact with the gate had not slowed the vehicle at all, its heavy metal plating more than a match for the far weaker barrier placed before the entry.

In the wake of the power surge, this phase of the operation carried the greatest risk. The distractions caused by the overloads and the other explosions set off by members of his team would buy him precious little time. The Starfleet ship was likely in the midst of recovering from whatever setbacks the surge may have inflicted. Unlike its civilian counterparts here in the spaceport, the *Narbonne* would be shielded from such occurrences to a greater degree, and even a vessel not intended for space combat would still have systems designed to remain functional if ever it found itself in such a situation. Its crew likewise would be trained and prepared to handle unexpected crises like this, perhaps more so than the spaceport personnel. Even if the ship itself was in no condition to act against this new infiltration, its crew could still be deployed as a defensive measure.

So we need to get the hell out of here. Now.

"We're here!" shouted the driver, Benjamin Islip, and Pakaski felt himself pulled to the right as the carrier turned left and began braking. Even before the vehicle came to a stop, Pakaski was pressing the control to open the hatch at the rear of the passenger compartment. Essentially a fortified ramp, the hatch swung down from its frame, its far edge clanging against the tarmac and allowing light from the nearby lamps to flood the vehicle's interior.

"Let's go!" Pakaski was the first through the open hatchway, brandishing his phaser rifle and aiming back the way they had come. He saw two figures in Starfleet uniforms and fired without warning. His first shot caught one of the figures and spun him around, dropping him to the ground as his companion lunged to his left in search of cover. Pakaski's second shot caught him on the run and the man collapsed to the tarmac in a clumsy heap.

Shouts of warning from somewhere ahead of the carrier were echoing in the night air and bouncing off the docking slip's thermoconcrete walls. Pakaski turned toward the new sounds as Islip, exiting the vehicle's driver compartment, dropped to one knee and brought up his own phaser rifle. Ahead of Islip, at least three figures wearing what Pakaski recognized as security forces uniforms were emerging from a service passage at the docking berth's far end, weapons drawn. One of the officers managed to get off a shot before Islip returned fire. That was enough to send the new arrivals scrambling, though two of the men fired poorly aimed shots in the carrier's general direction.

Pakaski turned back to the carrier to see the other two members of his team leading Soltani and Jenn to the ground. Turning his phaser rifle on the two Starfleet officers, he waved to Islip. "Go and get them. I've got these two."

Keeping to the plan, Islip led the other two men away from the vehicle and deeper into the docking bay, leaving Pakaski standing with his two prisoners.

"What's this all about?" asked the woman, Jenn.

Once again, Pakaski opted not to answer, and instead looked past her to see Hisayo Fujimura descending the ramp. Her face was a mask of worry.

"We can't stay here!" she shouted. Wielding a phaser pistol in her left hand, she was holding her satchel close to her right hip. The bag contained her portable computer, the instigator of the evening's events, and it had one more task to complete before they were well away from New Anchorage and Tarsus IV.

Pakaski offered her a grim smile. "Don't worry, we're not. Come on." With the front of his phaser rifle, he indicated for Soltani and Jenn to begin walking toward the docking bay. "Move."

"Hey!"

There was no time to react to the new voice behind him before Pakaski heard and saw the first phaser beam streaking past his right shoulder. He pivoted, bringing around his rifle toward the new threat, and saw two more Starfleet officers near the berthing area's gate. Without waiting he fired as they came abreast of their two stunned companions, and they dropped to the ground. One of them, a female, had taken a knee while aiming in his direction. Her male partner was also crouching near one of his fallen comrades with a phaser in his hand. The woman was the more immediate threat, so he fired at her. She realized too late that he was not backing down or surrendering, and by then his phaser beam struck her left arm. She spun and fell unconscious to the tarmac.

"No!" shouted Soltani from behind him, but Pakaski was already taking aim at the remaining Starfleet officer, who was trying to use one of his unconscious friends for cover. He could not hide, though, and Pakaski's next shot took him high in the chest and he pitched forward, coming to rest atop his already stunned companion.

"Tell me you didn't kill them," snapped Jenn. She glared first at Pakaski and then to Fujimura, who stood nearby, covering her and Soltani with her phaser as she had throughout the brief firefight.

Pakaski shrugged. "I didn't kill them. They're just stunned." As with the employees incapacitated at the power plant, he saw no need to add any more deaths to what was already a long list. The woman killed while apprehending Soltani and Jenn was an unfortunate accident, a careless act perpetrated by one of his men that Pakaski regretted. It was a mistake he vowed not to repeat, but for the moment he needed to keep up appearances. With that in mind, he turned his phaser rifle toward his prisoners. "Don't make me regret that decision. Move."

With the Starfleet officers leading the way, Pakaski and Fujimura once more headed for the docking slip. Pakaski saw that the transport that was their target appeared to be operational. As part of the sabotage plan, he had instructed Fujimura to ensure this ship was not affected by the massive power burst sent from the distribution plant. While the surge wreaked havoc with the *Narbonne*, the other transport as well as the rest of the spaceport, and a significant portion of New Anchorage, this single ship was insulated from the attack. It was time to make use of their prize.

"Pakaski!" shouted Islip from where he stood near the transport's forward boarding ramp. "They're coming!" There could be no mistaking the dark-haired man's agitation.

Directing Jenn and Soltani toward the ramp, Pakaski asked, "Who?"

"Scans show more than a dozen people coming from the Starfleet ship, and additional security forces are also coming. We can't hold all of them off forever."

"We won't have to. What's the story on the *Narbonne*?"

Islip smiled. "They're in bad shape. The surge hit them

worse than we thought it would. They might get backup power systems up and running, but they won't be able to fly for at least an hour. Their warp drive was offline when they made planetfall, so that alone will take at least thirty minutes to bring back up. The other transport won't fly, either. We've got an edge, but it won't last long."

Processing this, Pakaski liked what he was hearing. Their bold little scheme seemed to be working. They just needed to take it the rest of the way. "How many hostages do we have?"

Gesturing toward the ramp, Islip replied, "Counting those two, five. The other three are maintenance workers."

"The Starfleet people will be more valuable, but I'll take what I can get." Pakaski gestured to Fujimura. "Get started."

Scowling, the computer tech replied, "It could take a while. I don't know what kind of encryption or other lockouts they may have."

"It can't be too hard, because if it is, then we're all going to jail, assuming we don't die right here."

Making her way toward the boarding ramp, Fujimura glanced up at him. "Hell of a pep talk, boss."

Pakaski looked at her with a wry grin. "Better than the one you'll get from the warden of a Federation penal colony."

"Not helping."

"You'll be fine. Get to work."

From here, the plan was simple: seize control of the transport and fly it out of here toward the mountains. Once there, they would pick up Kodos and the others and bid Tarsus IV farewell. The hostages were only really useful in securing their escape from the spaceport. Once Kodos and the others were aboard, Pakaski would put them off the ship, where they soon would be found by a search party.

With the *Narbonne* and the other transport unable to give chase, the stolen transport would have a short interval of unchallenged warp speed travel that would allow them to make a couple of necessary course changes in order to obscure their flight path. This would hopefully be enough to throw off any pursuers until another ship or a place to hide could be secured. There were inhabited planets in neighboring star systems where such alternative transportation options were available, with few or no questions asked.

Just a few more minutes. That was all Pakaski needed for Fujimura to work her magic and get him and his people out of here. Could they hold off the approaching security forces that long?

For the first time, Pakaski considered the possibility of failure.

I guess we'll see what we see.

30

It was the silence that woke Lorca.

Having drifted to sleep listening to the chirps, clicks, whistles, and other odd sounds emanating from local Tarsus IV insect life along with the occasional report of some animal in the distance, the sudden lack of such ambient noise was enough to rouse him from slumber. His eyes open, he lay motionless while listening to the utter quiet now surrounding him. The moon was well past the midpoint in the sky, casting a faint bluish glow upon the area and telling him that they were in the very early hours of a new day.

His first thought, that someone had arisen to take care of personal hygiene needs, was dismissed when he realized that he could account for all of the other twenty-three men and women comprising the search party. All but two were lying asleep—or at least motionless—in their individual sleeping rolls. The remaining two members of the *Narbonne* security detachment were walking on opposite sides of a large circle around the rest of the group. They were the watch, assigned a two-hour shift to look and listen for anything that might pose a threat to the team, ready to raise an alarm if and when they detected something. Neither of the two men seemed to be breaking from the routine they had established.

Was he imagining things?

No.

The sound was faint, almost obscured by the gentle breeze blowing across the hillside, but he still heard it. It was from somewhere to his left, from a point farther along the sloping terrain than where the team made their camp. Something caught on a rock or stumbled into a hole before going quiet. Animals were seldom so clumsy, so that left only one real possibility.

We've got company.

Turning in his sleeping roll as though seeking a more comfortable position while still in the grips of slumber, Lorca attempted to get a better look up the hill. The moonlight was both an aid and a burden, playing tricks on his eyes as he searched the near darkness. He settled onto his left side, with a line of sight toward the source of the sound. The motion allowed him to retrieve the phaser from where he placed it next to his right hip, inside the blanket. From his new vantage point, he could also see nine members of the team, none of whom appeared to have responded to whatever it was he heard. Beyond them, there was nothing but uneven terrain and shadows.

Then, in the distance, one of the shadows moved.

It separated from a larger patch of black near a slab of rock protruding from the hillside, moving with deliberate slowness and stealth. Lorca's hand tightened around the phaser's grip, and he watched the shadow take on the form of a humanoid figure. A second one followed, moving a few paces behind its companion.

Phaser fire sliced through the darkness, shattering the silence. Lorca flinched in response to the abrupt noise and flash of light, watching as the energy beam washed over the first of the intruders. A second shot followed, and he traced its source to one of the sleeping rolls to his right. Within seconds, both figures were neutralized, and other members of the team were reacting to the sudden explosion of activity.

Throwing aside his own sleeping roll, Lorca pushed himself to his feet, aiming his phaser at the two intruders. He glanced to his right and saw Ensign Terri Bridges, phaser in hand, rising to one knee, and he realized it was she who had dispatched their unwanted visitors.

"What?" she said. "Didn't you hear them?"

The deadpan remark earned a smile from Lorca along with a nod of appreciation. "Nicely done."

More weapons fire to his left made him turn to see one of the *Narbonne* security officers falling as a phaser beam struck him. Two others were firing toward the source of the attack, and two more shadowy figures dropped to the ground.

"Secure the area!"

Lorca recognized Lieutenant Reece O'Bannon shouting the order, followed by other instructions as he went about organizing the rest of the team and assessing the situation.

"Spencer! Get me a perimeter. Are there any more of these bastards running around out here?"

Moving to the closest of the stunned intruders, Lorca saw that the man was wearing nondescript dark clothing designed to help him blend into his surroundings. A balaclava covered his face, and Lorca knelt beside the man to remove the mask. It revealed a dark-haired human of apparent Asian descent, his chin and jaw covered with beard stubble. He retrieved the man's phaser from where it had fallen next to his feet, and frowned as he noted the weapon's power setting.

"Bridges," said Lorca, "get your medical kit. I want this one revived."

He looked up as O'Bannon approached, and Lorca noticed that the man, along with lacking his uniform jacket, was also barefoot. This made him realize that he was dressed in similar fashion, as was pretty much every member of the search party. The scene might have been amusing under normal circumstances.

"Commander," said O'Bannon. He held out a rectangular device about twice the size of a standard-issue communicator. "One of the intruders had it in a pocket. It's a frequency jammer, and it was active when we found it on him." He nodded to where several of his people were moving about the camp's edges. "It's why the tricorders we had on the perimeter didn't give us a warning."

Taking the proffered device, Lorca eyed it with disdain. "Someone's crafty."

Bridges stepped between him and the unconscious man, having returned with her field medical kit. Cross-trained as a medic while still a cadet at Starfleet Academy, the ensign had kept up the necessary certifications and, like Aasal Soltani, used her secondary skills to take care of the outpost team's minor medical needs. Without waiting for Lorca to instruct her further, Bridges extracted a hypospray from the kit and fitted it with an ampoule of a pale liquid. She pressed the device to the man's neck and administered the medication, and a moment later his eyes fluttered open. Lorca made sure the first thing he saw upon regaining consciousness was the power emitter of his own phaser.

"Welcome back."

To his credit, the man remained still, lying on his back and saying nothing, though his eyes widened as he recognized the weapon pointed at his face.

"What's your name?" asked Lorca.

"Kuzeko. Odaka Kuzeko."

Lorca leaned closer. "Well, Odaka Kuzeko, we seem to have something of a problem. People sneaking around and trying to kill me tends to annoy me. Are you trying to annoy me?"

Raising his hands in a slow, deliberate manner to signify that he would not fight, Kuzeko said, "Take it easy."

Lorca waved the captured phaser before the man's nose.

"Is it dark out here, or are my eyes just that bad, or is this weapon set to kill?" He lowered his voice and made sure to add a touch of menace. "It's yours, so I'm hoping you can tell me. Otherwise, I may have to test it."

"No need for that." Kuzeko paused, swallowing as his gaze shifted between Lorca and the phaser hovering before his eyes. "It's set to kill."

"See what I mean?" Lorca tapped the phaser's emitter against the other man's forehead. "Annoying." Stepping away from him, he gestured for O'Bannon to help Kuzeko to his feet. The security officer stayed close, maintaining a grip on the man's arm.

"All right," said Lorca. "Who sent you? Or are you going to make me guess?"

Holding his hands away from his body to show he was not a threat, Kuzeko replied, "Governor Kodos sent me."

"To kill us?" asked Bridges.

Kuzeko was quick to answer, "I was instructed to investigate intruders in the area, and take whatever action I deemed necessary to . . . to protect our people."

"I've been shooting at friends of yours for the better part of two days, Mister Kuzeko, and I haven't killed anybody. Not yet, anyway." Lowering the phaser, Lorca stepped forward until mere centimeters separated his face from the other man's. "On the other hand, you people have been quite busy with the killing, haven't you?"

"I didn't have anything to do with—"

Lorca pressed even closer, gritting his teeth. "Don't even start." New rage was bubbling up within him, but he pushed it back down. It would do no good to lose control of his emotions and composure. For all he knew, this man was innocent, at least so far as participating in the massacre. Still, Kuzeko had already admitted to aiding Kodos, and that was enough to damn him in Lorca's eyes.

"Commander Lorca? Lieutenant O'Bannon?"

Moving back from Kuzeko, Lorca saw Ensign Dmitri Spencer walking toward them. He still carried his phaser pistol, along with a tricorder. The blond security officer held up the portable scanning device.

"We've checked the area, sir. There was only the four of them. The other three are in custody. We didn't find a vehicle, at least not as far as our tricorders can scan up here."

To Lorca, that last part was an unexpected bit of welcome news. Returning his attention to Kuzeko, he regarded the man with a grim smile. "So you came on foot? I'm guessing your camp can't be too far from here." Kuzeko did not have to answer. The way his eyes shifted from Lorca to the other people in his midst, as though searching for a potential weakness among the group or some avenue of escape, was a sufficient response.

"Where's your camp?" asked O'Bannon, giving the other man's arm a small shake.

Bridges said, "Simmons was right, sir. Before, I mean, when you grilled him after what happened to Lieutenant Giler. Their camp can't be too far from here if they detected our presence. Or maybe they heard the explosion that killed the lieutenant. Either way, they have to be somewhere close."

"Lieutenant Giler," said Lorca, almost to himself, before turning back to Kuzeko. "Who do we have to thank for the bomb that killed him?"

Kuzeko's eyes widened, his fear evident, and Lorca had his answer, which earned the other man a fresh look at his own phaser.

"Why."

It was not a question, but instead a judgment. There was nothing the man could say that would ever justify the barbaric act that had taken Lieutenant Jason Giler's life.

Kuzeko knew that, just as he seemed to be realizing that he may well have sealed his own fate.

"It's a good thing I still need you." Lorca gestured to O'Bannon. "Secure him with his friends, then get the rest of the team organized." He glanced at his chronometer. "We move out in ten minutes." Traveling in the dark was not his first choice, but sooner or later, Kuzeko and his team would be missed, and Kodos or whoever sent them would take action. There was a very slim window of opportunity here, but Lorca and the others would have to move fast. "Tell Simmons he's off the hook. Our new friend's going to lead the way."

31

Georgiou rolled away from her position atop the parapet overlooking the transport vessel's berth as phaser fire cut through the air over her head. The attack in her direction lasted only seconds before the torrent of energy beams swept to her right, razing the ground above and beyond the bay's confines.

"What the hell is that?" asked Haley Carroll. The SCE engineer had thrown herself to the ground along the grassy embankment leading away from the parapet, near Georgiou's left side. Her arms were over her head in what she and Georgiou knew was a futile gesture. Next to her, Ensign Dralax also lay flat, keeping his head away from the edge of the embankment.

"Phaser cannon," said Commander Larson from where she hunkered to Georgiou's right. "The ship has four, two up top and two below. From where they're sitting, they can cover pretty much any ground attack."

Carroll asked, "We're arming transport ships now? Did I miss a briefing?"

"We're out on the frontier," said Georgiou. "A long way from Starfleet. If one of these transports runs into Orion pirates or some other rogue ship, they're on their own. More merchant captains are choosing to arm their ships." She ducked as the cannon fired again in their direction. "Normally I'd say there's nothing wrong with the idea. Ask me again tomorrow."

Georgiou split her attention between her companions and the docking slip as she studied the ship and the area surrounding it. Bathed in the light of bright work lamps positioned around the bay's edges, the transport was a dingy, utilitarian affair. Essentially a squat rectangle with an angled forward hull section and a cylindrical warp nacelle tucked against either side of its main hull section, it was a design that dated back to the last decades of the twenty-second century. Hull plates of different colors, many of them featuring an assortment of dents and scars, were patched together in an odd, dilapidated mosaic. On the other hand, the nacelles appeared to be of far more recent vintage, likely replacements as part of an upgrade to give the ship a more powerful warp drive capable of achieving greater speeds.

The bay in which the transport was parked offered plenty of room for landing and takeoff, but it also prevented an approach by stealth. Anyone trying to get to the ship across the tarmac would be exposed and at the mercy of its phaser cannons, to say nothing of anyone on board who was also armed. That much was reflected in how the *Narbonne* and colony security people were reacting to the situation. All of them were keeping their heads down, and a handful were retreating away from the parapet, but it had become apparent to Georgiou that whoever was firing the phaser cannon was not seeking to kill or perhaps even hurt anyone. The barrage was meant to keep at bay anyone looking to advance on the transport. That, at least, gave her some hope that this situation could be resolved without further bloodshed.

Moving away from the parapet's edge, down the embankment, and out of the line of fire, Georgiou looked to Larson. The *Narbonne*'s first officer was consulting a tricorder in her hand.

"What's going on?"

"Their engines are online," replied Larson. "They're preparing for lift-off."

Carroll asked, "Do we know how many people are aboard?"

"I've picked up eight distinct life signs. Seven human, one Betazoid." Larson's expression conveyed she was thinking the same thing as Georgiou.

"Lieutenant Jenn?"

"Probably." Larson grimaced.

Standing next to Carroll, Dralax said, "She and Soltani were at the distribution plant where the power surge originated."

"They must have been taken hostage," added Georgiou. "That'd explain why we haven't been able to reach them."

Damn it.

Though Georgiou was buoyed by the knowledge that the two Starfleet officers had not been killed at the power plant, it complicated the immediate problem. The people seizing the transport seemed restrained with their actions against anyone standing in their way. If they felt pressured, cornered, or otherwise out of options, they would almost certainly use their hostages as leverage to achieve their ends. Aasal Soltani and Enamori Jenn were far from being out of danger.

Down in the docking slips, the transport's engines were powering up, their increasing hum growing louder thanks to the bay's natural acoustics.

"We can't let that ship take off," said Georgiou. "And we sure as hell can't stay here if it does." Thrusters designed to thwart a planet's gravity and lift the craft toward space would be more than powerful enough to kill anyone in proximity to the ship.

Larson replied, "There's no way to keep it on the

ground. If we had the *Narbonne*, then maybe, but they're a half hour from being ready to launch."

"And we can't assault the ship directly." Georgiou looked around, searching for anything else the spaceport might offer to thwart the transport's pending liftoff. "Is there a working transporter around here somewhere?"

"The ones on the *Narbonne* are the only ones I'd trust, but after that power surge, I wouldn't want to try them without running a full diagnostic."

Pulling her communicator from her belt, Georgiou flipped open the unit's cover. "Georgiou to *Narbonne*."

"Korrapati here," replied the voice of the ship's captain.

Her attention still focused on the ship below, Georgiou said, "What's the status of your transporters, sir?"

"They're online, but engineering hasn't run full checks on them."

"I need someone to beam me onto that transport."

Larson regarded her with disbelief. "Are you insane?"

"Ask me that tomorrow too."

Over the open comm frequency, Korrapati said, *"Commander, that's a risky proposition, at best."*

"We're out of options if we want to keep that ship here. If I can get aboard, I can force them to abort takeoff or get them back on the ground."

"Assuming they're open to negotiation," offered Larson.

Georgiou replied, "Then I'll find a way to disable it."

"Hold on," said Carroll. "I think I can go one better."

"I'm listening," said Korrapati.

Carroll grabbed her arm. "No time for that. Come on!"

Sprinting for the small building near the docking area's entrance, Carroll was the first through the doorway, and Georgiou saw upon entering that it was a small guardhouse. It was a single room with two workstations, each with computer interface terminals, communications equipment, and other components she did not recognize.

"Lieutenant Carroll," she prompted, watching as the engineer settled herself at one of the workstations.

"I think I can take remote control of the transport."

"What?" The immediate absurdity of the notion gripped her for a second or two, then Georgiou waved off her initial reaction as she realized where Carroll was going. "Prefix code access?"

Carroll, already setting to work at the console, nodded. "That's the idea."

"But don't you need the code?" The question came from Larson, who had arrived at the guardhouse. Georgiou looked to see the first officer and Dralax watching her and Carroll from the doorway.

Turning from the console just long enough to flash a knowing smile, Carroll replied, "This isn't exactly something they teach at the Academy, Commander. Join the SCE, and we can show you all kinds of tricks."

"I'm only interested in one," said Georgiou. Beyond the guardhouse's walls, she could hear the drone of the transport's engines continuing to increase. "How long is this going to take?"

"If the transport is still linked to the spaceport's communications and computer network array, only a minute or so," replied Carroll. "I can use that to patch into the ship's onboard computer. Once I'm past the security encryption, I'll have full access. Thankfully, the systems on these civilian ships aren't as tough as Starfleet computers."

"Commander," called Ensign Dralax. "The transport is lifting off."

Moving to the doorway, Georgiou peered outside the guardhouse as the rumble from the docking berth grew even louder. Shadows shifted along the embankment leading up to the parapet overlooking the bay as the transport rose into view. With her hand resting on the edge of the door, she felt the guardhouse's walls trembling in the face of the ship's powerful atmospheric thrusters.

"Larson to *Narbonne*," the first officer called into her communicator. "Are you seeing this? The transport's launching. We need to track it for as long as possible."

Through the device's speaker grille, Georgiou heard Korrapati say, *"We're on it, Commander, but we're not yet back to full strength. If they leave the atmosphere, we may be out of luck."*

Gritting her teeth as she watched the transport climb higher into the night sky, its silhouette bathed in pale blue moonlight, Georgiou said, "Carroll, where are we?"

"Working on it, Commander." A moment later, the engineer released a string of obscenities—human, Andorian, Tellarite, and a few Georgiou did not recognize. "They've severed their link with the spaceport and blocked their communications. I can't get in."

Her mind racing as she watched the transport rising higher into the sky, Georgiou said, "What if comm was re-established?"

"I just need any open frequency, but it has to be done from on . . ." The rest of the sentence faded, and she looked up from the station. "Oh. Wait."

Ignoring her, Georgiou said into her communicator, "Captain, it's now or never. Requesting immediate transport to that ship. I understand the risks, but if we don't try, we lose Jenn and Soltani anyway." If the worst happened, her own life would be just one more casualty of this entire tragic affair, but that at least was preferable to doing nothing and consigning two fellow Starfleet officers to almost certain death.

Was there really another choice?

His voice somber over the open channel, Korrapati said, *"Stand by for transport."*

"We're up," reported the pilot from the transport's cramped cockpit. "Doesn't look like anybody's trying to chase us."

From where she sat in one of four seats positioned in a section of deck behind the pilot and copilot's stations, Enamori Jenn watched as the man tasked with flying the ship—she had learned his name, Benjamin Islip, after probing his thoughts—moved his hands over the helm console and its various clusters of controls. Somewhere behind her, the transport's engines were rumbling under restrained power while the ship relied on thrusters to maneuver the ungainly craft while still within the planet's atmosphere. Beyond the cockpit's canopy, she could see flashes of light as the transporter lifted away from the spaceport, but she was not sensing the sort of acceleration needed for the ship to escape the planet's gravity and head for open space. Of course, Jenn knew that was not Pakaski's objective. At least not yet.

Standing behind Islip, Pakaski said, "Well, don't get too comfortable. You know they'll be trying to track us on sensors. So long as we're down here, they'll know where we are."

The woman seated next to Islip, Hisayo Fujimura, said, "Yeah, I'm already seeing that from the Starfleet ship." She released a loud sigh. "I have to give them credit. They're shaking off the power surge faster than I thought they would."

"You don't really think you can get away without them being able to follow you, do you?" asked Soltani. Like Jenn, he sat in his seat with his wrists still restrained behind his back.

Pakaski patted a nearby bulkhead with the flat of his hand. "There's a reason we picked this ship. Unlike the other transport, this baby can get up to warp seven. Your ship can only hit warp six. Once we reach our initial destination, we'll just disappear."

The man's confidence radiated from him as it had from the moment he and his people took her and Soltani hostage, but it was almost suffocating to her in the confined space. She already knew his plan, having retrieved it from his thoughts. Everything he knew, at least, as it appeared he did not possess knowledge of all of the scheme's various parts. He did not know the ship's destination after leaving Tarsus IV, and Jenn read his irritation at having that information kept from him by Kodos. She was tempted to talk to him about it and perhaps unsettle him with the knowledge he had unknowingly given her. There was little to be gained from that, and certainly not enough to justify revealing her abilities and putting herself and Soltani at risk. In addition to her and Soltani, they also had three workers from the spaceport, restrained to seats in the compartment behind the cockpit and under guard by the other two members of Pakaski's team. According to Pakaski's thoughts, he intended to leave all five of his prisoners behind once the transport arrived at its destination in the mountains east of New Anchorage. There, they would pick up the rest of their people, including Kodos.

What he did not know was that his partner, Fujimura, harbored no qualms about killing not just the hostages, but him as well if he got in her way or if she believed he represented a threat to her. Perhaps this was something Jenn could use to her and Soltani's advantage, and somehow pit Pakaski against Fujimura.

"Hang on," said Fujimura. She pointed to an alert indicator on the cockpit console. "Internal sensors just registered an incoming transporter beam."

Pakaski grunted in obvious irritation. "Are you sure?"

"Of course I'm sure." The woman did not bother to hide her disdain for the other man.

Exchanging looks with Soltani, Jenn sensed her companion's surprise and renewed hope that the situation could be changing in their favor. She also detected his concern that this development might cause their captors to take rash action against the prisoners.

Pakaski retrieved his phaser rifle from the deck beside his chair, and Jenn watched him check its power setting. Pushing himself from his seat, he eyed her and Soltani before casting a look toward the cockpit.

"Stay here. I'll check it out. Keep your eyes on our friends."

"Go," snapped Fujimura. "We've got this."

When the woman glared over her shoulder, Jenn felt contempt radiating from her, but she also registered Fujimura's growing worry. The unexpected arrival of an intruder in their midst would be at the very least a distraction from the mission they were attempting to complete. There was also the first hint of desperation creeping into the other woman's thoughts, and Jenn knew this might make her unpredictable, and perhaps even dangerous.

"Some of your friends are trying to be cute," said Pakaski, staring at Jenn as though able to read her thoughts. Gripping the phaser rifle in both hands, he began moving to the cockpit's rear access hatch. "They're going to wish they'd just left us alone."

32

Georgiou braced herself against the wave of dizziness that accompanied the fading of the transporter beam. The room around her reeled, and she reached with her free hand to steady herself against a nearby bulkhead. Her other hand lifted her phaser, aiming the weapon in front of her as she searched her immediate surroundings for threats. For now—and she knew the moment was fleeting—she was alone.

The *Narbonne*'s transporter officer had executed her transfer from the spaceport to the fleeing vessel with pinpoint precision, depositing Georgiou in one corner of a cargo bay. Packing containers of various sizes were shelved or stacked and secured to the deck around her, but the area in which she arrived was open space and yet protected on all sides either by bulkheads or cargo. None of that would matter if anyone was monitoring the ship's internal sensors, but at least there was no one waiting to shoot her the instant she finished materializing.

She stood motionless for a moment, verifying that she was alone in the compartment. The transport's engines droned with power, and the walls and deck carried a small yet noticeable vibration as the vessel continued its ascent toward orbit. There seemed to be no one else within earshot. With the last lingering effects of vertigo still gripping her, she fumbled for her communicator. She flipped it open and the unit's telltale chirp sounded like an alarm siren in the otherwise quiet bay.

"Georgiou to Carroll."

It took only a moment for the engineer to respond, *"I'm here, Commander. Glad you made it aboard okay."*

"What do I do?" Emerging from her place of concealment behind the stacks of cargo containers, Georgiou kept her phaser out and pointed ahead of her.

Carroll replied, *"Find a comm panel or computer interface. Anything that'll let you open a hailing frequency directed away from the ship."*

It took Georgiou only a moment to find what appeared to be an office tucked into another corner of the bay. Inside was a simple desk with one end mounted to a bulkhead and playing host to a simple computer terminal, which she was relieved to see was operational.

"I've found a terminal," she said, setting her phaser on the desk so that she could activate the desktop interface. The unit's screen flashed in response to her commands, its display coalescing into a menu of options, and she tapped one that indicated access to the ship's communications system. "The internal comm network has been deactivated."

"Unless they've overridden the option, you should still be able to send an emergency distress signal. That automatically opens up a frequency."

A quick check of the available options revealed the feature Carroll wanted, and Georgiou pressed that control. The response was immediate as alert indicators began flashing throughout the cargo bay, and alarm sirens wailed. Flinching at the sudden intrusion of light and sound, Georgiou found the icon to silence the cacophony.

"I think I found it."

"Hang on, Commander. This could take a minute."

Before she could reply, Georgiou sensed movement from somewhere outside the small office. A shadow fell across the bulkhead to the doorway's left, an instant before she saw the muzzle of a weapon. Instinct drove her free hand to reach for the phaser on the desk as she dropped into a crouch. She aimed it at the door, firing at the unknown new arrival just as he stepped into view. Her adversary, a bald man wearing dark coveralls and carrying a phaser rifle, also benefited from quick reflexes and managed to retreat as the phaser beam cut across the office to strike the bulkhead. He managed a single shot but it went high and wide, allowing Georgiou ample opportunity to move aside.

"Commander?"

Ignoring Carroll's call from her still open communicator, Georgiou closed the device and stowed it. She maneuvered around the desk and toward the open doorway, wielding her phaser in a two-handed grip. Noises from the bay told her the man was nearby, and she emerged from the office laying down covering fire. Three rapid shots from right to left zipped the length of the narrow passageway, striking the far bulkhead. Georgiou returned to her crouch, moving forward with short steps while listening for clues to her opponent's location. Back in the main cargo bay, she confronted the stacks of cargo containers and storage shelving units, most of which were tall enough to block her line of sight.

Fabric rubbing against metal somewhere ahead of her made her stop her advance, but as she stepped to her left between two stacks of containers, Georgiou realized she had miscalculated her adversary's movements. She had but a heartbeat to realize her mistake before the man was in her face.

Damn!

Too close to shoot her with his phaser rifle, the man tried swinging the weapon like a club at her head. Georgiou anticipated that attack, stepping back and avoiding the hit while trying to bring up her own phaser. He was quicker, swinging his rifle again and catching her weapon hand. The pistol flew from her grip, bouncing off a nearby cargo container before clattering to the deck.

Not bothering to retrieve the phaser, Georgiou pounced, closing the distance separating her from the man and driving the heel of her right hand up under his chin. He grunted in surprise and pain as her other hand closed around the phaser rifle's barrel and she pulled. Then she lashed out with a second strike, the edge of her hand catching him across the bridge of his nose. Howling, he released his grip on the rifle and pulled one hand to his face while trying to maintain a defensive posture.

Georgiou gave him no quarter, swinging the phaser rifle by its barrel against the left side of his head. The force of the attack was enough to send him slamming into another cargo container. He staggered from the impact, doing his best to recover, but a front kick from Georgiou to his chin thrust him backward. His head smacked against the container, and he sagged in a limp heap to the deck.

Verifying the man was unconscious, Georgiou retrieved her own phaser and holstered it before checking the power setting on her opponent's phaser rifle. She noted that it was set to stun.

"Small favors, I suppose," she said to no one.

All around her, the transport shuddered and the pitch of its engines changed, and Georgiou felt a slight tilting of the deck before the inertial dampers were able to compensate for the abrupt change in the ship's attitude. Even with the system's quick response, she was still able to sense the transport's ascent beginning to slow.

Way to go, Carroll.

From her vantage point behind Hisayo Fujimura, Enamori Jenn felt the other woman's anxiety spike, along with that of the pilot, Benjamin Islip, as yet another alert signal flashed on the cockpit console. She also heard the sound of the transport's engines shift as the vessel continued its climb toward orbit.

"What the hell is going on?" asked Islip, his hands moving across several controls.

Fujimura cast a worried look toward her companion. "It's some kind of computer glitch. Never seen anything like it. If I didn't know better, I'd say it was a system lag, but I don't know what process is causing it." She tapped several controls while blowing out her breath in frustration. Jenn felt her mounting unease.

"I don't like this," said Soltani, leaning closer to Jenn. The look in his eyes conveyed his thoughts and emotions without Jenn having to read them for herself. Was the ship somehow defective? Could Pakaski and his people have selected it for their escape without first verifying it was capable of ferrying them where they needed to go? That seemed unlikely, and Fujimura's thoughts told her she was asking herself the same questions and arriving at similar answers. She was as confused as everyone else.

"Son of a bitch," snapped Fujimura, slamming her hands against the edge of her console. "I get it now. Somebody on the ground is inside our system. They're trying to take over the ship."

"Whoa," said Islip, just as the entire transport shuddered around them. There was a new, distinct warble in the ship's engines, and Jenn's stomach fluttered as the artificial gravity system seemed to waver for a fleeting moment. "The helm's fighting me. It's not wanting to answer instructions. Are piloting and navigation systems green?"

"Yes," replied Fujimura. "Wait. There's something active in those processes too. Damn it!"

Islip scowled. "They can do that?"

"If they've got the right skills," replied the computer tech. "Whoever this is, they're pretty damned good."

"Can you stop it?" Islip's composed facade, which had seemed almost indestructible to this point, was beginning to crack around the edges.

Muttering a string of profanities Jenn found impressive as much for its variety as its colorful incorporation of adjectives and adverbs, Fujimura replied, "I don't know."

Islip, still struggling with the helm controls, added his own cursing to the mix. "We're being redirected. The engines are losing thrust. Whoever's doing this is forcing us to land." He glanced to Fujimura. "Come on, Hisayo."

"I'm trying!"

Leaning close to Jenn, Soltani whispered, "It has to be one of the *Narbonne* people, right?"

"Someone with exceptional computer skills," replied Jenn, wincing when Fujimura smacked her console a second time. Her growing anger at being challenged for control of this ship and its systems was making Jenn uncomfortable, almost nauseated, due to their proximity in the small compartment as well as the intensity of the other woman's emotions.

Islip all but shouted, "I've got no helm control *at all!*"

The warning came as the ship shuddered once more around them, accompanied by a renewed warble in the transport's engines and another dip as they lost power and altitude. Whatever was happening while Fujimura battled the demons being unleashed within the onboard computer systems was taking a toll. How much longer could the ship take being subjected to such stress?

"Yes!" shouted Fujimura. "I found the sneaky bastard. They were running some kind of workaround to access the ship's systems remotely. I think I can lock them out and shut down that program."

"I'd prefer you didn't."

Despite her restraints, Jenn was able to jerk her head around to see Commander Georgiou emerging from the connecting passageway. How had she not sensed her presence? Had she just been that distracted by the chaotic situation unfolding before her?

Georgiou was aiming a phaser rifle toward Fujimura and Islip, the latter of whom made the mistake of reaching for his own weapon. He never made it before Georgiou fired, hitting him in the chest. Islip slumped forward in his seat, already unconscious as he sagged against the console.

"You just knocked out our pilot," said Fujimura.

"I can fly." Moving forward, Georgiou motioned to the other woman with the rifle's muzzle. "Get up."

Moving almost too fast to track, Fujimura's hand struck out at the console and her fingers landed on one of the controls. Georgiou fired the rifle again, and the woman was thrown against the console and neighboring bulkhead, dropping to the deck, but by then Jenn could feel the transport reacting to whatever it was she had done. A distinct whine in the ship's engines radiated through the walls, deck plating, and even the seat she occupied.

"What's happening?" Soltani was shifting in his seat, turning so that Georgiou could undo his wrist restraints. She did the same for Jenn before moving toward the cockpit.

"I don't know." Setting aside her phaser rifle, Georgiou

pulled the stunned Islip from his chair just before the transport's deck shifted beneath their feet, and she all but fell into the seat.

Reaching for the back of the pilot's chair to steady herself, Jenn clawed her way toward the other chair, shifting Fujimura's unmoving form out of the way before taking her seat.

"I've got someone on the ground trying to seize remote control of the ship," said Georgiou. Pulling her communicator from her belt, she activated the unit. "Georgiou to Carroll."

"Commander!" said a female voice Jenn did not recognize. *"Something's wrong. My access has been blocked. I've still got no control down here."*

Georgiou tapped at an unresponsive console with her free hand. "I've got nothing up here. What can I do?"

"Open another comm frequency. I'm trying to get back in."

Through the cockpit's transparent canopy, Jenn could see that the transport's ascent through the thin, wispy clouds was slowing. Within seconds their upward course came to a stop before the ship began dropping back down through the planet's upper atmosphere.

After seeing to it that Islip and Fujimura were secured in the seats vacated by him and Jenn, Soltani moved forward until he stood between Georgiou and Jenn. "This can't be good, right?"

"No." Georgiou pressed another control. "Comm systems reactivated. Hailing frequency open."

Even with artificial gravity and inertial damping systems, the effects of the transport's accelerating fall through the atmosphere was beginning to have an effect.

"Lieutenant Carroll," said Georgiou into her communicator as she worked her way into the seat's restraints.

"I'm back in, Commander. Hold on!"

Despite the situation's heightening tension, Jenn's read of Georgiou's thoughts was that the commander was doing a superb job of keeping her emotions at bay. There was fear there, yes, but for the moment her focus was on the matter at hand, concentrating on the ship and the safety of the people aboard.

"Work faster," said Georgiou, her voice tight. With her other hand, she was checking other controls and indicators. "I'm trying to restore helm."

Having already belted herself into her own seat, Jenn examined the controls. "In her haste to block the unauthorized access, it looks like Fujimura has also locked out primary helm control."

"Why isn't the computer overriding all of this?" asked Georgiou. "It should be treating this like an uncontrolled descent and automatically taking emergency action."

Soltani said, "Try reinitiating the main computer oversight processes." Kneeling between the two pilot seats, he pointed to one set of console controls. "Maybe you can reset whatever she did."

"That will likely take too long," said Georgiou.

There was a sudden lurch as the ship shifted its angle of flight. Even the inertial dampers were unable to compensate, and Jenn felt her stomach lurch as the transport shifted its direction.

"*I'm back in!*" shouted Carroll over the open comm frequency. "*There's definitely some kind of security override in my way, though.*"

Georgiou placed the communicator on the console, freeing her other hand for the controls before her. "I'm still locked out. We've got to slow our descent. I'll take atmospheric or even orbital maneuvering thrusters. Just give me something." Jenn realized the commander was putting herself through a rapid familiarization with the ship's controls, not all of which translated to the Starfleet workstations with which she would be familiar.

"Our rate of descent is increasing," said Jenn, and her report was punctuated by a new alarm indicator from the cockpit console. "Impact in thirty-four seconds."

"Commander Georgiou," came the voice of Captain Korrapati over the open link. *"Stand by for transport."*

"No!" barked Georgiou, and Jenn nearly flinched from the sudden burst of anger clouding the commander's thoughts. "There are six other people on board, Captain. You can't lock on and beam us all out in time."

"I've disabled the lock on the helm controls," said Carroll. *"You should have access to maneuvering thrusters."*

Without acknowledging the lieutenant, Georgiou stabbed at the controls to activate the ship's atmospheric flight controls. A new high-pitched hum began filling the cramped cockpit as the newly available system came on line.

"Thrusters active," said Jenn, reviewing the console's status readouts.

Soltani said, "We're still falling way too fast."

"Hang on."

Jenn watched Georgiou's fingers jabbing at various controls, most of which Jenn did not understand. Through the cockpit's canopy, she could see that the ship had dropped far enough that the horizon and distant mountains were visible.

Over the comm frequency, Korrapati yelled, *"Pull up!"*

"Routing power from the main engines to thrusters and inertial damping," said Georgiou, not looking up from the controls. "I'm trying to put us down just outside the spaceport, away from any buildings or people. Soltani, buckle in." Jenn realized the commander likely was more aware of their present predicament than anyone, and was carrying the burden of trying to see them all to safety. Despite the mounting fear she emitted, Georgiou was fighting her own emotions and channeling that energy toward the task before her.

"You're still coming down too fast," warned Carroll.

Instead of answering, Georgiou punched another control and Jenn heard the sound of the ship's engines groaning in protest. Everything around them rumbled as the transport struggled against gravity and inertia, trying to force some sort of compromise. Jenn's stomach felt like it might barrel its way into her throat just as Georgiou hit one more button, and a thunderous roar echoed through the ship from somewhere beneath them. Just before she closed her eyes, Jenn caught a glimpse of one of the spaceport buildings, looming far too close as the ship fell.

The transport hit the ground, the force of the controlled crash overriding the damping systems enough to rattle every panel and component in the cockpit along with every tooth in Jenn's mouth. Her entire body felt like it was being jammed down into her seat and she gasped for breath, but the impact was far less than she had anticipated. The most surprising aspect of the entire thing, she realized seconds later, was that she was able to open her eyes and look around.

Turning to her left, she saw Georgiou sagging in her seat, looking as haggard as Jenn felt. She saw Soltani strapped into a seat next to the still unconscious Fujimura, offering a weak smile and a shaky thumbs-up gesture.

"Not the best landing, Commander, but I'll take it."

"So will I," added Jenn.

"Commander." It was Korrapati, speaking over the still open communications channel. His tone was sober. *"Commander Georgiou?"*

Not even bothering to lift the communicator to her face, Georgiou remained slumped in her seat. "Yes, Captain. We're here, but I'm guessing we'll all be pretty sore tomorrow."

"Our scans show all nine of you are still alive. You managed to put the ship down relatively unharmed, and with no damage to personnel or property. Hell of a landing, Commander. And, Lieutenant Carroll, they couldn't have done it without you."

"Nice job, Commander," replied the engineer. *"And thank you, Captain."*

Georgiou exhaled a long, tired breath, her gaze shifting to make sure Jenn and Soltani were uninjured. "We're a little beat up out here, sir; we could use a hand."

"Commander Larson is already on the way with a security and medical team," replied Korrapati. *"Is there anything specific you need?"*

Georgiou smiled, and Jenn sensed the wave of relief flooding the commander's thoughts. "Shore leave, for about a month."

33

Through the binoculars taken from his pack, Lorca studied the dark opening in the side of the hill. The moon was helping him identify terrain details, but at this distance the entrance itself remained a mystery. No illumination from within, which was as he expected. If there were sentries on duty, in or near the cave opening, they would have extinguished all light sources so as not to impede their own natural abilities to see at night.

"Are they using thermal sensors or tricorders to scan for unwanted visitors?" he asked, casting a sideways glance at Alexander Simmons, who like him was hunkered down behind a large rock outcropping. From here, about fifty meters from the opening and in the near darkness, they were for all intents invisible, but as sounds tended to travel better at night, Lorca kept his voice just above a whisper.

Simmons, still under the watchful eyes of Lieutenant Reece O'Bannon and with his wrists restrained in front of him, replied, "We brought them with us, but they don't work very well up here."

Assuming the man was being truthful—something Lorca was not prepared to do—the region's natural geomagnetic fields and the havoc they caused on scanning devices and communications were at least working in their favor. Even the electronic components of his binoculars were impeded, their targeting and distance sensors rendered inert thanks to the interference and leaving him only with the standard magnification feature. They might not be able to scan for their quarry, but the same limitations hampered those being hunted as well. Remove the technology, and this became more of a simple stand-up fight.

Lorca liked that. After walking in the dark for over an hour, every step bringing with it the possibility of discovering another explosive like the one that had killed Lieutenant Jason Giler, he was ready to face his quarry head-on.

Enough with the sneaking around. Let's get on with this.

"How do you want to do this, Commander?" asked O'Bannon.

Having resumed his inspection of the hillside with the binoculars, Lorca replied with a question of his own. "Is there another way in?"

"At least two other entrances that I know of," said Simmons. "One higher up on the mountain, and another on the far side."

Reaching either of those without being detected was unlikely, Lorca decided, and it would take too long. It would be dawn soon, and waiting for daylight to make a move on this potential hiding place was not a prudent tactic either. Assaulting this position was the proper choice, but what if this was all a ruse, or Kodos and his followers had simply vacated this hiding place in favor of a new refuge?

"O'Bannon," he said, still looking through the binoculars. "You and I will go ahead and get a closer look. We'll decide what to do after that." He was aware of the time factor even without consulting his chronometer. Less than two hours remained before the first glow of sunlight would begin peeking up over the eastern horizon. They would have to move fast, and hopefully without drawing unwelcome attention.

He was about to lower the glasses when movement caught

his eye. Pressing his face against the binoculars, he adjusted the magnification setting to its highest level. He waited, wanting to make sure his eyes were not deceiving him in the gloom, but then he saw the dark-clothed figure, walking from right to left in front of the cave opening. The figure stopped near the entrance's left side, and another figure stepped into view.

"I count two bodies," he said. "Both near the cave." Lowering the binoculars, he looked to Simmons. "Sound about right?"

"The man in charge of security did establish two-person sentry details at the outset," replied Simmons. "He is, or was, a member of the security forces, and that is their standard practice."

O'Bannon added, "He's right, sir. I learned that while touring a couple of their precinct locations."

After pondering these details, Lorca said, "Okay, new plan." He gestured to Ensign Terri Bridges, who had taken up a defensive position a few meters away and was still guarding Odaka Kuzeko, their newest informant, who like Simmons had his wrists fastened with security binders. Along with Simmons, Kuzeko had proven useful during their renewed advance up the hill, if for no other reason than Lorca figured they would be the ones to trigger any other booby traps set by the fugitives in order to hamper pursuit. On their way here, the team had found and disarmed three such devices without incident, but each one served to heighten the group's collective anticipation and anxiety.

"Kuzeko and I will go up there and scope the situation firsthand."

O'Bannon said, "Sir, with all due respect, are you sure that's a good idea?" He pointed to Kuzeko. "I don't trust this guy at all. We should've left him back with the others."

"I don't trust him either, but this is why we brought him." The other three members of Kuzeko's little raid-

ing party were at this moment being escorted back to the
base camp farther down the mountain, marching under
the watchful eye of two security officers from O'Bannon's
detail. Kuzeko, on the other hand, was of enormous use to
Lorca. Besides helping to detect potential hazards during
their march through the hills, he might be able to provide
another advantage: access to the cave.

To Kuzeko, Lorca said, "Did you establish a challenge
and password for your sentries when you and your team returned from your mission?"

The other man nodded. His nervousness was obvious.
"Yes."

"Good. I need a closer look, so you and I are going to
report in. Try anything stupid, and you know what happens."

Kuzeko's brow furrowed. "You'll kill me?"

"Not right away, but you'll wish I had."

After instructing O'Bannon to have his people ready to
advance on the cave at his signal, including stunning Simmons if the disgraced security officer tried anything like
warning his companions, Lorca and Kuzeko emerged from
hiding and began moving up the hill's gentle slope. It took
them just under two minutes to cover the open, uneven terrain while relying only on the moon's illumination to guide
the way. As they walked, Lorca reached for Kuzeko's wrists
and removed the security binders.

"Don't make me regret this," he warned.

The closer they approached, the easier it was for Lorca to
make out the cave opening. He thought he detected a faint
glow from somewhere beyond the entrance, perhaps a small
lamp or other portable light source within a subterranean cavern. Also easier to see were the two figures—males, so far as
Lorca could tell—standing at the edge of the opening. Both
men had noted the approach of someone from down the hillside, and Lorca could see them drawing phasers from holsters

on their belts. He made no attempt to conceal his presence, opting instead to walk just behind Kuzeko at a normal pace, as though their arrival was to be expected. As they walked, he kept his right hand at his side, close to Kuzeko, while holding his own phaser against his thigh. The ruse seemed to be working, as one of the men at the cave raised a hand.

"Hold it right there. Alpha Four."

Kuzeko seemed to hesitate before responding to the challenge. "Tango Seven."

Already on edge from the idea of walking into the proverbial lion's den, Lorca's every muscle and sense were keyed up in anticipation of a confrontation. As such, he was ready the instant he saw both of the guards beginning to raise their weapons. He was somewhat faster, lifting his phaser and firing at the first guard, who had no chance to react before the energy beam struck him and he fell against the side of the cave opening before sliding to the ground.

His companion was better on the draw, managing to let loose a single shot before Lorca's phaser found him. The second guard staggered, stumbling over a rock and falling in a heavy heap as he settled onto his back.

Only then did Lorca realize the guard's shot had found its own target.

Looking behind him, he saw Odaka Kuzeko lying faceup, his flat expression ashen in the moonlight. Though looking at the man's open eyes was sufficient evidence, Lorca knelt next to him to verify that he was dead.

"You got off easy."

Shouts of alarm from somewhere ahead of him made Lorca lift his phaser and aim it toward the cave. A half-dozen figures were emerging from the opening, spilling out onto the open ground. Each carried a flashlight, and he could make out the silhouettes of hand phasers as well as larger rifle versions.

Well, shit.

He was taking aim at his first target when a host of phaser beams streaked past from behind him, each finding one of the figures and dropping them to the sloping hillside. Within seconds, all six of the new arrivals were incapacitated, and Lorca heard running footsteps coming up the hill behind him. He pushed himself to his feet as Lieutenant O'Bannon and Ensign Bridges arrived, the latter pushing Alexander Simmons ahead of her. All around Lorca, the rest of the search party, *Narbonne* security people and civilian volunteers, were advancing in a skirmishers line, converging on the cave.

"You okay, Commander?" asked Bridges.

Lorca nodded. "Better than Kuzeko." He gave the fallen man a last look. Perhaps he did not deserve to die, and there likely was no way to ever know whether he had helped Kodos perpetrate the executions, but Lorca found himself unable to muster even the tiniest morsel of sympathy for Odaka Kuzeko, or anyone else who assisted the fugitive governor in any way.

"Come on," he said, directing his attention toward the cave.

Bridges gestured with her phaser toward the opening. "It's a safe bet they know we're coming."

Checking the charge level of his phaser, Lorca swapped the weapon's power pack for a new one. Satisfied that he was ready for the coming confrontation, he started marching toward the cave.

"So they know we're coming. It won't matter."

It was time to finish this.

"Governor! They're here!"

Having fallen into fitful slumber while sitting in the collapsible and utterly uncomfortable field chair serving as the only other furnishing within the small cavern he had made a temporary home, Kodos awoke to the sound of Ian Galloway's frantic shout of warning. He rose from the chair, pushing aside the canvas tarp that acted as a privacy curtain, and stepped into the larger chamber. The subterranean room was abuzz with activity, a handful of men and women carrying out all manner of tasks, but the bulk of the two dozen or so people who had come with him to their place of temporary sanctuary were not present. Those who remained were pulling weapons and other equipment from storage containers and offering instructions before taking off down one of the tunnels leading from the cavern.

"What's going on? Where is everyone?"

Galloway, standing at one of the six field desks arranged in a circle and forming a command center of sorts, looked up from where he was consulting a portable computer terminal. "We've got intruders, sir. Sentries near checkpoint two reported weapons fire on the surface, and none of the guards posted to that entrance are reporting in."

Search parties, Kodos reasoned. One of them must finally have found where he and his people had made their hiding place. Kodos cursed the unfortunate timing. Joel Pakaski and his team were supposed to be on their way after having secured a means of escaping the planet. Broadcasts from New Anchorage relayed reports of the massive surge that had incapacitated—albeit temporarily—significant portions of the city. What the reports did not provide was information on the status of the Starfleet vessel docked at the city's spaceport, though that was to be expected. Regardless of any detrimental effects stemming from the power surge, Kodos figured the ship's captain would elect not to share the extent of its damage, especially if he believed he was the victim of sabotage.

"Any updates on Pakaski and his team?" asked Kodos.

Shaking his head, Galloway replied, "No, Governor. None of the sentries at any of the entrances have reported any ship sightings, and there's been nothing on any of the broadcasts."

Something about that did not seem right to Kodos, but there was nothing to be done about it. For now, there were more immediate concerns.

From a weapons container near his desk, Galloway retrieved a phaser pistol and offered it to Kodos. It was a model used by the colony security forces.

"We can't stay here, sir. They're coming."

The echo of weapons fire from somewhere in the tunnels connecting to the cavern told Kodos the fight was moving ever deeper into his underground refuge. If they remained here, there was the distinct possibility they could find themselves trapped.

He frowned. "We only need to hold out long enough for Pakaski to arrive." As protection for their refuge, Pakaski had taken several precautions to provide the group with escape routes as well as options for defense. There were at least five exits to the surface from the underground cavern, some easier to access than others, but all would work if the situation called for it. To help cover their retreat in the event the subterranean hideaway was breached or overrun, Pakaski also had installed several explosive charges at key locations throughout the tunnels and connected caverns.

There would be no simple surrender, and Kodos had no intention of going quietly.

Echoes of a firefight from one of the tunnels was growing louder by the second, and then two of his followers appeared from the passageway, running into the cavern. Kodos recognized them both as former members of the security forces, assigned by Pakaski as part of a protection detail for the governor. Fiona Okafor, a lithe, statuesque woman of

African descent, was running right at him, while her male companion, a blond-haired man named Nikolaus Cohler, was turning to fire his phaser back the way they had come.

"Governor!" snapped Okafor. "We need to go. *Now!*"

She grabbed his arm, pulling him after her as she continued running across the chamber toward another tunnel.

"What's happening?" asked Galloway.

Calling over her shoulder, Okafor replied, "It's one of the Starfleet search parties. They've breached the outer defenses and are working their way deeper into the tunnels. We're moving you to one of the emergency stations until we can secure an escape route."

There were few such locations within the underground network of tunnels and caves, but Pakaski still managed to select and equip a handful of suitable positions. From these points, a defensive stand could be made while covering an escape to the surface or even deeper into areas of the subterranean network that could be used as hiding places. None of these contingencies would matter if they stayed here, however.

With Okafor leading and Cohler covering their rear, Kodos and Galloway made their way toward one of the other tunnels leading from the cavern. Behind them, the other passageway channeled with great efficiency the sounds of a firefight from somewhere close. Whoever was making their way into the underground passages was doing so with speed and efficiency.

The hunters were getting closer.

34

Lorca emerged first from the short tunnel connecting the surface entrance to a large cavern with a high ceiling, firing at anything that moved. His first two shots caught a pair of sentries before they could react, and both men fell to the cave floor. Another shot missed its mark, sending a third person scampering for cover and giving Lorca the opportunity to huddle behind a haphazard pile of rocks.

Ahead of him, he heard shouts of warning and other unintelligible instructions as people in the cave and connecting tunnels responded to the intruders in their midst. The search party's dispatching of the guards on the surface had, as Ensign Bridges predicted, not gone unnoticed. From concealed positions behind thick stone stalagmites or near the mouths of tunnels leading from the cavern, at least four or five people were firing in his direction. His place of concealment afforded him some protection, though he could hear the phaser beams chewing into the rocks in front of him. Lorca wondered why his adversaries did not adjust their weapons to their maximum settings and simply disintegrate whatever was between them and their target, but then he realized that destroying too many of the stone columns might well bring the cavern ceiling down upon them all.

There's a comforting thought.

Shuffling movement to his left preceded the arrival of Ensign Bridges. She was pushing Alexander Simmons ahead of her, and shoved him to the ground behind the pile of fallen rock.

"Where would Kodos be?" asked Lorca, eyeing Simmons as the prisoner shifted his position. His wrists, still restrained with security binders, hampered his movements.

"There's a larger cave, deeper inside the mountain. Several of the passages here connect to it."

Consulting her tricorder, Bridges asked, "Is everything down here a natural formation, or did you cut your own tunnels?"

Simmons shook his head. "As far as I know, it's all natural, but they may have cut new passages I don't know about."

"I wouldn't put it past them," said Reece O'Bannon, who had come up along Lorca's right side. "They've been pretty resourceful."

Lorca grunted in agreement. With just the small portions of the underground lair they had seen, it was obvious Kodos and his people had planned their hideaway and possible escape. They would have needed only a handful of days beforehand to make initial preparations and stage needed supplies, weapons, and other equipment. Now that they had been here for at least a few days since fleeing New Anchorage in the wake of the massacre, they would have spent a good portion of that time fortifying their positions. It spelled trouble for anyone attempting an infiltration, as the people already here would have terrain familiarity on their side, along with whatever surprises they may have set out for unwanted interlopers.

A quick check of his own tricorder offered Lorca a muddled reading of the underground network's interior. "The interference in here's messing with life sign readings. I can't be sure, but it looks to be about a dozen or so bodies running around down here, not counting our people."

Bridges added, "I've also got a partial map of the caves and tunnel layout. It's good for about fifty meters, but hopefully it'll fill in as we move around."

"It'll have to do," replied Lorca. At least they would be able to maneuver in here without being completely blind. He would take the small favors wherever he found them. Behind him, Lorca saw the rest of the search party beginning to make their way into the cavern, and he looked to O'Bannon.

"Spread your people out, Lieutenant. Teams of three." Lorca held up his tricorder. "Take that passage to the right, and use it to approach the next big cavern. We'll take one that lets us move in from the left. Anybody who's not one of us is a target, but stun only. We're taking these people back to New Anchorage."

"Even Kodos?" asked Bridges.

Despite himself, Lorca hesitated before answering, "Yes, even Kodos." Part of him did not want that to be his truthful response, but it was the correct one, regardless of personal feelings. Adrian Kodos would stand trial for his crimes.

And if he resists?

Lorca pushed away the question along with the feelings it stirred within him, focusing his attention on the matter at hand.

Resistance in the tunnel came in the form of three more people, a man and two women, all dressed in dark clothing, trying to mount a defense at the passage's far end. Lorca saw movement ahead of him, in the form of one of the women running away into the connecting cavern. Before her companions could fire, he threw himself toward one of the tunnel walls as the other woman let loose with the first shot. Bridges, pushing Simmons out of possible danger, returned fire, and Lorca heard a gasp of surprise as her single shot found its target. She ducked toward the tunnel's opposite side, and Lorca leaned into the passageway, firing his phaser toward their attackers. He knew his shot had missed, and the sound of the weapon's discharge was followed by running footfalls heading away from the tunnel.

"Come on," Lorca said, giving chase. With Bridges and the unwilling Simmons following behind him, he charged into the larger chamber and found it stocked with all manner of cargo containers, field equipment, and other miscellaneous items. Instinct told him this must have been the main gathering place for the fugitives, which made sense given this area's prominence within his scans of the underground interior. Choosing this as their base camp was not accident or even fortunate happenstance, but rather intentional design, for its space as well as the routes of escape it provided.

Clever bastards.

Across the massive chamber, Lorca saw four people, three men along with the woman he saw moments before, running toward the cavern's far end. There, another subterranean passage waited. It took Lorca an extra few seconds to realize he recognized one of the fleeing people, from an image provided by Commander Georgiou.

"Kodos! Stop right there!"

One of the men, with a muscular build and blond hair, was covering the group's retreat and was the last to disappear into the tunnel. A moment later he leaned back into view brandishing a phaser pistol, but Lorca ignored him. Instead, he focused on the man less than twenty meters in front of him, whose face he had committed to memory. At long last, his quarry was within reach, and he sprinted forward, firing on the run and splitting his attention between the retreating fugitives, the cavern's uneven ground, and the various obstacles in his path. None of his shots hit anything; he intended instead to instill fear and compel his adversaries to stop. So far, that was not working. He darted around cargo containers, leaped over cots and piles of equipment. Ahead of him, Kodos and the others disappeared into one of the tunnels. Lorca followed after them.

And then everything went to hell.

Following Fiona Okafor, Kodos ran for the tunnel that would take them from the cavern and deeper into the underground passages toward a somewhat smaller but still spacious chamber. That space could have served as the group's main camp, but for the water running from the ceiling and down the walls to pool in the chamber's lower areas. The water, originating from springs flowing from underground shafts, also fed the small river cutting through the valley to the north of Mount Bonestell.

None of that seemed to matter now.

"The fighting's moving in this direction," said Nikolaus Cohler. While covering their retreat, he stepped up alongside Ian Galloway and gave Kodos a small shove. "We have to keep moving, Governor."

From fragmented reports relayed over communications frequencies still impacted by the mountain valley's geomagnetic properties, Kodos knew that his people were on the defensive, retreating and attempting to provide cover for one another as they sought escape within the network of underground passages. The Starfleet search party, better trained and equipped for fighting in close quarters, was gaining the upper hand. How many people did Kodos have left? Fewer than a dozen, he guessed; likely far fewer. For all he knew, the three loyal followers currently escorting him to supposed safety were all who remained.

As for the Starfleet personnel, reinforcements from the

city were likely already on the way, and Kodos knew they would not stop until he was in custody. Though he had not said so aloud, he suspected that Joel Pakaski's attempt to secure transport from Tarsus IV must have failed. He was overdue, and there was no sign of ship activity anywhere in the region.

It's time to take more direct action.

From a pocket of his jacket, Kodos extracted the palm-sized device given to him by Pakaski. It was a simple keypad: a rectangle with a dozen buttons and a control dial embedded in a sturdy material suitable for the harsh demands of field use. A gift of sorts from Pakaski, it would allow Kodos to control each of the contingency devices deployed within the caverns. Each numbered control indicated a device planted somewhere in the caverns. Kodos had memorized Pakaski's deployment plan. The control labeled FIVE denoted the package set near the entrance to the tunnel through which the sounds of the fight were coming. Within seconds, someone would be—

"Kodos! Stop right there!"

The command preceded a barrage of phaser fire just as Kodos and the others reached the other passageway. They pressed themselves against the tunnel wall. Kodos gripped his phaser with one hand and the keypad with the other.

"We have to keep moving," said Okafor. Next to Kodos, Cohler dropped to one knee and leaned out of the passageway, firing his phaser at something the governor could not see.

"Starfleet," said Cohler, hauling himself back into the tunnel. "Two or three, I think, but more of them are coming."

"Let's go!" snapped Okafor. "Now!"

Instead of replying, Kodos set the keypad's dial to the fifth position, then pressed its corresponding control key.

35

The explosion was behind him. Despite its small size, the shock wave in the confined space was still enough to make him stumble, while the sound of the blast set his ears to ringing. Despite this, Lorca heard the rumble of displaced rock raining down inside the tunnel he had just exited. Chunks of stone and a cloud of dust began filling the air. He could see that the passage was clogged with stone debris, much of it far too large and heavy to move without assistance, but that did not concern him. Instead, his immediate thought was for the people following him through the tunnel.

"Bridges!" he shouted. Reaching for his communicator, he flipped open the unit's cover. "Lorca to Bridges. Are you there?"

A muted, garbled response filtered through the communicator's speaker. *". . . kay. Just missed . . . all right?"*

Relieved to hear the ensign's voice, Lorca said, "It looks like the tunnel's blocked. Can you find another way around?"

". . . annon on it . . . follow him. Wait for—"

The broken message still conveyed enough. Bridges wanted him to wait for O'Bannon or other reinforcements before continuing his pursuit of Kodos, but that was out of the question. The bastard had just tried to kill him and his people, and he was on the verge of getting away.

Not a chance.

"Commander!"

Lorca saw Reece O'Bannon emerging from another tunnel, waving to him. Two members of the *Narbonne* security detachment followed the lieutenant into the cavern, and Lorca gestured for them to keep moving.

"Are you all right?" he asked as O'Bannon and his men drew closer.

The lieutenant nodded. "We heard the explosion in the other tunnel. Glad to hear everyone's okay."

"That wasn't just a simple booby trap." Lorca pointed toward the tunnel used by Kodos and others. "He triggered it deliberately."

O'Bannon's eyes narrowed. "I think we need to have a chat with him. Ask him what the hell he was thinking."

"My thoughts exactly. Let's go."

Leading the way into the next tunnel, Lorca moved at a brisk pace, eyes and tricorder searching the passage ahead of him for threats. The only life signs he detected were several dozen meters ahead. As he approached the tunnel's far end, his scans registered the presence of something else. It was close to the ground, perhaps ten meters from the mouth of the underground corridor, and he signaled for O'Bannon and the others to halt their advance as he adjusted the tricorder's controls to refine its readings.

Another bomb.

Son of a bitch.

Without thinking, Lorca increased his phaser's power setting to maximum, took aim at the foreign object, and fired. The entire package disappeared in a flash of energy, disintegrated without detonating.

"Well," said O'Bannon. "That worked out okay. I guess."

Ignoring the lieutenant's commentary, Lorca pressed on. He moved to within a meter of the tunnel's opening, getting his first look at the cavern beyond. The sound of water dripping reached his ears, and there was a dampness to the air here. He stepped closer, resetting his phaser to stun and holding it in a two-handed grip before him.

The energy beam from a phaser fired at very close range streaked past his face and chewed into the rock wall to his right. He stumbled backward, flinching as bits of stone shrapnel peppered his legs and torso. Falling against the tunnel wall, he slid to a kneeling position as a figure stepped into the light afforded by the passage's opening. It was the blond man covering Kodos's retreat. Their eyes met and the man raised his phaser pistol, but Lorca fired first and his adversary's body went limp as the stun beam enveloped him. He dropped unconscious to the ground.

Reaching the tunnel mouth again, he confirmed that the other man, lying on the ground three meters from the passageway, was indeed stunned. Where were his companions? Where was Kodos?

"There's another tunnel on the other side of this cavern," said O'Bannon, having come up behind Lorca. "There are also a couple of outcroppings and ledges around the room, leading to other, smaller passages. My tricorder can't scan far enough to see where they go."

Lorca nodded, studying what he could see of the cavern. Everything about this situation—to say nothing of experience and instinct—told him he was walking into an ambush.

He was going anyway.

Pointing to a large, mineral-encrusted stalagmite, he said, "Once I get behind that column, follow me."

No sooner did he take his first step forward than someone fired from a concealed position ahead of him. Lorca had only a heartbeat to register that the angle of the phaser beam boring into the ground at his feet indicated a downward trajectory, and by then he was moving. Sprinting out of the tunnel, he fired blind, aiming his weapon in the general direction of the shot. He dashed to the blond man lying in a heap in a shallow puddle of water and scooped up his phaser with his free hand before changing direction and lunging for the stalagmite.

His wild covering-fire scheme seemed to work, as no one saw fit to shoot at him while he was on the run. Reaching the massive stone column, he put his back to it, giving himself a view toward the tunnel where O'Bannon and his team still hid. The lieutenant was trying to shift his position, searching for the danger, and was rewarded by a new barrage of phaser fire aimed in his direction. Lorca saw the other man duck from sight, but the intensity of the attack continued. Hunks of stone were falling from the tunnel edges and the surrounding rock walls, as though the person doing the shooting was trying to cause the tunnel to collapse. Then Lorca winced as the stalagmite behind him shuddered, and pieces of it were thrown in various directions. His quarry had not forgotten about him either.

"Commander!" It was O'Bannon, shouting from the tunnel, but whatever else he might have said was lost amid another assault on his position before something else was fired at the tunnel, impacting against the rock above the opening. The small, dull explosion echoed in the cavern, and Lorca realized it was some kind of grenade, followed moments later by a second explosive. The dual blasts were powerful enough to drop a large hunk of stone across the tunnel opening, sending a plume of dirt and water into the air.

His grip tightening on the phasers he held in each hand, Lorca pushed himself to his feet, darting to the left as he abandoned the stalagmite's marginal protection. He pivoted to face toward the source of the attack and caught sight of a phaser rifle firing from an elevated position toward the tunnel. For the briefest of moments he worried that O'Bannon and his team were dead, caught in the unrelenting barrage and perhaps buried beneath tons of fallen rock. He could not afford such thinking, as he was still a target. This close, he could see at least two faces, a woman and another figure he could not identify. Was that Kodos?

Then the woman saw him and began swinging her phaser rifle in his direction.

Uh-oh.

He fired toward them with both phasers, concentrating his efforts to keep them ducking for cover. Momentary glimpses of containers bearing the familiar markings of weapons and munitions caught his eye, and he knew from where the grenades had come.

A figure revealed itself above a portion of rock outcropping, and Lorca fired in its direction. The shot missed as the person dropped back out of sight, continuing on until it struck one of the containers, which exploded.

Only then did Lorca realize the phaser taken from the other man was set to a more lethal setting, as rock and fire belched outward from the outcropping, accompanied by screams as whoever was up there took the full force of the blast. Flames were everywhere as chunks of stone showered onto the cavern floor. The explosion thundered through the chamber, knocking Lorca off his feet and throwing him backward until he landed in a puddle of muddy water. Pain racked his body as he rolled onto his side, the cold, dirty water seeping through his uniform. He pulled himself to his knees, looking up to where the fire was continuing to grow as it consumed whatever was staged on the ledge.

Damn.

His communicator, somehow still attached to his equipment belt, beeped for attention. Retrieving the device, which dripped dirty water, he flipped open its cover.

"Lorca here."

"*. . . ander? This is O'Ban . . . are you?*"

There was no sense trying to have a conversation over

the faltering frequency. Instead, Lorca lowered himself to the cavern floor, sighing in relief as he listened to Reece O'Bannon's fragmented voice. Resting his back against the cold, wet rock wall, Lorca placed the still active communicator on a rock near his right hip. Bridges or someone else would eventually use the open channel to track his location. If he was lucky, they would find him within a half hour.

Until then, he was content to sit here and watch the fire burn.

Are you up there, Kodos? I hope so.

There would be questions, of course, and at this moment he had no idea how he might answer some of them. His actions, brash as they were, saved at least some of his team, and that gave him no small measure of comfort. It was obvious to him that Kodos and his remaining followers were more than happy to kill in order to secure their escape, as just another extension of the tragedy they had wrought upon the Tarsus IV colonists to reach this point. Was there something he, Lorca, could have done to prevent further loss of life? Perhaps, but that was for other people to decide.

And what of Kodos? If indeed he was caught in the explosion and fire that claimed his final place of refuge, had death helped him escape punishment for his crimes? That, too, was a question best answered by those qualified to render such judgments.

At the end of all of this, Balayna Ferasini was still dead, along with thousands of other people, all victims of one man's horribly misguided sense of sacrifice and noble intentions. With respect to Kodos, he knew it was wrong to feel as he did rather than wondering if justice had been served, but he did not care. As he continued to watch the fire, he was satisfied that Adrian Kodos—if he was up there—was receiving exactly what he deserved.

Enjoy your funeral.

36

Getting her first look at Lorca, Philippa Georgiou thought the man might be dead.

"How is he?" she asked as she moved closer to where the commander, dirty and bloodied, his uniform wet and torn, sat leaning against the cavern wall. Kneeling next to Lorca was Ensign Terri Bridges, who also looked more than a little the worse for wear. She had pulled an emergency dermal patch from a field medical kit and applied it to the left side of Lorca's face, and was fitting a hypospray with some kind of medicine.

Bridges replied, "Despite his appearance, he'll live, Commander. We found him sitting here like this, and so far our conversation has been a series of grunts and point-ing." She held up a diagnostic scanner. "I don't think he's in a coma, at least according to this." Her smile was forced, as was her demeanor, and Georgiou knew the woman was holding herself together in the face of fatigue and grief.

"I'm just tired," said Lorca, his voice low and quiet. "I'll get to the coma later."

The comment was enough to ease Georgiou's concerns. "It's good to see you, Commander."

"Good to see you too."

There was no emotion in the man's voice, owing to more than simple exhaustion, which by itself would be more than just cause for Lorca to want to sit quietly. Both he and Bridges knew that there still were matters requiring attention before they would be allowed even the briefest respite.

"We don't know how many people were here," she said, "but we're making a full sweep of the entire underground network. We've got twenty-two people, either in custody or else their bodies were recovered." She pointed toward the collapsed tunnel entrance. "We found one body just outside that passageway, buried under rubble. Lieutenant O'Bannon and his people were damned lucky."

"You can say that again," replied Lorca.

Looking around the cavern, Georgiou took note of both Starfleet and civilian personnel working on various tasks. Most of the activity was taking place on the ledge overlooking the cave floor, which Georgiou knew was where Adrian Kodos made his last stand. Scorched rock walls and the smell of burned composite materials bore testimony to the destructive force of the explosives detonated in that contained space.

"Thermite grenades," she said, for Lorca's benefit. "A case of them, up there. I didn't even know they made those things anymore."

Lorca grunted. "They don't. They were outlawed over twenty years ago. Those must have been surplus ordnance, either brought here by someone immigrating to the colony, or else something shipped in under the radar by a member of the security forces."

"Well," Georgiou said, "you're lucky they didn't bring down the whole cavern around your ears."

"Just my day, I guess." He gestured toward the ledge. "I don't suppose they left much up there, did they?"

"I doubt it, but the forensic techs are checking everything."

Rubbing the side of his head, which still ached even with the medication Bridges gave him, Lorca said, "Until I see proof, Kodos isn't dead."

Doubt clouded Georgiou's features. "I don't think the thermite left all that much."

"Proof, or we keep going," he said with total seriousness. "After everything that's happened, nothing less than absolute confirmation of his death is sufficient." He glanced once more to the ledge. "If he's not up there, then I'm getting my gear and we're starting this all over again."

"Commander Georgiou."

It was Captain Korrapati, crossing the cavern toward her. He was walking alongside Governor Gisela Ribiero and another man in a Starfleet captain's uniform. The man, in his mid to late forties, was tall and fit, with wavy auburn hair that to Georgiou's eyes was somewhat longer than regulations typically allowed. His brown eyes burned with the intensity and wisdom earned from a long Starfleet career, but Georgiou thought there was a bit of playfulness there too. She guessed he commanded one of the two starships that had assumed orbit above Tarsus IV just over an hour earlier.

"Captain," she said, nodding to Korrapati while noting that Lorca had pushed himself to his feet. She offered greetings to Ribiero before turning her gaze to the other command officer. "I'm sorry, sir. We've not met. Commander Philippa Georgiou, temporarily assigned to the *Narbonne* under Captain Korrapati."

The other man smiled as they shook hands. "Oh, I know very well who you are, Commander." He extended his right hand. "Robert April, *U.S.S. Enterprise*." His British accent was crisp, though there was also a lilt in his voice that gave it a youthful quality despite his apparent age. "As I was telling Aurobindo, you've done tremendous work here." His gaze shifted to Lorca, and he offered his hand again. "Commander Lorca, it's good to meet you as well. I only wish it was under better circumstances."

"As do I, Captain," replied the commander. "Still, we're damned glad to see you."

April said, "We come bearing gifts, after a fashion. Food stores for the entire colony, for starters. They'll want for nothing. It's the least we can do. We've also brought a full staff of grief counselors and other therapists, and we're prepared to ferry anyone who needs additional or extended medical attention to Starbase 11 or their destination of choice." He shook his head. "None of that comes anywhere close to compensating these people for their losses, but it's a start, and hopefully it shows that somebody gives a damn about them the way you've obviously been demonstrating. You lot have left me with tremendous shoes to fill. I hope my crew and I can measure up."

Taking that as an apparent cue, Ribiero stepped toward Lorca. "Commander, I wanted to thank you personally for everything you've done for us. It's a debt we'll never be able to repay." She reached for his hand, taking it in both of hers. "I've been made aware of the personal loss you've suffered, as well as the deaths of your fellow Starfleet officers. You have my deepest sympathies."

"Thank you, Governor," said Lorca. "I appreciate you making time for me. As for the rest of it . . ." He cast his gaze toward the cavern floor. "I was just doing my duty, the same as Captain Korrapati, Commander Georgiou, and the rest of the *Narbonne* crew."

"It was not a jest when I said filling your shoes was a tall order," said April. "You all have accomplished so much in such a short period." He looked to Ribiero. "Governor, that the colony is far more stable than I expected to see upon arriving is a testament to the people themselves, but also your leadership."

"More the former, Captain," replied Ribiero. "We've been through a lot, and I need to earn back the trust of my fellow citizens, but we'll persevere, and this colony will soon be thriving once again. I've never been prouder of this community than I am now."

April nodded in unabashed approval. "And the progress being made toward isolating and fighting the contagion is most impressive. My chief medical officer expects to have a viable counteragent ready to deploy in less than a week, but that wouldn't be possible without the work you started. I long ago learned to take whatever estimate she provides for anything as nothing less than the gospel truth."

"For future reference," said Korrapati, "the *Enterprise*'s chief medical officer is also the good captain's wife."

"Sarah." April smiled. "Captain Korrapati's statement makes mine no less true."

Activity elsewhere in the cavern caught their notice, and Georgiou saw a pair of Starfleet officers, both dressed in pale blue coveralls, emerging from the space above the cave floor. She recognized them as the civilian forensic technicians dispatched by Korrapati as part of the team sent to support Lorca and his search party. Rather than using the crude ladder rungs hammered into the rock wall, the techs were descending a ramp installed to facilitate movement to and from the cave floor. Between them was an antigravity sled, atop which rested a black bag that Georgiou knew was large enough to accommodate a humanoid, but which appeared to contain something far smaller. Once on the floor, one of the technicians, a woman of Latino descent, made her way toward Ribiero and the group of officers.

"Good morning," she said by way of introduction. "My name is Amelia Cardoso. I'm a forensic pathologist. I know you've been waiting for information, and I'll give you what I have." She gestured to the ledge. "We found two bodies up there. Both human, one male, the other female. There wasn't much left. As you can imagine, the thermite was pretty efficient, though we were able to secure genetic samples from both victims."

Lorca, stepping closer, asked, "Were you able to make an identification?"

"Yes. The woman's name is Fiona Okafor. According to the colony administration databases, she's a maintenance worker assigned to one of the city's hydroponics farms." Cardoso paused, and Georgiou saw something in the woman's eyes. Relief? Sadness? Some odd combination of those two emotions?

"The man is Adrian Kodos."

Georgiou asked, "You're certain?"

"As certain as we can be." Reaching into a pocket of her overalls, Cardoso extracted a compact medical scanner. "We were able to run genetic comparisons between samples retrieved here and the colony medical databases. It's a match, no question. We can run more comprehensive tests once we take the bodies back to a proper lab, but even our field tests are ninety-nine percent reliable."

"It would be good to share this news with the colony," said Ribiero. "I'd like to make a formal address later this morning."

Lorca asked, "Is that wise, Governor? I mean, if we're not absolutely sure—"

"Regardless of the less-than-ideal outcome," said Korrapati, "the people need to know that there's a resolution to all of this. While it would've been preferable to have Kodos stand trial, this still provides a measure of closure."

"I believe you're right," added Captain April. "For the good of the community, I don't think you should sit on this."

Georgiou eyed Lorca. "Are you okay with this?"

"I suppose I'll have to be." The commander frowned.

"After everything that's happened, it just doesn't seem real somehow."

April said, "It seems real enough to me."

"Indeed." Ribiero placed a hand on Lorca's arm. "You can stop worrying about this, Commander. You've done us a great service. Thanks to you, Kodos is gone forever."

"But he still has supporters, Governor," countered Lorca. "Maybe we got the most committed followers, but what about those who cowered in the dark, silently cheering on the bastard and those who helped him? Those are the same people who celebrated your removal from office and got behind Kodos, whether or not they were brave enough to demonstrate that allegiance. What about them?"

"It's a complicated question, Commander," replied Ribiero, "and it's not one we'll answer today. We'll find those people, sooner or later, but for now? You've earned yourself a much-deserved rest."

Despite the praise and assurances, which Lorca accepted with aplomb, Georgiou saw that the man was not convinced. Something, whether it was determination, anger, dissatisfaction, or simple grief, was gnawing at him, and he would have to purge these personal demons in his own way and in his own time. Sooner or later, he would come to accept what science and common sense were trying to tell him.

Adrian Kodos was dead.

37

Containers of varying sizes covered most of the warehouse's floor. Some stood alone, while others were stacked atop one another or occupied shelving units along the walls or arranged in rows and clusters. From where she stood on a catwalk extending from the warehouse's second level, Georgiou regarded the haphazard maze in which one could lose themselves if they were not careful.

Whether issued by one of the Federation colony support entities or provided by the *Narbonne* or the other Starfleet vessels providing assistance, each crate, capsule, or other vessel held within it the household effects and other personal items of someone taken far too soon. Though hundreds of such parcels were amassed here, Georgiou knew there would be many more coming in the days ahead. Teams of people were working around the clock to inventory and package the possessions of each slain colonist, ensuring that everything was handled in a careful, reverent manner as it was prepared for transport. Each item would be delivered to family members or other designated parties, carrying with them fond memories as well as the embodiment of loss. From experience, Georgiou knew such keepsakes would forever harbor a dull, lingering ache of grief but also—if the fates were kind—some small measure of closure.

The full magnitude of the tragedy inflicted upon the people of Tarsus IV was put into some semblance of perspective. While the amphitheater offered its own perspective on the horror unleashed there, this vast sea of orphaned belongings was a blunt, profound indicator of the sheer number of lives so monstrously ended. To Georgiou it was a hammer striking without mercy, demanding that the senselessness of the atrocity committed here should neither be forgotten nor repeated.

Never again. We owe these people at least that much.

Not just them, she reminded herself. There were the men and women who died later, after the executions, as a consequence of the hunt for Kodos. Their sacrifices also needed to be observed and honored.

Footsteps on the catwalk to her left made Georgiou turn to see Gabriel Lorca walking in her direction. Like her, he wore a dress uniform suitable for the day's observances. His beard stubble was gone and he had received a haircut, so he now presented the epitome of a squared-away Starfleet officer.

"Commander," he said by way of greeting. "I was told you wanted to see me."

"Yes. Thank you for coming. I saw you at the memorial. I wanted to say again how sorry I am for your loss."

Lorca nodded. "Thank you." Rather than sit with the *Narbonne* crew who were mourning the deaths of their own people, he, Lieutenant Aasal Soltani, and Ensign Terri Bridges had instead attended the service with a small group of colonists, which Georgiou assumed to be friends or other acquaintances. Given Lorca's relationship with one of the women who perished, this was more than understandable.

"I thought it was a lovely service," said Georgiou.

Lorca nodded but did not reply, and she saw the pain that still lingered in the man's eyes. She also noted something else. Was it acceptance, or perhaps resignation? After all, he had to know why she had called him here.

"I let you continue the search for Kodos even though we both knew you weren't at your best. You were carrying a lot of emotional baggage, Commander, but I want to believe you when you tell me you didn't let your grief affect the way you carried out your duty."

Frowning, Lorca replied, "It didn't."

"You're sure?"

"I won't deny I was personally affected by all of this, but everyone who died here—the colonists, Meizhen and Piotr, Jason Giler, Balayna, all of them—deserved nothing less than the full measure of justice." Lorca looked away, casting his gaze over the warehouse floor. "I don't know that we'll ever be able to provide that for them in the proper measure, but hopefully it was enough so that they can rest a bit more peacefully."

"Did your feelings get in the way of bringing Kodos to justice?"

Anger flashed in Lorca's eyes. "If you're asking whether I deliberately killed him, Commander, the answer is no. Do I regret that he didn't live to stand trial? Of course, but am I sorry he's dead? Absolutely not."

Persuaded by his answers, Georgiou had to acknowledge that Lorca had done a tremendous, even superhuman job keeping his personal feelings at bay while carrying out the task of hunting Kodos and his followers. It was easy in hindsight to see how much the effort weighed on him, and yet he had soldiered on, putting aside grief and even a desire for vengeance in order to complete the assignment given to him. With the mission over—Kodos was gone, and some small parcel of justice had been served—Georgiou wondered if Lorca might finally allow himself to mourn.

"What's next for you?" she asked.

"They're temporarily assigning a new staff to the outpost. The four of us are to report to Starbase 11 for debriefing and extended shore leave. That's probably for the best, I think."

What he did not say, and what Georgiou knew, was the outpost's surviving team members, and Lorca in particular, would undergo psychological evaluation in order to determine if there might be any residual and potentially harmful consequences to what they had endured. Such reviews were normal after any personal loss, and varied in scope and intensity depending on the nature of the incident in question.

As for the remaining colonists, several hundred were scheduled for transport away from Tarsus IV at their request, aboard either the *Narbonne* or one of the other ships attached to the relief effort. She was not surprised to hear that the overwhelming majority of the population was electing to remain. The reasons varied, of course, from a desire to maintain some connection to a lost loved one, to a simple wish to not feel as though they were being forced from the home they had made here, to a renewed commitment to the goals embodied by the colony and the potential it represented. There was much encouragement and inspiration to be taken from that.

"What about you, Commander?" asked Lorca. "Where are you headed?"

"I was on my way to the *Defiant* before all of this. I suspect that's where I'll end up once we're back at Starbase 11 and I get my debriefing." So hectic was the situation since arriving on Tarsus IV that there was little to no time to consider her pending new duty assignment. The science vessel was a good posting, and would provide all manner of new challenges unlike those faced aboard a patrol ship. What she learned aboard the *Defiant* would offer insight into another aspect of Starfleet's overall mission of exploration and the expansion of knowledge. The experience would serve her well as she continued her pursuit of one day commanding a ship of her own.

But enough about me.

"I haven't asked how you're doing," she said.

Lorca replied, "I've already had an extensive conversation with Captain Korrapati about all of this. As I told him, the mission is over. Kodos is dead. I know there are those who would've preferred he was brought back to stand trial. I understand their feelings and as a Starfleet officer I did everything in my power to affect that outcome, but Kodos made his choice. He pushed the fight, and he's dead as a result. As far as any official reports are concerned, I'm disappointed that he died before we could take him into custody, and saddened that our attempts to capture him resulted in the loss of even a single life."

"But unofficially?"

"I'm sorry he didn't burn longer and live while doing it."

Her eyebrows rising at the cold, harsh truth lacing his words, Georgiou nodded. "Best to keep that out of the report."

"Absolutely." Then, Lorca offered a small smile. "I appreciate your concern, Commander. Honestly, and I'd be lying if I told you I'm fine and there's nothing to worry about. The truth is that I'm a long way from being fine, but I'm better than I was a few days ago. A few days from now, I'll be better still. But I know it will be a while before I get past it." He placed his hand on the catwalk's guard rail. "I may never be completely past it. Balayna was . . . something very special." The smile returned, and Georgiou could tell it was not forced for her benefit. "She was everything I wasn't. Spontaneous, serene, maybe even a little too wild on occasion. Balayna was a free spirit, and a caring soul unlike anyone I've ever known. She was a descendant of the

original settlers, but she wasn't caught up in all of the isola-
tionist talk and the movement to declare the planet free of
Federation oversight. When relocation happened, she was
one of the strongest supporters once the influx of refugees
started. There were all kinds of committees and task groups
designed to help with the transition into the community,
and from what her friends told me, I think she volunteered for all of them." He paused, his features softening as
though he was recalling a pleasant memory.

"I wish I could've met her," offered Georgiou.

"You'd have liked her. She made me want to be a better person, to do something worthwhile with my life, and
maybe even make life just a little better for someone else."

Lorca was staring ahead, though perhaps not focusing
on anything in particular, and Georgiou heard him utter a
short, quiet laugh. "She convinced me to try orbital skydiv-
ing. Do you know how insane and ridiculous that sounds
to me? I would never have done something like that before
meeting her. I wouldn't have tried a lot of things before
meeting her." He sighed. "Balayna was good for me."

"She still is," replied Georgiou. "She sounds like an
amazing person, and it's obvious she had an influence on
you, beyond the obvious attraction. You haven't given
yourself the time to properly mourn her, but now you can.
Do that, hold on to the good things, and don't let what
you shared go to waste, Commander."

Returning his attention to her, Lorca cocked an eyebrow. "After everything we've been through, ranks seem a
little stuffy, Philippa. I'm Gabriel."

"Don't let everything you shared with Balayna go to
waste, Gabriel, for her sake."

Lorca straightened his posture. "I don't plan to. I just
don't know how to go about it. For a while, I was even considering leaving Starfleet to stay here with her." He shook

his head. "Staying here doesn't seem right anymore, but I'm not sure Starfleet is the right place for me anymore either."

"Starfleet needs good officers like you," Georgiou countered. "They've also invested a great deal into your training and career. It'd be a shame if you didn't give them an opportunity to get a decent return on that investment." She suspected he knew this, just as she suspected he knew that he still had much to offer Starfleet. While some joined the service because they wanted to or believed they could contribute to something greater than themselves, there were those who answered what they felt was a higher calling: a mandate or even destiny of sorts, for which an ordinary life would never be able to offer a worthy substitute. Did Gabriel Lorca view Starfleet this way? Of that, Georgiou could not be sure. In her experience, it was a question best asked and answered by the person it most directly affected.

"Deep down, I know you're right," said Lorca. "Just as I know it's likely the best place for me. I can't run away from what happened, or go hide somewhere and hope for the pain to pass or that I might forget. I don't want to forget." He gestured to the warehouse floor. "And I don't want this to happen anywhere else."

Behind the grief he still felt, Georgiou heard his conviction. With only her gut instincts to guide her, she felt he would not turn his back on Starfleet. However, what he endured here would stay with him. His heart had hardened in the face of what he had suffered and lost, and in the actions he had taken to bring Kodos to justice. The experience would fade, but would always lurk just within the shadows. It would forever weigh on him without his conscious knowledge, the way living through any extreme event affected a person's psyche. How Lorca accepted or rejected this unavoidable change within would define the type of person he was to be from this time forward.

"Ever since that last fight with Kodos and his people," he said, "I've been asking myself how things might have gone differently. I honestly did want to bring him in. I wanted the families and friends of those he killed to see him, along with those who helped him, face the full weight of Federation justice. But there was a small part of me that just didn't care." He turned to meet her gaze. "And an even smaller part that wished I could've killed him with my bare hands. It would've been wrong, and I'd like to think reason and duty would've won out, but . . . if I had it to do over again, I wonder what I would've done."

Georgiou shook her head. "I think you know." She looked toward the containers of personal effects. "Upholding a set of ideals can be difficult, and sometimes it's damned cruel. Being able to do that, especially during times of adversity and crisis and even great personal tragedy, is the true test of anyone privileged to wear this." Reaching up, she tapped her chest to indicate her Starfleet uniform. "We're bound to uphold and defend those ideals, but the harder job is living up to them."

His expression falling, Lorca said, "I don't know if I'm capable of that anymore." He sighed. "For that matter, I don't know if I ever was."

"Balayna knew." Georgiou smiled. "Something tells me the woman you described was a pretty good judge of character, and wouldn't bother with someone who wasn't of a mind similar to hers. What do you think she'd say to you if she were here?"

Again, Lorca smiled. "That I should quit sulking and get back to work."

Sounds like good advice, Georgiou decided. *For all of us.*

38

Resisting the urge to grab on to a handrail or anything else to help her maintain her balance, Georgiou waited for the turbulence engulfing the *Narbonne* to wane as it clawed upward through the last vestiges of Tarsus IV's atmosphere and pushed into open space. Her stomach was the first to register the almost imperceptible shift when the vessel's artificial gravity systems kicked in, replacing the natural pull of the planet itself.

"We've achieved orbit," reported Lieutenant Melissa Parham from where she sat at the helm console. "Securing launch thrusters, and adjusting trajectory for standard orbit departure course."

Seated in his chair at the center of the bridge, Captain Korrapati said, "Nicely done, Lieutenant. Commander Larson, secure from atmospheric operations and let's get ready to head home."

"Aye, sir," replied the *Narbonne*'s first officer from where she sat at the aft engineering monitoring station. She tapped the control to activate the ship's intercom. "Commander Larson to all hands. Commence postlaunch systems checks."

Korrapati turned in his chair to face Georgiou, who managed to withstand the atmospheric buffeting without resorting to taking a seat. Smiling at her, he said, "You're getting the hang of this, Commander. We may just make a planet hopper out of you yet." He gestured toward the screen. "However, I promise it'll be smooth sailing from here on out."

"Sounds good to me, Captain." The return trip to Starbase 11 promised to be routine, followed by whatever debriefing schedule awaited her with officials from Starfleet Command who still were trying to wrap their heads around everything that had transpired on Tarsus IV. According to a message from Admiral Anderson, her assignment to the *U.S.S. Defiant* was still on track, with her orders revised to include the layover at the starbase. At this point, she was looking forward to starship duty. The demands placed upon the first officer of a science vessel were bound to be less taxing than what she and the rest of the *Narbonne* crew had just undergone.

Don't jinx it.

At the communications console, Ensign Richard Doherty turned in his seat. "Captain, we're being hailed by the *Enterprise*."

Pushing himself from his chair, Korrapati stepped around the helm console, putting himself directly in front of the main viewscreen before gesturing to the younger officer. "Put it on screen."

A moment later, the image of Tarsus IV and the space beyond the curve of the planet disappeared, replaced by the visage of Robert April. Now that he was back aboard the welcoming environs of his own ship, April was making good on the reputation that preceded him. Georgiou almost smiled at his nod to eccentricity, with the captain sporting a wooly gray cardigan, the front of which was open to reveal his Starfleet uniform tunic. His hands were jammed into its pockets, giving him something of a professorial appearance that was exacerbated by his unkempt hair. Behind April, the *Enterprise* bridge was a hive of color and activity, with men and women manning consoles that seemed jammed to over-flowing with controls and display screens.

"Aurobindo," said April, offering a smile as he eschewed proper protocol. *"I just wanted to wish you and your crew safe travels."*

"Thank you, Captain. It's been an honor to work with you. I just wish the circumstances could have been better."

"Likewise. You and your people can be proud of the work you've done here. There's still a lot left to do, but we wouldn't be where we are without everything you did. I suspect a great many souls—of the dead as well as the living—will rest just a bit easier, thanks to you."

Though she was anxious to get on with her next assignment, a part of Georgiou wanted to remain on Tarsus IV, to see how things progressed in the weeks and months to come. The people of New Anchorage and the other settlements were well on their way to returning to their normal lives, but the scars left by Kodos would be a long time healing. Several of his supporters were aboard the *Narbonne*, berthed in isolated quarters and under constant watch by the ship's security detail; at Starbase 11 they would be remanded to station security while they awaited trial. Georgiou would be keeping tabs on those proceedings, as well as checking on the planet and the status of the recovery effort.

"Between Governor Ribiero, her people, and you and the other ships helping her out, I think Tarsus IV is in good hands, sir," said Korrapati. "Best of luck to all of you."

April smiled. *"Fair winds and following seas,* Narbonne. *This is* Enterprise, *signing off."*

The connection was severed and April disappeared, returning the main screen to its image of the planet, only now Ensign Doherty had engaged the *Narbonne* sensors to provide a view of the *Enterprise* as it pursued its own standard orbit of Tarsus IV. It was Georgiou's first up-close look at a

Constitution-class starship, and the mighty vessel was a sight to behold.

I guess that's the future. That's my future.

Excusing herself from the bridge, Georgiou headed down the companionway toward the crew recreation and mess areas. Her stomach reminded her that she had missed breakfast, and it was well past time to correct that oversight. With no official duties awaiting her now that the *Narbonne* was on its way to Starbase 11, the only activities demanding her attention were the after-action reports she would be submitting to Admiral Anderson and Starfleet Command, and precisely none of those appealed to her. On the other hand, a workout in the ship's gym followed by a long, hot shower and a nap held greater attraction.

Come to think of it, that nap's sounding better by the minute.

"Commander!"

The young voice stopped Georgiou in her tracks, and she returned to the corridor junction she had just passed to see Shannon Moulton, familiar Andorian plush doll in hand, running toward her. Shannon's mother, Eliana, followed close behind, smiling in apparent embarrassment.

"Shannon," said Georgiou. "What are you doing up here?" From what she had been told, civilians were not supposed to be allowed into this part of the ship.

Blissfully unaware of any protocols she may have been breaching, the girl ran up to Georgiou and wrapped her short arms around Georgiou's legs.

"I apologize, Commander," said Eliana. "Commander Larson said it would be all right if we came up here to find you. Shannon's been wanting to see you."

Dropping to a knee so that she was eye level with the girl, Georgiou smiled. "I didn't get to see you before we left, but I knew we'd run into each other sooner or later. It's not that big a ship, after all. So, what brings you up here?"

"We're going to see my grandparents," replied Shannon, changing the topic of discussion with no effort in that way only children could. "They live on Mars."

Georgiou had seen the Moultons in the boarding area at the spaceport prior to the *Narbonne*'s departure. A quick check of the status reports from the colony informed her that Shannon and her mother were among those opting to leave Tarsus IV in favor of a fresh start. No doubt, Eliana Moulton was hoping to bury the pain and grief she felt at the loss of her husband. Shannon, on the other hand, was insulated from that anguish thanks to the merciful innocence of childhood. It would be a while before she came to understand what she had survived, and why her father had not.

"If you're going to Mars," said Georgiou, "then you should ask Captain Korrapati about it. He was born there, you know."

Eliana replied, "We'll be sure to do that. Shannon, don't you have something for Commander Georgiou?"

Instead of replying, Shannon held up the doll in her right hand. The stuffed Andorian companion now sported two antennae thanks to Georgiou's repair efforts, and she noted that it had been cleaned since she last saw it.

"I want you to take him. Maybe he can bring you luck now."

The simple gesture was enough to elicit tears, and Georgiou reached up to wipe her eyes. "Thank you, sweetheart. I promise to take good care of him."

Reaching to brush the girl's hair, she marveled at how this child had somehow weathered everything cruel fate had thrown at her. It gave Georgiou hope that everyone who had survived the Tarsus IV incident—along with those who came to help—might learn to live with what they experienced.

She gazed at the doll. While it represented enormous loss, perhaps it also served as a reminder for the future.

Despite the actions of Kodos and his followers, Georgiou remained heartened by how so many of the colonists were able to come together in the face of such tragedy and help one another. Her belief in the empathy and willingness of intelligent beings to bond even during times of extreme hardship may have been tested, but not broken.

Could anything positive come from what the Tarsus IV colonists experienced? At the moment, Georgiou was hard-pressed to see what, or how that might happen, but Shannon Moulton gave her hope.

After promising the girl and her mother to meet up again on Starbase 11, Georgiou took her leave of the Moultons and started back down the passageway. Descending to the crew level, she passed the large open area of deck space that housed the ship's gymnasium and other recreational facilities. Separate rooms around the larger chamber's perimeter offered a small library and audiovisual entertainment alcoves, all of it surrounding a collection of fitness equipment.

A few members of the *Narbonne*'s crew were working out on different machines, while one man stood alone on the room's opposite side, exercising in frenetic fashion against a person-sized mannequin designed for boxing and other hand-to-hand combat training. The man was attacking the simulated opponent with what Georgiou thought to be barely restrained fury.

It was Gabriel Lorca.

He landed punch after punch, feeling the training model's padded, synthetic outer shell give beneath his knuckles with each impact. Every landed strike elicited a tone, indicating a point added to his score. Lorca preferred training simulations like this one to simple boxing bags, for the feeling of facing off against an actual person. The mannequins could be programmed to simulate any of over a hundred different humanoid life-forms, presenting each species' respective vulnerable or soft spots and adjusting the difficulty setting automatically.

For sessions like this, Lorca normally preferred to square off against a Klingon simulation, which tended to present one of the programs more challenging options. Today, however, he had elected to combat a standard Earth human. Whereas the computer assigned no identity to his manufactured opponent, Lorca already had a particular persona in mind. Not satisfied with standard boxing training, he had switched to a sparring method first learned years earlier, before joining Starfleet. A mix of techniques mastered in martial arts classes during his youth was later augmented by his Academy and security school training. He had taken to it all, relishing the challenge of developing his skills to their limit, and testing them against his instructors and other opponents. The victories in such situations were rewarding, but so too were the defeats, as he almost always came away from those matches having learned something new about himself or discovering yet another improvement he might pursue.

Another thing he had learned over the years was that there was a time and place for form and technique, usually in a training dojo or formal competition. When it came to real-world situations, Lorca preferred a blended fighting style that relied on fast, violent attacks designed to incapacitate his opponent as quickly as possible.

Then there were the times when he just wanted to beat on something.

He shifted his attack away from the mannequin's torso, focusing each strike on the target's head. The pings announcing points augmenting his score meant nothing. Tones bleating that he had landed blows sufficient to stun or even kill his imaginary opponent went unheeded.

All he saw was Kodos, the face of the executioner, pum-meled and bleeding at his hands. Every strike was retribu-tion. Every perceived cry of pain or plea for mercy was fuel to drive Lorca harder.

You got off lucky, you bastard.

Lorca pressed the assault, holding the vision of Kodos in his sights and inflicting that much more imaginary pain upon the dead governor. If he continued doing this, it might keep the images of Meizhen Bao, Piotr Nolokov, and especially Balayna Ferasini from haunting him for just a little longer.

Not the best plan, but for now I'll go with it.

Only after he realized the sparring target was no longer reacting to his punches and a voice was calling to him from somewhere did he force himself to stop. His hands aching and his lungs on fire, Lorca drew deep breaths as he stepped away from the mannequin before noticing the pair of wide-eyed crew members staring at him. The pair—a man and a woman, each dressed in fitness attire emblazoned with the *Narbonne*'s name and registry number—regarded him with obvious concern.

"Sir?" prompted the female crew member. "I think you killed it."

Taking another step back from the training target, Lorca saw that the mannequin was standing at an angle, rocked back off the base anchoring it to the deck. Indenta-tions from his fists were still visible in the model's chest re-gion, and its face was misshapen and even collapsed inward several centimeters.

"I didn't even know you could do that to these things," said the younger male officer, before turning his gaze to Lorca. "Are you all right, sir?"

The ache in his knuckles making him look at his hands, Lorca saw fresh blood soaking through the thin sparring gloves. He flexed his fingers. They would hurt for a while, but there was nothing broken.

"I'm better now."

He really was a far cry from being "better," let alone "okay" or "fine." But these two junior officers, looking for a workout free from distractions, did not deserve to be the brunt of his emotional outbursts.

Without another word, he turned and made his way from the gym floor, stripping off his sparring gloves and giving his fingers another tentative flex. The blood there was still oozing, but it was nothing a dermal regenerator could not handle. Moving toward a bench where a towel and a bottle of water waited for him, he noted the figure standing near the doorway on the room's opposite side: Philippa Georgiou. Her face was a mask of concern, doubtless heightened by the sight of his bloodied knuckles. Despite the dull throb beginning to radiate through his hands, he felt better than he had in days.

"Good evening, Commander," he said, exchanging the water bottle for his towel. "Something I can do for you?"

"I was about to ask you the same question." Her tone was flat, but her features still communicated the worry that had greeted him upon noticing her presence in the gym.

"Just working off a little excess energy." Lorca wiped the towel across his face and over his hair. He stretched his fingers again. The pain was already beginning to ebb. In a few minutes, he might be up for another round with the bag.

Georgiou asked, "Anything you want to talk about?"

Instead of replying, Lorca wiped his face again. As he did so, he noted a trio of obvious civilians entering the gym. He knew that Captain Korrapati had offered the use of all of the ship's exercise and other facilities to the hundreds of passengers the *Narbonne* carried, and that the invitation extended to those areas of the ship normally reserved for the crew in order to help with potential overcrowding. There already were a few people—colonists who decided to leave Tarsus IV for transfer to Starbase 11 and eventual transport to some other destination—making use of the gym, and Lorca expected to see still more during the days it would take the ship to make the journey.

"I figured we discussed everything back on the planet," he said after a moment, and from the look in Georgiou's eyes, it was obvious he would not get off that easy.

"And I got the sense you were holding something back."

Releasing a sigh, he sat on the bench, leaning against the adjacent bulkhead as he took another sip of his water. "You read people pretty well, Commander."

"It's a gift." Without waiting for an invitation, Georgiou took a seat next to him on the bench. "So, what's bothering you?"

Lorca released a small, humorless chuckle. "Everything."

"Give me an example."

Drinking from his bottle, Lorca pondered her request for a moment, and decided there was no reason to be coy any longer. By this point, Georgiou had more than earned a straight answer.

"We should be evacuating the entire planet. To hell with what some of the colonists want. We should pull every last soul from there and relocate them, and then mark Tarsus IV as off-limits. I'd suggest obliterating the damned thing, but even I think that might be a bit extreme."

"At least you'd be waiting for us to get the people up before you pulled the trigger."

"And don't think I didn't consider leaving at least some people behind for that."

Georgiou rested against the bulkhead, crossing her arms. "Fair enough. As for this idea of yours, what about the people who've decided to stay and rebuild?"

"Screw them." It was a simple, blunt statement, uttered almost without conscious thought, and for a second or two Lorca considered offering something to soften it. Then he dismissed that notion before taking another sip of water. "From this point on, any mention of Tarsus IV in any history book or database will start and end with what happened here. There's nothing left to rebuild, except a legacy of poor leadership, lack of simple damned humanity, and avoidable tragedy, and that's the way it'll be, forever."

When Georgiou said nothing in response, he added, "It's not just about Kodos, but also the environment that allowed him to do what he did. He didn't act alone, or in a vacuum." It was all well and good that those followers of Kodos taken into custody would face justice for their aiding and abetting him. On the other hand, it had taken Lorca a bit of time and reflection to realize that such action only addressed part of the problem.

"Where the hell did we go wrong? Two centuries ago on Earth, we damned near bombed ourselves out of existence, and those people lucky enough to survive that *still* found ways to keep fighting over what was left. We got lucky that the Vulcans showed up and opted to give a shit about us. They handed us a second chance on a silver platter, and for a while there we looked and acted like we might deserve it."

Finishing the water bottle, he tossed it across the room in the general direction of the recycler. It bounced on the floor and rolled toward the far bulkhead.

"Imagine what those first Vulcans to visit Earth would say if they could see what we let happen on Tarsus IV. What about those who raised hell when we finally decided to take that first warp flight out of our solar system? It's not like we didn't give them reason to worry, and yet they stuck with us. They stood beside us during the Xindi crisis, fought a war with us against the Romulans, and helped us found the Federation because they finally believed we were ready to act like a mature species capable of standing like grown-ups on an interstellar stage. How do we betray that trust? By panicking in the face of crisis and killing four thousand of our own people because it was the 'expedient' thing to do. The four thousand people who survived that purge don't deserve the gift of survival they were given."

"It wasn't everyone," countered Georgiou. "It wasn't even a significant percentage of people on his side."

"But there were enough of them." Lorca shook his head. "There were those who either believed as he did, or found they could live with it because it helped save their own asses. Some of those people are dead, and we took a lot more of them into custody, but you and I both know that hiding among those survivors are people who are thanking deities or random chance or the fact that Kodos found them useful enough to keep alive. Some of them believed in what he was doing, even if they never admit that for as long as they live. Tell me how any of that espouses our lofty Federation values."

Georgiou said, "It doesn't, but you can't blame an entire group of people for the actions of a few extremists. History is full of dire consequences brought on by that sort of thinking."

Sighing, Lorca looked down at his hands as he bent his fingers. The pain was all but gone, and the blood had dried on his knuckles.

"Thinking about another round?" asked Georgiou.

"Yes, I am. At least the bag and I have an understanding."

"If you want to talk, I'm happy to listen." She pushed herself from the bench, straightening her uniform tunic. "Don't give up on those ideals just yet, Gabriel. If I've learned anything, it's that after a test like this, we seem to do well at remembering what makes us who we are, and we rededicate ourselves to those things we hold dear in a quest to do better. History also has its share of those stories, and it may well prove you wrong here too."

Lorca stood. "Believe it or not, I'd be very happy to see that." The smile, small and tired though it may be, was genuine. He admired Philippa Georgiou, who despite everything she had witnessed on Tarsus IV still found room to hope not just for the present, but also for the future.

Wiping off his hand, he reached into his pocket. He remembered how Balayna at first thought it strange when he gave her fortune cookies. It was an affectation he acquired years earlier, and it became something of a game between them. Later, she insisted the fortune was the best part of their dates. She kept them, in that wooden bowl in her apartment, and every so often pulled one at random to read aloud. Sometimes, she would joke that she was searching for inspiration, or that she was selecting an attitude by which she would face the coming day. It was yet another of her delightful eccentricities.

The paper resting in the palm of his hand, Lorca studied the words it contained.

Hate is never conquered by hate. Hate is conquered by love.

It seemed Georgiou and Balayna shared the same outlook.

One day, Lorca hoped he might feel the same way.

39

Excerpt from *The Four Thousand: Crisis on Tarsus IV*

Following the departure of the *U.S.S. Narbonne*, other Starfleet vessels operating under the joint command of the *Starship Enterprise*'s captain, Robert April, remained at Tarsus IV for another seventy-nine days. Through their work with Governor Ribiero and the leadership council, order was quickly restored, and the remaining colonists attempted to turn their attentions to the future. Part of that process was addressing still important matters that lingered in the aftermath of the tragedy, which required immediate attention if the surviving population was to move forward.

While Kodos was killed during the attempt to capture him, many of his supporters were taken into custody. After careful deliberation with Federation legal experts, it was decided that those charged with aiding Kodos to carry out the executions would face trial at a neutral location well away from Tarsus IV. The demands of justice and fair treatment under the law were observed; separation from the scene of their crime was deemed necessary. All twenty-seven men and women who faced charges were convicted of their roles in the Tarsus IV massacre. Each went on to serve life sentences in a handful of Federation penal colonies.

Following the eradication of the fungal infection that ravaged the colony's food supplies and inhibited the production of farming and other food production operations, the effects of the plague would continue to be felt for months. Even after the crisis itself was declared "over," memories of what happened here would never truly fade.

Ten years after those horrific events, for those who survived the brief yet deadly reign of Kodos, the scars still run deep. Talking with colonists who bore witness to the events of that dreadful night reveals a host of haunted memories. Those who lost friends or family members still speak with great affection and sadness about those whose lives were cut short in such brutal fashion. Even younger men and women who were children on the night of the massacre carry disquieting memories of that time, able to process their individual experiences only years afterward and with the support of family members, friends, or professional counselors.

For anyone who opts to leave Tarsus IV, this almost always invites curiosity once it's learned that person lived through the tragedy, or is the offspring of a survivor. Given the state of modern society and the many luxuries we take for granted, unless an individual was caught up in the incident or has a personal connection to a victim or a survivor, there are no points of comparison. The actions undertaken on Tarsus IV, even if motivated by supposed purity of purpose, are simply too far outside mainstream thinking to fully understand or appreciate.

Those on Tarsus IV left behind to pick up the pieces of shattered lives found themselves at a crossroads. Many people, either descendants of the original settlers or people transplanted from Epsilon Sorona II or other colonies, chose relocation to Earth or another Federation world. However, the vast majority of the planet's surviving population elected to stay. Not content to rebuild just their own lives, there began a growing movement among the community to ensure the massacre, along with the harsh lessons it imparted, was not forgotten. Monuments would be constructed, and memorial services were and continue to be observed each year.

Further, there was and remains a concerted effort to make certain such an incident is never visited upon another population, anywhere. In the years following the Tarsus IV incident, numerous strides were made in improving adaptability and compatibility testing for plants and seeds transferred between worlds, with an emphasis on verifying agricultural suitability on existing as well as new colony worlds. Thomas Leighton, himself a teenager during the massacre, is currently studying to be a scientist, learning to improve farming techniques so that crops from ecologically disparate worlds can be cultivated side by side. Leighton, who was not actually among the colonists gathered for the execution, was able to get close enough to the venue to witness the massacre firsthand. Injured during the ensuing chaos, he still bears the marks of his wounds, with the left side of his face covered by a form-fitting shroud to hide mangled flesh and bone as well as his missing eye. For reasons he chooses not to share, he years ago opted against reconstructive surgery to restore his features.

"When I'm alone, or if I'm lying in bed before drifting off to sleep," says Leighton in an interview conducted for this book, "I can still see his face and hear his voice. It's as clear as when I heard it that night in the amphitheater." According to the official reports, fewer than a dozen people are still alive today who saw Adrian Kodos on Tarsus IV with their own eyes, so for them the pain runs even deeper, as they are able, firsthand, to put a face to the man who inflicted so much pain and fear.

Driven to prevent another incident like Tarsus IV from ever happening again, Leighton has spent years devoted to his studies. His successes, along with those of so many others like him, will continue to expand colonization efforts on worlds across the quadrant. New settlements enjoy levels of cultural and technological diversity that could only be dreamed about just decades ago.

Not satisfied with these achievements, Leighton and others continue to expand their research into other areas, such as creating fool-proof means of combating or even preventing ecological dangers like the plague that ravaged Tarsus IV. For the past three years, Leighton has focused his research on developing synthetic foodstuffs in order to curb famine and ensure that nothing can endanger the food supplies or production abilities on any populated world. His work with zenite, a mineral indigenous to the planet Ardana and primarily used to mitigate the effects of plant diseases on worlds throughout the Federation, has yielded promising results with his new research. Despite years devoted to this effort, Leighton will tell you that it does little to assuage the pain he still feels about the events on Tarsus IV.

"Even though they say he's dead, he and the heinous acts he committed are forever seared into my memory. All of it will haunt me for the rest of my days."

Disregarding the official reports detailing the fate of Kodos, Leighton is one of a small number of people who wonder if the tyrant really is dead. Having seen all of the information submitted by Starfleet personnel who participated in the manhunt for Kodos and who were there during the final skirmish that brought about his death, people like Leighton still wonder if the story of Kodos really ended ten years ago on Tarsus IV. The topic is one of moderate popularity in circles that entertain conspiracy theories of every sort, though official circles give the idea no public credence. As for Leighton, he actually eschews such unsubstantiated gossip.

"I don't really believe he's still alive," offers the scientist, aware that holding such beliefs might prove detrimental to his work. "But he'll live on in my memory, and the memories of everyone who survived that bloody, horrible thing he did to all of us."

U.S.S. SHENZHOU NCC-1227

MARCH 16, 2256

40

Resting the padd on her desk, Philippa Georgiou leaned back in her chair, eyeing with great admiration the author of what she had just read.

"Well, that was a hell of a thing."

From the couch set against the ready room's far bulkhead, Shannon Moulton set aside the data slate with which she occupied herself while the captain read in silence. She straightened her posture, lifting her gaze to meet Georgiou's.

"Do you really think so?"

"Absolutely." Georgiou tapped the padd with the fingers of her left hand. "I've read other books about Tarsus IV, and even a few interviews from survivors, but none of them carry this level of personal detail." She laid her hand on the padd. "This is a wonderful tribute, to the living as well as the dead. It's the story they've deserved to have told for ten years. You did a marvelous job capturing so many different perspectives and memories, and giving the entire narrative a proper balance. Each of the people you interviewed brought something unique to the overall picture you were painting. I admit I was surprised at your inclusion of Fujimura and other Kodos supporters, but after reading the whole thing, I see that you were right to have them represented as well."

It would be difficult, Georgiou decided, for some readers to appreciate the viewpoints offered by anyone who aided or otherwise sympathized with Adrian Kodos, but she believed the proper chronicling of any historical event required insight from all sides of the issue. This included the losers as well as the winners of any conflict, and in the case of Tarsus IV, this meant the accounts of perpetrators as well as victims. What would Kodos himself have thought of Shannon's efforts? It was an interesting question that would, of course, never receive the answer the author or her work deserved.

Her face flushing with obvious embarrassment, Shannon reached up to cover the smile she was doing her best to conceal. "Thank you, Captain. That means a lot, coming from you."

Sitting with her hands clasped in her lap, she was showing signs of the nervousness that seemed to plague her upon her arrival aboard ship. Georgiou considered the possibility that this might well be Shannon's first visit to a Starfleet vessel since leaving Tarsus IV. At eighteen Earth years of age, with loose-fitting civilian clothing and long blond hair flowing past her shoulders, Shannon Moulton was very much out of place aboard the prim and proper *Shenzhou*. Even if she opted for a career in Starfleet, she was at least four years away from earning the right to wear a uniform and serve aboard a vessel like this one, but Georgiou knew the girl's future lay along a different path. That much was obvious from her manuscript, which still lingered in Georgiou's mind.

Has it really been ten years since I last saw her? How is she not still that little girl with dirty clothes and a broken leg?

On the other hand, there seemed to be a wisdom lurking behind Shannon's blue eyes that belied her youth. Hers was a childhood marked by tragedy, and that she emerged from the calamity of Tarsus IV able to process the sights she had witnessed and the memories she still carried was a testament to her character and inner strength. Even as an adult encountering only the aftermath of what Shannon and her fellow colonists endured, Georgiou remained haunted by those memories.

Pushing herself from her chair, Georgiou stepped around her desk, crossing the ready room to take a seat next to Shannon on the couch.

"What made you decide to write about this?"

Shannon's hands fidgeted for a moment before she replied, "It's something I was thinking about for a while. At the time, I only understood some of what was happening. I didn't comprehend the magnitude of it all until much later. I remember asking my mother about it once or twice, but she was always reluctant to talk about it." She paused, a small smile teasing the corners of her mouth. "I'm sure she thought I was still too young to hear about such things."

The smile faded, and Shannon fell silent, her head tilting downward until she was staring at her own clasped hands. "Then she got sick, and the end came so suddenly that those sorts of things just weren't important. Later, when I was in high school and living with my aunt on Benecia, few people where I lived even knew about what happened. It's like it was already being forgotten." She lifted her head, returning her attention to Georgiou. "That's when I decided I needed to learn and understand as much as I could, and write about it, not just for me or the other survivors, and not even for the people we lost. It's a story that needs to be told, and it needs to be heard, by as many people as possible so that nothing like it ever happens again. Maybe someone, somewhere, will someday do a better job than I have, but I think this is a good start." Reaching out, she placed a hand on Georgiou's. "I can't thank you enough for agreeing to be a part of it."

"I'll admit I was reluctant at first." Georgiou recalled her surprise several months earlier upon receiving the subspace message from Shannon, asking for an interview as one of dozens that would comprise the book. "I wasn't sure mine was an appropriate voice to be included, as it's not really my story to tell, the way it is with you and the other survivors."

Shannon shook her head. "But you and the others who came to help us are as much a part of that story as anyone. You helped us get through it, and not just by bringing food and other supplies. Finding Kodos and his followers and bringing them to justice was an important part of helping us all heal." Her expression turned somber. "Unfortunately, not everyone I contacted agreed to be interviewed."

"Captain Lorca." It was an easy deduction, given the lack of an interview from one of the few Starfleet officers who witnessed the massacre and its immediate aftermath.

"He politely declined," said Shannon. "At least, that was the message I was given. I was never able to contact him directly, but a representative from Starfleet Command told me he'd received my message."

Georgiou sighed. "I'm not surprised he turned you down. It affected him more than he was willing to admit." It had been years since she last saw Gabriel Lorca, and she had no idea as to his present whereabouts. "I don't know if he was ever able to come to terms with what happened."

"I understand, but I'm still disappointed. His story deserved to be in there, too, but it's his to tell." She sighed. "Maybe one day he'll change his mind."

Rubbing her hands on her uniform trousers, Georgiou said, "Want to get out of here for a minute? I need some air."

"On a spaceship?" asked Shannon.

"It's an expression, young writer. Come on, and humor me."

They exited Georgiou's ready room and emerged on the *Shenzhou*'s bridge. Her first officer and the rest of the prime bridge crew were officially off duty, having been relieved by beta shift while Georgiou was reading Shannon's book. Despite the hour, the captain was not surprised to see Lieutenant Saru standing at the science station just behind the captain's chair, engrossed in some task he likely preferred to complete now rather than wait until his next scheduled duty shift. Sitting in the command seat was Ensign Danby Connor, who rose from the seat upon noticing Georgiou's arrival on the bridge.

"Good evening, Captain," said Connor. "Is there something I can do for you?"

Georgiou shook her head. "As you were, Ensign. I'm guessing this is part of Commander Burnham's training regimen?"

"Yes, Captain. I volunteered to stand an extra watch."

In addition to her regular duties, her first officer, Lieutenant Commander Michael Burnham, also oversaw a comprehensive cross-training program for all of the *Shenzhou*'s junior officers. It was Burnham's belief that a successful Starfleet officer was proficient in multiple disciplines outside their normal range of responsibilities. Georgiou agreed with the sentiment, endorsing Burnham's initiative and giving her exec free rein to implement the program.

"Carry on, Ensign. I'm just showing our guest around a bit."

As Connor returned to the center seat, Georgiou walked around its raised dais and the conn and ops stations until she and Shannon stood before the bridge's oversized forward viewscreen. Just visible off the *Shenzhou*'s port bow was the curvature of M-11, the remote world that was home to the ground-based installation Starbase 11.

"It's beautiful," said Shannon as she took in the planet's violet-hued atmosphere.

"From up here, sure. It's not really much to look at on the ground, though." Georgiou smiled. "I guess I'm just more comfortable in space."

Shannon asked, "You've been in Starfleet for, what? Thirty-five years? Haven't you thought about retiring and settling down somewhere?"

"After this long, I don't know that I'm suited for anything else." Turning from the viewscreen, she regarded her bridge crew. "Starfleet is my home, and my crew is my family."

"The Benecia colony is mostly people from Earth," said Shannon. "Or their descendants. There aren't that many people from other worlds. The funny thing is that I had to go back to Earth to get a true sense of how diverse the Federation really is." She stifled a small laugh. "You'd be amazed at how many people from so many planets travel to Earth for college."

"Starfleet is getting there. For a long time, it was mostly humans, either from Earth or one of the colonies, and to be honest it's still largely that way." She gestured to Saru. "My science officer is the first Kelpien in Starfleet, and there's a Vulcan and a Lirin on the *Enterprise*. The *Intrepid* is crewed entirely by Vulcans, and other worlds are starting to send their own candidates. What better example of Federation values can we offer to a newly encountered alien species than a crew with representatives from every Federation planet? I look forward to that day."

She moved away from the viewscreen, nodding to the officers on duty before leading Shannon back to her ready room. Returning to her desk and dropping into her chair, she saw the younger woman stop just inside the entrance, stepping far enough into the room to allow the doors to close behind her.

"If only we'd had that sort of understanding and co-operation," said the younger woman after a moment. "We should have, but instead we forgot all of that when things got tough. When push came to shove, we reverted to the worst parts of ourselves, by embracing fear and being satisfied with finding someone else to blame for our problems. What happened on Tarsus IV was a test of everything we're supposed to hold dear, and we failed miserably."

Georgiou recalled similar sentiments uttered by others ten years ago, in particular Gabriel Lorca, who had left the planet with a decidedly low opinion of the people and circumstances that allowed the massacre to take place. Given the personal tragedy he endured, she could not blame him for his views. Instead, she could only hope he had not allowed them to blacken his soul.

"The rescue mission to Tarsus IV was a lesson for me too. It reinforced how I feel about everything we're supposed to stand for. Starfleet values. Federation values. It's when they're tested by extreme circumstances that we see just how important they truly are, and how we need to work that much harder to uphold them. Otherwise, they're worthless."

Shannon stepped closer. "You didn't say any of this during your interview. Your answers to my questions made me think you'd prefer to keep all of that in the past."

Instead of replying, Georgiou reached to a drawer of her desk and retrieved a wooden box. She set it down in front of her, caressing its smooth, worn surface before raising its lid and extracting the lone item it contained and setting it on the desk for Shannon to see. It required only a moment before the other woman recognized the object.

"Vran," she said, gazing at the Andorian doll. When she smiled, Georgiou noted her eyes beginning to moisten. "You kept it all this time?"

"Of course I did. It was a gift." Rising from her chair, Georgiou stepped around her desk. "For me, it's also a reminder that we can't let the tragedy of Tarsus IV consume us. Instead, we have to keep in mind the harsh lessons it taught us, and make sure something like it never happens again. We owe it to the people Kodos took from us. We owe it to the Four Thousand."

FEDERATION COLONY PLANET
TARSUS IV

2247

Epilogue

"Good morning, ladies and gentlemen. This is Captain Gershen speaking. All passengers and cargo have been loaded aboard, and I've just been informed that we've received our clearance from Spaceport Control. We should be breaking orbit in just a few minutes. Flight attendants: please make your final checks and prepare for departure."

The female voice filtering through the passenger compartment's intercom system exuded self-assurance and control, the speaker no doubt an experienced pilot who viewed the coming voyage as just another routine launch and flight between distant points in space. In her defense, and perhaps that of everyone else in the cabin, she was almost certainly right.

But for Adrian Kodos, it was another matter altogether.

Sitting in the private cabin aboard the transport vessel *Philomela*, Kodos, now traveling under a new identity he had taken great pains to create, looked out the ports set into one wall of his compartment. The view offered was that of Tarsus IV, curving away above and to his right, toward the aft part of the *Philomela* as the ship continued angling itself toward breaking orbit. He had come to this planet in the hopes of establishing a new life, far from the demands and trappings of modern Federation society. That he had been able to live that dream even for a few short years was its own reward in his eyes. However, that gift served to remind him of what he was forced to leave behind.

Also visible in the window, thanks to the cabin's recessed lighting, was his own reflection, and Kodos could not help taking it in one more time. Almost without conscious thought, he reached up to rub his bald head, his fingers playing across the surface of his shaven dome. He let his hand drop down to stroke his face, which was free of the mustache and beard he had worn for more than two decades. Contact lenses had changed his dark brown eyes to a brilliant, piercing blue. He had lost weight over the course of the numerous weeks spent living in the wilderness after escaping their mountain hideaway with a handful of remaining loyalists, consuming meager food rations while foraging for whatever else they could find. His face had lost some of its roundness, particularly under the chin and along his jawline. The transformation of his appearance was near total. There was no way the man looking back at him could be mistaken for Adrian Kodos.

Kodos the Executioner.

He scowled at the very thought of the moniker bestowed upon him—or, rather, the man he used to be. Whether an invention of some journalist or a nickname given to him by one of the colonists, it was an appellation that took almost no time to stick. Despite the three months that had passed since the Sacrifice and the ensuing manhunt that led to his presumed demise, "Kodos the Executioner" still featured in Tarsus IV news broadcasts. These days, it usually was in connection to reports of men and women taken from the planet to stand trial in Federation court for their part in aiding Kodos's "Revolution" and his escape from capture. He regretted that people loyal to him were forced to endure such hardship, but each of them knew the potential for risk, ostracizing, and even punishment as a consequence for what they did. It did not matter whether he or they believed in the cause they pursued, or if the means employed to achieve it were righteous. Theirs was always doomed to be a minority opinion, regardless of how the Tarsus IV crisis played out.

As for his own situation, it had taken him months to reach this moment, a point where he felt confident he could finally make his escape from Tarsus IV. Each component of his plan and task performed, every risk taken and bet hedged had come to this. He had worked with considerable advantages, beginning with the fact that he was believed to be dead, and of the limited number of people who had recently seen his face, very few remained alive. A handful, at most, and it was a big galaxy. Within moments, Kodos would be free of this world, and in two days he would be gone, blended into the vast tapestry of interstellar space. There were hundreds of inhabited planets and moons out there, most boasting large populations in which it would be a simple matter to lose himself.

Before all of that could happen, the *Philomela* had to break orbit, and that would not occur until the ship's flight and passenger support staff made their final checks of the travelers in their charge.

"Mister Galloway?"

The voice from the doorway to his private compartment belonged to a young human man in his early to mid-twenties. He wore smartly tailored and pressed dark green trousers and jacket, the latter of which was fastened up to the man's throat. Gold piping accented the uniform down its front closure as well as around the collar. Epaulets on each shoulder bore some sort of insignia Kodos did not recognize, and the symbol of the Spaceways Interstellar Transport Company decorated the jacket's left breast pocket.

"Yes, that's right," replied Kodos, keeping his voice low.

The man, whose name tag read NATHAN, said, "Welcome aboard the *Philomela*, sir. I'm just conducting our final check before departure. Are you comfortable? Is there anything you need?"

Kodos shook his head. "I'm fine, thank you." He gestured to the food processor set into the cabin's opposite wall. "I was hoping for a glass of water."

"All food processors are deactivated until we break orbit, sir, but Captain Gershen is usually pretty accommodating to straightforward requests." Stepping into the cabin, Nathan entered a code into the keypad next to the food processor's access door and a moment later the door slid upward to reveal a carafe that looked like glass but which Kodos suspected was transparent aluminum or some other unbreakable material. Next to the decanter was a single glass composed of similar material.

"Here we are." Retrieving the carafe and the glass, Nathan placed both into recesses built into the table positioned in front of Kodos. "Can't have it spilling all over you and everything else, now, can we?" He stepped back to stand once more in the open doorway. "The override on the passenger cabin doors will be rescinded momentarily, so you'll be able to close yours for privacy. Once we've left the solar system and are at warp, passengers will be permitted to move about the ship. Shopping, restaurants, and all the other activity areas will be available at that time." He pointed to the intercom set into the wall near the door. "Meanwhile, if there's anything you need, just hit the blue button on your cabin comm, and you'll be connected to me or one of the other attendants assigned to you. Enjoy your flight, Mister Galloway."

Kodos offered an appreciative nod. "Thank you, Nathan." Despite the interruption and the unease he felt at the unlikely possibility of the attendant recognizing him, he was enjoying this small slice of normal life. For a moment, he was able to forget why he was running, or even that he was running at all.

The younger man tapped two fingers to his right temple in an informal salute before disappearing into the corridor, likely heading to visit the adjacent cabin in order to go through the same speech and ritual with other passengers. Waiting until the attendant was gone, Kodos filled his glass from the carafe and closed his eyes as the cool water coursed down his throat.

Nathan, like everyone else he had encountered since boarding the *Philomela*, suspected nothing.

At this point, Kodos believed there was little chance of anyone discovering his true identity. He had proceeded through the passenger boarding and screening processes without incident. The identity he co-opted was solid, or at least robust enough to gain him passage offworld. Between that, the amount of time that had passed since his apparent death, and his altered appearance, the hardest part of his escape was already behind him. The man once known as Adrian Kodos no longer existed. All traces of his former life were wiped away, replaced with that of Ian Galloway. He only needed to exercise patience and prudence from this point, until he was well away from Tarsus IV. Once he departed the *Philomela*, he would inhabit yet another new persona, one he had been crafting for weeks in preparation for this day.

Creating a new identity that could withstand the scrutiny of modern technology presented a challenge, of course, but even there Kodos had planned well ahead. One of his earliest preparations was to update the colony's computer records even before his hasty departure from New Anchorage as the first Starfleet vessel was making its approach toward the planet. The building blocks of his new identity were already there, including swapping personal information, retinal scans, and DNA data with that of his late aide, Ian Galloway. Despite pledging loyalty to Kodos in the early days of the crisis, the young, naive man never knew that he might one day serve as a stand-in should "the Executioner" ever have need to cover his escape. Kodos was thankful that he was not forced to kill Galloway himself. Fate had seen to that unenviable task, so helpful to Kodos in his bid to evade capture. The genetic scans that almost certainly were conducted on his aide's body in the mountains would be compared to information on file with the New Anchorage medical department. It would serve as the only point of comparison, as Kodos had never been required to submit such data to anyone before his arrival at Tarsus IV. So far as anyone would have need to be certain, the scans of Ian Galloway would show a match and a positive identification for Adrian Kodos.

More problematic were those few people still living on Tarsus IV who could identify him on sight. Kodos had considered attempting to deal with such loose ends before departing the planet. Doing so would only invite enhanced scrutiny, including the likely closing of the spaceport and a renewed prohibition on anyone traveling to or from the planet. The last thing Kodos wanted was to remain on Tarsus IV any longer than necessary. He had, by any measure, overstayed his welcome on that world. That was fine with him, as he had no intentions of ever returning, either to the planet or this sector of space. There was, after all, an entire Federation out there, with borders expanding almost by the day, that offered him a chance at a new life.

Another major aspect of inhabiting his new persona was severing all ties to his former life. That meant discarding or forsaking all of his possessions. Holding on to anything that might provide a link to his true identity was a tremendous risk, at least until he was well away from Tarsus IV and able to solidify his new life. Only one item was spared that purge.

Opening his travel bag, Kodos extracted *The Complete Works of William Shakespeare* and laid the worn book on the seat next to him. His fingers traced the book's edges, which were burned, and there was a new gouge in its imitation-leather cover. He would have to obtain a new copy at some point, but for the moment he was content to once again lose himself in the Bard's writings.

Surely you'd have enough material to write about me now?

As for what came next? His travel itinerary would take him to the planet Deneva, another Federation colony world with a large population. From there, he would catch another transport vessel, to a destination he had not yet selected. His Ian Galloway identity was a temporary measure, a bridge between Adrian Kodos and the name that would soon replace his current moniker. For the moment, the destination was not so important as the journey. Somewhere, out there, was a place Kodos—or whatever name he ended up using—could call home for the rest of his days, living in obscurity and eluding a chapter of history in which he would be forever cursed.

He could live with that.

Acknowledgments

There are several people to thank for inviting me to this particular party:

First, there's Kirsten Beyer, one of the staff writers for *Star Trek: Discovery* and the production's designated "*Star Trek* Continuity Cop" for tie-ins like the novel you've just finished reading. It was she who first championed my writing this book, and she's the one who worked with me to flesh out several ideas as I developed my outline. I still smile when recalling some of our more animated phone conversations. Kirsten's been an absolute joy to work with every step of the way.

Next are my editors, Ed Schlesinger and Margaret Clark. 2018 marks twenty years since my first *Star Trek* story was published by Pocket Books, and I've been doing it on a pretty regular basis since then. Two big reasons for that are Ed and Margaret, both of whom have been in my corner for a very large chunk of that time. They keep calling me back to play in the *Star Trek* sandbox, so of course I'm going to keep saying "Yes!"

Likewise, there are the good people at CBS Consumer Products, namely John Van Citters, who reviews and approves all our wordy shenanigans. He's been doing it almost as long as I've been writing for Pocket, and he was another vote cast in favor of my coming on board for this project. Not gonna lie to you people: It's nice to be loved.

Finally, there's you, the most important piece of this puzzle we call publishing: Loyal Reader. A lot of you out there have been with me for all these years, and it's because of your continued support of my work that I was in a position to be selected for this book. Don't think for a minute that I don't appreciate it.

Until next time!

About the Author

Dayton Ward understands and forgives readers who skip over these "About the Author" pages. It's easy to gloss right past them. Besides, a lot of them can be kind of pretentious, with the author listing everything they've ever written along with the names of every cat they've ever rescued from a tree. Dayton hates being that guy, even though he digs cats.

But if you've made it this far, let Dayton know by visiting him on the web at www.daytonward.com, where you can read about all the stuff he's written and thank him for sparing you the pain of yet another long, drawn-out "About the Author" page.

ELSEWHERE

He was already awake when the lights came on.

The first flickers of illumination made weak attempts to chase away the darkness before the room's internal lighting flared to life. Still lying on the metal slab with a thin mattress that was his bed, he used a forearm to shield his eyes while they adjusted to the change. He looked past his feet toward the force field that served as his cell's forward wall, watching as the lights in the adjacent corridor went out. Darkness.

Be it ever so humble . . .

A guard moved outside his cell. He did not recognize the new arrival's form. Maddeningly, he had never seen any of their faces. They were either shrouded in darkness or he would wake with a hood tied over his head. Each guard carried a sidearm and a small, narrow cylinder that could be extended and used as a baton.

No stranger to those.

"Good morning," he said to the guard. Already dressed in his drab gray prison shirt and pants, with soft shoes covering his feet, he rose to a sitting position on the bed.

The guard paused at the force field, as if staring at him through the invisible barrier. He was used to such scrutiny. He wondered if this was the guard who foolishly did not shackle his hands and ankles—not likely.

He waited until the guard turned and continued down the corridor before pushing himself from the cot and walking toward the force field. Once he was alone, he shook his head and smiled to himself. Standing this close to the force field, he could hear clearly the minor hum it emitted, and he could feel a slight tingle on his exposed skin. It was a subtle warning not to approach the barrier, and direct contact with the energy field would of course incur an immediate and painful response. He had tested it once or twice in the early going, and was satisfied it would defy any attempt at escape.

Likewise, he had inspected every centimeter of his cell, searching for any flaw or point of access to anything he might turn to his advantage. Welded to the bulkhead, the bed slab was the room's only furnishing save for a toilet and sink, which at the press of an embedded control emerged from the wall opposite the bed. As expected, a careful study of that mechanism revealed no sign of weakness or points of possible exploitation. There was no food slot, and therefore no interface panel with which he might tamper. A small ventilation shaft, too small to accommodate a person, was set into the ceiling and provided the cell's only other point of entry. When it came to plotting escape, the designers of this facility seemed to have anticipated every contingency.

Another day in paradise.

Whoever these people were, violence seemed to be a way of life for them. That much was obvious from his first hours in this place. Wanton brutality up to and including summary execution was commonplace. This attitude extended to members of the staff, an unpleasant reality he had witnessed twice since his arrival. With such casual disregard for anyone in their custody as well as soldiers under their command, it made him wonder why those in power bothered with incarceration. On the other hand, with a few notable exceptions, he was treated in a far different manner. The guards, while still cold and intimidating, exercised great restraint when dealing with him.

They still want me alive. I guess that's something.

How had he even come to be here? What was this place? Who were these people?

He sensed a common malevolence. These were not explorers, or even a military force mobilized by Starfleet for some unknown reason.

With only the hum of the force field to keep him company, he dropped with a heavy sigh onto the cot. He maneuvered himself so that his back rested against the bulkhead, and waited. As with everything else, waiting had become part and parcel of his existence here.

Still certain he was alone, he let his fingers trace over the lump in the bottom hem of his shirt. It was small, not even two centimeters in length. Reaching to the underside of the hem, he searched for the small opening he had made, and with a few deft movements extracted the item hidden there. It was a thin white cylinder, which he unrolled to its true length of nearly six centimeters. Long ago he had memorized the inscription it contained.

Hate is never conquered by hate. Hate is conquered by love.